Give Way to Night

Also by Cass Morris

The Aven Cycle
FROM UNSEEN FIRE
GIVE WAY TO NIGHT

GIVE WAY TO NIGHT

TO

NIGHT

◆ BOOK TWO OF THE AVEN CYCLE ◆

CASS MORRIS

DAW BOOKS, INC.
DONALD A. WOLLHEIM, FOUNDER
1745 Broadway, New York, NY 10019
ELIZABETH R. WOLLHEIM
SHEILA E. GILBERT
PUBLISHERS
www.dawbooks.com

To My Parents,

Bruce and Mary,

with Love From Your Little Bird.

DRAMATIS PERSONAE

In Aven and Stabiae

Aulus Vitellius, a Popularist Senator
Aula Vitellia, his oldest daughter, a widow
Vitellia Secunda, called **Latona**, his second daughter, a mage of Spirit and Fire
Vitellia Tertia, called **Alhena**, his third daughter, a mage of Time
Numerius **Herennius**, Latona's husband
Lucia, Aula's daughter
Helva, a freedwoman, mage of Time, and Aula's personal attendant
Merula, a Phrygian slave, Latona's personal attendant
Mus, a Cantabrian slave, Alhena's personal attendant

Vibia Sempronia, a mage of Fracture, sister to Sempronius Tarren
Taius **Mella**, her husband
Galerius Orator, consul of Aven
Marcia Tullia, his wife, a mage of Air
Aufidius **Strato**, Galerius's co-consul
Marcus Autronius, a Popularist Senator and a mage of Earth
Gnaeus Autronius, his father

Ama **Rubellia**, High Priestess of Venus, friend to Latona
Quintus **Terentius**, a Popularist Senator
Quinta Terentia, his daughter, a Vestal Virgin and a mage of Light
Terentilla, called **Tilla**, her sister, a mage of Earth
Maia Domitia, of a Popularist family, friend to Aula and Latona
Vatinius **Obir**, client to Sempronius Tarren, head of the Esquiline Collegium
Ebredus, a member of the Esquiline Collegium
Eneas, a freedman sailor
Moira, a priestess at the Temple of Proserpina in Stabiae

Arrius **Buteo**, an Optimate Senator
Decius **Gratianus**, an Optimate Senator

Memmia, his wife
Gratiana, his sister
Glaucanis, wife to Lucretius Rabirus
Licinius **Cornicen**, an Optimate Senator
Pinarius **Scaeva**, a Priest of Janus and mage of Fracture
Salonius Decur and **Durmius** Argus, members of the Augian Commission
Aemilia Fullia, High Priestess of Juno

In Iberia

Vibius **Sempronius** Tarren, Praetor of Cantabria, a Popularist Senator
  and a mage of Shadow and Water
Calpurnius and **Onidius**, generals commanding legions
Autronius **Felix**, a military tribune, brother to Marcus Autronius
Corvinus, a freedman, mage of Water, and Sempronius's steward
Eustix, a mage of Air

Gaius **Vitellius**, a military tribune, son to Aulus Vitellius and brother to
  Aula, Latona, and Alhena
Titus **Mennenius**, a military tribune
Calix, a centurion
Bartasco, chieftain of the Arevaci, allied to Aven
Hanath, his wife, a Numidian warrior

Ekialde, chieftain of the Lusetani
Neitin, his wife
Reilin, **Ditalce**, and **Irrin**, her sisters
Bailar, a magic-man, Ekialde's uncle
Otiger, a magic-man, Neitin's uncle
Sakarbik, a magic-woman of the Cossetans

Lucretius **Rabirus**, Praetor of Baelonia, an Optimate Senator
Cominius **Pavo**, a military tribune
Fimbrianus, former Praetor of Baelonia

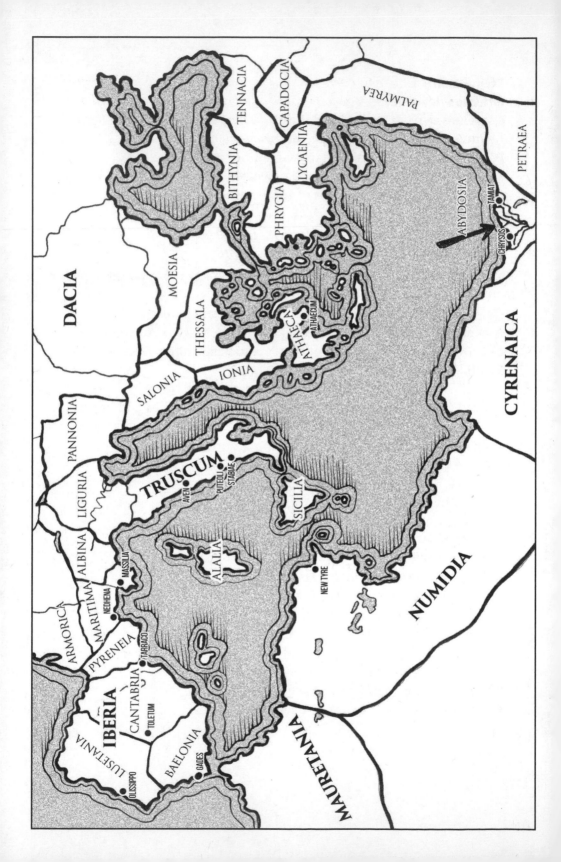

"*Longa mora est, quantum noxae sit ubique repertum, enumerare: minor fuit ipsa infamia vero. Maenala transieram latebris horrenda ferarum et cum Cyllene gelidi pineta Lycaei: Arcadis hinc sedes et inhospita tecta tyranni ingredior, traherent cum sera crepuscula noctem.*"

"*It would take too long to tell what wickedness I found everywhere, for rumors were less than truth. I had crossed Maenala, those mountains bristling with wild beasts' lairs, steep Cyllene, and the pinewoods of icy Lycaeus. Then, as the last shadows gave way to night, I entered the inhospitable house of the Arcadian king.*"

—Ovid, *Metamorphoses, Book I*

PROLOGUE

In the deep of winter, hundreds of miles from her own village, from the broad flat river and gently sloping hills of her home, Neitin of the Lusetani clung to the arms of the birthing stool, trying to bring forth life in cold and desperation. When the pangs faded, Neitin hung her head, sobbing helplessly, her sweat-soaked chestnut curls hanging like curtains on either side of her face.

"Good, good!" The midwife rubbed between her shoulders. "Not far to go, I think."

Neitin wanted to protest that she couldn't possibly do this, not a moment longer, that if this child didn't get out of her right now she would walk into the dark shadows of the underworld gladly, but she held her tongue. Another woman might make those protestations. Neitin was the wife of the *erregerra*, the Lusetani war-king, and she could not admit to such weakness. Choking her sobs back into her throat, she scraped her feet against the deerskins that covered the ground inside her tent, trying to get them solidly underneath her. "I want to walk."

The midwife helped her to stand properly, nodding. "That will be good for you. Walk until the next pains hit."

One hand rubbing at the back of her neck, Neitin paced the length of the tent, from her bed to the flaming brazier, stoked hot to chase out the hard winter chill. Small comfort, to catch her breath, when she knew the agony would return.

Before it could strike again, however, the thick woolen tent door jerked open. Neitin looked up sharply; everyone she wished to see was already inside the tent, with the exception of her husband Ekialde, who would not be allowed in until after his child was born. When she saw the dark-headed man who had entered, her lips pulled back from her teeth in an instinctive snarl.

Bailar, uncle to her husband and leader of their magic-men, sidled in, letting the tent flap snap in the wind behind him. Reilin, first of Neitin's younger sisters, rushed to hold it closed, but as she skirted around Bailar, she bowed her head in respect.

Neitin had no intention of showing such deference. "This is no place for you. Why have you come?"

Bailar's shoulders hung low, giving him a demure appearance that ill-suited his true nature. "I knew your husband had sent for a woman from a nearby village," Bailar scarcely gave the midwife a glance, "but I feared the assistance might be . . . insufficient."

The midwife gave no indication that she took umbrage, but Neitin took plenty on her behalf. "This honored lady has been dedicated to divine Nabia's heart and magic for thirty years," she said. "I assure you, she has things well in hand."

Bailar's mild expression did not change. "We heard a great deal of screaming."

"And have you never heard women in childbirth before?" Neitin growled. "No doubt your own mother shrieked fit to split the heavens, bringing forth one such as you." She had long since outgrown civility with this man, the fiend she blamed for their current predicament, out in the wilds of the central forests, so far from home. *He* had led her husband in this madness, *he* had lured Ekialde with promises of grand victories in the name of the war-god, *he* had convinced Ekialde that dark magics, so long disused by civilized magic-men, were appropriate. Neitin pleaded for Ekialde to set this man aside, or at least to take equal counsel from others, to no avail.

She might not be able to pry him away from her husband, but she could damn well forbid him her own company.

"There is nothing here for you." She staggered toward him, nostrils flared. "I stand at the threshold of Nabia's realm. It is *nothing* to do with you."

Bailar regarded her coolly, impassive in the face of her panting breath and flushed, sweaty face. "You are in a great deal of pain, Lady. I take no offense, of course."

She spat at his feet.

This, too, Bailar ignored. "You may yet have need of aid. Endovelicos sees all things, as the sun and the moon do. We are never out of his realm."

"If I need Endovelicos's assistance," she said, swiping at the damp locks of hair falling in her face, "I will send for *my* uncle. Not for you. I would never—" She grimaced, silenced for a moment as her whole world narrowed to the agony overtaking her body. The wracking cramps could not fully divert her fury away from Bailar, though, and when the pain ebbed, she found her tongue again. "I would never invite your darkness so near this sacred moment. You pollute everything you touch, but you will *never* touch this babe. You understand me? *Never.* Not at the moment of its birth and at no time in its life."

"Your husband may—"

"My husband may respect you in matters of war, but this is hearth and home!" Neitin's words stampeded over his. "I will not be gainsaid in this, and he will neither persuade nor overrule me." She could hardly stand unaided, but she made no move to lean on either her sisters or the midwife. She was determined to face Bailar with her spine as straight as she could manage and the earth solidly beneath her bare feet. "So get out." When he did not move, she screamed, "Get. *Out!* Or I swear, I will devote the rest of my waking days to seeing you brought as low as you deserve to lie!"

Bailar gave her a mocking little bow. "Women in childbirth are often frantic. I understand."

He left then. Neitin wanted to throw something at his departing back. That he should have the nerve to treat her with such condescension, such smugness—but the thoughts would hardly string together. Her knees buckled, and the midwife's arms were swiftly around her, keeping her from falling. For a moment, the pain obliterated all other thoughts in her mind, and another ragged scream tore from her throat.

Only when the anguish receded could she regain herself to speak. "You keep that man out of here," Neitin snarled at her sisters, her dark eyes wild with rage. Her face contorted as another spasm wracked her, but as she huffed through the pain, she pointed at the door of the tent. "You keep him out, and you keep him away."

"Sister—" the youngest began.

"You have heard me! Do you think I speak in jest?"

Her sisters exchanged worried glances, no doubt debating who they should be most afraid of: the magic-man whose powers grew by the day or their beloved sister in the throes of childbirth. Their tribe held that this was a time of great power, wrapped in Nabia's arms. A mother could tell no lies in these hours, with her soul in full flood, and her wishes were to be heeded as though they came from Nabia herself.

In the end, religious conviction outstripped the mingled fear and respect they had for Bailar. The youngest sister went to tie the tent flaps shut, but Reilin, only a year younger than Neitin, halted her. "Stay here with her. Ditalce and I will stand guard outside, that neither Bailar nor any of his men approach the tent." She walked over, with her long warrior's stride, and kissed Neitin's dewy forehead. "These hours are yours, sister, and they are blessed. Nabia's grace will see you through them."

Neitin felt little grace in the next hour, but as dawn approached, so too did her babe. Outside the tent, the blackness of night gave way to the eerie cobalt-blue that raced ahead of the sun. All at once, the buffeting winds calmed, just in time for another scream to join Neitin's: tiny lungs, shrieking their indignation at so rude an introduction to the world.

A moment later, Neitin's youngest sister raced out of the tent. "A boy! A son!" She did not pause as she shouted this to her sisters, but rather raced across the camp toward the tent where her brother-in-law and his war-band had kept vigil. "The *erregerra* has a son!"

As a cheer went up throughout the camp, inside the tent, Neitin half-swooned on the birthing stool, watching through heavy-lidded eyes as the midwife cut the cord of life and swaddled the babe. Somehow, she found the strength to grab the woman's arm. "The afterbirth—"

"It'll be along in a moment, my dear, never fear. I looked to the stars last night; they said you are in no danger, so it should come away clean. No risk of fever."

"No, that's not what—" Neitin blew out her breath. Tears had rushed to her eyes; she felt exhausted and elated at the same time. "Wretched Bailar will want it for some foul purpose, I have no doubt. He must not have it. You, you must keep it safe, and cast it in the river for Nabia."

The midwife stared at her a moment, eyes wide. "Of course," she said. "That is what is right and proper—"

"Right and proper have little meaning in this camp, honored lady," Neitin said, hoping the earnestness in her voice and eyes would be convincing.

This mattered, more than she could express. She belonged to Nabia, mother-goddess, not to Bandue, the war-god, and so would her son. Whatever hell Bailar led them into, Neitin could at least keep her son's soul safe from his perfidies.

"He may order, or he may resort to subterfuge, even threats of violence. Whatever happens, he must not have it."

The midwife nodded. "I understand, little mother."

VER

SPLINTER THE FIRST

The world was full of broken things.

Promises. Dreams. Plans. The stones of the road leading south from Aven. The wings of the bird in Corinna's hands, snapping under the pressure of her thumbs.

It struggled in agony, pecking and slashing, but Corinna's grip remained firm, despite the scrabbling feet scratching her wrists, the sharp beak assaulting her fingers. She held the bird as long as she could stand it, drawing in the power of its shattered pieces, its pain.

These were the constants of the universe. Anything that was built would be broken. Anything born would suffer and die.

These were a Fracture mage's strength, her succor.

'Through this,' Corinna thought, as the pigeon's fear and fury crackled through her own bones, *'I can reshape the world.'* In a swift twist, she snapped the bird's neck. *'Through this, I can find grace.'*

I

NEDHENA, PROVINCE OF MARITIMA

With slender green stalks of unbloomed lavender on one side and the murky blue of a flat river on the other, the General of Aven's Legio X Equestris rode toward his camp.

As praetor of Cantabria, the northern of Aven's two provinces in the vast expanse of Iberia, Sempronius Tarren had not technically arrived in his appointed domain yet. He wanted to gather his full forces before proceeding south into Iberia. Opportunities would not be lost in waiting, however. The centurions were drilling the troops, preparing for whatever they might face in the Iberian wilds. The quartermasters, under the supervision of Sempronius's tribunes, were restocking and setting up the supply chains that would support the legions going forward. Sempronius took it upon himself to speak to the locals, to find out what challenges they faced that Aven might help them rise to meet. Maritima was, technically, no business of his, but it was against his nature not to take an interest.

This day, he had gone upriver to inspect the local dye factory. They were doing remarkable work with the materials available to them. *'A more secure trade network would enable them to apply their processes to finer products. Saffron and indigo, kermes instead of red madder—they could have the beginnings of a flourishing industry here, if Aven would support the necessary infrastructure.'*

Sempronius had wanted to learn from the dyers themselves what about the trade routes needed improvement. The conservative Optimates in the Senate sneered at tradesmen's matters, but they were the lifeblood of any nation. *'I would see these veins pumping vigor into every extremity of the Middle Sea, and Aven the beating heart.'*

The river Atax flowed flat and slow through this part of Maritima, impressing itself between low hills. It was not a clean-flowing channel, and that troubled Sempronius. Practically, it cut down on the channel's navigability, making it a less reliable trade route—one of the complaints of the upriver dyers. That alone would be reason to see it cleared, but Sempronius had another, though one he wouldn't admit to even if he could. How ridiculous would it be, to try and explain that the river was *unhappy*?

Yet that was his sense of it. With the strain of Water magic flowing through him, he could feel the Atax's choked flow, too clogged with duckweed and silt to move with any speed. *'Stagnant water is not healthy.'* The slower it moved, the more prone it was to fostering disease and decay.

Sempronius's other element was Shadow, and that side of his nature argued that even disease and decay had their place. Rot was an essential component of the world's life cycle. For the Atax, though, Water won out. It yearned for a freer flow, a course that could roll through Maritima, strong and true and clear. Sempronius could feel the goddess Lympha, lady of springs and rivers, calling to him, directing his attention.

'If it is in my power to help, Lady, I shall,' he vowed. *'If I can find the way to set this river free, I will.'* He could rely on the trade-related reasons for doing so, since he could not reveal his magical insights. His whole life, Sempronius had kept his blessings a secret. Mages were prohibited by the *lex cantatia Augiae* from holding any political office higher than that of a senator, and the Augian Commission, responsible for keeping Aven's mages in adherence to all magic-governing laws, would ruthlessly punish any offender, if he were caught.

Such restraint had never been in Sempronius's plans, and he believed the gods were behind him. They *wanted* him to build Aven into the city of his dreams, that heart of a vibrant and thriving world. He could not do so if stymied by prohibitions of men who feared the misuse of such power.

In any case, he would not have the time to free the Atax now. That would have to wait until after the Iberian venture was finished. *'So much needs fixing. One problem at a time.'*

As he approached the rows upon rows of tents, pitched outside Nedhena's low earthenwork walls, he thought over the months of his praetorship thus far, and what would need doing in the future. It had taken months to bring the legion this far. The road from Aven to Iberia went through four provinces. First, the high plains of Liguria, where Sempronius had drilled the Tenth Legion until the spring thaw allowed them to get through the mountain passes of Albina. Sempronius had started in March, as early as he could deem reasonable, grateful for the predecessors who had seen to it that an unbroken road crossed the continent from Aven to Nedhena. The passage through the Albine Mountains had been one of the grandest achievements of the previous century. Now, instead of having to wait for the snows and ice to thaw the upper elevations, the army could march at lower altitudes, closer to the coast. The campaign season could start earlier in the year, with a shorter route and fewer accidents and casualties on the road.

On the other side of the white mountains, they had found respite in an easy march to Nedhena. Decades of serving as a reliable western outpost had grown Nedhena from a soldiers' camp to a thriving city in its own right, though it was yet nothing to rival the ancient majesty of Massilia, Maritima's largest city, founded a thousand years earlier by refugees fleeing the sack of Ilion.

'*It could be, though,*' Sempronius thought, riding along the riverbank towards the settlement. '*It could be every bit as grand.*' He felt again that familiar twinge that was not quite ambition so much as an innate desire to see the most made of everything. Wherever Sempronius looked, he tended to see potential, and where he saw it, he could not avoid wishing it achieved. '*Proper walls, real streets laid out along the camp's grid system. Better sanitation, to be sure. Build some Aventan-style baths, a promenade like they have in Massilia, and this could be a resort to rival any on Crater Bay.*'

"Praetor Sempronius!" Sempronius lifted his eyes to see Autronius Felix hailing him from the eastward-facing praetorian gate. Sempronius waved him down, not yet ready to abandon the relative quiet of the grassy bank for the tightly controlled chaos of the camp itself.

As the highest-ranking of the military tribunes under Sempronius's command, Felix had been put through his paces over the past four months. Sempronius had made a promise to Felix's older brother Marcus that he would keep the high-spirited young man out of trouble. It was, in some ways, much like training a horse. Felix would snort and shake his head and chuff, but he didn't grumble too much and generally settled to his work quickly and capably.

While they were on the road, if there was nothing more complex to be getting on with, Sempronius had Felix run orders up and down the long column of cohorts, and the effort generally left him too tired to find much mischief at the end of the day. '*All he really needs is discipline, and the weight of a little responsibility on his shoulders.*' Autronius Felix was headstrong and passionate, but a stallion in need of curbing, not breaking.

Keeping Felix out of trouble had been more of a challenge in Nedhena than on the road. The town was as famed for its vibrant population of camp followers and women of negotiable affection as for its merchants and Fire-forgers. Between the brothels, the taverns, and the gaming dens, Felix might have been as dizzy with carnal indulgence and moral depravity as he ever was in Aven, had Sempronius not found plenty of ways to keep him busy. He could commit only so much debauchery in the few hours that Sempronius left him.

Oddly—or perhaps not—Felix did not seem to mind. Sempronius wondered if he got into mischief out of boredom, idleness his true undoing. He was not half the fool he sometimes played. Felix had a mind in his head, and though it was not a particularly imaginative one, it was a mind constructed with a talent for finding the simplest solution to a given problem. When put to the test, Felix was efficient and focused, and Sempronius had hopes of shaping the young man's loyalty into reliability as his second. *'The fact that doing so will put Optimate noses out of joint is an amenable side benefit.'* Not everyone in the Senate had approved of Sempronius's decision to make Felix, with his up-and-coming plebeian family, his senior tribune instead of a well-pedigreed patrician.

Sempronius swung down off of his horse as Felix drew near. "We've had word from a messenger," Felix said, jogging closer. "General Sallust should arrive by evening."

"Excellent!" With the Fourteenth under General Calpurnius already encamped, that would make for three legions at nearly full strength— minus the two cohorts already in Iberia. That vexillation, under the direction of Young Gaius Vitellius, had been the first Aventan force to engage the Lusetani in battle. The Lusetani had begun their attacks over a year earlier, first targeting the merchants traveling through central Iberia. They claimed their purpose was to drive out Aventan influence from their territory, but they had swiftly progressed to assaulting not only Aventans and Tyrian traders, but also any of the other Iberian tribes who did not accept their dominion.

'Over fourteen thousand fighting men.' Sempronius prayed they would be enough, and that he would not need to rely on the Second and Fourth coming up from Gades. Those legions were under the command of Lucretius Rabirus, Sempronius's enemy in the Senate. Taking praetorial command of Baelonia and its legions was far from the worst of Rabirus's crimes, but he had done so with the explicit goal of being a thorn in Sempronius's side. *'So much the better if I need never give him the opportunity of thwarting me. We need a swift, strong strike, not a lingering campaign.'* Sempronius wanted to prove to Aven's allies that Aven could be depended on to defend their interests.

"Should I give direction to be ready to break camp in the morning?"

"Yes—for the Fourteenth. We'll send Calpurnius on ahead first." They had arranged passage from Nedhena to Tarraco, the capital of the Cantabrian province and the seat of Sempronius's praetorship, but the fleet was not enough to carry all three legions at once. With the winter storms passed, the trip to Tarraco and back should only take four or five days. Even with the boats making a few trips to ferry them all, it would still be faster than trekking over the mountains. "That'll give the Eighth a chance to rest—and adjust to Onidius's command." Sallust was giving up his command of the Eighth to his subordinate, Onidius Praectus, who had ridden ahead of the main forces to meet Sempronius in Nedhena. Sempronius was glad he had, for it had given him time to consult and plan with both of his sub-commanders.

"He seems solid enough. Quieter than Sallust, though! Their ears might need more adjustment than anything else." Felix drew a deep breath, looking appraisingly at the countryside. "Did you have a good ride?"

"I did. Would that we had the time to explore farther. Even with as long as we've held Maritima, we haven't made full use of it."

"Personally," Felix said, "I don't think Nedhena will ever be quite the city of culture and grace that Massilia is, but the farmland is good. It'd be an excellent place to settle legionaries upon retirement." Felix's voice was casual, but his dark eyes had a knowing spark in them.

"You read my mind," Sempronius said.

"I read your *intent*, sir."

Sempronius handed the horse's reins over to Felix. "It would be a different kind of colony. The waterways need improvement."

"Fortunately, old soldiers are good at digging trenches."

"True enough. It's no Truscum, but the land does have its charms."

Felix snorted. "Well, if you convince the Senate to approve such a measure, you'll have achieved something extraordinary. Speaking of Nedhena's charms, have you sampled the locals' honey?"

Sempronius arched an eyebrow. "Rather a personal question, I think."

Felix blinked a moment, then barked a loud laugh, nearly doubling over in mirth. "Oh, sweet Bellona, I did ask for that, didn't I? No, no— though that's as sweet as anything, too, if you do want to know, and I can highly recommend a few delectable sources." Though not a paragon of male beauty by typical Aventan standards, Felix had rough charm to go along with dark curly hair, merry brown eyes, and a grin that had, no doubt, coaxed much flowing honey from the local ladies. "But no, I meant the real honey. The bees here make a nectar like you wouldn't believe. Something about the lavender. I'll bring some to dinner tonight, if you invite me."

Even Sempronius was not immune to Felix's charm. "Very well, tribune. I could have worse company."

"Too true you could." He jerked his head toward the stables. "I'll see to the horse, speak to the centurions about our schedule, and then see you at dinner."

"My thanks, Felix."

"Oh!" Felix said, rounding back about, again with a too-casual air. "Letters came for you as well. I had Corvinus take them to your tent. The usual Senate dispatches, for the most part, but I do believe there was something of a more personal nature from . . . let's see . . ." He tapped his chin mock-thoughtfully. "From the Lady Vitellia Latona."

Felix was not grinning, but Sempronius could feel the amusement coming from him nonetheless. *'And how much more amused he'd be if he knew the full extent of it . . .'* Felix teased Sempronius in private because he had seen the emerald-eyed beauty saying farewell to Sempronius on the Field of Mars—he had no notion of the intimate interlude that had occurred at his own house during the Saturnalia, the one night of passion that Sempronius Tarren and the Lady Latona had shared.

'One night?' Sempronius thought, striding toward his tent. *'One hour. One sweet, stolen hour . . .'*

The stack of messages on his desk was high. His fingers itched to sift through it for Latona's letter. But duty's demand was ever heavy upon him, and he selected the first of the Senate dispatches instead.

∞∞∞∞∞∞∞∞∞∞∞∞

CITY OF AVEN, TRUSCUM

Latona of the Vitelliae sat on a bench, basking in warm spring sunlight. The leaves were still coming in on the sycamore trees that lined the walk, and at this hour, the nearby Temple of Tellus did not cast a long shadow. All around Latona, the oleander bushes were half-flowered, spots of pink dotting the deep green shrubs. A nipping breeze had many of those strolling through the garden tugging their mantles close around their shoulders, but Latona hardly noticed it. She was practicing, and it kept her warm within and without.

Her attendant, Merula, sat next to her on the bench, alert as ever for any potential menace, and a copper dish with a few glowing embers in it rested at Latona's feet. Latona drew energy from the nearly-banked flames, drawing in the Fire magic and breathing it out again as Spirit.

It was delicate work, transmuting the elements within herself. The first time she had done it, it had been an act of desperation, during the fires on the Aventine that had disrupted the previous year's elections. Now, she was learning to control the process. As people passed by her, she flicked out her Spirit magic, testing how quickly she could get a read on their emotions. Bolstered by the Fire magic, she found that the empathy of Spirit came swiftly—but less accurately. Emotions came in sharp bursts: a flare of desire, a twinge of worry, frenetic sparks of distraction, the gray haze of listlessness, but if a pair or a group passed her, she wasn't always certain which of them was experiencing the particular feeling her magic had picked up on.

'Less than ideal,' she thought, mentally giving the embers a prod to keep them from guttering out. *'But something I can build on. Perhaps the influence of Fire makes Spirit less predictable, or scatters the focus? I should ask Rubellia.'* The High Priestess of Venus was Latona's close friend and had become something of a thaumaturgical mentor, even though she controlled Fire alone. There were other mages in the city who controlled two elements, as Latona did, but no one else with her strength in Spirit, and so in that, she often had to forge her own path. The gods bestowed some gifts more frequently than others, and Spirit was a rarer talent. Latona's early education had been foreshortened, and for years, she had suppressed her talents, fearful to draw too much attention to herself.

No longer.

The past year had taught Latona that since she had the ability to do good with her magic, she had the moral imperative to act.

Merula's callused fingers touched Latona's wrist. "Domina," she said, her voice tight, "that woman is approaching, that priestess, from the Capitoline—"

Latona snapped her focus out of metaphysical contemplations and the wounds of the past. She followed Merula's dark gaze and saw the slight figure of Aemilia Fullia, High Priestess at the Temple of Juno Maxima, moving purposefully in her direction.

With effort, Latona managed not to frown. Her bad blood with Aemilia went back years, to Latona's childhood, when Aemilia had been a pitiless woman sending a grieving girl away after the death of her mentor.

Fresher was their dispute over Latona's "unwomanly ambitions"—precisely the end goal of the practices Latona was in the middle of trying to perfect. *'Juno's mercy, what does she want now?'*

"Vitellia Herenniae," Aemilia said, looking down her thin nose at Latona. She always used the marital form of Latona's name, and Latona wondered if it was genuinely strict adherence to form or done deliberately to aggravate her.

Custom dictated that Latona rise to greet Aemilia. To remain seated at the onset of a conversation was a mark of superiority, and Aemilia *was* a High Priestess, whatever Latona thought of her occupation of the office. So Latona rose—but she took her time in doing so, nudging the bowl of embers to the side with her foot first, so that her skirts wouldn't risk blowing into it. At her side, Merula was even more grudging, not bothering to disguise that she was glaring daggers at the older woman.

It mattered little. Aemilia didn't spare Merula so much as a glance.

"Aemilia," Latona said, in as warm a tone as she could manage. "Pleasant day."

"Still a bit cool for my liking," Aemilia said, her eyes flicking significantly over Latona's shoulders, their golden skin bared to the sunlight. Aemilia was, of course, dressed with exacting and modest perfection: a pale pink gown pinned over a long-sleeved white tunic, her hair caught up underneath a purple band. She pressed her lips thin, clearly on the verge of saying something—and yet no words were forthcoming.

She knew it was unlovely of her, but Latona almost enjoyed Aemilia's obvious discomfiture. "Is there something I can help you with?"

"I understand—that is, I have *heard*—that you've made a practice of working your gods-given gifts out here." Aemilia gestured to the garden around them, as though the idea of magic in such a space was somehow unfathomable.

Latona furrowed her brow. "Do you have someone spying on me?"

Aemilia gave a hollow laugh. "How over-dramatic," she scoffed. "Though perhaps that shouldn't surprise me."

"I should rather call it analytic." Latona's hands settled on her hips. "What I'm doing is Spirit work. Invisible. *You* don't have any magic." She gave that a beat to hit and was somewhat gratified to see Aemilia's cheek twitch in irritation. "So I have to wonder who informed upon me." Latona felt her lip curling slightly; the idea that someone was reporting on her use of magic to an authority figure reminded her too nearly of the days of the Dictatorship, when Horatius Ocella had done all in his power to cajole, threaten, and suborn mages to do his bidding—and when he ruthlessly persecuted those who refused his commands.

"A concerned citizen, that's all," Aemilia sniffed. "Someone who knew I would take an interest in a devotee of Juno who had strayed outside her proper bounds."

Latona thought about pressing the issue of the informant's identity further, then decided against it. If it seemed necessary, she could put her older sister Aula on the scent. There were few enough mages with reason to report to Aemilia; fewer still who could have seen Latona's magic in effect. Not all elements bestowed the ability to see magical signatures: Spirit, Air, Water, and Light owned that talent. The field would be narrow, and Aula would relish ferreting out a tattletale. "I can't see where it's any concern of yours," Latona said. "I'm a free woman, exercising my gods-given talents in accordance with the *leges tabulae magicae*."

"Just because what you're doing is permissible doesn't mean it is right."

Lucretius Rabirus had said something similar to her the year before, and Latona hadn't liked it any better then.

"It is my duty," Aemilia continued, drawing herself up pompously, "to *counsel* mages blessed by Juno, even if they are not under my direct supervision in the temple."

"Consider me counseled, then." Latona could not keep sharpness out of her voice. A silken touch and deference had never worked with Aemilia before, and she was tired of futilely resorting to such measures just for the sake of civility. "You disapprove of my intentions. I intend to act nonetheless. We are at an impasse." She spread her hands. "What more is there to say?"

Aemilia's expression was somewhere between irritation and condescension. "Your humors are still clearly unsettled, which is why you remain determined to impose yourself on affairs that do not concern you. I am only trying to spare you a great deal of frustration and embarrassment."

Latona clenched her jaw so tightly that it sent a line of pain up into her temples. "I find myself unable to understand," she said, forming every word carefully, lest less-gentle ones escape her lips, "why a devotee of Juno should *not* interest herself in public affairs. She is the Queen of Heaven. She rules on Olympus."

"Second to her *husband*," Aemilia said pointedly. "He rules the public world, and she the private. *That* is what we should seek to emulate."

Latona shook her head, though more in dismay than anything else. It was *exhausting*, encountering this opinion in a woman who had the power and position to do so much more, who could open so many doors, if she would only take the trouble to do so. "We are not Athaecans, to keep women mewed up behind walls." She gestured in vain at Aemilia herself. "We can do better, Aemilia. Nothing you say will convince me that is not what Juno intends."

Aemilia's dark eyes flashed bitterly. "It is not for you to tell me what Juno intends. *I* interpret the goddess's will here in Aven, not you."

'It might have been me,' Latona thought, with no less acidity than she saw written on Aemilia's face. *'If you hadn't chased me out. If you hadn't been so scared of a child's potential to become a rival. I might have been High Priestess of Juno, not you.'*

She said only, "Your view diverges significantly from Gaia Claudia's. She taught me. You declined to do so. Is it so startling that I absorbed her philosophy rather than yours?"

II

Another several minutes of conversation with Aemilia yielded nothing fruitful, except in giving Latona a few choice morsels of Aemilia's sanctimonious condemnation to chew on as she walked home. Aemilia had departed, annoyed that Latona had refused to conciliate herself to continued hobbling of her talents; Latona had departed, annoyed that she could not give the High Priestess of Juno a thick ear.

Her mood was not improved by encountering her husband almost immediately upon re-entering their domus on the Caelian Hill. Just the sight of him provoked an internal sigh. Once, tolerating him had been easier. Their relationship had never been particularly cozy, but at first, Herennius had treated her with honor and regard, and she had been able to muster up a species of affection in return. Over the years, that cordiality had deteriorated under a number of stresses. Some she could lay at Dictator Ocella's doorstep—or, rather, at the base of his mausoleum. Others were the natural result of their opposing personalities and goals. Now, having tasted true passion, knowing what it felt like to have the true admiration of a worthy partner—Latona could no longer pretend in the way she once had.

Yet she chided herself for her lack of patience with him. Herennius could be no other than he was: a man of middling attraction and minimal ambition. Many women would have been grateful for such a husband. If he was not handsome, neither was he ill-favored, and his broad face was honest. *He* was honest, if only because he lacked the guile and intellect to be aught else. He had money enough to keep any woman content, which would more than make up for his lack of political initiative in most women's assessment, and he did not have a voluptuous nature. He insisted on his husbandly rights infrequently, and if Latona ever managed to produce a child, would likely avail himself of them even less.

'*The right man for someone else, perhaps,*' Latona thought, '*but not for me. Not now.*'

All the same, she tried to put on a smile for him. If domestic felicity was too much to hope for, she could at least aim for tranquility. "Good afternoon, husband," she said, unwinding her mantle from around her shoulders. She had to unpin it from her hair herself; Merula's hands were still occupied with the bowl they had placed the burning embers in, and neither of them wanted Herennius asking questions about that.

"Where were you?" Herennius asked, in his usual abrupt fashion.

"The garden behind the Temple of Tellus." That much, at least, she could be honest about—even as she draped her mantle over Merula's shoulder, allowing Merula's quick hands to shift the bowl underneath it. "It's a pleasant day, don't you think?" Herennius grunted in response; he'd been out, Latona knew, with his clients, but he was not a man to observe the fragile blossoms on the trees or appreciate the playful vernal winds. "We've an invitation to dine with my father tonight," she said, crossing the atrium toward her husband. "Aula's note said she had fresh lamb, and—"

"I've already accepted an invitation to dine elsewhere," Herennius said, and named his host as one of his friends with a neighboring estate in Liguria; no one of importance in the city. "You should go to your father's, though," he said. "Give him my regrets."

They were both trying, Latona could tell, not to show their relief at having an excuse not to dine together. "That's very thoughtful of you," she said. "I'm sure my father would be pleased to share a couch with you some other time."

"There's mail." Herennius's voice had a sudden hard edge. He gestured to a table at the side of the atrium, where a folded packet of papers sat waiting. "I believe some of it came from Iberia." Latona felt her heartbeat speed up. "From your brother, I presume?"

"It must be," she said, infusing her voice with a casual airiness she did not feel. She forced herself to walk slowly to the table, lifting the packet without looking at it. "No doubt Father has one as well." She graced Herennius with another smile. "That Gaius can get letters out at all must be good news. Last we heard, he was worried the Lusetani were cutting off the couriers' routes."

"I only wondered," Herennius said, his tone still sharp, "because the messenger said they'd been delivered by way of the *Tenth* Legion." Latona allowed herself only a blink in response. "Not the Eighth. And Gaius Vitellius is with the Eighth, is he not?"

"A portion of it," Latona said, affecting unconcern. "Perhaps the messenger was mistaken."

"Sempronius Tarren is leading the Tenth, is he not?"

Latona's heart suddenly felt too large, too loud inside her chest. "I believe so." She lifted one shoulder in a shrug. "Or was it the Fourteenth? Aula would remember, I'm sure. I can ask her tonight, if there's some reason you'd like to know."

Herennius's eyes flicked down to the papers held in Latona's slender fingers, then back up to her face. "Just a husbandly interest," he said, the edge in his voice turning toward a snarl, "in who my wife corresponds with."

Latona raised her chin. "I correspond with many people. I can't imagine what interest you would find in the vast majority of my letters." She held the packet out toward him. "By all means. Investigate further, if it would put your mind at ease."

Herennius's fingers twitched. For a moment, Latona thought he might call her bluff—but then he seemed to determine that it would be undignified to do so. "Just have a care," he grumbled, turning away from her. "You and I both know you can't afford to be the target of unseemly rumors." With that last loosed arrow, Herennius shuffled back into his room, summoning a slave to help him change for dinner, and Latona finally released the sigh that had been caught at the back of her voice.

Magical energy prickled in her right hand. Fire and Spirit, ever rooted in a mage's emotions, asserted themselves more forcefully on days she had been deliberately practicing. *'A year ago, I might have set the room on fire after that conversation.'* A year ago, she *had* set the room on fire when her magic spiraled out of control after a pique. Not directly; no mage since the Age of Heroes had been able to create fire out of nothingness, to snap their fingers and summon it. Latona could, however, increase the size of an already existing flame, and the previous summer, in the wake of Dictator Ocella's death and the turmoil that followed, Latona's powers had fallen into the habit of overheating lamps until they exploded.

She gave her hand a sharp shake, dispelling the swelling energy. The lamps on the nearby altar flared gently, then subsided.

Control was important for all mages, and for those blessed with volatile elements most of all. But control, she had learned, did not have to mean suppression.

◇◇◇◇◇◇◇◇◇◇◇◇◇◇

Latona read the letter in the privacy of her own room. Herennius had been mistaken—or else deliberately trying to trap her. The letter had not been posted from Iberia, but from Nedhena, the legion-founded town on the north side of the Pyreneian Mountains. The paper was cheap and flimsy, the hand imperfect with too-quick strokes, but just the sight of it warmed Latona. She took delight in knowing that Sempronius had written the letter himself; she could tell the difference between his slightly smudged strokes and the precise lines his scribe inked onto the messages sent to her father. Thinking of his fingers gripping the stylus, imagining his face as he composed the words, an unbidden smile found its way onto her lips.

"You keep looking like that every time he is sending you a letter," came Merula's accented voice from behind her, "and I am thinking you are not keeping secrets much longer." Latona submitted to her attendant's chiding as readily as to her quick hands, which moved to unfasten the copper-tipped ties on her gown. Merula, a Phrygian-born slave, had been given a gladiatrix's training to act as bodyguard to her mistress, in lieu of the decorative arts or household management skills that a lady of Latona's class would typically seek in an omnipresent servant. Merula considered it her duty to protect Latona in ways other than the physical, and lately, that concern extended to reminding Latona of the legal perils of adulterous behavior. Latona knew the dangers, knew how foolish and incautious she had been the previous winter, when for once she had chosen to give her heart free rein.

She could not be sorry for it. That Saturnalia had liberated more than her fleshly desires. In letting heat and passion consume her, Latona had discovered just how much of Venus's fire truly lived within her—and how small and sad she had allowed her world to become.

As Merula worked around her, stripping off her day garments and tying her into a gown more suitable for dinner, Latona lifted the letter and read.

Its tone was the same as the others she had received from Sempronius since his Januarius departure from Aven: friendly without overt intimacy, no hint of impropriety, no pet names or endearments. Much though she might have wished for messages of greater passion, the absence of ardor was safer. If Herennius did take it into his head to open his wife's mail, he would find nothing incriminating.

'. . . Eager as I am to reach the Iberian plateaus, I admit that Maritima is not without its charms. One can easily see why the Tyrians settled here when they fled burning Ilion—and why plundering pirates have been drawn to the region equally as long. The land is well-watered and verdant, and the sea at Massilia is even bluer than that of Crater Bay. We did not tarry long in Massilia herself, but I liked the feel of the old place. Not as large or messy as our beloved Aven, but it seems all the peoples of the Middle Sea have left residue of themselves here, carved into the white rocks of the Maritiman shoreline.

'I hope your studies continue well, and that you have not yet had need to strangle Aemilia Fullia or anyone else standing between you and improvement.

'I remain,
'Yours in friendship,
'V. Sempronius Tarren'

Tsking, Merula jabbed a pin into Latona's hair a tad harder than was necessary to secure the mantle among her golden curls. "Blushing, Domina."

"I can't control my *skin*, Merula."

"Should be trying."

Merula only meant it for her safety, of course; she cared, if possible, even less for Herennius himself than Latona did. Latona hated the sound of those words nonetheless, echoing Aemilia's insistence that she should be trying to be a better wife. Somewhere in the last year, her impetus to make the marriage work had burned away like morning fog under a swiftly rising sun. Now she hoped only to endure it until she could either convince Herennius to surrender his claim to her family's wealth and connections or else persuade her father to agree there was more advantage in a divorce than safety in the continued bond. *Blessed Juno, just let us be rid of each other before things grow worse.*

She wished that her father would see the unsuitability of her match and suggest a divorce. It would look so much better if it was Aulus's idea. That would pass it off as his pragmatism, rather than risking any aspersions being cast upon her character.

'Then, if Sempronius comes home safe from Iberia, we might—'

But she stamped down hard on the thought. It did no good to yearn for that which was not yet within her grasp.

◇◇◇◇◇◇◇◇◇◇◇◇◇

OSTIA, TRUSCAN COAST

The curse had to be carefully crafted.

Vibia Sempronia Mellanis wished no misfortune upon the soldiers of the Second Legion, nor upon the sailors ferrying them across the Middle Sea to Gades. At least, no more than ill luck had brought them already, placing them not under the command of Vibia's brother, Sempronius Tarren, but instead that of Praetor Lucretius Rabirus. *'Tribulations will find them soon enough under his leadership without any help from me,'* she thought, tucking wind-stripped wisps of dark hair back beneath her mantle. She stood in Ostia's market, near the temple to Volturnus, waiting.

Getting to Ostia had been simple enough. Her husband, Taius Mella, had many mercantile interests in the city at the mouth of the Tiber, which served as Aven's main port. As a senator, he had to stay one step removed from operations, working through a freedman client, but he liked to check in once a month to keep an eye on things. As luck would have it, this trip coincided with the day that two legions were set to board ships on their way to Iberia.

'Luck.' Vibia almost smiled. She did not have magical strength enough to affect the laws of chance, as some Fracture mages could, but she had prayed to Fortuna, and the goddess had answered. All Vibia had to do then was express a fancy to come along, and her husband had been more than happy to make the arrangements. When she told him she needed to slip away for a bit, Mella had kissed her forehead, told her to take care, and sent a trio of slaves along as her escort. "Some business for my brother," was all the explanation Vibia had given, and it was all that Mella had required. He knew, of course, that he had married a Fracture mage, but Vibia had always felt it more dignified to keep him one step removed from her thaumaturgical endeavors—particularly those which some might characterize as unsavory.

Vibia suffered no crisis of conscience, however. Rabirus deserved everything she could throw at him. He had tried to have Sempronius assassinated at least once, had set fire to Aven to try to invalidate elections that were not going his way, but worst of all, he had engaged the services of the Discordian devotee Pinarius Scaeva. Remembering the foulness that Scaeva had let loose, Vibia almost shook with rage, even months later. *'Perverted, corrupted souls, the pair of them.'*

Scaeva had abused the gifts of the gods, had sworn his allegiance not to Janus or Fortuna, as a Fracture mage ought, nor even to one of the lesser cults, but to Discordia, the lady of strife and misrule, who had no place in civilized society. Had been *banished* from it, her worshipers driven out of Aven—out of all Truscum. Yet this aberration had remained. For the harm he perpetrated, Vibia had exacted justice, fierce and swift.

Lucretius Rabirus, though, had escaped the initial reprimand. All through the winter, while Sempronius trained his troops on Ligurian fields and while most of the city settled into doldrums, Vibia had contemplated the right way to reach him.

A curse tablet was the surest method. A sheet of hammered bronze, inscribed with a lead stylus, so that Vibia could be excruciatingly specific. Sitting in a doorway one cool spring evening, with lavender twilight streaking the sky above her garden, Vibia had channeled all her fury, her affront, her horror at what Rabirus had done and had driven it into the metal. The gods would see him punished for his perfidies, she was certain; they could have no cause to deny her petition, rendered with righteous fury and precise piety, and they would deliver to him mishaps, ill fortune, and the frustration of his most dearly-held goals.

The trouble then was delivering it. A curse tablet *might* work if buried at a crossroads or cast into the river, but best of all was to get it into the possession of the cursed individual.

As a slender youth with dark curly hair crossed the forum toward her, Vibia considered that for once she had cause to be grateful for her brother's habits of associating with the less rarefied elements of Aventan society.

"Hail, Domina," the lad said as he pulled his gawky limbs to a halt in front of her and gave what was clearly meant to be a respectful bow, though it came off as a bit of a spasm.

Vibia inclined her head in a nod of acknowledgment. "You are Eneas of the *Pipinos*?"

"Indeed, Domina." Another awkward bow. Taking pity on the young man, Vibia tried to relax her posture a bit. "I am here to fulfill my obligation to your noble brother."

Young Eneas was a freedman—one of Sempronius's, and his client still. As a child, he had worked at the family's country estate, but in his tenth year, he manifested magical gifts, earning him his freedom and setting him on the path to a new career. Eneas's talents lay in Water and

Fracture—weak, but enough to give him a keen sense of storms, when they would appear, how they would move, how to avoid them. Valuable skills on the seas, and he had made good use of them. Young Eneas would likely gain a captaincy of his own before his twenty-fifth year, if he could muster some *gravitas* to go along with his magical gifts, but for now, he served as sailing master upon the ship that would carry Rabirus to Gades.

More luck, or more of Fortuna's favor, Vibia hardly cared which. Had it been Sempronius being ferried across the Middle Sea, he would have gleaned the names and personal histories of all the ship's officers within two days. But Vibia knew her target; Lucretius Rabirus was unlikely to trouble himself with even the captain's name, much less the lower officers, and so he would never know that one Eneas Sempronianus guided his path to Gades.

Vibia waved her attendant forward, took the basket she carried, then dismissed her along with Taius Mella's escorting guards. "Wait by the temple steps." Her attendant was a good girl, and Vibia had no cause to distrust her husband's men, but the fewer ears that heard a thing, the fewer tongues that could ever speak of it. Only once they were out of earshot did Vibia draw the curse tablet from the bottom of the basket. Though it was no longer hot to the touch, as it had been while she worked on it, she kept it wrapped in a simple homespun cloth. She never liked to touch her own works once they were complete; it seemed impolite, as though it implied that she needed to keep tampering rather than trusting the gods to keep up their half of the bargain.

Eneas put out a hand to receive the tablet, but Vibia did not hand it to him immediately. "Look at me, Eneas," she said, in a tone meant to impress upon him the gravity of the situation. "Your patron's life may depend upon this." The lad's pale eyes went wide. "Praetor Rabirus means him harm. I do not intend to let that harm come about, and I don't think you would wish to, either."

"Of course not, Domina."

Vibia nodded, pleased by the earnestness in the boy's voice. The loyalty Sempronius inspired was sometimes unfathomable to her, and gaining it led to what Vibia considered indignities beneath his station, but it had its uses, she did admit. "You will have access to the man and his quarters, no doubt. I need you to make sure this ends up in his possession, but beneath his notice." She held the tablet towards Eneas, who reached reverently for it. "In his trunks," she instructed, not yet releasing the tablet. "Something he will take with him if he leaves Gades. Something that he will share a roof with, at all times. Buried and hidden as best you can."

Eneas ducked his head, blushing. "I think I can do you one better, Domina." When her fingers finally released the tablet, he turned it over in his hands. "This is thin enough . . . I have a friend on board who knows how to fit a false bottom onto a trunk, or a false top into its lid." Vibia forbore from asking how Eneas's friend knew this; smuggling was a time-honored illegality at the Ostian port. "It may take some doing, to get enough time . . . but it will be done, Domina. I swear to you."

Vibia smiled, glad the boy was cleverer than she had initially assumed. "Praetor Sempronius will be most grateful," she said, "and I will be sure he knows to whom he owes that gratitude."

The lad slipped the tablet into the pouch hanging at his waist. "I know he does not forget his friends, Domina. I was so happy I became a man last year, so that I could vote for him. The whole crew—we journeyed to Aven just for the election."

'Baffling,' Vibia thought, *'but useful.'* Aloud, she said, "Your trust is well placed, Eneas, and we thank you for your bravery. Go with the gods, and Fortuna bless you."

Eneas nodded his farewells and darted away, and Vibia returned to Ostia's forum, where Taius Mella greeted her warmly. "All is well, I trust?"

"Quite so."

"Excellent! Glad to hear it."

And that would be the end of it. Taius Mella was, in Vibia's opinion, an excellent husband: devoted without doting, supportive without interfering.

Vibia liked it when her life arranged itself tidily.

∞∞∞∞∞∞∞∞∞∞∞∞

City of Aven

For an old man, Arrius Buteo had a powerfully resonant voice, carrying across the Forum, high and sharp over the conversations of lawyers and tradesmen.

"—These foreign luxuries, these decadent indulgences, they degrade our moral character! You may think, good citizens, that there is no harm in a silken tunic, no danger in a gold chain, no threat in saffron and snails—but these are the weapons with which cowards fight their wars!

Nations which cannot defeat us in battle seek to corrupt us from within! Such excess, such extravagance, it makes us weak. How long can Aven stand as the moral example of the Middle Sea, when we invite such unseemly opulence into our homes?"

Aula, eldest of the Vitelliae daughters, clucked her tongue. *'What a pompous fool. Aven was founded by thieves, brigands, and harlots. And if I were a man, I'd tell him so right now.'*

She stood as near the Rostra as she could manage without getting glared at. She had dressed with care to look virtuous, her gown modestly draped and her mantle drawn up over her bright copper hair, though she knew it would not be enough to deflect criticism. There were still those in Aven, particularly among the Optimates, who thought the Forum ought to remain a thoroughly masculine space, tolerating only the strictly necessary priestesses and slaves. When matrons like herself took an interest in public affairs, they considered it an inappropriate intrusion at best, a sign of imminent social collapse at worst. Her mere presence was a disruption, so far as Buteo and his ilk were concerned; her voice, upraised to challenge Buteo, would be utterly intolerable. An impish twitch inside almost prompted Aula to present just such a provocation—but no, that would be a step too far. However richly Buteo deserved a dressing-down, Aula would not risk a brazenness that would shame her family and jeopardize her father's and brother's careers. Aulus's position as censor was secure for the next few years, but it was an office that attracted a great deal of scrutiny, and while Gaius's campaign in Iberia had already made him something of a legend, he would need a solid grounding when he came home to stand for office himself. So Aula held her tongue.

Aula considered it her duty to her family to listen to the talk in the Forum, even when it was Buteo's moralizing drivel. "I thought perhaps he'd have changed topics by now," she commented to Helva, the Athaecan freedwoman who served as her attendant and managed much of the Vitellian household.

"No," Helva commented dryly. "He's even using the same phrases, word for word." Helva would know. She had the magical gift of a perfect memory, bestowed upon her by Saturn, one of the patrons of Time. "He might at least switch up the adjectives."

"I suppose there are only so many words for 'indulgent' in our language," Aula said, rolling her eyes.

Buteo had been on this theme for long days now, an effort to muster support for the sumptuary laws he was gamely trying to promote in the

Senate. Having failed in his effort to stop Aven from going to war in Iberia, thus expanding their influence and trading networks around the Middle Sea, he had determined to convince the Aventan people that they did not *want* the resources—and, yes, frivolous luxuries—that such expansion would provide. The Lemuria had put a temporary halt to his public haranguing, and to all civic business. The festival was a time to honor one's ancestors, but the days were also *nefasti,* considered unlucky. No legal or civic matters could occur on days that were *nefasti*, and so, for a few days, the Forum was free of Buteo's stentorian lectures.

Not that anyone was around to enjoy the quiet. Many citizens in Aven kept within doors during the Lemuria, as they often did on those days in the summer and autumn when the *mundus* was opened at the Temple of Janus. On such days, the *lemures*, the spirits of the unquiet dead, could return to earth. Aula herself had stayed at home during the Lemuria, not even venturing out to visit friends. She had never met a wrathful spirit walking abroad, and she had no intention of opening herself to the possibility. She had hoped, upon walking out again, to discover that Buteo would have transferred his vitriol to a new topic, but he appeared to have gone right back into the same stride.

"Well," Aula said with a little sigh, "I suppose if he's not going to say anything new, we can go along. I want to see if anyone has any new dangerously indulgent foreign fabrics for me to make some summer gowns out of." Even though Buteo could not hear her, Aula crinkled her nose in his direction, before pointing herself and Helva toward the markets on the northern side of the Forum.

She was picking through summer-weight linens in a sky blue she quite fancied and a butter yellow that she thought would suit her daughter, Lucia, when she first noticed the man. At the time, she thought nothing of it. He was dark-skinned, Numidian or Mauretanian, but that was hardly unusual, especially in the mercantile parts of the city. He stood out more because he was uncommonly tall. Aula caught him staring at her, but he turned swiftly away when he noticed her looking back. Aula beamed, always happy for her beauty to be the subject of regard.

But then she saw him again, after she and Helva had walked over to the spice markets. Aula had wanted to look over the selection, in case there was anything new or unusual to pass along to her cook. And there he was again, about the same distance away, still watching her.

And then *again*, another block over, while she was sampling olive oil blends from a Ligurian merchant.

Three times was too many. She had Haelix and Pacco with her as bodyguards, of course; Aula rarely ventured forth without a cordon to announce that she was a protected patrician lady, unlike Latona, who had developed the habit of slipping around the city with only Merula at her side. She wasn't afraid for her physical safety in this moment. *'But why on Tellus's green earth would someone be following me?'*

Stomach fluttering, she caught Helva's elbow. "Helva, turn slowly and look at the tall, dark man over by the garum stall."

Under the pretense of tucking the fabric of Aula's gown more firmly into the belt, Helva negotiated herself so that the stranger was within her sight. Her eyes flicked up only briefly as she fluffed Aula's mantle. "He is familiar, Domina. Give me a moment." Her brow creased, and Aula knew she was shuffling through her immense mental catalog of every name and face she had ever known.

'What must it be like, to have a mind with so many library niches, to pull information out of and slot it back in at will?'

Helva smoothed her kerchief back, glanced once more in the man's direction, and said, "Vatinius Obir, of the Esquiline Collegium. Formerly of Mauretania. Veteran of the Numidian Wars. Granted citizenship for his service. Client to Sempronius Tarren."

At that, Aula's posture softened. "Oh! Well, that's all right, then." No client of Sempronius's would mean her harm. She jerked her head in Obir's direction. "Go and tell him to stop skulking." Helva arched a thin eyebrow, but she turned away, returning a moment later with Obir in tow. A broad grin indicated he was evidently unworried to have been caught out in his stalking. Aula cocked her head at the man, her hands settling on her hips. "Hail and well met, Vatinius Obir of the Esquiline," she said, her words a bit clipped. "Do explain why you were following me."

Pressing a hand to his chest—which, Aula could not help but notice, was rather impressively muscular beneath the goldenrod-yellow tunic and loose green cloak he wore—Obir gave her a respectful little bow. "Honored lady," he said, his consonants tapped with the accent of his homeland. "I am sorry if I alarmed you. And, with the greatest respect, I must confess that, lovely though you are to gaze upon, you were not, in truth, my target."

Aula threaded the edge of her mantle through her fingers. "Whatever do you mean?"

"I must explain much." His warm brown eyes darted around. "And this is, perhaps, not the best place? May I accompany you to your next destination?"

Aula found herself smiling. "Well, I do adore an intrigue. By all means, let us walk. I suddenly fancy a stroll in the shade." Behind a nearby temple, they found a broad and open walk, shaded by sycamores. Haelix and Pacco could follow close behind, but so long as Aula and Obir didn't shout, they were unlikely to be overheard by anyone else.

"I am, as your woman told me you know, client to Praetor Sempronius Tarren," Obir began his confession. "I served under him in Numidia towards the end of my years as an auxiliary."

"And you didn't want to sign on again to join him in Iberia?" Aula teased.

He laughed. "No, no, I have had enough of warfare for one lifetime. War gave me opportunities, true, but now, I am an Aventan businessman, and I am happy with the life I have built here." He grinned sideways at her, with a familiarity that a prissier patrician lady might have taken as an insult. "Besides, an old fellow like me, to go tramping through the Iberian Mountains?"

'Old?' Obir could not have seen forty years, from the look of him, and he did not appear to have gone to seed in the decade since the Numidian Wars had ended. Aula bit back the unladylike commentary, and instead offered, "I can hardly blame you for preferring a life of comfort to the hardships of the legions."

"Indeed, indeed. And here I am relied upon, a figure of stability in my neighborhood. So, my friend the praetor marched off to war, with all those young men following him, their blood afire, and I stayed behind. But he asked me a favor, before he went." Aula quirked an eyebrow; he was coming to it, but there was a hitch in his amiable bluntness before he continued. "Praetor Sempronius, he . . . has a great regard for your sister, Lady."

Aula blinked a few times, but his statement only caught her off-guard for a moment before triumph replaced bewilderment. 'So the good praetor has set a watch over my sister, has he? Now what in Juno's grace might have prompted that?' A question for Latona, as soon as Aula could ask it.

"He asked that I would keep my eyes and ears alert for danger to her," Obir continued.

"Danger?" Aula's laugh was not quite as unconcerned as she might have wished. A beautiful mage from a prominent family, Latona presented many temptations to the unscrupulous, as they had all learned during Ocella's reign. "Whatever trouble she might find herself in, I can't see how it would be enough to warrant monitoring from the leader of a crossroads collegium." Aula arched an eyebrow pointedly. "Surely you have a great many demands on your time, no matter what favor your patron might ask."

Obir chuckled softly. "No, Lady, I confess it is not often I doing the watching. The collegium has a great many young lads who need occupation, and they do what I tell them. Good lads, all," he hastened to add, "have no fear of that. They would run to me, quick as lightning, were there any threat to the lady. I only happened to see you in the market today, and as it is known that copper and gold often walk out together . . ." He shrugged expressively. "My legs were in need of exercise, in any case. I thought I might keep watch a bit, see if the Lady Latona joined you."

"Reasonable," Aula murmured. "Does Latona *know* you and your boys are shadowing her?"

"Ah—no, Lady." Obir looked only mildly sheepish. "We thought it best to keep a distance."

"Well, you might do yourself a favor and warn her—or allow me to do so. Otherwise her girl might shove a dagger into someone's valuable territory if they get too close. Honestly, it's a marvel Merula hasn't gutted anyone already."

Obir laughed. "Yes, I have seen the little Amazon. Your advice is as wise as you are lovely, Lady Aula." He winked. "I shall give her no reason to use me for target practice."

Something about that wink put a flush on Aula's cheeks. Obir reminded her a bit of Autronius Felix, always an audacious flirt, but at least the Autroniae were of the senatorial class. They might not be accepted in the stodgier houses, thanks to their plebeian background and generations-distant slave ancestry, but they were a usual component of the Vitellian social circle. A man of a crossroads collegium, on the other hand—well, there was a social gulf between them, and no mistake, yet he spoke as warmly and freely as though they were good friends. *'Sempronius's influence, perhaps.'* He was known to be quite friendly with his clients, whatever their origins, and perhaps that had worn off on such an amiable creature as this Vatinius Obir seemed to be. *'And it isn't as though he's been disrespectful, for all his forwardness.'* Many patrician women, of course, would have considered his so much as looking her in the eye to be an unforgivable presumption—but Aula didn't see what harm could come from it, and she certainly intended to fill her gaze with a well-built man in return.

They reached the end of the garden, where it opened out onto the north side of the Carinae Hill. Obir came to a halt, and Aula turned to face him. "Well, Vatinius Obir of the Esquiline, I give you leave to protect my sister and any other member of the family that you or Praetor Sempronius deem fit." She weighed her next words on her tongue a moment before offering, "If ever you need anything, particularly while your patron is out of the country, stop by the Vitellian domus. My father will be happy to stand in Sempronius's stead."

"You are kind and gracious, Lady Aula," Vatinius said, giving her another little bow. "I shall remember it."

'And I,' Aula thought, watching him stride back between the trees, *'would not be unhappy to see you again.'*

III

The swirling waters were tinted faintly purple and smelled of lavender. No mere perfume, this, which would fade if Latona and Aula lingered too long; the pool was enchanted by Aven's foremost Water mage, a woman called Davina, who had made a fortune from her gift. Nor was a pleasant scent the only magic at work. The warm waters had a healing effect, and as Latona sank down to her chin, she could feel the tension unknotting from her back and shoulders.

"What a lovely idea this was," she said, leaning her head back against the edge of the pool. She and Aula were alone, in one of the bathhouse's private chambers, having already traversed the larger public rooms of warm, hot, and cold water. Those baths, too, had enchanted waters, but of less intensity. Latona had never asked Davina about it, but she assumed it was easier to sustain magic of higher intensity on the smaller pools.

"I do have them occasionally," Aula tittered, fluffing at the damp copper curls piled atop her head. "I'm just glad Davina had a private room available. I don't know that I could've taken much more of Crispinilla's wittering." The Vitelliae had, as was common in the baths, run into several women they knew in the public rooms. "I don't know why she thought we'd be impressed with her brother's letters from Cantabria. As though our own brother hadn't been in the very thick of it over there for the past year! Proculus's legion hasn't even been met in battle yet."

Latona knew that well enough even without Crispinilla's boastful report. Sempronius's latest letter indicated they had, at last, begun their trek into the interior of Cantabria, but they did not expect to meet resistance until they were much further south. "She just wants to feel important," Latona said. "You know she was jealous as anything for all the attention Gaius's letters got last year." Their brother had been, though a thousand miles away at the time, a primary force in motivating the governing bodies of Aven to vote in favor of supporting their Iberian allies against the suddenly rapacious Lusetani.

"So—" Aula began, in a high and too-casual pitch that immediately had Latona arching an eyebrow. "You'll simply never guess who I ran into while shopping the other day."

"I'm sure I won't," Latona allowed. "Do you mean to tell me, or would you rather make a game out of my guessing?"

Aula giggled. "No, I'll tell you. A most interesting man, really. I wish I could get away with inviting him to a dinner party sometime, because I'd love to hear his life story, I'm sure it's *fascinating*."

"Aula."

Aula's pretty lips curved in a sly grin. "Vatinius Obir, of the Esquiline Collegium."

Latona remembered him. His men had helped Galerius Orator and Sempronius put down the riot that had erupted on the Esquiline Hill just after the Dictator's death the previous year. Latona felt sure enough of their Popularist loyalties to have summoned them when a fight had broken out in the Forum—a fight spurred by a Discordian curse that had netted Autronius Felix in its power, though no one had known that at the time. The older brother ran the collegium alone now; his brother had died before the elections—murdered, it was said, during an assassination attempt on Sempronius Tarren. "I know of the man," Latona said, carefully, "but I had no idea you were acquainted."

"We weren't." Aula's eyes, mirrors to Latona's own, crinkled impishly. "Tell me, what on earth did you do that Sempronius decided he needed to tell an entire collegium to be watchful over you and guard your welfare?"

Latona blinked a few times. "I should have known," she drawled after a moment. "'Come to Davina's with me,' you said, 'my treat, a private room, oh and let's give Helva and Merula a treat, too, and send them off to enjoy their own baths once we've settled in here.' Of *course* you had a reason for it."

"I am hurt, *hurt*," Aula said, clutching a hand to her chest, "that you think my generosity had any premeditated ulterior motives." But there was a grin twitching at the corner of her mouth and a laugh caught in the midst of her voice, giving her away. She splashed water in Latona's direction. "Come on. Tell me."

Latona shrugged, her shoulders sending ripples through the water. "I'm sure I don't know."

A bigger splash, this one sending a bit of floral-scented water up Latona's nose. As she sputtered, Aula chided, "I'm sure you *do*. Now talk, or I'll hide your clothes until you do."

Latona wiped at her face with the back of a hand. "Beast."

"Obir said he was told to be alert for dangers to you. I think I deserve to know if there's some genuine threat to my beloved sister's well-being."

It was the concern threading through Aula's voice that tugged on Latona's conscience. She reached out with her Spirit magic and was answered by the clarion ring of sincerity beneath the playful cover.

She could have continued to demur. She *didn't* know, for certain, what had prompted Sempronius to make such a request of his client. But denial would be disingenuous.

Latona drew herself up slightly, sitting more solidly on the bench rather than letting herself slump into the salubrious waters. Where to begin? "You remember the day of the fire, by the Aventine docks?"

Aula shuddered. "I'm not likely to forget *that*. You running off to use your magic to help the brigades." One look at Latona's face, and Aula went ashen. "That wasn't all that happened, was it?" Latona shook her head. "Sweet Juno."

Latona had trouble forcing the words off of her tongue. It was meant to be a secret; no one but she, their younger sister Alhena, Sempronius Tarren, and his sister Vibia knew what had happened in that warehouse. But she could no longer look at Aula's imploring eyes, feeling the surge of sisterly protection emanating from her, and hide the truth. So she told the story of the Aventine fires and her part in quelling them: how she had not just assisted, but been able to extinguish whole buildings at a time. How she had taken the energy into herself through Fire, then transmuted it to Spirit, which she could spin back out to help others when their energy or vigor flagged. How she had poured out so much of herself that way, with so little regard for the toll it took, that she became easy prey for a Fracture mage who siphoned her power, knocked her unconscious, and dragged her into a warehouse.

The tale did not come easily. Love for her sister warred in Latona's heart with her awareness of her sister's flaws—chief among them, a propensity for gossip. Strangely, the pallor that had come over Aula's skin was reassuring. She was less likely to chatter if she was truly afraid. Still, Latona felt it important to underscore the severity of the situation. "Aula, if I tell you this next part, you must keep it locked between your teeth and lips, I mean it."

"I promise," Aula said, her big eyes serious. "Latona, I know I'm a frivol, but I *can* keep my mouth shut when it matters."

"I know you can. I'm sorry. It's just—" A sigh. "This could be dangerous, in more than one way." But she drew a deep breath, and told Aula what she had learned in that warehouse of Rabirus's role in orchestrating the Aventine fires—and of the attempt on her life made by Pinarius Scaeva, secret devotee of Discordian magic, the dark side of Fracture that ripped and tore and devoured, rather than maintaining a fragile balance in the world.

Fury swiftly replaced the concern on Aula's face. "Rabirus set the fires? And set that—that *beast* on you?" She stood abruptly, propelled by her anger, water streaming off her ample curves in violet-tinted rivulets.

"And set him on Felix earlier in the fall, we fear," Latona said. "And was likely responsible for the poisoned arrow that hit Sempronius on that hunting trip."

Aula sat again, sloshing water over the side of the pool. "I can't believe it. I mean, of *course* I believe *you*. It just seems incredible, that he should stoop to such depravities over—" A mirthless laugh bubbled up in her throat. "Over a praetorial election!"

"I hardly wanted to believe it, myself. He thinks it a far more dire issue than a simple election. He thinks he's fighting for the soul of the nation." Latona gave a little shiver, remembering how vulnerable she had felt, kneeling on the floor of the warehouse, kept prone by Scaeva's magic, as Rabirus made his mad devotion to ancient customs so clear. "The worst part was . . . he knew it was me he was coming for. Scaeva had worked out my magical signature from other things I'd done in the city." Aula nodded slowly; Latona knew she was on the verge of outstripping her sister's knowledge of magical workings. Aula had not been blessed with magical gifts as her two younger sisters had, and she had turned her natural cleverness toward understanding political machinations rather than thaumaturgical mysteries. "He told Rabirus how I'd thwarted him. Suffice to say, Rabirus was . . . displeased to have been outmaneuvered by a woman."

Aula's lips twitched slightly. "The more fool him."

"Yes, well, he made some unkind remarks as to the nature of my reason for protecting Sempronius." Latona crinkled her nose. "None of which were true at the time."

"At the time?" Aula squealed, her face transforming in an instant from pinched concern to effusive interest. "What do you mean, *at the time*?"

"Do you want this story in the proper order or not?"

"Not!" Aula said with glee. "That part sounds far more—"

"*Au*la."

"Fine. Go on." Aula was fairly wriggling in anticipation, but then her expression turned serious again—a reminder that she was *not* a frivol, whatever aspect she might put on for society's sake. "But, my honey— Rabirus knew about Ocella—he didn't—"

Shaking her head vehemently, Latona said, "No. No, he seemed to consider it, then to determine that I was soiled goods." Latona gave a self-deprecating smile. "Or perhaps he merely surmised there would be no wooing me over to the Optimate cause. But then he made threats against Alhena." Aula gasped, squeezing Latona tighter. "I'm afraid that's when I quite lost control of myself."

"And no wonder! What did you do?"

"Tried to bite him."

Another laugh, though not jovial. "Quite rightly, too."

"After that, he left me to Scaeva's mercies. And *he* was . . ." Another shudder moved Latona's shoulders. "He *enjoyed* it, Aula. He had me in the palm of his hand, an insect to squish at will, and he was rejoicing in that power. I could feel it . . ." Her hand came up to her chest, pressing hard against her breastbone. "Like a fishhook, sent into the core of me, and I could do nothing but dangle."

Tears were clinging to Aula's eyelashes. "Oh, my honey," she sighed. "That must have been . . . I can't even imagine."

Latona had no words to comfort her sister, and so determined that the best course of action was to keep talking. "He meant to kill me. I'm certain of that. He said as much, that he would drain me of everything I had, everything I am . . . and he could have. I had no strength left to defend myself." Latona could still feel it, the cold chasm seeping deep in her chest as her magic flooded out of her, taking her very essence along with it. "Perhaps because he was so certain he would kill me, he revealed that he was no mere priest of Janus, but a devotee of Discordia."

Aula's cheeks were damp now, but Latona could see her mind working behind her eyes. "Discordia." The cult had been banished from the city several times over Aven's history, most recently by the Dictator Ocella, but they always seemed to creep back. "Do you think," Aula began hesitantly, touching her lips as though fearful of letting the words past them, "that Rabirus knew?"

Latona nodded, then shook her head, then shrugged. "I'm not sure. I know he didn't want me dead, he said as much. He just wanted me terrified and taken out of play, as it were. Scaeva went rogue on that. It seems incredible that Rabirus wouldn't know about his Discordian devotion, but I cannot confirm it. Neither of them addressed it in front of me, and I lost consciousness soon after. I don't remember anything else until . . . until Sempronius was carrying me towards the Temple of Venus."

"He rescued you!" Aula sighed, her emotions rapidly turning toward the more agreeable component of the story. "Latona, if that isn't the most romantic—"

But Latona cut her off. "Sorry to disappoint you, but it was *Vibia* who bears that honor."

Aula's face shifted from sentimental swoon to utter perplexity with comical speed. "What? Vibia?"

"Alhena fetched her. And Sempronius, but it was Vibia who had the power to intervene. I suppose Alhena knew that no one else could battle a Fracture mage so well as another of that element."

Aula's nose and lips were still curled in confusion. "I had never thought Vibia to have so much power, to combat someone capable of laying you out as Scaeva did."

"Nor I," Latona shrugged. "I don't know how she overcame him, to be honest, or what part Sempronius played. Perhaps he was a distraction, or fought him physically. It *would* be hard to fight physically and magically at the same time."

Aula was actually quiet a moment, considering. She cupped a bit of water in her hands and splashed it on her face. "It's this Scaeva that Sempronius fears, then?"

"I don't know. Something went wrong with Scaeva's magic, when Vibia intervened, Alhena said. His mind broke. He's being kept in seclusion now, but . . ." Latona shrugged. "Perhaps Sempronius fears he'll restore himself somehow. Or that he has allies."

Aula nodded. "A sensible assumption. You'd think if there were other Discordian cultists in the city, we'd know, but . . ." She shook her head helplessly, and Latona took her meaning. They hadn't known about Scaeva. Aven held many secrets, particularly in the disarray that followed the dictatorship. Then, Aula's eyes turned keen and teasing again. "So . . . about Sempronius Tarren and true or untrue reasons for protecting him?"

Latona felt heat coming to her cheeks, and she sank back down in the water a bit. "You can't be but so surprised. You've been pushing me at him ever since he returned from exile."

"It never occurred to me that you would actually take my advice."

Aula's lips screwed up at one corner. "In fact, I doubt my nudging had much at all to do with it. How *did* it start?"

Latona hardly knew, herself. Certainly it had not begun in the Autroniae's garden, with Saturnalian revels chiming in the background, nor even when Sempronius and Vibia had rescued her from Scaeva, with the city smoldering around them. That was but a ripple outwards from whatever had set them on this path. So when had it been? That chilly day, standing atop the Palatine Hill after the Cantrinalia, when he had disclosed his hopes for their vagrant little city? Or when she had seen his generosity at the Aventine temple complex? *'Or,'* she thought wryly, *'when he demonstrated so aptly that altruism and political acumen are far from bad bedfellows?'* For much of his appeal, she owned, was in his cleverness—in that always-working mind, so swift and fierce.

But no—it went back further than that. Her heart had raced from the moment she had greeted him at her family's feast, after Ocella's funeral. It had heated that night on the Esquiline, when she saw him stand up against a riotous crowd.

Or further yet, to a day when they had stood together on the Capitoline, with the city in the throes of Dictator Ocella's depredations. Latona, huddled against the cold, tangled up in her own anguish, on her way to beg Juno for guidance. Sempronius, making a final sacrifice to Jupiter before fleeing the city, already wearing his travel cloak and boots. Something had leapt between their souls in that moment, and though years passed, she never stopped thinking of him.

Latona hardly knew how to explain that to Aula, though, so she began with the moments in-between those that Aula already knew of. Aula listened, rapt, as Latona explained how their friendship had blossomed into something more. *'No,'* Latona thought as she told Aula of the terror that had gripped her when Sempronius had been wounded at Galerius Orator's hunting party, of the connection she had felt while healing him. *'No, not blossomed. Nothing so gentle—nor so predictable.'* Their passion for each other had taken strong, sudden flame, like dry brush struck by lightning.

Latona noticed that Aula was grinning a bit madly. "What?"

"You're blushing," Aula said. "Stars and sun, my honey, you're in a world of trouble."

Latona cast her eyes up at the ceiling, painted to resemble the starry firmament. "Funny, Rubellia said almost the same thing."

"Well, she would have the right sort of wisdom and insight to—Wait." Aula folded her arms in front of her chest. "You told Ama Rubellia and not me?"

Latona winced, remembering the circumstances under which her friend, the High Priestess of Venus, had learned about her tryst. "I didn't so much tell her as she walked in on me with my gown pulled down halfway to my navel—"

"She *what*?"

"Shh!" Latona cast her eyes toward the door. "This is a private room, Aula, but that doesn't mean no one could overhear—"

Grinning impishly, Aula gave Latona a nudge with her foot. "Then I suppose you'd best hurry up and tell me the rest of the story before anyone wanders by."

"It's not funny," Latona insisted. "I committed—if Herennius were to find out—"

"Are you sorry for it?" Aula asked, leaning forward. "Put aside Father and your ill-matched husband and everything else. Are you sorry for what you did?"

Latona bit her lip. Wrong though it had been, by the strictures she was meant to live by, it had also been *right* in a way that made her soul sing. Never before had she found such use for Venus's blessings on her. She could not be sorry for having taken that pleasure.

She shook her head.

"Well, then, *I'm* certainly not going to shame you for it. So *tell* me."

Leaning in and voice hushed, she did. Latona told her sister of her Saturnalian transgression, the ivy in the Autroniae's garden, the chill in the air, the heat in the little guest room Rubellia had pointed them toward. Aula, as was her wont, allowed her no dignity in the retelling, pressing for the prurient details. "It's only fair," she pouted. "I told you everything when I first discovered pleasure." And so, blushing, Latona yielded.

"Oh, my darling," Aula said, when she had finished. "Well, I'm still cross as anything with you for not telling me, but I'm so . . . so *glad*." Her pretty lips turned in a small smile. "You deserve happiness. You always have."

Latona shrugged that assertion off. "It was a madness that took over me. I don't know what comes of it. Even if he returns from Iberia, which is by no means certain, there's still Herennius . . ." Aula gave a snort: her usual way of imparting to Latona that marriage was by no means an inescapable conundrum. "But I do . . . I *miss* him, Aula," Latona went on to confess.

"He's well worth missing, I should think!" Aula laughed, kicking her legs beneath the water. "Sweet Venus, *I've* missed the sight of him, and all the other handsome men out on campaign, and I haven't your reason for it."

Latona smiled, thinking of her lover. He *wasn't* the most handsome man in Aven, in truth, whatever Aula said. He was well formed, but not particularly notable for his looks. Average of height, with sable hair and deep brown eyes, it was Sempronius's presence that impressed, the aura of certainty with which he walked through life. "It isn't only that. Talking to him feels . . . different." She fidgeted, drawing circles in the surface of the water with one finger. "He has such grand dreams. Such immense, impossible dreams, but he approaches every day as though he cannot fail to bring them out of Morpheus's realm and into the light of reality. He knows what he's capable of, and he sees something in me that . . . that I confess, I had quite forgotten might be there. I feel stronger around him. I feel like . . ." Unexpected, the impulse to weep tickled at the back of her throat. "Like I matter."

Aula swam over to her side, putting an arm around her sister. "You have *always* mattered. And you've always been strong. Don't think that I ever forget, for a moment, that your strength and sacrifice saved me and Lucia from Ocella." A sideways smile. "But if Sempronius has helped you to remember that you have that fortitude in you, then I'm afraid I must come down even more firmly on the side of your adulterous behavior."

Latona snorted and leaned her head against Aula's, temple to temple. "It's just so much to deal with. Father married me to Herennius to keep me out of trouble, and he wasn't entirely wrong." She remembered all the words that had passed between her father and herself when last she had questioned the arrangement. "Using my power attracts danger. Ocella, Rabirus . . . and Sempronius has many enemies. If I throw my lot in with him . . ." Her voice trailed off. Would it be worth it? Could she keep her family safe? Or would it be inexcusably selfish, to endanger them for the sake of her own pleasure?

Haunting questions, all.

IV

Tagus River, Central Iberia

The storms came too early that year.

Strange heat baked the spring, crisping flower blossoms and green leaves before they could flourish, and vicious sandstorms whipped across the plateaus without warning. And when the dust cleared, as often as not, thunder and lightning followed in its wake.

'Ill omens,' Neitin thought, clutching her child to her chest. *'I cannot be the only one who sees that. How, how can they not see it?'*

Neitin, wife of the *erregerra* of the Lusetani, beloved of the war-king blessed by divine Bandue, felt the hot wind drying her tears as soon as they left her eyes. Any moment now, one of her sisters would come out and chide her for exposing herself and the babe to the elements. But she could not stay in her tent, not so near to where her husband and his cursed, cursing uncle were playing at summoning demons.

Oh, Bailar the magic-man swore they were no such thing, but Neitin knew in her bones that they had crossed a line—or were, at least, trying to. Though the gods themselves were screaming their displeasure, Neitin would not stay inside, not when it meant staying so near Bailar's abominable efforts. So she had wrapped herself in a light cloak, her babe swaddled close to her chest, and stood with her back to the wind, gazing toward the west, toward where home should be.

'If you can hear me, Nabia, if we have not wandered too far from you, if you know this river like the rivers of home, then I beg you, intervene. Come between my husband and the war-god, come between him and this dread purpose, Nabia, please.' Prayers, she had to hope, would be heard even above Bailar's magic.

It was not the reassuring voice of the river goddess, protector of women, that reached her next, but the continued eldritch keening. It started out low and thrumming, then rose in pitch to a whistle higher than the wind, and far more chilling. No wolf, this, no natural creature at all, but an *akdraugo*, a fiend, a dark and hungry spirit eager to break through from its world to theirs, howling its frustration at impediments. Fresh tears broke out from Neitin's eyes, dewing her cheeks only for a moment before evaporating and leaving their tracks behind. *'Why, Ek-ialde, why do you do this?'*

But she knew. She did not understand the compulsion, but she knew his reason. He thought the *akdraugi* would be a boon to him in battle, spirits to sap the strength of the enemy, to dishearten them, to poison their minds. *'But at what price, husband?'*

Neitin stood for a moment, transfixed, looking back at her husband's tent. Strange shadows danced on the walls, lit by the fires within. Faster and faster they moved until, in a sickly orange flash, the light brightened, obliterating the shadows—and then failed entirely. The wind carried the sound of Bailar swearing to Neitin's ears, reassuringly mundane.

It hadn't worked.

Neitin's momentary relief was quickly dashed away by the horror of knowing that they would keep trying. She did not know what would be worse: that they fail, and Ekialde sicken or even perish in the attempt, or that they succeed, loosing monstrosities upon the earth. Every time Bailar failed to bring the *akdraugi* through from the nether realms, he read in it a message that he and Ekialde had simply not done enough—not spilled enough blood, not sacrificed enough of their enemies. No matter how Neitin pleaded that it was, instead, a sign of denial from Endovelicos, king of the gods, who held dominion over life or death, Bailar insisted that she, a woman with no magic, could not possibly make such a judgment. And Ekialde let himself be persuaded by Bailar again and again. In Bandue the war-god's name, he opened his veins and he breathed in smoke and he let the magic take him to the very threshold of that dark world.

He would die of it, Neitin was certain. She did not know how or when, but she was sure this would kill him, someday, this bartering his soul for unholy powers. When he drank Bailar's blood-potions, he would be strong, so strong, for a day—and then as weak as a kitten for a night, his energy thinned out in sacrifice to Bandue.

It was an *erregerra*'s duty, Ekialde insisted, to suffer thusly on behalf of his people, on behalf of his cause. Who else but their war-king should bear the burden?

Neitin did not understand why the burden needed bearing at all. There was still time. Their warriors were fierce and skilled, but no match for the iron-clad Aventan legions, if they came in force. If the Lusetani disappeared back into the wilderness, if they retreated to their own vil-lages and orchards and riverbanks, surely the Aventans would not bother to pursue them.

The child stirred, squawking objection to being out in the harsh elements. Neitin wrapped her cloak more securely around him, protecting him from the buffeting winds. As she rocked the boy, she gave thanks to Nabia and Trebarunu that their child had been conceived before Ekialde had started indulging in these dark magics. She could not bear to think of what kind of monster might have come forth, had it been conceived with such horrors abounding.

"Sister!" Ditalce, rushing out from a nearby tent, with Reilin close behind her. Neitin ignored her, staring forlornly at the horizon. "What are you doing?"

Still she answered only with silence. Neitin knew her sisters too well; they were all under Bailar's spell, as sure as Ekialde was. They all *believed*. She tried not to despise them for it, prayed to Nabia to make her heart compassionate and forgiving. Some days, it worked better than others.

"Sister," Reilin said, "you must go back to your tent. To have brought your child out into this wind, this is dangerous—"

"Better the wind and sand," Neitin said, "than what's in there." Reilin tried to take her by the arm, but Neitin shrugged her off as strongly as she could without jostling the babe too much. She would not be led docilely back to a comfortless bed, and when Ditalce added her strength to Reilin's, Neitin dug her heels into the hardened earth. "No. I will not go back. Not while Bailar is there."

Her sisters exchanged nervous glances. They were for Ekialde, heart and soul, and her reticence troubled them. Reilin and Ditalce would have laid down their own lives, if Ekialde asked. They believed, as Ekialde did, as his warriors did, that the Lusetani were on a sacred quest, a charge from Bandue himself, to eliminate the Aventan threat from all of Iberia— even if that meant turning on tribes that had long been allied with them, even if it meant destroying groves and orchards that fed their own people, even if it meant straying so very far from home. Ekialde was god-touched, the reasoning went. Whatever he decided, it *must* be so.

Neitin was his wife. She been at his side long before Bailar had proclaimed him *erregerra*. She knew his fears, knew he had questioned, once, the path before him. *'And now he has been swallowed up . . .'*

The winds picked up, carrying even more stinging sand with them, with such a roar that Reilin struggled to be heard above it. "Neitin! Come to our tent, if you do not wish to return to your own! Ditalce and I will keep you and the babe safe."

It was offered with an indulgent tone—the sort one used with an unreasonable child. The sort Neitin had used herself, on these younger siblings of hers, in other times. Now she was the one to be treated cautiously. Now she was the one who had to be delicately reasoned with. Her sisters would write it off as maternal stress, no doubt, or the result of traveling in such hard weather. They would fabricate excuses and treat her as though she were the youngest, not the eldest of them, to be coddled and corralled in equal measure. They would do this so that they did not have to think her disloyal.

'*I am,*' Neitin thought. '*I am disloyal, and I can not even bring myself to be sorry for it.*'

The lights in Ekialde's tent flickered, and Neitin's heart sank. "Do they think to try again? So soon?" Neither Reilin nor Ditalce answered, and as her sisters bundled her away, Neitin discovered that she was too tired even to weep.

∞∞∞∞∞∞∞∞∞∞∞∞

Every muscle in his body burned. The sensation was familiar, in a distant way. When Ekialde had first learned to shoot a bow, his father had made him draw over and over again, until the muscles in his arms felt like they had come apart from his bones.

This was worse.

Blood dripped from his biceps and his thighs. Bailar had not cut deep, but he had made thirteen cuts, one for each month of the year. Ekialde's blood, the blood of the *erregerra*, mixed with that of their fallen foes and scattered upon the earth. It should open the way between the worlds. It *would* open the way. Bailar had sworn it. The blood of life together with the blood of death, to show the *akdraugi* the path from the netherworlds.

"We can try no more tonight," Bailar said.

"We must."

Bailar fixed him with a stern look. "We mean to bring the *akdraugi* into our world, not send you into theirs. That uncle of your wife's is a decent healer. Have him bind your wounds. You will rest for three days before we try again."

Though dizziness threatened him, Ekialde set his jaw. "I am the *erregerra*. I decide when we are done and when we try again."

Folding his arms over his chest, Bailar arched an eyebrow expressively. Then he stepped forward, extended one arm, and gave Ekialde a gentle prod on the shoulder.

It was hardly more than a nudge, but in Ekialde's depleted state, it was enough to throw him off-balance. He slid a foot back, trying to steady himself, but his head swam heavily and black spots pattered over his vision.

Carefully, slowly, Ekialde seated himself on the nearest bench.

"I have decided we are done for tonight," Ekialde said. "I will tell you when I feel strong enough to try again." Two nights, at most, he would allow himself. An ordinary man might need three to recover, but Ekialde knew he was not ordinary.

Bailar snorted, likely knowing his young king's mind. But he made no further mention of the necessity of rest. Instead, he sopped a rag in a waiting basin of water and began sponging the blood off of his own arms. "It will not always take so much effort," he said. "Once we have opened the way for the *akdraugi,* they will know how to follow it again. Very little of your blood will be necessary, after that." He bobbed his head, considering, as a cook might contemplate the balance of ingredients in a delicate dish. "More of your enemies' blood will always be beneficial, though. Your blood opens the way, but theirs is what the *akdraugi* will feed upon."

"That is all very well," Ekialde said, "but first we must open the way."

"We will. And that will only be the beginning, blessed *erregerra.* And there may be a way to strengthen you for future endeavors." Bailar tossed the rag aside and plucked at his long beard thoughtfully. There was more white in it now than there had been when they began this war.

'He likes all our men to think him impervious,' Ekialde realized, *'a conduit for the gods' power who does not suffer for bearing that burden. He likes me to think that. But he is still just a man. It costs him, as it costs me.'*

"I will need to consult the stars," Bailar went on. "Find the right time, when you can take the strength of your enemies into yourself."

"I thought I was doing that already." For a year now, he had been drinking Bailar's tinctures, thick wines with drops of his enemies' blood in them.

An acknowledging nod from Bailar. "True. But I think . . . I think there is a way we can do better." Another thoughtful tug on his beard. *"Akdraugi* first. Then we will see what other gates we can open."

V

STABIAE, CRATER BAY

One by one, Alhena of the Vitelliae plucked the seeds from the core of the pomegranate, placing them gently in the offering bowl in front of her. Her mind was meant to be on matters sacred and devout, but by the time her fingers were stained as red as her hair, her thoughts had wandered. It was easy to let them, here at the Temple of Proserpina, with azure sky at her back and the goddess's serene eyes looking down on her from the painted wooden statue. Here she could be calm enough for contemplation, a mage of Time sheltered beneath the gaze of her patron deity.

Only in the bucolic surroundings of seaside Stabiae did Alhena realize just how much the size and bustle of Aven intimidated her. *'It's not as though I hate the city . . . but I do not have my sisters' affection for it.'* She had never been able to get a handle on how the thing *worked*. So many people, all vying for their own sorts of power, all jostling and negotiating and elbowing each other—often as literally as metaphorically. Alhena did not think she would ever have Aula's affinity for political maneuvering, nor her social graces, nor did she feel Latona's joy in the chaos of the city, her pleasure in going among the markets and forums and meeting new people.

'Somehow Latona managed to learn the proper things, even though she spent her early years at a temple . . .' Latona had gone to Juno's keeping at the tender age of four. Not all priestesses and acolytes lived in the apartments that stood behind the temple, of course, but Gaia Claudia, the High Priestess of Juno who had seen Latona's potential, had done so, and she chose to keep Latona with her. Latona might have stayed there her entire life, had not Claudia been taken away by the fever that ravaged the city seven years later.

Then, at Aula's elbow, Latona had received a different kind of education: social graces, household management, and the intricacies of personal relationships that formed the chaotic spiderweb of patrician life. Between Aula's profitable gossip-mongering and Latona's Spirit-given empathic insights, it seemed there was nothing her older sisters didn't know about the city: who was courting whose daughter, who was an un-faithful spouse, who hated whom for what reasons—fresh insults and generations-old grudges alike lay themselves open before the elder two Vitelliae sisters. *'Me, though . . .'*

Aulus had resisted attaching Alhena to a temple—first, because his trust in them had been damaged after Latona's experience, and second, because during Ocella's reign, temple life was less safe than homebound seclusion. Too many priests and mages were in the Dictator's pay or had been coerced into cooperating with him, and a budding young prophetess from a prominent family might have been an irresistible temptation. As a result, Alhena had grown up cloistered, rarely venturing out into pub-lic. It had never occurred to her to be bothered by it. She knew she would marry someday, to a nice young man from a good family, and go from one home to another, secure all the while.

Then the Dictator had died, and her intended husband not long after-wards, and Alhena found herself suddenly thrust into a world she felt ill-prepared for. Her father was censor, her brother famous for holding Iberia against the barbarians, her sisters maneuvering to secure alliances, and the family more in the public eye than ever. Parties, dinners, conversations . . . Aven was a constant suffocation of expectations.

So it had been both a triumph and a relief when she had convinced her father to bring her to Stabiae early this year. Aula and her daughter Lucia would come along later in the summer, and Latona, too, if she could get away from her husband without it causing a stir, but Aulus had traveled down to make Stabiae his base of operations while he saw to censorial duties around Crater Bay, and he had allowed Alhena to come along. In Stabiae, she could *breathe,* and peace came to her under the eaves of the Temple of Proserpina.

In truth, the temple here was little more than a shrine. A large one, with mosaic floors and brightly painted walls to house the statue of the goddess, but nothing to rival the grand temples in Aven. Alhena didn't mind. A smaller temple meant fewer rituals and fewer ways to put a foot wrong. She had grown fond of the local priestess, Moira, an Athae-can woman with considerable gifts in Time and Earth—a natural histo-rian as well as a steady mentor. A few other girls and young women frequented the shrine, though none of them had magical blessings. Moira introduced her to a few of them, and Alhena had overcome shyness enough for a few short but genuine conversations on the goddess's doorstep.

Perhaps because she felt safe enough to let her guard down, Proserpina's gifts came rolling to the surface, swift and unbidden, after she had finished with the pomegranate and while she was lighting incense at the base of the goddess's statue. A waking dream. Alhena was grateful the goddess's touch had chosen an opportune moment to come upon her, rather than felling her in the street, as had happened before. The wafting musk from the incense made her head feel heavy, and before she knew it, she had sunk to her knees, the room around her blurring.

A blink, and she was no longer in the temple under the clear light of a warm afternoon; she instead stood on a wide green hill under a gray, cloud-streaked sky. It was no place she recognized—not a place at all, she realized, as the hill started to roll beneath her. Alhena felt her limbs shaking, trembling as the ground shook. She whimpered, looking around the vacant landscape for anyone, anything that might help her—but there was nothing, only an endless, shaking earth.

"Shhhh . . ." Alhena could hear Moira's voice, though it seemed to be coming from far away, and she could not see her. She felt a soft pressure on her back, too—a reminder that not all of her was Proserpina's to direct. "Ride it. Don't let it ride you."

Alhena swallowed and tried to focus her attention. She could do it, sometimes, in dreams, but here she was groping for purchase with nothing to hold onto. But she took a steadying breath. *Show me, Lady Proserpina . . . What is it you want me to see?*

The green earth stopped shaking and began to peel back, like a citron rind, revealing a shining white interior to the hill before Alhena. No, not shining—glistening. Alhena had seen this kind of white before, at sacrifices. It was the white of bones, hewn from flesh, still gleaming with fat. Stacks and stacks of them, locked together, beneath the soil, forming the bonds of the hill itself. Somewhere behind her awareness, Alhena's stomach roiled. But she forced her mind to focus.

What for? Show me.

The bones began to clack and clatter, pulling apart from each other in jagged lines to reveal a set of bronze doors, deep underground. Alhena had no wish to draw closer to the tangle of bones, but there was something etched on the doors, and a nudge in the back of her mind told her she needed to see it. Her feet were bare, she realized as she padded along the not-quite-path of torn grass and disturbed earth, and when she grew nearer the hill of bones, she could smell the rankness, putrefying in the buried viscera.

The doors had words upon them, but at first they were in no language Alhena could recognize, not even in Tyrian characters, but strange triangular shapes, then glyphs that she thought might be Abydosian. After a moment, however, they began to morph, reforming first into Athaecan words. She recognized a few—strife, quarrel, pain—before they, too, disappeared, and long chains of Truscan appeared before her. None of the words stayed put; they wandered all over the bronze doors, so fleet that Alhena's eyes could hardly follow them, and every time she blinked, new ones seemed to appear, etching their way to the surface and pounding the previous sentences down. Her skin felt hot, as though a great fire burned behind the doors, ready to open like an oven, but Alhena forced herself to stand still, bearing the discomfort, and not take her eyes from the doors.

"Chaos is the constant," one line read. "Her wrath is relentless, she hurls down bitterness from heaven," said another. "The elder daughter of dark Night" faded before Alhena could catch the rest of the sentence, as did "a man grows eager." Soon there were so many words that Alhena could hardly separate one from the other, and her eyes watered with the strain of trying. "Reviled" flashed across her vision in searing shapes, and "wrathful," "justified," "needing"—"vengeance," "fury"—"alarms," "blood," "city"—Alhena could make no sense of the rolling verbal tide.

Then, just as Alhena thought the swirling scripture would become entirely illegible, it resolved into a single, bright-burning phrase, lit up as though molten: "All worlds shatter."

At that moment, the ground shook, and around her were other hills, likewise splitting to reveal gleaming bones and bronze doors. The doors opened and clanged shut, never in unison, but nor with any discernible pattern, raising up a bruising cacophony. Underneath it, though, was another noise: a harrowing howl, rising up from within the earth itself.

"The fiends hunger, little mage."

Alhena whipped around, looking for the source of the voice. It had spoken low but perfectly audible, even amid the banging doors and the keening, as though the speaker were right at her elbow. "Who's there? What do you want?"

An eerie laughter echoed through the ravaged hills, and for a moment, the banging of the doors seemed to join in its chortle.

"The fiends, little mage, the fiends . . . how hungry they are . . . what a feast your city is . . . the fiends, the fiends . . ." Something snatched at

Alhena's hair, and she whirled again, looking for the speaker. But there was no one there, only a rising wind, plucking at her curls and her clothes, and the echoing words, "The fiends, the fiends, the fiends . . ."

Alhena sat up with a gasp, unsure for a moment where she was. Her skin still felt hot to the touch, as though she had been too long out in the sun, and her throat felt parched. "I need—!"

"Shhh." Moira, supporting her shoulders. Alhena realized she had been brought to the small garden beside the shrine. Her already red-stained fingers were smudged with the incense she had been lighting, but she had no recollection either of setting the incense cones down or of walking to the garden. "You fainted, dear. Take some water."

Alhena's hands hardly seemed to belong to her, but somehow she managed to wrap her fingers around the cup that Moira offered, grateful for the older woman's presence. Moira's cool voice and thick, graying curls put Alhena in mind of the mother she hardly remembered. She liked to think, had Vipsania Vitelliae lived, she would have been like this: steady and serene.

Once Alhena had sipped away half the cup of water, Moira spoke again. "That was quite something, my dear. Can you speak of it, what you saw?"

"I think . . . I think so." Many of her visions dissipated like dreams when she surfaced from them, but this one went on resonating in her brain, and she had no trouble recounting it to Moira. "It was . . . unusual," she said at the end of the tale. "I so rarely have anything . . . well, anything so *animate* in my visions. Almost never anything that talks. It's usually just . . . images, feelings . . ."

Moira nodded in understanding. "That is often the way with Time mages, particularly when young. Have you had much training in shepherding your visions?"

"The usual," Alhena said, then blushed. "Maybe somewhat less. I've been close kept. I had a tutor in Aven, but she focused more on controlling the gift, not interpreting what came of it." Aulus Vitellius had been anxious that Alhena's talents not make themselves too noticeable.

Moira frowned. "I'm not sure what this might mean—either the vision itself or that it seems to have exceeded your usual gift. But it may be, Alhena, that Proserpina is asking more of you than she has before."

Alhena held in a sigh, unsure whether that might be a blessing or a curse.

◇◇◇◇◇◇◇◇◇◇◇◇◇

TOLETUM, CENTRAL IBERIA

Gaius Vitellius, Tribune of the Eighth Legion, walked the ramparts of Toletum's walls, with the rumbling Tagus River far below on his left and a scattering of red-and-brown rooftops to his right.

Toletum stood in a deep bend of the Tagus River, almost in the dead center of Iberia, where a narrow valley provided passage between the high central mountains and the seeming-immeasurable plateaus in the south. It derived its only importance from that position: a crossroads, a meeting-place, and a trading post for Iberians from the Arevaci and other tribes, Tyrian merchants, and intrepid Aventans.

When Vitellius had arrived the prior year, its walls had been a haphazard mix of stonework and earthwork where the city faced land, and hardly anything at all along the river. He was proud of the improvements. *'We did rather well, for not having any engineers in the vexillation.'* Now all of Toletum was encircled by timber structures, in some places built upon earthworks and in others atop the original stone. The improvements showed he had not been idle, nor allowed his men to be.

Vitellius had come up to the wall with the intent of checking for faults in the mortar, or any place where the underlying earthworks might have shifted with the recent rains. His gaze, though, kept wandering toward the horizon. Not east, though, not towards Aven and his father and sisters, so many thousands of miles away. Downriver went his eyes and his thoughts, down the snaking path of the Tagus.

A figure ascended a ladder and bounded onto the wall a short distance in front of him: Hanath, a tall woman with deep brown skin and an athletic physique. She was Numidian-born, but her husband, Bartasco, was the leader of the local Arevaci tribe, the staunchest allies Aven had in central Iberia.

Both Bartasco and Hanath had proved their worth a hundred times over during these months, within Toletum as well as without. Bartasco had been invaluable in keeping the people of Toletum happy, working with the magistrates to administer rations and adjudicate disputes, while Hanath often rode out with the cavalry to check on the local villages and make sure they were properly supplied. *'And Hanath,'* Vitellius reflected, *'has a unique talent for promoting courage.'* Like a lioness cuffing her mate, she had stirred Bartasco into action the previous year. The Numidian-born woman seemed to have a similar effect on the young men of every town she visited, and she almost always returned with more riders than she had left with, new recruits to freshen the patrols.

"Tribune!" Hanath called as she approached. Her voice had the high vowels and clipped consonants of her homeland. "I have been speaking with the men and women whose homes border that empty space near the tinsmith's." She settled her hands on her hips, giving Vitellius a satisfied smile. "They are quite amenable to our plan of turning the plot into a garden."

"Good, good." Food was beginning to be a worry—ironically more than it had been through the winter. Vitellius had rationed well, and the Lusetani had retreated to less-contested areas, away from the tribes who had allied with Aven. They had set up camps in Vettoni lands, along-side their blood-forged allies, and there they had waited through the snows and rains, rather than facing harassment throughout the lean months.

But spring had come, and with it, new troubles. Reports deluged Toletum, of attacks on towns, villages, mines, fields, and orchards through-out the Iberian plateaus. It was hard to convince anyone to go out to plough or plant with the threat of raids hanging over them, and the weather had been unpredictable ever since the season turned. Vitellius had taken to dispatching cohorts alongside the farmers for the peasants' peace of mind, and some of the legionaries could even make themselves useful with farming implements. The roads to the east were open yet, and Vitellius had called for grain and other supplies to be brought up from the coastal towns, as much as could be gathered before the Lusetani or Vettoni cut them off.

From downriver, they heard more and more stories of fields set ablaze, towns ravaged, and worse. Strange tales, carried by fleeing peasants, of haunting wraiths, howling the names of the living, crying to them in the night. Vitellius might not have given the tales credence, but he remembered the strange potion Ekialde had tried to use on him, how it had nearly robbed him of his will until countermanded by his sister Latona's protective magic, woven into his clothing. Thinking of that, anything seemed possible. *'All downriver . . .'*

Hanath cocked her head. "You are distracted, Tribune."

"Hmm?" Vitellius realized a moment too late that the mindless response had proved her point. "Oh. I suppose I am." He cleared his throat.

"I apologize. I did not mean to be inattentive. I'm very glad to hear it, about the empty plot. I know the herbalists want a portion of it, but we should ask the farmers what will give the best yield for the rest." They had discussed all those details previously, but Vitellius used the repetition to ground himself back in the present moment.

Hanath's perception, however, would not let him off so easily. "You are missing your friend."

Vitellius scuffed his boot on the rampart, hobnails scraping against the wood. "I am worried for my cohort." Then, at Hanath's knowingly arched eyebrow, he added, "And yes, I am worried about Mennenius. He should have been back long before now."

Tribune Titus Mennenius had been due back in Toletum five days before the Kalends of Maius. His cohort was on patrol, marching from a village on the Tagus River up toward the mountain line, while Vitellius's cohort stayed in fortified Toletum with the few Fourth Legion men sent up from Gades the previous year. It was a path they had marched before, one of several that Vitellius had determined necessary to maintain awareness of the enemy's movements and to protect the nearby farmers as best they were able. An easy path, a familiar path. But now they were on the third day past the Kalends, with still no sign of Mennenius.

"I should have . . . I don't know, I should have found a better way, to keep *everyone* safe." Vitellius passed a hand over his brow and scrubbed it through his gingery hair. "But I needed men in the field to protect the villages. If we'd all stayed holed up in here, we'd have been no better than Fimbrianus, damn his coward's heart." He still hadn't forgiven the ex-governor of Baelonia for refusing to march north all the past year. "There are simply . . . there are not enough of us, Hanath." A plaintive moan was perilously close to entering his voice. *Not* the sort of tone a commander hoped to affect.

Hanath, though, was strangely comfortable to be around. She was a comrade now, but neither under his command nor someone on whom his advancement depended. He could be honest with her, and with Bartasco, in a way he could risk with few others. Even with Mennenius, he tried to put on a brave face.

"It is a hard task the gods have set us, Tribune," Hanath said. "We are all doing the best we can. And you are right—if you did not send a cohort out to patrol, we could not guarantee the farmers a safe perimeter, and our survival depends on theirs. You made the right choice."

"I could've gone out myself."

"You are the ranking Aventan," Hanath pointed out. "What happens if you die out in the wilderness, eh?" She clapped his shoulder lightly. "This is the curse of authority. I had to learn it when I married Bartasco. You must learn it now."

She had the right of it. Vitellius *did* consider it his duty to stay and fortify the stronghold. Toletum was the largest settlement for a hundred miles; from here, the Aventans could hope to hold out until reinforcements arrived. And they *would*. In Aprilis there had been news from Aven: the legions, on the move, into the heart of Iberia. Sempronius Tarren, leading the Tenth and the Fourteenth, and Onidius Praectus, bringing the rest of the Eighth to finally rejoin their comrades-in-arms. They heard, too, that Lucretius Rabirus was headed for Gades to relieve Fimbrianus of his command—welcome news to the cohort from the Fourth, who likewise sought reunification of their legion. Vitellius knew enough about Rabirus to be skeptical that his command would yield favorable results. But whenever *someone* did arrive, Vitellius would need to be on hand to coordinate further efforts.

"Mennenius is only here because of me," Vitellius confessed. "He's younger than me, you know. Most junior of the Eighth's tribunes; he'd never have been sent on a vexillation like this. But I asked for him to join me." His lips twisted slightly, a tiny smile. "We met as boys." He could picture the day so clearly, the bright sun baking the Field of Mars. "I was already halfway through training. He was so eager to learn. I suppose you could say I took him under my wing."

"He is a man grown now, my friend," Hanath gently reminded him, "and a tribune of the Aventan military, with that same training. He does not need your protection, and he has sense enough to think his way out of trouble."

"You're right . . ." Vitellius sighed. "You're right, of course. If it hadn't been so long . . ."

Hanath jerked her head toward the ladder. "You are lonely, Tribune." She said it so flatly and without judgment that Vitellius could not be ashamed for having shown such a weakness. "Come and take lunch with me and Bartasco. We shall eat salt-fish and speak of how to grow crops inside city walls." She leveled a commanding gaze at him. "We shall speak of things that can be *done*, things we have power over. It is always better than to dwell on the dread of fates beyond our control."

That was easier said than achieved, in Vitellius's experience, but he accepted the invitation.

Just after the guard on the half-improved walls changed, the cry of an Arevaci horn cut the evening air. The patrol, coming in from afar. Vitellius tensed, then recognized the sennet: one of aid requested, not an approaching threat.

Vitellius raced to the wall with Bartasco only a few steps behind him, both of them mounting the ladder with the swiftness of goats. "What's going on?" Vitellius asked one of the sentries.

The young man pointed. "Riders returning, there, sir," he said. "Looks like Sotir's group."

One of Hanath's fierce maids, leading a group of cavalry. "They had gone—"

"West, I believe, sir."

Vitellius exchanged looks with Bartasco, then gestured him forward. Sotir was barreling toward the gates; the others were still scarcely visible, coming through the tree line. She pulled her gallop to a halt within shouting distance, but her words were in the Arevaci dialect, too swift and desperate for Vitellius to catch all of it, despite half a year's tutelage. He thought he caught the word the Arevaci used for "cohort," though, and turned to Bartasco for confirmation. "What does she say? Did they find—"

Bartasco nodded rapidly. "Tribune Mennenius and the others . . . somewhere near the town of Libora, she says, and . . ." Bartasco's face had gone pale, his usual bluff manner turned to waxen alarm. "There's been trouble."

"What kind of trouble?"

The horsewoman shouted something else, and in it, Vitellius made out Mennenius's name. "She says something of Mennenius." Vitellius caught Bartasco by the sleeve. "Mennenius, she says, and something else. What does she say?"

"She does not explain. She says you should hear it from the Tribune." Bartasco's brow creased; he was evidently having trouble following the scout's scattered message. "She cannot tell, she did not see enough herself. You will need to hear the truth of it from Mennenius."

"So Tribune Mennenius lives?" Flooded with gratitude, Vitellius released Bartasco and leaned out over the wall, peering as far to the Tagus's southwestern bend as he could. Straggling up from the south was a cohort, though nothing like in proper formation. The lines were uneven, their steps shuffling, not the even, steady beat of a proper legion on the march. Some were even slung over saddles; others pulled on improvised sledges. This was an army routed, an army in retreat, and Vitellius felt a cold pit settling into his stomach.

"Sons of Dis . . ." Vitellius muttered, then shouted, "Open the gates! Immediately!"

Vitellius's instinct was to dash across the field to meet the incoming men, but he knew the foolishness of such exertion. Instead, he sent more riders out to assist them, while he forced himself to stand in the gateway, Bartasco at his side, until they drew nearer.

Titus Mennenius, in tattered tribune's garb, was at the front of the lines, as he should have been—but he looked a dead man walking. His hollow, haunted eyes could barely focus on the city he trudged toward. His face and limbs were dirty, caked with some strange muck, and he shuffled as though he had no strength in him. Once Vitellius could make out his features enough to identify him, he could hold back no longer. "Water!" Vitellius bellowed, breaking out into a sprint. "Bring water!"

"Water, yes . . ." Mennenius did not seem to see Vitellius right in front of him; his eyes drifted to the open sky. "We crossed the river at . . . at Libora . . . we thought that putting water between us would . . . but it didn't . . ."

"Easy, easy," Vitellius said, clutching his friend by the shoulders.

"Water . . . we needed . . . but it didn't . . ."

Bartasco was shouting orders to his horsemen, and what centurions had wits left to them were shepherding the other fighting men within the safety of Toletum's walls. "Mennenius, where have you been?" Vitellius asked. "We were—that is, we thought—Hellfire, Mennenius."

Mennenius's head lolled, and for a moment, Vitellius thought he was going to faint. He snapped back to himself, though, the fog going out of his countenance. "We were lost. Not on the land, I mean, but the land around us . . . We knew where we were, but could never get where we were going . . ." Mennenius frowned, as though he knew how little sense he was making. "Get me in, Vitellius . . . the sun is . . . I am overwhelmed . . ." And saying so, his eyes rolled back and he half-sank in Vitellius's arms.

VI

"I lost sixteen men," Mennenius said some time later, inside the tribunes' quarters within Toletum's walls. He had been scrubbed clean of what had turned out to be muck from the Tagus, then wrapped in a warm blanket. With that and some bread, Mennenius was regaining sensibility, but Vitellius had given up trying to ask questions. Mennenius was spinning the story around in his own good time, and no impetus from anyone would hasten the telling. "I don't . . . I couldn't even tell you why. It was like the will to live just got . . . got drained out of them . . ." He tore off another hunk of bread with savage eagerness as Bartasco came through the doorway; Vitellius gestured with a hand for him to come in, but stay silent. He was worried further interruption might put Mennenius off the tale. "I haven't slept in days, none of us have," Mennenius continued. "We—we were wandering. I don't know how we got so far off-course."

Mennenius's hands came up and raked through his hair, then pulled slowly down his face. Bartasco stepped in quietly, closing the door behind him.

"I'm sorry." Mennenius's voice was much quieter when he continued. "I know I sound mad. I've been . . ." A heavy sigh. "It's been a rough few days. At times I thought I was going mad for certain. Or that I'd died and been swamped in Lethe's waters."

"Breathe easy, friend," Vitellius said. "I just need to know what happened."

Mennenius's eyes were still far away, and he spoke as though relating a tale that had happened to someone else. "The first few days were uneventful. We made it to the mountain line without encountering anyone. Then we heard . . . there was a scout, one of the . . . one of the Cossetans, I thought. He found us as we were marching back towards the river, told us there was a group of Lusetani a little ways to the west. So we went to see . . ." Another sigh, this one shaky. "It was their bastard war-king, Gaius; I'm sure of it. Him with the yellow eyes, that engaged you last year."

Vitellius let out a slow breath through his teeth. "Sons of Dis. So close?"

Mennenius wagged a slow affirmative. "Not with his whole force, though. Fewer men than he brought to Libora last year. A small band, smaller than our cohort, I think . . . but that didn't matter . . ." A tremulous laugh burst out of him, startling Vitellius. "What need you men when there are demons on your side?"

Vitellius and Bartasco exchanged worried looks. "You don't seem as though you're speaking metaphorically, friend?"

Mennenius shook his head vehemently, then winced, as though the sudden jerking movement had pained him. He let his head fall into his hands, cupping his brow with his palm. "No, no, there were demons. True demons."

"Demons?" Bartasco asked. "What demons fight for this Ekialde?"

"Shadows," Mennenius replied, with a shudder. He dragged himself to sit upright again. "Shadows, following us for days, driving us into a mist . . ." His hand passed over his eyes. "I thought there was a mist, at least. Maybe there wasn't. We were all so tired. The shadows followed us everywhere, always whispering. I couldn't understand what they said, but I never needed to." His eyes flickered over to the jug of water standing near Vitellius's bed; Vitellius rushed to provide him with a fresh cup. Only after swallowing several gulps did Mennenius go on. "Howling of death and destruction, but with a feeling like . . . like having your family's *penates* smashed in front of you. Your ancestors' death masks trodden upon. A wrenching sense of sacrilege, that crawled up inside of us, like a poison of the soul . . ."

Bartasco gave a low hiss.

Vitellius turned to him. "Speak."

The Arevaci leader's face was grim. "I know whereof he speaks," Bartasco said. "At least I think I . . ." His features twisted in consternation. "It makes no sense! No man in a dozen generations has raised them."

"Bartasco?"

He huffed through his thick reddish-brown beard. "*Akdraugi*. Soul-poisoners. Spirits torn from the netherworld."

"That, I can easily believe," Mennenius said, draining the cup of water and reaching out for more. "It felt like having Pluto's own breath on the back of my neck." He shuddered, spilling the water; Vitellius steadied the pitcher, but Mennenius continued to tremble. "I'm sorry. I can't . . . Sixteen men just . . . stopped living. Just gave up. Haunted to death." He shook his head incredulously. "I watched it happen and I still can't explain it. It was like . . . like something was feeding on each man's *anima* . . .

and some men were meals more quickly devoured than others. Sixteen men . . ." A shaky half-sob, then he looked up at Bartasco. "What defeats them?" Mennenius asked, panic and desperation written on his face, as though he could take Bartasco's answer across the river and back in time, to save his fallen men.

"It varies," Bartasco replied. "In some stories, song will drive them off. In others, pouring rain. But in most of the stories, what works best are . . ." He hesitated. "I do not know what word you would have for it, in Truscan. To us they are the *besteki*. Good spirits, where the *akdraugi* are evil. Protective of humans, where the *akdraugi* feed on them."

Outside, the wind had picked up, clattering the shutters of the building the tribunes had commandeered for the officers. "Well," Mennenius ventured, voice quavering, "where do we get some of the good kind?"

"I shall ask the magic-men of my tribe what they know of them," Bartasco said, "and I shall ask the Edetani to do the same. But I can promise nothing." He made a helpless gesture. "The *akdraugi,* these are stories to us now. Things the heroes of legends encountered, but I would no more expect to run into one than you would one of Ulysses's cyclopes or Jason's harpies." Despite himself, Vitellius smiled; the long winter nights had been rife with storytelling, and Bartasco seemed a sponge for a good tale. "But the memory of magic-men is long. They may know something."

Mennenius wrapped his arms around himself as shivers began to course through his body. "You have to find out. You have to."

"You should rest," Vitellius said, clapping his friend on the shoulder. "Bartasco, would you walk him to his quarters?" Something had been tickling at Vitellius's mind as Mennenius described the *akdraugi*— something that made them seem not so foreign, not so inexplicable. Aventans, too, had haunting wraiths and protective spirits. Aventans, too, had magic to command them and magic to expel them.

Vitellius needed to write a letter to his sister.

∞∞∞∞∞∞∞∞∞∞

CITY OF AVEN

Latona did not have an office or a study in her husband's home. He would have considered that ridiculous. What use could a woman possibly have for such a space? But she did have a room off of the garden housing her loom, and she had had Merula set up a table and a small rack which she could fill with scrolls. It was not private, but if Herennius decided to snoop, he would only discover a small trove of religious and thaumaturgical texts, and Latona did not think he would guess at her true reasons for investigating them.

Nor would he suspect that Latona, in truth, had been barred access from these very papers. *'I owe my baby sister a great deal.'* Aemilia Fullia had apparently convinced half the temples in Aven to deny Latona access to their libraries, but she had not thought to have them bar little Alhena as well. Before she left with their father for Stabiae, Alhena had gone to the Temple of Saturn and borrowed a number of dusty tomes. These were mostly histories of mages and their deeds, from epic tales of the heroes to mundane records of mages using their talents to help build aqueducts, revive crops, or dispense justice. Some other texts, Latona had begged off of Quinta Terentia, the Vestal Virgin. Her friendship with Quinta's younger sister, Terentilla, had given her some insulation there from Aemilia's spite. The Vestals had a carefully curated library—curated and, in some ways, limited. The official doctrine, the heart of the *mos maiorum,* dictated what could be found there. The *mos maiorum* set out how all things in Aven should be, not laws, but guiding principles and customs, based on the philosophies of the revered men who had founded the Republic almost five hundred years earlier. Latona knew how little that could sometimes resemble the way things actually were.

Few of the books were the practical treatises that Latona was hoping for. There had been a stray reference in one text that seemed as though it should have been expanded in another—but hours of searching had left Latona still unable to locate the source.

Absorbed in the texts and in her thoughts, Latona uncharacteristically lost track of who passed in and out of the garden. Usually her Spirit magic gave her a constant background awareness of other peoples' presences, particularly when they were as familiar to her as the household staff. So it came as a shock when two soft hands landed on her shoulders and pulled her out of her slumped posture. "Mustn't slouch!" came her older sister's chipper voice.

Latona looked, instead of at Aula, over at Merula, who was on the floor nearby, midway through some complex series of stretches. "Aren't you meant to be defending me from menace? How did she slip by you?" With a little grin, Merula shrugged unapologetically.

"Merula knows your darling and devoted sister would never mean you a moment's harm," Aula went on, as Latona twisted to face her. "Speaking of harm, you're going to strain your eyes, you know, all these hours squinting in poor light."

"I do not squint." But she could hear the familiar anxious note in Aula's voice, commenting on a little worry because a larger one was niggling at her mind. "I'll find what I'm looking for, sooner or later. But in the meantime, some of these stories . . ." Latona shook her head. "It's no wonder the Republic has turned towards limiting what mages may do. If even half of these tales are even half true . . . Mages who could hold fire in their palms, even create it out of nothing—" But as soon as she spoke the words, she winced, feeling the *wrongness* of them. "No, not out of nothing, out of the *potentiality* of fire. Others who could not just read but control the weather, not with our charms and implorations for rain, but with sea-tossing storms and blistering droughts . . ." She reached back to her desk, seizing a scroll embellished with a black border. "And this one! You wouldn't think Earth could turn vile, but there are stories of ground-rotters, and this Ionian cult of Echidna, mages who wanted to be the mothers of monsters . . ."

Aula shuddered. "No, thank you. Birthing Lucia was quite trauma enough. I can't imagine if she'd come out with eight limbs or tentacles."

Latona smiled, grateful for Aula's leavening presence, even if she had interrupted. No one recognized better than Aula that sometimes Latona *needed* interrupting, lest she fall too deeply into whatever had currently fixated her attention. She stood up, pushing tendrils of golden hair back where they had fallen from the simple coronet that Merula plaited for her on quiet days, when she didn't expect visitors. "Yet in all of this, there's so little on Spirit mages."

"There are fewer of you," Aula reasoned. "Didn't the old Athaecans eschew the intangible elements entirely until the age of Teracles?" Latona nodded. "Well, there you have it. Nothing to write of, for so long." She bumped her shoulder against Latona's lightly. "And it's not up to you to unravel the mysteries of the ages in a single sitting, you know."

"I know." She wasn't sure how to explain the pressing need that had driven her to such intent study. The gods had plans for her, she felt sure, wanted her to use her magic to better purpose. *'But how?'* The answer remained murky.

Aula put out a hand slightly behind her, gesturing her attendant forward. Not Helva today, Latona noticed, but a small fair-headed woman, who put a folded piece of paper into Aula's hand. "A letter came for you,"

Aula explained, passing it over to Latona. "From Alhena. I had one as well, though all it said was to give this one to you, because she didn't trust sending it here, lest your husband meddle." Aula's lips twitched in amusement. "A directive you might give some of your *other* correspondents, come to think of it."

"I have nothing to hide," Latona said airily as she popped the plain blue seal. "And it's not as though you're above meddling with the post, yourself." While Aula squawked in protest, Latona read.

It wasn't much of a letter, only a note, in Alhena's carefully elegant hand:

'Dearest sister,

'Your husband is receiving a letter, too, from Father, asking if you'll join us in Stabiae, even though it's still not quite the season for it. He's asking for you both, but it's you I want. Please come, even if Herennius won't. Find a way. You're needed. And I know this will sound strange, but I think you should invite Vibia Sempronia along with you. I can't explain in a letter. Just come.

'Ever your faithful,
'Alhena'

Frowning, Latona held it out to Aula. "Do you know anything about this?"

After a quick perusal, Aula shook her head. "I haven't the faintest. *Vibia*? Why on earth would she want you to—" And then Latona watched as something clicked behind Aula's eyes. "She counted on Vibia once before, with Scaeva. You don't think this could be . . ." Her voice trailed off, as though she were unwilling to put words to the thought.

Latona was scarcely more eager. "Something to do with him?" The idea shot a cold bolt straight through her. "But—in Stabiae? How? Why?"

"Maybe not him, specifically," Aula said, "but . . . related? Other . . ." Her eyes flicked left and right, then she dropped her voice to a low whisper. "Other Discordians?"

"I don't think any are hiding behind the trellis, Aula."

"Well, pardon me for caution, but I didn't think your household was privy to such dealings," Aula shot back. Latona's head wagged in concession to that point. "So . . . what will you do?"

"Tell Herennius I'm going to Stabiae, and he can come or not as he likes. If he tries to make a fuss, I'll tell him Alhena begged my assessment of some young man she's mooning over there." Latona shrugged. "He'll want no part of such feminine fuss, but he's not likely to deny me."

"And what about Vibia?"

"I suppose I'll go speak to her." Latona took the letter back. There were no braziers burning on this warm spring day, and it was too early for the lamps to be lit, so she passed the paper to Merula. "Toss that in the kitchen's fire when you get a chance, please." She looked back to Aula. "I can't imagine Alhena would mention her if she didn't truly think it necessary. I've no notion whether I'll be able to convince her to make a trip to Stabiae on short notice, but . . . if Alhena thinks I must, then I'll at least try."

"Well, it's not a conversation I envy you," Aula snorted. "She's been more prickly than usual ever since Sempronius left the city."

⬦⬦⬦⬦⬦⬦⬦⬦⬦⬦⬦⬦

The following afternoon, with Merula at her side, Latona went to the Mellan domus on the lower slope of the Palatine.

Whether by his influence or his wife's, Taius Mella's home was kept up in elegant fashion, modern but not trendy, the walls painted in geometric patterns of bright colors. The mosaic on the atrium floor paid tribute to the family's tradition of excellence, depicting famous landmarks and creatures from the various regions the family had conducted trade expeditions in, prior to their elevation to the senatorial class: tigers, leopards, and elephants all danced about the impluvium in a tile-blocked parade. Now, Taius Mella had to conduct his business through an intermediary, but unlike many senators, he felt no shame in his family's mercantile roots. Latona found herself wondering at the differences between him and her own husband. Both men had more wealth than ambition, both had married pedigreed patrician wives, but Taius Mella had always struck Latona as a pleasant-spirited man, content with his lot and proud of his clever wife.

"What a pleasant surprise," Vibia said, as the steward showed Latona into the back garden, where the plants stood in neat rows, each leaf and blossom clipped and angled to perfection.

'That control, so prim and precise . . .' Latona doubted that Vibia did her own gardening, but this was her domain nonetheless. A place to feel secure, where limitation could be channeled.

Vibia was in some ways so different from her brother, and in other ways so similar. They did not have as much in common physically as siblings could. Vibia was slightly built, with narrow, angular features, while Sempronius was broad and solid. Her skin was pale as Abydosian alabaster, while Sempronius's was naturally darker, and further weathered by his time in the military. They shared thick sable hair, however, and they both had keen eyes; that was where they looked the most alike. It was not just in the coloring, bistre and enveloping, but in the sharpness, in the way they had of looking at you in a way that suggested they could see through to the soul.

'Of course, in Vibia's case, that might literally be true.' Fracture mages had that talent, to peel away layers of pretense and scoop out the truth beneath, however flawed or ugly it might be. For a Spirit mage, accustomed as Latona was to creating the version of herself that the world saw, it was somewhat discomfiting. *'Perhaps that's why we've never been quite at ease with each other.'*

But Latona wanted to be—and not only for Sempronius's sake, nor because Vibia had saved her life. They were mages, women of the same class, and closely connected politically. They ought to be friends. That, too, was a Spirit-born impulse, to seek amiability where one could.

But if she was right about Alhena's summons, she needed an ally far more than a friend.

◇◇◇◇◇◇◇◇◇◇◇◇◇

A shiver of anxiety sloughed off of Latona, and Vibia found the twitch of it distracting. Something had rattled the lovely Spirit mage, and her glamour was inadequate to the task of covering it. At least, she could not hide it from a Fracture mage. Pure empathic talent was not within Vibia's domain, but she could often feel the fragile edges of another's soul, and Latona's were fluttering. "Is this purely a social call?" Vibia asked, as soon as the niceties of greeting and small talk had been done away with.

Fortunately, Latona did not look offended by Vibia's preference to get straight to the matter. "I'm afraid not," she said, then flicked her eyes around the garden at the slaves standing nearby, ready to offer cherries or water or a fan, if needed.

Vibia caught her meaning and looked to the pair waiting near the door. "Dana, pour us each a cup of water. Aganthus, leave a plate of cherries. You are all excused."

After they had gone, swishing away in their matched linen tunics, Latona said, "Thank you. It's not that I would mistrust your staff, but—"

Vibia held up a hand. "No need to apologize. If it is a sensitive matter—"

"It is." Latona's hand hovered over her cup for a moment before she continued. "At least, I think it is. I had a very strange letter from my sister Alhena—"

As Latona explained the letter and its summons, meant for the both of them, Vibia's mind churned. The youngest Vitellian had made more of a positive impression on Vibia than the rest of her family combined. Oh, Aulus was a solid enough man, she supposed, and a good ally to Sempronius in the Senate, but Aula was a meddlesome chatterbox, Gaius's involvement in the Iberian matter was too knotty to be an accident of fortune, and Latona—

Vibia *wished* she thought better of Latona, but she could never entirely quell the suspicions lurking in her heart. Trouble clung to the woman's skirts. Even if she had no ill intentions of her own—and Vibia had to credit that Latona seemed almost painfully earnest in her altruistic endeavors—she ended up right in the thick of mayhem too often for Vibia's comfort. Vibia might have been able to overlook that if she could have kept Latona on the outskirts of her social circle, but Sempronius had formed an attachment. How desperate of one, Vibia hadn't fully winkled out of him, but she read the situation as dire enough to warrant concern. *'The woman attracted the attention of a Discordian cultist, for Fortuna's sake.'*

And that, it seemed, was the problem that had brought her to Vibia's doorstep.

"I don't know the full story yet, obviously," Latona was explaining, "but the fact that Alhena didn't want to commit it to paper worries me. You may be one of the only people in Aven who can appreciate the significance of that." Latona bit her lower lip briefly. "I'm worried she's stumbled into some Discordian . . . something out in the country. I can't think of any other reason she would beg for me to join her and bring you along."

Despite the warmth of the day, the garden suddenly seemed considerably cooler. Vibia's hand pressed against her stomach, as though that might soothe the ache that Latona's words had provoked. "If you're right, the implications would be—"

"Terrifying," Latona finished. "If Pinarius Scaeva wasn't just a single maniac, some deranged remnant of the cult, if there are more of them out there—"

"It's not impossible," Vibia admitted. "Ocella killed as many as he could and banished the rest. I'd heard they went to the East, Bithynia and Parthia, places where their perfidies might go unnoticed. But if they stayed, or returned after his death, and found each other again . . ." She shuddered.

"It might not be so!" Latona rushed to say, though Vibia wasn't sure who she was most trying to convince. "Maybe I'm wrong and it's something else entirely. And I know it's mad to ask you to take a spontaneous sojourn to Crater Bay before the summer even properly begins, but . . ." Latona's face took on slightly pained lines. "I couldn't just ignore my sister's words. And, well, she was right before."

A stab of guilt joined the faint twist of horror in Vibia's gut. Alhena *had* summoned her alongside Sempronius, when Latona had been prone and helpless in that riverside warehouse, but Vibia's contribution had been slight enough. Her powers in Fracture, openly known to the world, were tepid things next to what her brother could wreak with Shadow, in secret. Latona, unless Sempronius had been far more indiscreet than Vibia guessed, did not know about his talents. Unconscious during his efforts, she woke to think Vibia her savior. She did not mean to call attention to Vibia's insufficiencies. She thought she was doing just the opposite. It stung, nonetheless.

Still, she knew Alhena had a considerable gift for foresight, and Latona was correct—she *had* been right before. Vibia's presence had been necessary, if in a small way. *'I wonder how much Alhena knows about who was more valuable in that warehouse.'* They had left the girl outside, for her own protection, but also so that she would not see Sempronius's magic at work. A girl blessed by Proserpina could see with far more than her eyes, however. The thought that she might learn the secret Sempronius had kept for so long, the hidden blasphemy that could undo his entire life—*'These Vitellians are dangerous, even if they don't mean to be.'*

But Discordian cultists were more so. Vibia remembered the nausea that had swelled in her when she had seen Scaeva working his profane magic. If more of that was going on, Vibia owed it not just to Aven but to her element—to the reputation of Fracture mages everywhere—to do what she could to eliminate the foul practice.

"So," Latona asked, with a pathetic glint of hope in her voice, "will you come? Your husband would be welcome, too, of course, and any of your people—"

Vibia's breath caught briefly. "I can't. I'm sorry." Vibia hoped her voice conveyed sincerity. "At least, not right away. I have commitments through next market day." It was the truth, and a hasty rearrangement of her plans might draw nosy questions, which Vibia would rather avoid. She pressed her lips together, then added, "I could join you afterwards, perhaps."

Latona, who had wilted slightly upon her denial, straightened a bit. "Or, if I get down there and discover there's nothing to this, I could write back to spare you the trip."

"We may hope," Vibia said, then hastily amended, "Meaning no offense, of course." She might not be eager to enjoy the Vitelliae's hospitality, but neither had she intended to slight it. "I only meant, better for everyone if there's nothing unsettled there, so we may hope for that. But I agree with your assessment. Vitellia Alhena seems little inclined towards histrionics. I don't think she'd summon you for nothing, let alone beg my attendance."

VII

Lucretius Rabirus disliked travel.

He had never seen the point in it. Oh, going to his various country estates dotted around Truscum was one thing. None were more than a few days from the great city of Aven, and he had many comfortable options for staying the night along the way, whether with friends or at posting houses of excellent reputation. Once arrived, he could enjoy the same comforts as he did in his domus in Aven: furniture he had chosen himself, his own clothes, his own books, food prepared by his own cooks, the attendance of his own docile slaves. His wife and son, if he desired their company; solitude, if he did not, for they could easily be left in Aven or packed off to a different estate.

Familiarity, in his consideration, was a vastly underrated concept.

You never knew what you might run into, out in the provinces. That was the trouble. Rabirus had served time as a military tribune, as nearly all men of political ambition did, but his father had arranged a suitable position for him. Rather than spending his early twenties baking in the Numidian heat or growing mold in the Albine forests, Rabirus had enjoyed a comfortable posting in Thessala. It had blooded him, he was quick to point out if anyone raised an eyebrow. He had seen combat. There had been a riot in the city of Polidaea. The legion—the two cohorts the governor had sent to deal with the crisis, at least—had had to act quickly, to put the unrest down. Rabirus knew what it was, to wade through blood in the streets, but gratefully, he had then been able to return to a well-built house in a city of decent, civilized people, rather than a tent in the wilderness.

As his ship approached Gades, he felt a lip curling in distaste. Things would not be so simple here, practically at the end of the world. They had passed through the Pillars of Hercules that morning, and Rabirus had felt an awful shiver course through him when he realized he could see Iberia to one side of him and Mauretania on the other. That marked the moment they were no longer on the Middle Sea, which, as far as Rabirus was concerned, encompassed all of the world worth knowing about. Gades faced out to the Endless Ocean and its lurking horrors.

Despite a hundred years of Aventan governance, Gades was still Tyrian at its heart. Rabirus knew what he was likely to find among its people: Eastern decadence, for all that they were on the edge of the western wilderness. Men wearing jewelry. Snake-worshipping cultists. Courtesans sitting at table with prominent citizens, as though they had any right to mingle with their betters. *'The gods know how many uncouth beards I'll be forced to endure the sight of.'* And *commerce*, invading every conversation. Such a mercantile people, the Tyrians, and the Athaecans and Aventans who had settled in Gades and the nearby Iberian cities had picked up the disease. Like any proper Aventan senator, Rabirus despised merchant-talk. It was beneath him, and yet he knew he would be forced to dine with men who would speak of nothing else, as though profit and gain crowded all other ideas from their minds.

He had come to regret the position he had put himself in. Keeping Sempronius Tarren's arrogance in check *required* his presence in Iberia, but it was an unpleasant duty. *'For Aven,'* he reminded himself. *'To protect the city from his predations, you must keep him from covering himself in glory and riches as Dictator Ocella did. Deny him the advantage of grand military victories, and you deny him power in the city itself. Then, perhaps, we can withdraw swiftly from this wretched misadventure and go back to tending our proper domains.'* The far-flung provinces were a drain on Aven's resources, in Rabirus's opinion, and ought to be left to their own devices. *'Would that we had never expanded out of Truscum.'*

Gades looked pleasant enough from a distance. It was built on a peninsula only barely connected to the mainland, Rabirus recalled, and it seemed to take up the entire spit of land. As the ship pulled toward the harbor, Rabirus took in the low skyline. The buildings were of a sandy white stone for the most part, and most did not rise even as high as some Aventan insulae. Only a few stretched toward heaven, and those looked to be built in the Athaecan style, with pointed pediments.

As they drew nearer, the crash of waves grew louder. White spray shot up from gray-brown rocks, not all of which were the natural coastline. Gades had built itself out, at least near the harbor, with artificial walls dropped into the sea. When he disembarked, Rabirus was surprised to see a knot of togate men waiting at the far end of the dock. Even at a distance, Rabirus could see the thick purple stripe on the tunic and toga of one of them: the mark of the praetor, the same stripes Rabirus himself wore. Governor Fimbrianus, it seemed, had come to greet him.

Governor Fimbrianus—*ex*-governor, that was, since Rabirus had been formally invested with the title at the New Year and would now assume the position in truth—was a weedy man, handsome in his youth but now well past his prime, limbs shrunken to spindles through inactivity. He still wore a toga well, keeping his back straight and his arms in the proper posture, not allowing the weight of the wool to bend his back. Rabirus's lip curled, though, to see the golden chain around his throat. If he indulged in such ornamental excess to greet a fellow Aventan in a public place, what depravities might he have sunk to in private?

As it happened, Rabirus was soon to find out. Fimbrianus had, with evident goodwill, arranged a celebration, which he was eager to rush Rabirus to. "Oh, I know you'll want to bathe and change into fresh clothing, no need to worry, we've some time yet," the older man chattered as he led Rabirus through the streets toward the governor's domus. "Though I'm afraid it's nothing like the baths in Aven. No aqueduct, you know!"

He had not expected Aventan-style bathhouses here, but the reminder of the lack of civilization rankled him nonetheless. But he attempted to be gracious. "After ten days at sea, I shall simply be grateful to feel clean."

"Yes, yes, I know the feeling!" Fimbrianus laughed. "The domus the city provides us is a treat, though, even if it does lack some amenities. Take it from me, though, you'll want to invest in some property on the mainland for a respite. All the wealthy folk have estates over there, where there's more room to spread out. Though perhaps—" Fimbrianus's already-wrinkled brow creased further as he seemed to remember the reason for Rabirus's arrival. "Perhaps best to make that investment once you've sorted out the trouble with the locals. Just in case."

Rabirus wanted to ask Fimbrianus's opinion of those locals, but they had arrived at the domus, and he found himself swiftly bundled off to clean up before dinner.

An hour later, Rabirus joined Fimbrianus in the dining rooms. Even the furniture was odd in this foreign place, a mongrel configuration of Aventan, Tyrian, and what Rabirus assumed were Iberian practices. The arrangement of the tables was familiar enough—three set in the shape of a horseshoe, with the greatest men seated at the top of the room. The tables were unnaturally high, though, and after further scrutiny, Rabirus saw why: there were no couches set around them, but a series of high-backed benches. *'At least they have cushions . . .'* The native Iberians, no doubt, would be happy to sit on bare wood, as though they were no better than beasts of the wild.

The company was likewise as mismatched an assortment as Rabirus would have expected to find in a Popularist household back in Aven, with men of all sorts mingling freely. Rabirus could not keep his eyes from drifting over toward one stranger in particular. His clothing was of neither Aventan nor Tyrian design, nor did he have an Iberian look to him. His tunic was striped blue and brown, and secured with strangely knotted cords that formed an X over his chest. Rabirus had never seen the like.

"Ah!" Fimbrianus said, seeing Rabirus glance at the odd dinner guest and mistaking the look for one of interest. "You've noticed my Asherite friend. There's a small population of them in the city. Mostly keep to themselves, you know, or else they deal with the Tyrian traders. Well, they came over with the Tyrians, generations ago. Some of them live up near the Ligustine Lake now. Good textile workers!" He flapped a hand, as though waving away the stray thoughts that buzzed through his conversation like so many flies.

An Asherite! A thing almost anathema to the Aventan way of life, utterly inexplicable, lounging in an Aventan triclinium! Rabirus could hardly countenance it and was unable to contain his shock from distorting his expression. The Asherites were considered strange even in their native lands, a people who eschewed all gods but one—and that one, from what Rabirus had heard, seemed a harsh and thankless taskmaster. Even the Parthians and Abydosians were wary of the Asherites.

"You know," Fimbrianus said, lowering his voice and leaning toward Rabirus. His tone became almost conspiratorial. "If I might offer a suggestion, friend Rabirus." Rabirus bit back an insult, challenging Fimbrianus to prove that they had ever been friends. "You would do well to make sure the people of Gades see you take the Tyrians and Iberians, and even yon Asherite, into your council. They will like you for it, and, if you do not . . ." He lolled back into his chair, eyebrows arcing as his eyes went exaggeratedly wide. "Well . . ." Fimbrianus spread his hands.

Rabirus had no patience for this. "If I do not, *what*?" he demanded.

Fimbrianus gave no visible response to his sharp tone. "They will think you . . ." After a moment of searching for the right word, he laughed. "Well! As we would call it, provincial."

Recoiling, Rabirus glanced around the room. *These* men? This ragged collection of eastern hedonists and western barbarians, they would dare to deem *him* provincial, when he hailed from the finest city in the world? The center of all morality, the republic which had stood for hundreds of years?

Fimbrianus noticed his shock. "I know, I know. When you've hardly been out of Aven, it seems impossible." The man's reasonable tone irritated Rabirus all the more. "But a few years of living here taught me how much more there is to the world. Well! It's on our own doorstep, if we could see it!" Now he looked amused, laughter playing at his lips. Rabirus suppressed an urge to punch him in the nose. "Hard to tell, from the Palatine or Caelian, but Aven is very like Gades, in some ways."

"You sound," Rabirus said, ice in every syllable, "like a Popularist."

That proclamation made Fimbrianus chortle without restraint. "Oh, friend Rabirus, I've been away from Aven too long to consider myself aligned to any particular faction. Popularist, Optimate, I've had no need to care about it, out here. But I think, perhaps, I've become a bit more cosmopolitan." He winked—actually had the audacity to *wink*—at Rabirus. "I hope it does you as much good as it did me."

"If it's advice you wish to dispense," Rabirus said, "then bring me up-to-date on the barbarian uprising."

Fimbrianus's merry features melted into a scowl as he plucked apart a partridge wing. "I told that boy messing about in Toletum to leave well enough alone," he said. "He stirred up trouble, if you ask me. Those Lusetani would have gone back to their villages once the winter set in and raiding lost its appeal. Now they feel they've something to prove, so they've dug in all up and down the Tagus River." He waved a grease-covered hand dismissively before reaching for his napkin. "I sent a cohort that needed blooding, but I haven't seen any need to move anyone else out of the city. We're best off protecting Aventan interests here."

As inclined as Rabirus was to agree, there was one hole in Fimbrianus's reasoning. "But what became of that cohort?" he asked.

This time, Fimbrianus hesitated before replying. "They're still in Toletum. Stayed there through the winter."

Rabirus stared at him a long moment. Fimbrianus's shoulders had drawn together, and his eyes were fixed determinedly on his plate now, not expansively enjoying the room, as he had been. "There's something you're not telling me."

"It's rumors, that's all!" Fimbrianus huffed. "Mad rumors, you know how it is. Young men listen to too many stories and start thinking they see specters out there in the wilderness." Rabirus continued to stare at him, and under the scrutiny, Fimbrianus sighed and continued, less dismissively. "The last I heard from the centurion posted there, he claimed the Lusetani had summoned *lemures* against them."

"*Lemures*?"

"Or something like them. Iberian spirits. I'll—I'll show you the letter, you'll see what nonsense he talks. He called them 'soul-drainers,' said they make a man feel like he lacks the strength to stand . . ." Fimbrianus sucked his lower lip up under his teeth for a moment, making Rabirus suspect he credited these tales more than he let on. Denial had become a convenient excuse for not placing himself in jeopardy—all the more convenient when he also had the excuse of waiting for Rabirus to arrive and take over command. "More likely some horrible fog crept in around them and they all started hallucinating out of boredom! The Counei—they're the local Iberians, along the coast from here to Olissippo—they told me they'd heard nothing of the sort. That it was quite impossible, in fact! It's nonsense, I tell you, plain nonsense." But his voice trailed off into uncertainty.

Rabirus had intended to do as Fimbrianus had done: hole up in Gades, refuse supplies to Sempronius's efforts, starve the war effort as passively as he could manage. The new praetor of Maritima was a friend of his and had agreed to do what he could to slow Sempronius's supply lines. Waiting games—that was how Rabirus liked to achieve his ends.

This, though—these rumors caught his attention. These *lemures*, or soul-drainers, or whatever they were, they sounded like something Pinarius Scaeva had spoken of. *'They might be worth seeing.'*

Swift and sudden, that thought grew into a compulsion. Rabirus went from feeling as though he might like to witness this to feeling that he *must*. Even if it took him into the wilderness, he had to see this foreign work—whether it was magic or trickery. Perhaps it would prove something he could turn against his opponents while keeping his own hands clean, as he had so nearly managed to do with Pinarius. A way to counter Sempronius, or to deal with the troublemaking tribune up in Toletum—who was, after all, brother to the meddlesome woman who had spoiled his efforts back in Aven. Or perhaps it would be nothing at all, as Fimbrianus said, and Rabirus could cut through the rumors and thus undermine the *casus belli* for the entire Iberian endeavor.

But of all that, Fimbrianus needed to know nothing, and so Rabirus turned his attention back to his meal.

✧✧✧✧✧✧✧✧✧✧✧✧✧✧

EBRUS RIVER, CENTRAL IBERIA

By the Ides of Maius, Sempronius's legions were well into the Iberian interior. Sempronius left a single tribune in Tarraco as an anchor, to pass messages to and from Aven, and went himself upriver toward Salduba.

The legions cutting their way through the provinces made for a considerable sight: fields of crimson fabric and shining iron armor, a river of men, flowing for miles at a time. As they marched, their standards bobbed encouragingly above them: For the Tenth, a horse rearing on its hind legs, looking as though he had fire in his mane and at his hooves, homage to their long-ago origin as a mounted auxiliary unit. For the Eighth, marching to rejoin their beleaguered vexillation in Toletum, the barking dog, testament to their history of serving as Aven's protective guards. The Fourteenth's standard displayed an upraised fist. Along the poles of each were hung the awards won in battle by generations past. And with them all, the eagles, the standard of all Aventan legions.

More than a standard, the eagles were a talisman of luck and glory. The men looked to them and took heart. To lose them was an almost-unsurvivable shame. Legions who lost their eagles could be disbanded—if any had survived the battle to begin with. The eagles stood for the legions' honor, their fortitude, their devotion, and their piety, all wrapped together. The eagles marching with Sempronius's legions were polished until they gleamed in the sunlight and had been blessed by Nedhena's foremost Spirit mage before the legions had started south.

The plateaus of central Iberia were not without challenges, dotted with forests and cut with ravines. The legions had to adopt a new marching formation. Their lines were stretched out across miles, in places no more than four or six men across. A vulnerable way to march, and one which agitated Sempronius. The thinness of the lines kept him up at night and had him watching like a hawk during the day.

He strove to keep his anxiety from showing, but Felix picked up on it anyway, demonstrating the clever intuition that so easily disappeared beneath his irreverent demeanor. "You're worried," he said in a low voice, pulling his black horse up alongside of Sempronius's dapple-gray stallion. He had sense enough not to bellow loud enough that the troops would hear.

"I am," Sempronius admitted, in the same subdued tone. "Perhaps without reason. But this formation is a weak one."

"How else would you have us march?"

The question was sincere, not flippant, and so it bothered Sempronius all the more that he had no ready answer. "There is no alternative, truly," he said, with a shrug more casual than he felt. "The terrain dictates us at times. If we had a good Aventan road through this territory . . . but it may be many years before the region is secure enough for us to see that project through." He gestured at the men just ahead of them, marching only four abreast. "When the lines are this thin, they are easier to break, easier to scatter. We have not drilled enough for these conditions. Worse, the tribunes and centurions are too far apart to give orders effectively. If anyone attacks, cohesion could break down. We'll be little better than the brawlers we face."

Felix's face was set seriously. "So what do we do?"

"Wait," Sempronius said. He did not say hope, for with each passing day, he was becoming more convinced that an attack would find them, sooner rather than later. If the rebels had any scouts in this territory, they would be fools if they missed the significance of how the Aventans were being forced to march. All it would take was one intrepid tribesman to repeat the information back to his chieftain, and the Aventans would be in for sport.

◇◇◇◇◇◇◇◇◇◇◇◇◇◇◇◇

When it came, not long after the legions passed the outpost of Salduba, it hit hard and fast, and from both directions at once. The legions marched through a thick patch of evergreens, and though they took advantage of every spare foot, so that the prickling needles brushed against the armor of the men marching on the outsides of the column, they could still not march more than six abreast.

The tribesmen struck from left and right simultaneously. A hail of arrows and slung stones rained on the legionaries like a sudden rainstorm, and several men went down before anyone had realized what was happening to them. "*Testudo!*" Sempronius shouted, and to his gratification, the men immediately raised their shields, moving into the tortoise formation—so named because they used their shields to create a shell-like barrier around the entire legion. Sempronius swung down out of his saddle and under the shields of his lictors, the small contingent of personal guards he had by virtue of his praetorial office.

The tribesmen must have been waiting for quite some time. They had set themselves up in the higher elevations before the army had even begun to pass through this part of the forest, and they had waited patiently until they could strike at the middle of the seemingly endless line. *'How did our scouts not realize—'*

The tribesmen on the left flank were less organized than those on the right; he could see that in an instant. On the right, they advanced in a wedge formation—more sophisticated than Aventans generally expected out of supposed barbarians. On the left, they continued to fire arrows intermittently, but more were throwing stones from slings. A primitive weapon, perhaps, but a formidable one; a hard enough strike could dash a man's brains out or break his arm. *'Thank Mars and Bellona we march in full armor.'*

The tortoise was an excellent defensive formation, but poor for fighting, and it would not hold forever. Sempronius stuck two fingers in his mouth and whistled a short code. Several of the centurions picked up his signal and repeated it down the lines, and in response, the men adjusted their formation, splitting down the middle so that half faced out to the left, half out to the right. The men on the outer edges held their shields before them, while those in the middle stayed above. "Hold the lines!" Sempronius bellowed. "Hold!"

His men were well-disciplined. Even with the Iberians howling for their blood, rushing down from the hillsides, they held their lines, unshaking. When the first of the Iberians slammed into those outward shields, many of the leather-covered wooden barriers shuddered, but did not give way. The centurions knew their business; without any direction from Sempronius or the other commanders, their whistles called for methodical stabs of hundreds of short swords, perfectly in synchronization, up and down their lines. Iberian chaos crashed against stalwart Aventan discipline. Sempronius believed, with everything in his soul, that discipline would triumph—*if* it could last long enough to do so.

"Second line!" Sempronius yelled, "shields down!" The tribesmen were using fewer projectiles now, with their own men engaged in the action; hopefully the shields of those innermost would provide enough cover to protect them all. The second line needed to be ready to move forward. After a moment, he gave another short whistle, which the centurions dutifully echoed. At that signal, the first line of fighters on each side slid expertly back to the center, with the second line moving up to take their place.

This was ugly formation, and Sempronius knew it; they would tire quickly, rotating through the lines so fast. Legions typically deployed much deeper, so that a man might only fight for a few minutes out of an hour before cycling back through the ranks. With their forces only three lines deep, they would scarce have chance to catch their breath. Worse, there might be places where weaker men were grouped together without stronger fighters to support them.

Still, the legions had a plethora of built-in advantages, and what tribesmen had dared to rush them were swiftly falling to the Aventan blades. Their curved weapons looked to be made of bronze, no match for Aventan shields or the sturdy iron short sword that every legionary could use as efficiently as his own arm. Nor did the tribesmen have much armor to stand up to a legionary's scale-like plate and chains. But what the Iberians lacked in military technology, they made up for in numbers, falling upon the narrow strand of legionaries like massive waves upon a spit of sand.

At a shout and noise of clashing armor, Sempronius looked to his left, seeing with horror that part of the line was collapsing. Too many legionaries had taken wounding blows, or perhaps the sodden ground had given way beneath them, making them lose their so-crucial footing. "Lictors, part!" Sempronius shouted, hauling himself back up into the saddle. "Auxilia! On me!" The cavalry, a mix of those brought along from Truscum and local Lacetani picked up in the foothills, moved into formation behind him as he charged along the right side of the column, where part of the line had given way. "Ride them down!" he bellowed, and the cavalry eagerly complied. Sempronius's horse plunged through the swarm of hollering tribesmen, kicking and crushing men beneath its hooves, and Sempronius lashed out with his sword. He felt a hot spurt of blood on his arm and knew he had made contact with someone, but there was no time to see what damage he had wreaked. He pivoted his steed back around, trampling another tribesman, and made another pass.

In this way, the cavalry cleared the assault on the weak point long enough for the foot soldiers to recover themselves and reform their lines. Sempronius could take no time to breathe before giving another call to the rest of the cavalry. As the centurions mustered the infantry back into a solid position, Sempronius wanted to make sure there were no other weak points along the lines. "On me!" he cried again, raising his sword so that it caught the sunlight through the trees, and the riders bellowed their understanding.

Up and down the lines they rode, driving the tribesmen back from any place where the legionaries were faltering. Once, Sempronius came around a cluster of pine trees and nearly collided with Autronius Felix, also ahorse. Felix's dark eyes shone with bloodlust, and his sword bore the proof. He had evidently taken the same initiative as Sempronius, and Sempronius was glad to see it. He wasted no time on orders or commendations; he merely nodded, and they both swung back around to their respective units.

And then, as quickly as it had begun, it was over. The tribesmen sounded a retreat from their lugubrious horns, and those that had not fallen to the Aventan swords rushed back into the trees. "Should we pursue?" asked a cavalryman from Sempronius's side, but he shook his head.

"It could be another ambush if we do."

And so the legions stood, braced for another assault, until General Onidius Praectus came down the line. He had taken a gash to the chin, and there was blood pouring from his left calf, but he did not seem to notice either injury. "There's a clearing two miles from the front of our line," he said. "If we can make it that far, we can make camp as quickly as possible—and then maybe find out what the hell happened here."

Sempronius refrained from saying that he knew exactly what happened—they had been ambushed and could expect to be attacked in this manner again. Three Aventan legions crossing through the forest would be easy to track, but General Onidius was right; the best thing they could do now was to get out of this narrow passage and fortify themselves. "Our men can still march," he said. "I'll pass the word back to General Calpurnius. With luck, the Fourteenth may not have been hit at all."

Onidius nodded. "They only got the back end of our line—there can only have been so many of them, after all."

Sempronius hoped, rather than believed, that would prove true.

VIII

When Aulus came to greet his daughters, Alhena hovered just behind him, shifting herself from one foot to the other. All she wanted was to have her sisters to herself. She knew from the letter they'd sent ahead not to expect Vibia, not yet, and perhaps that was all to the good. However necessary the Fracture mage might be, ultimately, Alhena could not be sorry for a little time alone with Aula and Latona.

If she could *get* that time alone with them.

During the long days that her sisters were traveling south, Alhena had debated telling her father about the visions. Twice more, the same imagery had visited her. Maybe, *maybe* if she confided in her father, he would be able to do something about it. Instinct intervened—and so did observation. This was a mage's problem; Aulus could not solve it. And she had seen his attempts to clip Latona's wings, just as he had sought to keep Alhena safely mewed up. No, this would need to be a secret between sisters, at least for now, lest their father's well-meaning interventions keep them from the gods' design.

"Come in and sit," Aulus said, after kissing first little Lucia, then Aula, then Latona on the cheeks. "I want to hear about your trip. And *you*—" He fixed Latona with a hard stare. "I didn't think you'd be along without Herennius."

"He may join us after he's completed some business in the city," Latona offered airily, "but he told me to go on ahead." Alhena wondered how much truth was in that tale.

Aula's eyes met Alhena's over Aulus's shoulder. She might not have had Latona's empathic gifts, but Aula had a canny intuition all her own. "Father, we've been in the carriage for *days*. I feel jounced half to pieces and my legs are aching. You *know* how restless I get." Aula spent most of her days wandering up and down the seven hills of Aven on errands, social calls, and various missions conniving for her family's political careers; spending several days cooped up in a carriage was a trial for her. "I need a walk before I settle in."

"And I," Latona said, looking nearly as desperate as Alhena felt.

"Me too, me too!" Lucia crowed, bouncing up and down at her mother's feet.

Aula, however, was swift with an alternate plan for her daughter. "But my darling, you wanted to see if there were any new kittens in the stables, didn't you?"

"Oh! Yes!" Lucia's face split in a gap-toothed grin. "And *you* said maybe we could bring one home!"

"I said I would *think* about it," Aula said, settling her hands on her hips. "And I shall continue to do so, if you behave yourself. So why don't you go help Gera set up your room, and then have her take you to the stables?" Lucia's agreement was so swift that her fleet feet had already taken her halfway to the house before she finished promising her best behavior.

"Very well, stretch your legs, then," Aulus said, raising his hands in defeat. "We've got leerfish and plover for dinner, so work yourselves up a hearty appetite."

Alhena burst forward, seizing Latona's hand and fairly dragging her toward the tree line. But Latona held back a moment, looking to Merula. "Would you help with the unpacking, dear? See if you can set up a desk in my room so I can keep working on the texts we brought."

Merula's boxy face set in a frown. "Domina, I would not like you to be going alone in the woods. There may be—"

"I think we can chaperone ourselves on a short walk," Latona insisted. "And I would trust no one but you with my papers."

Alhena didn't miss the look that passed between Merula and her mistress. No doubt they had discussed Alhena's letter, and no doubt Latona would share whatever revelations Alhena had with her girl as soon as they returned. But she appreciated the gesture. It was ever easier to speak with fewer people around, and having only her sisters was best of all.

◇◇◇◇◇◇◇◇◇◇◇◇◇

Once they were out of earshot of the villa, Latona cast her gaze over her shoulder at Alhena. "All right then, pet," she said, with a wry smile. "Tell me what had you so rattled that you begged me to come down."

Though this had been her entire reason for summoning her sisters to Stabiae, Alhena struggled to fit her words together. "I—I had a vision. At the temple." She worried her lower lip. "Three times, actually. The same each time. I mean—only the first time, at the temple. The other times, I was at home. It scared me. And I thought . . . I thought you should know. Because I think it means something's going to happen, here." She glanced at the shady pines around them, wishing Proserpina had sent her images a bit more literal. "Or near here."

"What sort of a something?"

"Something . . ." Alhena bit her lower lip. "Something tearing a hole in the world."

As Alhena shared her vision of torn earth and hills of bones, bronze gates and fiendish voices, the women continued walking. Instead of setting their usual pace, with Aula charging ahead and Alhena dreamily bringing up the rear, the three sisters drew nearly shoulder to shoulder, as though that might afford them some protection from the terrors Alhena had seen.

By the time she finished, Alhena had tied a number of knots in the fringe of her mantle. "'All worlds shatter,' those were the last words on the door, and I swear, it felt as though the hills around me were ready to shake themselves to bits. And those doors . . . something was behind them, something wanted through." She shuddered, hearing their howling cry in her mind again. "They said they were hungry . . ." Alhena wrapped another loose thread around her finger and yanked hard. "I wish I could tell you better what it means. I only *think* it's to do with Fracture magic." It made sense to her, it *felt* right. All that bronze, and the gates, the words of chaos and fury. "And I don't know if, even if I'm right about that, there might be one mage or many. Or how close they're getting. Getting or . . . might get, in the future." Her nose crinkled and her shoulders sagged. "I'm sorry. A better mage would know for sure . . ."

Latona reached over to cup her chin. "A more experienced mage, pet. Better has naught to do with it."

Alhena shrugged off the reassurance. Latona always tried to lift her spirits with encouraging words, but it didn't alter their situation. They all would be better off if Alhena could make herself of more practical use, and the frustration of ineptitude nibbled at her nerves. "I feel so sure something's going to happen. Or it's already happening. And I thought, if I got you down here, well, you can *see* magic. And if Vibia comes, she might not be able to see it like you can, but if it's Discordian, then it's a kind of Fracture, and she'll be able to sense it, at least."

"And maybe make sense *of* it." Latona's gait was uneven, as though she were trying to walk within the patches of warm sunlight rather than in shadow. "Yes, that may be. I only wish . . ." Latona's lips twisted slightly. "Well. Vibia Sempronia is not the most . . . comfortable of companions."

Aula snorted. "That's an understatement. I've met more congenial geese."

A defensive stab prompted Alhena to say, "You should be easier on her. She's wound so tightly to keep from falling into chaos."

"You're right," Latona said. "We should be more generous with her. But that wasn't quite what I meant. More that . . ."

But before Latona could find the words, Aula supplied, "You don't think she likes you very much." Aula laughed as Latona sputtered the beginning of a denial. "No, no, don't even bother, you know it's what you're hinting so elegantly at. And it's of no concern. I *know* she doesn't like me." She tilted her head to one side. "But the political art is learning to work with those with whom we have a common purpose, no matter the distaste, is it not? And you are a daughter of the Vitelliae. So, fix yourself to the purpose."

"Vibia was ready enough to believe Alhena, however little she thinks of you or me," Latona said. "She was as disturbed by Pinarius Scaeva as I was. Maybe more. Feeling someone misuse your element . . ." A shudder moved down Latona's back. "It's a wretched thing."

Alhena almost wished she would say more. She had heard some whispers of what went on at the Dictator's court: mages who had delighted in depravity, abusing their gifts at Ocella's behest. Some had been compelled, of course, responding to threats to themselves or their families, but others, rumor had it, needed no such persuasion. No one had ever spoken of the details around Alhena, however. Aulus had kept her as far from such things as he could manage. *'Ignorance is comforting,'* she thought, reading the echoes of agony on Latona's face, *'but it is not safe.'*

Latona settled her shoulders back, as though shrugging off the memories. "So I believe we may count on Vibia to help us dig out the problem at the root." She rolled her eyes, her tone turning lighter. "I just wish I knew why, even when she's agreeing with me, she always looks at me like she'd rather I went away."

Aula's eyes shot wide. "Does she know about your deliciously torrid liaison with her dear brother?"

"No!" Latona cried, coming to a halt in a patch of sun between two pines. Then she turned a horrified gaze on Alhena.

For the first time that day, amusement instead of desperation took hold of Alhena. But it was tinged with annoyance. *'They really do forget*

I'm not a child, sometimes.' Clearly they'd discussed this with each *other*. Why not with her?

Alhena flicked her gaze to Aula—who was blushing a fierce red, mouth agape and at an uncustomary loss for words. She arched an eyebrow at her older sister, asking with sardonic innocence, "What? Is that something I'm not supposed to know?"

"You *knew*?" Latona gasped, in the same moment that Aula croaked, "They're dear friends," in a frantic attempt to mend her slip of the tongue, "who hold each other in the highest esteem and—"

"*Aula*," Alhena said, rolling her eyes. "I do wish you'd stop treating me like a taller version of Lucia." She turned her gaze back to Latona, who had gone as pale as Aula had red. "I mean, I didn't *know*-know. But I suspected."

"I confess," Latona said through a dry throat, "that I was rather hoping it wasn't so obvious."

"It's not," Alhena said. "At least, not to everyone. Not to most people, even. Maybe to no one. But . . ." She shrugged. "Well, I *told* you." Latona's gold and Sempronius's darkness, intertwined. Alhena had never been able to convince Proserpina to give her more detailed or literal information. Perhaps the future was still too uncertain, but it seemed Alhena's instincts about the haziness had been correct.

"*Anyway*," Latona said, starting to walk again, "Vibia doesn't know, I'm sure. I can't imagine we wouldn't have heard about it, if she did. And she's disliked me since long before that."

"Well," Aula said, "there's no accounting for taste."

∞∞∞∞∞∞∞∞∞∞∞∞

Latona wished they'd walked down to the shore, rather than into the forest. Even before Alhena had told her story of bone-built hills and fiendish voices, she had felt unsettled. In fact, the disquiet had been growing since they had passed beneath Vesuvius and onto the curving southeastern coast of Crater Bay. After hearing the substance of Alhena's vision, the shade provided by the verdant carob trees and brushy pines no longer seemed cool and inviting, but ominous.

At least the air was sweeter here than in Aven. The breeze whipped in from the water, and without the dust from carts, the smoke from thousands of hearth fires, and the refuse of three hundred thousand lives, it stayed clear as it drifted through the town and into the wooded groves beyond the seaside ridges. Latona paused for a moment as the three sisters ascended a hill, drawing a deep breath and trying to quiet her mind. She heard the crunch of grass and underbrush beneath Aula's feet, Alhena's softer and more careful footfalls, the calling of birds chattering in the trees above, the rustle of leaves. *'An Earth mage would appreciate this more than I do,'* she mused, thinking of her friend Terentilla, as near an incarnation of the goddess Diana as she could imagine. *'I wouldn't put it past Tilla to go for a jog through these woods bare-breasted if she felt moved to do so.'*

Aula and Alhena strode a little ways ahead of her. Aula was interrogating Alhena about the temple and her friends there. In an attempt to shake the baleful mood that had crept under her skin, Latona took a deep breath, and in a slow, deliberate push, she sent her Spirit magic out into her surroundings.

It was calming, grounding. There was Aula's familiar aura, bouncing lightly along the path; there, Alhena's, a sense of cool water disturbed by pebbles. Non-human life was muted to nothing more than a soft glow of energy, the quiet thrum of forest life all around. She wondered if she might be able to sense someone else nearby—a hunter, perhaps, or someone foraging for nuts or berries. Nothing else hit her, until—

Latona winced and started, reflexively, to draw her magic back into herself. But she stamped down on that instinct and reached out again, more tentatively, to probe the strange presence she had encountered. Not a person, though Latona could not say why she was sure of that. The energy lacked the cohesion she associated with a person, yet it was stronger than that of an animal. Instead of emotion, she simply felt force. *Magical* force.

"Well, we should have them over for dinner sometime," Aula was saying. "This Moira, at least, since you like her so well. Shouldn't we, Latona? And maybe if Father sees—"

"Wait."

"—how well you're doing at—what?" Stopping mid-sentence had physical force, and Aula halted. "Latona, what?"

Latona closed her eyes. "Just . . . quiet, please. I'm trying to—"

To her credit, Aula actually managed to remain silent for a brief moment before saying, "Trying to what? Latona?" But Alhena hushed her.

Whatever it was, it didn't like Latona probing at it. Latona had to swallow her fear and the inclination to back away: that was what it, whatever it was, wanted her to do. Initially, it tried to divert her attention, spinning her magical tendrils away. As she pressed on, though, it responded with anger—not a human sort of anger, still, but the red-hot sizzle had a familiar aspect. And then it began pushing back against her. A strange buzzing leapt along her fingertips, like miniature bolts of lightning within her skin.

"I recognize this . . ." Her eyes snapped open, finding Alhena's. "You were . . . Oh, this is not . . ." Latona started wandering, peering into the trees around them.

"Latona?" Aula asked, trotting after her. "You realize you didn't finish any of those sentences?"

"Yes."

A cold chill crept along Latona's spine. More afraid than she had been at first, she nonetheless knew she had to investigate. She had realized *why* the sensation felt familiar. A place where the world felt like pottery overheated in a kiln, brittle and cracking. A defensive pulse, encouraging panic to overtake her rapid-beating heart, urging her mind to turn away, look away, look anywhere else.

Fracture magic, warped and twisted and set to ill purpose. Alhena's visions confirmed, and Latona's fears realized.

With Aula and Alhena in her wake, Latona trekked up the hill, as though following a map only she could see. The magical fissure acted as a lodestone; when she turned in the right direction, it reacted more strongly; when she stepped the wrong direction, the sensation faded.

Finally, they came around an outcropping of stone and into a little grove. Latona's head ached. The sensation that the Fracture magic was actively fighting her own power increased with every step, but she pressed on, determined to find the source.

As she rounded a bend in the path, the stench of rotting flesh assaulted her nostrils, yet that was not chiefest among her concerns. Something else, beyond her usual five senses, cried out a warning. Then, on the far side of the outcropping, she saw it: a desiccated animal carcass hanging from a carob tree, its entrails heaped beneath where it dangled from a branch.

Aula gave a little shriek when she saw it, then clamped her fingers over her nose. "What in Jupiter's name could have done that? A—A leopard?" She almost sounded hopeful. There weren't leopards in these woods, of course, but considering the possibility looming over them, it would have been the preferable answer.

Latona's sensibilities were less delicate than Aula's, and she drew closer to the grisly scene. The carcass was not merely slung over a branch, but tied there with blackened rope. The entrails were piled over tree roots that had been deliberately exposed, dug out from the safety of the ground. "No. No, this was done intentionally, and by human hands." She pressed a hand to her stomach, trying to settle rising nausea.

"Do you think—" Alhena began, her voice thin and piping. She paused, swallowed, and tried again. "It's so near our home. Do you think that's . . . intentional?"

"Maybe." Latona's eyes drifted from the carcass to the tree itself, and what she saw concerned her. All along the branches, the bark was cracked and peeling away from the sapwood. Here and there, leaves had shriveled, crisped to black at the edges, but the effect was sporadic; some were still a verdant green, almost over-bright. The joints where the branches met the trunk were starting to split. Left much longer, the whole tree would slough to pieces.

Latona forced herself to take another step toward the gruesome spectacle—and immediately reeled, her magical senses recoiling from what they encountered. Like poison with sharp edges, like suffocation in a thundercloud. An arm curled around her waist. Alhena, steadying her. Latona's hand went to her throat, memories swirling through her, memories of feeling drained, bled dry of all her power. "I recognize this." She could barely scrape the words past her lips; her throat had gone dry, her lips numb.

"Oh, no . . ." Alhena sighed, but her voice seemed far away.

Hunger. Endless, yawning hunger, too great to ever be satisfied, always demanding more, more, *more*. "I recognize this magic, the signature. I remember it." Her power, splayed out as a delicious morsel next to an eager abyss, ready to snap her up. A voice in her ear, telling her to *burn*, because the brighter she did, the better meal she made for the gaping maw. *'I will leave you behind, a colder corpse than most.'* The fear, the terrible certainty that this was how she would die . . .

"Here, with me." Alhena's voice, gentle in her ear even as her arm was tight around Latona's middle. Then Aula pried her fingers away from her neck and grasped her hand: softer flesh than Alhena's, but no less fierce. "With us."

Latona thought about her heartbeats; about her blood, the same that ran through her sisters' veins; Aula's pulse in her palm, beating in time with her own; Alhena's lemon-clean scent. *'Here. With them.'* With a shuddering breath, Latona hauled her mind and soul back to the present moment. *'You are not dying. You did not die, there in that warehouse, and you are not dying now.'*

As her head cleared, Latona was able to distinguish the nuances in the Fracture magic. It wasn't *precisely* the same as Scaeva's: hungry, destructive, but not as fixedly predatory. She raised her head, shaking her hair back from her shoulders. "I recognize the magic, not the signature, quite. But this is absolutely Discordian magic."

"Yes," Aula drawled. "We gathered as much."

"It's so near the villa," Alhena said. "Do you think it was—was meant for you? Or us?"

"I don't know." Latona's body sagged. Fighting off the ill effects of the Discordian charm had enervated her limbs. "It seems too much to be coincidence, and too little to be intentional. If it *were* Scaeva's signature, I'd be sure it was meant as a message to me, or a threat."

Alhena's hands went to her head, her fingers smoothing back her brilliant red hair. "I saw so many shattered hills. If each one of them means something like this . . ."

"Then surely someone else will have noticed," Aula said. Her brisk tone, familiar and reassuring, put some strength back into Latona's blood. "We can put our ears out, see what the locals have encountered. Then we decide what to do next." Her arm slid around Latona's shoulders, steering her back toward the path. "For now, we are going home."

"No!" Latona cried, her body lurching back at the horrific remnants. "No, I have to fix it—"

Aula jostled her sharply. "Latona, look at me." Latona obeyed. "Do you know how to fix this, right now?" Though she hated to do it, Latona shook her head. "No. I have every faith that you can figure it out, my honey, but I don't think you can manage it here, before dark." Her rosy lips twisted in a wry smile. "And I certainly don't want to find out what Merula would do to me for letting you try."

"Aula's right," Alhena said. "We need more information. Then . . . then maybe we can fix it."

Warring instincts pounded in Latona's chest. Half of her wanted to flee as far as she could from the Discordian sacrifice, and the other half yearned to set things to rights. The Spirit of her nature was terrified, revolted, and indignant in equal measures; the Fire was simply angry. "Very well," she said. "Home. But—give me a moment." Latona turned back toward the grove, sending her Spirit magic out again. *'Whatever you are, wherever you came from, this is not over. I will be back, to cleanse this place.'* A malevolent pulse sent her skin prickling up, but she glared at the grisly display. *'That is a promise.'*

IX

Even a man who knew little of walled cities could see that Toletum's defenses had been freshly built.

"No," Ekialde said in a whisper, peering closely upward. He had come by night, and without torches, bringing only a handful of his war-band, his most trusted warriors, along with him. They moved quietly, slowly, creeping toward the city like a wildcat on soft paws. They kept well out of the circles of light cast by the Aventan torches, and they kept a cautious eye open, in case the Aventans sent out patrols. He did not want to engage the Aventans this night. He wanted to learn. "Not fresh-built, but improved upon. Do you see, Angeru?" He shouldered his second-in-command and pointed halfway up the walls. "They've built on top of the old walls, and extended them all the way to the river bluff."

This Aventan commander was a clever man, and he had not wasted the winter. Nor were those walls their only preparations. The tree line had been cut back, so that the Lusetani warriors could not leave the shelter of the forest without coming within arrow-range of the city. The Aventans had tried to dig trenches across the field between the walls and the tree line, but only in patches. The ground was too rocky, and in most places, the Aventans had only managed shallow ditches. Not enough to stop a charge, but enough to slow it, forcing attackers to negotiate a jagged path toward the city, all while stones and arrows rained down upon them from the walls.

'No doubt such a clever, careful man will have prepared his stores as well as he prepared his defenses.'

Another commander might have been daunted. Ekialde only smiled. He still did not understand what had protected his Aventan opponent from his magic the previous year. Bailar had been so certain the charm would work, and that Ekialde would have an ensorcelled Aventan leader under his control. *'Bailar is not infallible.'* As his wife was ever reminding him. Precious Neitin, she begrudged Bailar his every failure nearly as much as she resented his successes.

Ekialde was willing to be tolerant. Much of Bailar's work was experimental. He was attempting things no other magic-man of the Lusetani, or of any other tribe, had reached for in many generations. There would be some errors, as when a child first learned to use a bow.

This, though. *This*, he was sure would work. He had already seen it enacted, against the straggling legionaries they had harassed along the river. More difficult, certainly, to bewitch a fortified town of two thousand souls, but more worthwhile, as well.

"Fear not, my friends," he said. "Our magic-men have beaten the path for our allies from the netherworld, and no walls can keep *them* out."

◇◇◇◇◇◇◇◇◇◇◇◇◇

CENTRAL IBERIA

As the crash of swords rose like a tide on all sides of the cart, Corvinus decided he most definitely did not enjoy warfare.

He had not been with Sempronius when the dominus had served in Numidia. Junior officers didn't bring servants with them on campaign, so Corvinus had no prior experience of the battlefield. *'Or the battle road, as the case has proven to be.'* Long, hot marches interspersed with brief periods of violent action: thus did the Eighth, Tenth, and Fourteenth legions cross central Iberia. Since they had turned south, away from the Ebrus River and down toward the tributaries of the Tagus, few days passed without some contact with the rebellious tribes—not the Lusetani, they had learned, but their allies, the Vettoni. The legions rarely had trouble driving them off—in fact, the Vettoni seemed perfectly eager to retreat after a little blooding—but it slowed their progress, and it shot ripples through Corvinus's usually placid nerves.

He rode in one of the carts of the command train, behind the vanguard and the commanders but ahead of the main body of the legions. He hadn't yet decided if this was preferable to riding farther back with the baggage train. The commanders attracted plenty of attention, but they were also better protected. The baggage train relied on the rearguard, and those were mostly local auxiliaries, not the relentlessly drilled Aventan legionaries.

Corvinus's cart had high sides and a roof, for which he was particularly grateful whenever he heard a sling-bolt crack against the wood. All too easy to imagine what that stone could have done to his skull. Outside, horses shrieked, in outrage or in agony, but the cart remained motionless.

The mules which drew it were difficult to impress, unlike their high-strung cousins. Corvinus had developed an affection for the glumly suffering beasts.

He wasn't alone in the cart. Apart from the trunks of the legion's paperwork and the staff officers' gear, Corvinus had the company of a pair of clerks, both slaves owned by the state, and the mule-driver, a grizzled man from Tarraco. One of the slaves was muttering prayers in a ceaseless whisper. Irritating, but Corvinus couldn't blame the fellow. *'At least I chose to be here. After a fashion.'*

For no one else would he have made the choice. As Sempronius's steward, he could have remained behind in Aven. There, he had a comfortable house, predictable duties, and the company of his handsome lover, Djadi. But the dominus needed an attendant he could trust. *'Not to mention a cooler-headed adviser than Autronius Felix generally proves.'*

The bond went back decades. Sempronius had seen the marks of magic on Corvinus even before Corvinus himself had known his gifts for what they were. The next day, Sempronius had arranged for Corvinus's manumission under the mandate of the *tabulae magicae*, though Corvinus had been only a boy of ten and Sempronius still a stripling lad, not yet wearing the toga of manhood. It had necessitated a trick, to reveal Corvinus's magic without letting on that Sempronius knew about it thanks to his own hidden gifts—but he had let Corvinus in on his secret, the only person in the world so trusted besides Lady Vibia. Then he insisted that his father pay for Corvinus's education, so that a learned man would grow out of the enslaved child who'd been born in a muddy Albine farmhouse.

Only the bone-deep loyalty such actions inspired could have brought Corvinus to the Iberian hinterlands, to sit in the dark while fury-driven raiders harried them on all sides. *'Exile in Abydosia was a seaside vacation by comparison,'* he thought, as one of the horses shrieked. Yes, they'd had to flee Truscum with assassins on their heels, and he hadn't enjoyed the sea voyage, but life in Tamiat had swiftly developed a routine. One knew what to expect from the days, the people, and the politics.

That routine, of course, had bored Sempronius to distraction, but Corvinus did not have so restless a soul. He *liked* a day where you woke up and knew, for a certainty, that a horde of bearded maniacs wasn't going to try to murder you. *'Admittedly, that was mostly because the Abydosians were far more interested in murdering each other.'* The Vettoni tribesmen, alas, had no such inward-focused interest.

Corvinus wished he had light by which to inspect a map, but of course they had closed all the cart's shutters. He had been trying to determine if there were any patterns to the attacks. They came at all times of the day, sometimes just as the legions were setting out, sometimes when the sun was highest and hottest, sometimes late in the afternoon when the men's vigor had begun to flag. Corvinus's inner sense of order told him there had to be *some* underlying reasoning—something that would lead them to the Vettoni stronghold, or provide information about their scouting tactics. *'And,'* he thought, as the song of swords and shields beyond his wooden barrier seemed to reach a crescendo, *'having a map to focus on would be a pleasant distraction.'*

As soon as the attack had begun, it ended. The sound of horns was muffled by the cart's walls, but Corvinus's ears had grown practiced in listening for the Vettoni call to retreat. In its wake, the shouts of the fighters and the banging of weapons faded away. Then, the "all-clear" from the Aventan horns, far closer and louder. The mule-driver kicked open the flap at the back of the cart, resolutely returning to duty, and Corvinus followed him, desperate for fresh air.

∞∞∞∞∞∞∞∞∞∞∞

The Tenth Legion stopped to make camp in a large meadow between two strips of spiky trees. The clearing did not look natural, dotted as it was with small stumps where saplings had been cut away. The vexillation from the Eighth, perhaps, had stayed here back in the autumn. It was not large enough for all three legions to camp together, so the Fourteenth had gone on an extra mile to another clearing, while the Eighth lagged a little behind.

Corvinus helped to set up the command tent, swiftly unpacked Sempronius's essentials, then went to wait at the camp's main gate for any approaching messengers.

As anticipated, a rider came from each of the other legions, reporting on their status. Corvinus thanked the messengers and sent them to get water for themselves and their horses while they awaited any replies from Sempronius. Then, as the Tenth's rearguard trooped in with the auxiliaries, Corvinus sought out a gangly, wide-eyed youth called Eustix. "Any birds today?" he called out, before the young man had even hopped down from his cart.

"Yes, sir, yes!" Eustix reached into the sack at his side, pulling out several sealed parchments. "Parvus and Paullus both came back today, dear things, I think they must've gone through a storm—"

Sempronius had hired Eustix in Nedhena. The boy's father was that town's greatest Air mage, and the son had inherited the talent. Like Marcia Tullia, Consul Galerius's wife and the foremost Air mage in Aven, they had the ability to direct letter-bearing birds to the appropriate destinations. Sempronius might have had to lay out more money, had the youth not been so eager to leave home and see some adventure. As it was, the payments were not so much wages for the boy as a bribe for his father's indulgence.

Through the young man's power, Sempronius had birds making daily circuits to Tarraco, to pick up any messages delivered locally. Others went all the way to Aven, bearing regular reports of the action in Iberia and bringing missives back, so that Sempronius could receive news from the Senate in a few days rather than the half-month or more it might take a ship-borne letter to find him. An expensive venture, but Sempronius considered it worthy—and Corvinus was not sorry that the messages originating in Aven all passed through Djadi's hands. Every packet included a personal note for Corvinus, even if it was nothing more than a few lines: *'Be well. Be safe. I love you.'*

Eustix prattled on as he pulled the letters together. "Wouldn't it be a fine thing if they could talk to us?"

"Talk?" Corvinus echoed, a pale eyebrow lifting in confusion.

"The birds!" Eustix grinned, holding out two packets. "If they could tell us, 'Oh yes, it was raining in Maritima yesterday, so I flew a little further north.' I think that would be fascinating." Still smiling, he leaned back toward the cart, wiggling an affectionate finger at the nearest bird.

"Indeed." Corvinus withheld any other commentary. *'Strange boy.'* The lad was pleasant enough, dutiful to a fault, and had given no complaint during the occasionally harrowing journey south, but he was, undeniably, a bit odd. Sometimes Corvinus thought he rather resembled his birds, with dark eyes set slightly too far apart, a beakish nose, and a tendency to chirp without prompting. *'They say the magic shapes the mage, sometimes,'* Corvinus thought, glancing through the papers as he walked toward the command tent. *'I wonder if Marcia Tullia ever tries to converse with her birds.'*

When Corvinus entered the tent, he found Sempronius already there, sharing wine with Autronius Felix. "I don't like having to release the Lacetani without reinforcements to take their place, but I don't see any way around it," Sempronius was saying. "They have their own people to defend—and our supply trains."

"They've promised safe passage, then?" Felix asked. Sempronius nodded, rubbing at his chin. "Well, let's hope gratitude for being released keeps them honest."

"We're entering Edetani territory. Tribune Vitellius wrote of them as solid allies, quite helpful."

"If we can find any," Felix said, with a little snort. Every village they'd encountered in the past two days had been either pillaged by the Vettoni or abandoned in anticipation of such treatment.

"We will." Sempronius's eyebrows arched as he caught sight of Corvinus. "Letters from Tarraco?"

Corvinus nodded. "I haven't sorted them yet." Sempronius gestured for him to proceed, so Corvinus went to the desk and pulled open the cord that held the leather packet closed. "Generals Onidius and Calpurnius checked in. The Eighth is well-settled and will be ready to march at first light; the Fourteenth has leveled the ground for their camp and expects the tail of their train in another hour."

"Good."

"Their riders await any messages you may have for the other camps." As Corvinus shuffled the papers, he examined the seals and any notations scribbled onto the edge. "Two from Consul Galerius Orator," he said, setting them to the right. Senate business, no doubt, which the dominus would be eager to stay abreast of. "A few messages from our suppliers in and around Tarraco." Those, he set to the left, to be passed along to the prefect, though he knew Sempronius would glance through them first. "One from Marcus Autronius—no, two, but one's for the tribune." Corvinus passed that one over to Felix, setting the other with the letters from Galerius. "And one from—" Corvinus's brow arched; he recognized the name, but could not imagine what would be making the man write to Sempronius here in Iberia. "Shafer ben Nissim? Is that not the Asherite we dined with in Tamiat?"

Sempronius's dark eyes lit with pleasure. "Indeed!" he said, striding forward and holding out a hand for the letter. As he popped the seal, grinning, he explained, "My friend Shafer has taken up residence in Gades."

Corvinus's head bobbed in understanding, and Felix laughed. "I confess, Sempronius, I thought it might take you longer to establish a spy in Rabirus's camp."

"Not a spy, merely a good friend and loyal correspondent. And not in his camp, precisely," Sempronius said, as his eyes scanned the words printed in a slightly heavy hand. The letter was written, Corvinus noticed, in both Athaecan and Petraean, alternating line by line. Corvinus suspected the dominus would write back in the same fashion, in the Athaecan he and Shafer shared and in Truscan, that both men might have the opportunity to practice reading in languages less familiar to them. "But close enough, at least until Rabirus takes the field."

"If he even intends to do so, rather than holing up just like Fimbrianus did," Felix commented, lifting his eyes from his brother's letter.

"He will," Sempronius said, with quiet surety. "However little he likes this fight, he won't allow himself to be called a coward while *I'm* fighting for the honor of Aven."

SPLINTER THE SECOND

She was close, so close, to having enough power. She had importuned Discordia in the north and the south, the east and the west. She had begged favor at sunrise and sunset, at the turning-edge of the half-moon, in the midst of late spring storms. Every advantage she could seize, Corinna had taken.

It was not, yet, enough.

Corinna took up her stylus.

There had been a time when she might have made a fine poet. More usual for those blessed with Light or Air, but not all of humanity's gifts came channeled through magic. Corinna had loved words for themselves. She could have been quite happy, left alone to that love.

The Fates would not permit her to only love words.

A girl with talents like hers, she had been told, could not languish in seclusion. Peace was not her destiny. How could it be, for one gifted by Discordia? Fortuna, Janus, no, those were not the gods watching out for Corinna. Certainly not Felicitas or Sors, the gods of luck.

No. The Fates had made themselves clear. Discordia and Discordia alone had laid a hand upon Corinna's brow.

But she could still use her neglected talents of composition in that lady's honor.

Arise, o daughter of dark night,
Flashing-eyed mother of hardship and pain,
From exile come to rule again.
Arise, dreadful mistress of bane and blight,
Quarrel's dam, Lady of Sorrow.
Ascend until all earth lies in your shadow
And from those heights, hurl down all strife,
All bitterness, all blots to precious life.

This gift we make, of blood and bone,
And supplicate ourselves before your throne,
To call you forth where you might thrive
And feed where you have been so long deprived.
Arise, o daughter of dark night.

X

"Burn it all," Latona instructed, "and dump the ashes in the river." The two slaves Latona had brought along to clear the Discordian sacrifice nodded, but Latona could see confusion on their faces at what seemed a wasteful order. Bones and sinew were always useful, and some of the entrails might still be edible, for those who weren't too picky. But these remains were cursed, and Latona would take no chances on Discordian madness spreading into someone through them. "Then make sure you wash yourselves, thoroughly. Evil has been at work here." She would venture no more explanation, but none was needed. The slaves nodded their understanding and set to work.

Latona would have done it herself, however gruesome the spectacle, but her head swam when she drew too close to the desiccated remains. *'If I actually tried to lay a hand on them, I suspect I could not long remain conscious. Or sane.'* While the young men worked, she sat down as near as she could manage and gestured for Merula to bring her the scrolls they had hauled up the hill.

She might have waited for Vibia to arrive and offer advice. Latona had dispatched a letter as soon as they had returned home the prior evening, but it would still be several days before her ally reached Stabiae. Latona could not stomach the notion of letting this wretched display remain intact, so near her home, for that long. *'And if Alhena's visions are any indication, we won't be wanting for horrors for her to turn her hand to.'*

Discordian magic had never been particularly well-regarded in Aven, but the cult had had its periods of popularity throughout the centuries, and so she hoped some of the historical texts on Aventan magical theory would mention them. *'One of which will hopefully give me some idea of how to cleanse this place . . .'* Spirit and Fracture were inimical elements: each dangerous and vulnerable to the other. If anything could wipe away the miasma, it would be Spirit magic. But Latona had to figure out how to apply it.

One of the texts in her lap was medicinal in nature, a text used by the

priests, magical and mundane, of the Temple of Asclepius. It had occurred to Latona that the procedure of cleansing the grove might not be
unlike what she had done the previous year, purging poison when Sempronius had been shot with a tainted arrow during an autumn hunt. That
had been Fire magic, not Spirit, but the principles might be similar. *'Seek
it out, chase it down, then burn out . . .'* If she could find the right pattern,
the push and pull that had guided her in healing Sempronius, then perhaps she would meet with luck in healing the grove.

With Merula at her side, occasionally handing her another text to
reference, Latona kept her head bent over the scrolls while the two men
worked to clear away the physical remnants of the Discordian rites. She
had set out early in the morning, to give them as much time to work as
possible—and herself as much time after they were done. She had no
desire to be caught in this place after dark, particularly if her attempts to
cleanse it failed.

"Domina?" After some time, one of the young men, his hands reeking
with viscera, approached her. "Domina, we've completed the work."

"Mm?" Latona surfaced from her reading. "Oh. Excellent. Thank
you. Oh!" She stopped them before they could wheel the remains away.
"The ground, too. Any dirt that the remains touched." The two men
looked at each other, then set to work scraping away at the ground. Latona looked up at Merula. "I suppose it's about time to try, then."

"You are knowing what to do, Domina?" Merula said, gathering the
scrolls back from her.

Latona laughed. "Knowing? Of course not. But . . . I think I have a
good guess."

Once the men had taken away the cart with the remains of the carcass,
and with Merula standing protective watch, Latona found herself pacing
back and forth within the grove, sending out tendrils of Spirit magic to
test the energy of the place. A sense of oddness hung amid the leaves,
setting a prickle up on her neck. *'A distortion, that's what it is. Whatever
the natural energies are here, they've been warped.'* As surely as if someone had stuck a knife's point deep into the heartwood of a living tree, the
energies here had been ruptured. That had been the effect of the sacrifice, its power channeled into the tree's destruction. *'But why? What purpose could someone having blighting this single tree?'*

A warning to her, perhaps, as her sisters worried. But Latona wasn't
sure.

Fracture magic, by its very nature, played with boundaries—points of change, of chance, the thin line between reality and dreams. Mages like Vibia spent their lives trying to keep hold of the balance; Fracture mages who didn't fell to madness. *'Or worse. Or this.'* The place where change became catastrophe, where boundaries opened up into chasms and a little disorder whorled into utter chaos. *'That there are mages who seek to loose this on the world . . .'*

Latona went to the base of the tree, where the ground had been scraped away from the roots. She ran her hands over the gnarled brown twists, then tried to scoop some of the earth back toward them. "Poor thing . . ." she murmured. There was little she could do for it directly. *'If Terentilla were here, or Marcus Autronius . . .'* Setting the grove entirely to rights would be the domain of an Earth mage; all Latona could do was try to get rid of the lingering, pestilent Fracture magic, lest it poison the ground any further.

Latona made herself stand just where the carcass had hung, slipping out of her sandals so her bare feet touched the freshly exposed earth beneath where the entrails had lain. The *wrongness* hit her like suffocating incense, cloying and dizzying. *'You're not scaring me off, whatever you are.'* She closed her eyes, held her hands out, palm-up, and began an invocation. "Blessed Lady Juno, hear me, help me. Look on me with favor, help me to right the wrong that has been done here . . ."

The overhanging trees were thick, allowing hardly any sunlight through, but as Latona chanted, warmth blossomed on her shoulders. Her skin began to heat, and she tasted cinnamon on her tongue—magic at work, building up in her and then flowing back out. She let it ebb from her, trying to soothe the land as she had sometimes soothed her sisters, or as she had influenced the mood at dinner parties. It was a different thing, a strange challenge, to use Spirit magic to affect a place rather than a person. Reaching out to the plants and earth felt in no way like reaching out to a person's emotions. Those all had a similar shape, even with a stranger. The tree was something else entirely. *'I wonder, if I had Tilla here . . .'* Mages did sometimes combine their talents toward a common purpose, and Latona suspected that channeling Spirit's energy to dispel Fracture's curse from the earth would be much simpler with her Diana-blessed friend to help direct her efforts.

'Although Spirit can see the workings. It's not a skill I've much practiced, but maybe . . .'

Worrying her lower lip, Latona thought of all she had read regarding the visualization of magic. She was so used to operating on intuition above all else that it felt odd, calling on her eyes to aid her. It happened incidentally sometimes, usually when many mages were working all at once, as at the Cantrinalia rituals, or when so many had joined forces to fight the Aventine fires. Sheer magnitude would bring the proof of magic to her sight. Recalling what that felt like, Latona focused on summoning it to the forefront of her mind.

After a few moments, Latona chanced opening her eyes a bit, then gasped at the swirl of color in front of her: chains of gold emanating from her own form, twisting and twining around a hazy column of bronze that spurted up from where the entrails had been spilt. As her attention fluttered, the gold faded for a moment, until Latona refocused.

Her instinct was to pull the chains tight, squeezing the remnants of the Fracture magic into oblivion. *'No . . .'* she thought. *'No, see if you can find a signature . . . anything that might help you recognize this again . . .'*

Upon closer examination, it was no column: more like a jagged rock, jutting up out of the ground, uneven, cruelly broken, half-crumbling. Latona could get a feel for it as she wound her own magic around it, slowly sliding her way over the cracked edges—more crumbling now, with the locus of the spell removed from proximity. The sense of taint and invasive festering was similar to Pinarius Scaeva's, but she could not find anything more specific, nothing that might allow her to tie this working to a particular mage, should she encounter it again.

Latona sighed. *'Another thing I must learn more of.'* But now was not the time to lament the gaps in her magical education. Instead, she took a deep breath and closed her eyes to concentrate, focusing on her own magic. *'Burn brighter, burn harder. Burn it out, hunt it down, restore balance to this place.'*

The curse fought her, reminding Latona unpleasantly of facing Scaeva. The jagged edges spiked at her, like slivers of shattered glass trying to work their way beneath her skin. Now, though, there was no one to direct the Fracture magic, much less to set it on her blood like a hound. Spirit's strength attacked Fracture's weak points, and without the anchor of the sacrifice to reinforce it, the remnants of the Discordian curse began to crumble.

The sun climbed high above her, and Latona could feel its heat piercing through the trees, but she stood still, murmuring invocations. Each time the Fracture magic shivered or shuddered and tried to slip her grasp, she spun the net of her own magic another direction. She could give it no quarter, no avenue for escape.

Slowly, the wound that the terrible sacrifice had left in the world began to knit back together. Slowly, the sense of pollution dwindled.

Latona kept her eyes closed until her lingering nausea faded and she could no longer feel the taint of poison in the land around her. Tilla, she was sure, would have felt the ground give a sigh of relief; Latona simply had to keep pushing until nothing pushed back at her, and hope that was enough.

As she released the flow of magic, Latona felt a stiffening pain taking over her muscles. *'Oof.'* Some of the ache was from standing in one position for too long, but much of it was also from the exertion of magical energy. She made a mental note to have Ama Rubellia work with her on guarding against the negative effects of using her powers so strongly. Her calves would ache for days, she was sure, and she already felt lethargic, heavy-lidded. *'There must be better ways of replenishing one's energy than simply falling asleep for the better part of the day. That's not just pathetic, it's dangerous.'* For she remembered, too, what had made her so vulnerable to Pinarius Scaeva's predations: pouring too much of herself out through her magic, without a core of strength left in reserve to hold her up.

Groaning, Latona rotated her shoulders and stretched her neck. She ruffled her hair and looked around the grove. She grasped Merula's hand, taking comfort in her attendant's solid presence. *'Let this land be at peace, by Juno's grace.'* Peace such as she knew she would not find for herself, so long as Discordian mages freely roamed.

∞∞∞∞∞∞∞∞∞∞∞∞

TOLETUM, IBERIA

"Will it happen again tonight, do you think?"

"Shades of Dis . . ."

"I wish we had a mage with us . . ."

"What could a mage do against those demons?"

"Well, *something*, surely!"

Vitellius hated to hear the fear in his centurions' voices. These were battle-hardened men. Nearly all had fought the blue-painted Armoricans, the sound of their horns and war harps reverberating in the chilly air. Some had ventured across the border into Vendelicia, where ber-serker warriors fought while under the thrall of maddening potions. Oth-ers had been in Numidia years earlier, where arrows could come rushing down at a man out of a sandstorm.

They did not scare easily.

But now, they huddled together as the sun eased its way below the horizon, whispering about the terrors of the coming night. Vitellius hated to hear it and hated more knowing how rational the fear was.

Nearby, the centurions continued their fretting. "We've got the Arevaci mages, and they haven't figured anything out yet."

"Yeah, but that's barbarian magic, not good Aventan magic. We need good Aventan magic . . ."

"Can't use it in battle, thick-head. We'd offend Mars."

"We're not in battle *now*, are we? Anyway, he doesn't mind it as pro-tection. Good Aventan magic, I'm telling you—"

'*Good Aventan magic.*' Vitellius touched the focale at his collar, the scarlet neck-scarf that had, he was sure, saved his life by protecting him from Lusetanian ensorcellment. His sister Latona's magic infused it— good Aventan magic in no uncertain terms—and though he had no idea how it worked, it seemed to be guarding him still.

"*North wall, section eight!*"

The shout came, but Vitellius did not turn his head. The necessary men would move to reinforce that portion of the wall without his direc-tion. The legions were becoming as well-practiced at this as at setting their camp, thanks to near-nightly repetition.

The wind changed direction suddenly, a fierce gust out of the north, far colder than it should have been—a wind for Januarius, not Junius, and in its wake came the unnatural mist, sour-scented and heavy. Across the walls, a thousand men muttered prayers and readied their weapons. Vitellius glanced down toward the eastern sally gate, where Hanath and the rest of the auxiliary cavalry, Arevaci and Edetani men and women, waited. Hanath's face was serious, her horse's reins tied around her waist and a spear sitting across her lap. If there was a chance—

They had led sorties before, not that it did much good. The invaders turned tail and fled at the first hoofbeat, proving that they were no fools. Tonight, the cavalry had different instructions.

Still the mist rose, higher than any normal fog, rolling like waves against Toletum's walls, piling on itself until it crested the battlements.

The first few nights, men had dropped to their knees immediately, all their strength overcome by the fiends. Trial and error, though, had helped Vitellius and Mennenius discern that some men were less susceptible, and those were the men who now stood on the walls at night. The rest took day shifts and additional other responsibilities; Vitellius had let it be known that there was no shame in being among those who could not stand against the *akdraugi*—but they would work their share, all the same.

Still, even the hardier men were not proof against the roiling nausea and mind-swamping horrors that the *akdraugi* brought with them. Even at a distance, their chill set into Vitellius's bones. He had never yet succumbed to their power, thanks to the Fire magic in his focale, but that did not mean he was entirely unaffected. The Aventan charm granted enough power to keep his head above the churning magical waters that threatened to drown the other men, but not enough to keep him dry.

Vitellius gripped the wall hard, but more in anger than in agony— anger at the futility of the situation, at his inability to protect anyone but himself. And yet there *was* power, of a kind, that he could pass on. The men had noticed that the *akdraugi* could never quite reach Vitellius. He had gotten a reputation for being invincible against them, and while he knew that was not true, he did not wish to dispel the hope that the legionaries drew from his perceived strength. *'Good Aventan magic.'* If only they had more of it.

Here and there, the mists coagulated, though never into anything like the form of a man or animal. Sometimes demonic faces would appear— or were they only imagined?—sharp and pointed, with fathomless eyes, only to whirl away as the mist throbbed like a beating heart. Then the noise rose, a distant keening—higher than a moan, lower than a whistle. Vitellius gestured sharply to the men standing in the nearest tower: two Arevaci horn-blowers and an Aventan drummer, who set up a jaunty rhythm. It was terribly out of place, this triumphant and sunny tune, played in the dead of night with a haunting mist all around them, but the Arevaci magic-men thought it would help combat the eldritch howls of the *akdraugi*, and Vitellius was minded to try anything that might negate the fiends' advantage over them.

Still, the lugubrious wailing was difficult to ignore. Whenever he heard it, Vitellius found himself thinking of funerals, and some nights it seemed as though he were hearing mourners at his *own* funeral. His mind's eye conjured images of his father's careworn face, his sisters' tears, his own corpse hoisted on a funeral pyre, his own death mask placed among those of his ancestors . . .

With a violent shake of his head, Vitellius forced himself to focus. Dreadful as the *akdraugi* were, they were not all-powerful. He had kept himself away from the thick of them tonight for this reason: so that he could stand back and see, with a clearer head, their scope.

They were thickest near section eight of the northern wall, and the mist hardly thinned for two sections on either side. From there, though, it grew much more sparse. Hardly more than a wisp moved near the western corner, where the wall met the sharp cliff above the River Tagus. Toward the east, the fog was patchy: here thick, there thin, and shifting. Impossible though it was to pick out a single *akdraugo* from the whole, clearly, their numbers were finite. They might not have discrete bodies, but they could not stretch themselves indefinitely, either.

'The Lusetani do not have enough of the fiends to cover the whole wall. Or not enough magic-men to summon them.' Vitellius wondered which it was—and which the Lusetani might have an easier time procuring more of.

The men atop the walls stood against the *akdraugi* as long as they could, but what could a legionary do against an enemy that had no body to attack? Even the strongest of them could only hold fast against the miasmic terror for so long. As men began to drop, centurions at the base of the walls gave whistles, ordering them down to recover and fresh men sent up the ladders to replace them. The *akdraugi*'s effect lessened the farther one got from the walls, though so long as the mist hung in the air, no one could escape it entirely.

This rotation had kept the *akdraugi* from claiming more than a few lives; Vitellius could not bear to watch men hounded to death by dark magic as those who had died with Mennenius's cohort had been. But it was then, as the defensive line ran ragged, that the Lusetani charged.

They came from the tree line, and so they should have been visible a long way off, but the mist of the *akdraugi* concealed them until they were nearly at the base of the walls. Some had ladders; others used hand-picks to scale Toletum's defenses.

'If they could remain silent,' Vitellius thought, *'they might have a chance of summiting.'* But their enthusiasm for the fight always gave them away. The Lusetani could not seem to keep from whooping their war-cries as they approached, giving the Aventans some warning. The sheer

earthiness of it also seemed to call some of the legionaries back to themselves, breaking the spell of the *akdraugi* enough that they could rally a fight.

The Lusetani concentrated their attack where the *akdraugi* had been thickest, there at the northern section, for that was where the line of defenders had grown thinnest. Vitellius had given strict orders to the centurions only to pull reinforcements from below, not from other points along the wall; he would not risk creating multiple weak points for the Lusetani to take advantage of. A few enemy warriors avoided the arrows and stones sent their way as they ascended and managed to summit the wall, hurling themselves onto the battlement with victorious cries. Vitellius wanted enough men left hale that such threats could be quickly dealt with.

As swords and shields clashed, as men shouted in fury or in pain, Vitellius looked down at Hanath, whose eyes were fixed only on him, with nary a glance for the hideous mist hanging above her head nor the fighters on the walls. He gave her one sharp nod, gesturing toward the sally gate, and in reply, Hanath raised a fist in the air, drawing the other riders' attention. Two of the townspeople cranked the gate open for them, and with no cry nor call, Hanath and the two dozen riders behind her rode out of Toletum's protection. Not toward the attackers on the wall, but rather toward the northeast, away from the tree line, following the river, far away from the fighting. With any luck, the Lusetani would not even notice them go. *'Mercury give you swift passage, my lady,'* he thought. She might be their only hope of relief.

After that, the skirmish went on as they had almost every night for the past month. During the fighting, the *akdraugi* grew thinner and thinner until the mist dissipated. Whatever power was used to summon them, it seemed it could not hold them over so large an area for long. *'Or perhaps at such a distance from the casters . . .'* He wished he knew more, to explain the differences between what Mennenius described and how the *akdraugi* behaved here, but the Arevaci magic-men were at a loss. So much knowledge lost to time, they said, and perhaps so much invented by the warking Ekialde's people. It frustrated Vitellius, but he tried to keep from showing that to the Arevaci. *'It must feel to them as it would were some mage in Aven suddenly to demonstrate the powers of Hercules or Circe, unlike anything we've seen in centuries. We wouldn't know how to respond to that, either.'*

To the Aventans' advantage, the Lusetani knew even less of siege-craft than the tribes living closer to Tyrian and Aventan settlements. Troops with any idea what they were doing might have stood some chance of scaling Toletum's walls with the assistance that the *akdraugi* distraction provided. But the walls would hold; Vitellius had no doubt of that. Over the spring, they had grown by several feet, thanks to the ceaseless labor of his legionaries. The River Tagus wrapped around three sides of the city, leaving the northern approach as the only option for the attackers. Even when the *akdraugi* brought many of the defenders to their knees, enough remained to repel the corporeal assault.

'But,' Vitellius thought, as he heard the Lusetani horns, calling off the attack. *'Ekialde might not need to win by frontal assault.'* Vitellius had provisioned Toletum as well as he could, but now they were cut off from the surrounding farms and the coastal towns, reliant only upon their stores and what the gardens within the city could yield. Occasionally, some brave souls would take the switchbacking path down to the river to try to fish below the city, but they could never gather enough before the Lusetani noticed and chased them back up the hill. What cover Vitellius had been able to build along those shallow, rocky paths was not enough to allow the fishermen to ply their trade meaningfully.

'Neither their warriors nor their fiends alone would be enough to hold us in here,' Vitellius thought, staring out until the Lusetani disappeared back into the tree line, *'but together, they make a siege.'* It was clever work, Vitellius had to give the Lusetani that.

Vitellius, Mennenius, and the quartermasters had done the math. Two months, and then Toletum's provisions would run low; three, and they would be in danger of starving.

'And then what?' Vitellius yanked off his helmet and flung it aside, then rubbed irritably at his hair, near-plastered to his head with sweat. *'Turn out the civilians whose home this is? Try and fight our way through a few thousand barbarians, while hoping their wretched fiends don't snatch our souls?'*

He had sent Hanath and the cavalry out to find help, whether Aventan or Iberian, but there was another benefit: getting the horses out of the city would stretch the food stores a little longer.

'She'll find help. She has to. She'll be able to tell the governors what to expect. They can smash into the Lusetani from behind, and this nightmare will end.'

The last letter Vitellius had received before Ekialde cut off the messengers' routes had promised that help was on its way. Vitellius could not spare the meat for a sacrifice, but he prayed daily to Mars and Jupiter that it would come soon enough. And he had sent letters out with Hanath, too—including another to his sister, since the courier bearing the first had never returned, likely never reached the coast. Another letter, telling Latona not only of the *akdraugi*, but what had happened with the focale she had woven for him, how it protected him even now—and begging her, if she could, to send a little more of that Aventan magic his way.

◇◇◇◇◇◇◇◇◇◇◇◇◇◇◇

Lusetani Camp, Outside Toletum

He could only pretend the eldritch howls did not trouble him.

The first time Bailar had summoned the spirits, Ekialde had nearly jumped out of his skin. Fortunately, the rest of his war-band had been too similarly alarmed to notice his momentary lapse in control. He had asked for horrors worthy of wringing out Aventan souls, and Bailar had delivered, far beyond what Ekialde could have thought to ask for. And this—this worked so much better than the potion he had tried to use on the Aventan leader.

Now, he stood at the front of his war-band, unflinching, as the dread spirits rose not from the earth but through it, summoned from their homes in the netherworld and condensing in the hot Iberian air.

Bailar promised it would only get better, the more they had the fresh blood of their enemies to work with. Old blood was weaker, and the blood of farmers summoned less vigorous spirits than that of warriors. Ekialde had witnessed that; however harrowing the specters, they lost cohesion after a few moments. Bailar had worked around that by staggering his summonings, lengthening the effect. He assured Ekialde, though, that once they broke the siege and had the fresh lifeblood of Aventan legionaries, his spirits would linger much longer. *'The Aventans would have to be made of much sterner stuff to endure that.'*

He knew he should be glad. Bailar was delivering what he asked, a way to rout deadly Aventan steel and their possibly deadlier discipline. Yet something about it niggled at the back of his mind, tugging at his conscience. Would Bandue approve? A voice in his mind asked if this was right and proper, if the gods sanctioned such use of the magical gifts they gave.

The voice quite often sounded like his wife's.

It troubled some of his allies, too; the Lusetani trusted him, but the Vettoni had begun to whisper. Iberian magic typically relied on the stars, the trees, the rivers. Magic-men read the will of the gods and reported it to the chieftains and their warriors. They did not intervene in these matters themselves. Seeing what Bailar was doing made many of the southern and eastern tribes uneasy, and sometimes, in quiet moments, alone with his thoughts, Ekialde could not silence the questions he had about this path's rightness.

'Just because no one has used magic in this way in some time does not mean it is improper,' he told himself. 'Bailar is gifted. Endovelicos has smiled on him, as Bandue has smiled on me. We are exceptional men in an exceptional time.'

<hr />

The main camp was downriver, around a bend to the west, though Ekialde kept his war-band camping in the forest just outside Toletum. The women, the magic-men who were not summoning the *akdraugi*, and other hangers-on stayed further off, and it was from that camp that Ekialde also dispatched the raiding bands, both Lusetani and those of the tribes who had allied with them. While he kept his strongest warriors focused on besieging Toletum, he sent parties out to harass the local villages— what remained of them, at least. The Vettoni had already picked clean or burned much of the surrounding terrain, and those who had thus far escaped death or slavery had fled to the arms of the Aventans. Many were now sheltering in Toletum; others had gone further south and east, out of the mountains and toward the port towns. The raiding parties had to go further afield now, and they returned to seek Ekialde's direction less frequently.

'If my husband does not break this siege soon, or find new territory to plunder,' Neitin thought, looking at the fractious assembly, 'some of these allies may cease to return here at all. They will grow bored and wander back to their homes—or go looking for new trouble to make on their own.'

Neitin paced up and down the length of the camp, with her infant boy swaddled tightly to her chest. There was more activity than usual today; some of the raiders were packing up goods and slaves to transport back to their hometowns, or to the northern and western port cities, those not yet subject to Aventan control. A knot of captured Cossetan civilians stood in the hot sun, their expressions varying between dull and mutinous. *'More of our neighbors' blood on my husband's hands.'* For all that Ekialde preached of ridding Iberia of the Tyrians and Aventans, most of the true fighting had involved other Iberians, those whom Ekialde deemed traitors. Their crime: maintaining too friendly a relationship with the traders from the east.

The Cossetans were one of the tribes who made their home along the Baetis River, as it wound its way down to the Tyrian-turned-Aventan port of Gades. Neitin had not known so much geography before her husband began his Bandue-bestowed mission, but she had had cause to learn, and this observation concerned her. *'I did not think they were raiding so far south as Cossetan territory.'* Would Ekialde turn his full attention there, if they broke Toletum? Would they march on Gades itself? Neitin knew almost nothing of that city, save that it was said to be both ancient and extremely well-fortified.

She sighed, gazing over the Cossetans. *'Foolishness, all of it. We have plunder enough to satisfy us for years. If we went home now, the Aventans might be happy to see the back of us and just leave us be.'* But even as she thought it, Neitin knew things had gone too far for that. *'We abandoned hope for clemency when Bailar summoned his fiends against the Aventans. They will not forget that, nor forgive it.'*

As Neitin started to turn away from the Cossetans, one woman caught her eye. She was perhaps forty years old, skinny and pale as the moon, with glossy black hair hanging in limp ringlets around her face. Her eyes had a touch of yellow mixed in their hazel. Not as much as Ekialde's, which could look golden in a certain light, but something in them compelled Neitin's attention. The woman lifted her hands—bound at the wrist and tied to the women on either side of her—and gestured Neitin to approach her. When she did, Neitin saw dark patches on her arms. *'Burns, or scars?'* But no; when she looked closer, she could see they were the patterned markings that the magic-men and magic-women inked into their skin. Neitin's heart beat faster, recognizing them, as the woman continued to beckon her.

Curiosity brought Neitin forward, though good sense had her stop a few steps away.

"Handsome lad," the woman said, giving the boy an appraising look. "How old?"

"Nearly four months," Neitin answered.

"Oof." The woman clucked her tongue in sympathy. "It was a hard winter to bear a child in."

Neitin suspected it would not have been so hard had she been at home, in a warm and cozy mud-bricked house, not in a tent in the wilds. She bounced the boy a bit; he seemed to be enjoying the stranger's attention.

"Have you named him yet?"

Neitin had, but only in her own heart, and she was not willing to share that information with a magic-woman belonging to what Ekialde had decided was an enemy tribe. "We're going to have his naming ceremony at the solstice."

"Mm. Auspicious day for it," the woman said, nodding. "Pick a good one. Poor lad's going to need it."

Instinctively, Neitin's arms tightened around her child. "What do you mean?" The woman shrugged, but Neitin would not be dissuaded. "I saw the markings on your arms. You are one of the magic-women of the Cossetans, are you not?"

"I am." The woman's eyes had a shrewd look to them. "Or I was. Who knows what I will be, when these traders tear me away from the soil and rivers of my home?" She nodded at the boy. "But I've seen enough to know that child will need as much strength as the gods can give him."

"Why?" Neitin demanded. "What is it you've seen?"

The magic-woman's thin lips curled into a smile. "Information has a price. See to it that I go no further from my homeland, *erregerra*'s wife, and I will tell you what I know, and do my best to protect that boy of yours, conqueror's whelp though he may be."

Neitin bristled a bit to hear her son described so. "Why should I trust you?"

"You have no reason," the woman admitted, still holding Neitin with that unblinking stare. "But I will make you a solemn vow by the star that has watched over me since the hour of my birth. I have heard your story on the wind, little wife, little mother. I know that not all here pleases you." Only now did she look away—to nod in the direction of Bailar's tent, all its flaps tightly closed despite the heat of the day.

Neitin swallowed. "And you are strong enough to stand against him?"

The woman laughed. "I wasn't strong enough to protect my people. But one woman and one child?" She wagged her head in consideration. "I can give you the knowledge the stars have passed to me. There is protection of a sort in that, is there not? And it would be far easier to break this fiend-waker's power if I had the chance to observe him." A quick cloud of sorrow dimmed her expression. "We had no chance to defend ourselves. No one knew how to counter his magics when he descended upon our village." Her cheeks tightened as she looked back to Neitin, the defiant fire again in her eyes. "But here, I might stand more of a chance. I think you would wish that, yes, little wife? To free your husband from the seduction of blood?"

Neitin's son fidgeted, sputtering nonsense syllables, and she had to readjust her hold on him. "I am a loyal wife," she said. "I do not wish my husband harmed. But yes, I would wish him to find a different path to the glories the gods intend for him."

The woman's upper lip twitched. "Then take me in your service, and I swear by every star in heaven, my magics shall work only against the fiend-waker and his helpers. I shall lift no finger against you, your babe, or even your warlord husband." She nodded at the child. "And I shall do what is within my power to protect the innocent."

Distrust warred with temptation in Neitin's breast. Her uncle had proved a disappointment, unwilling to stand against Bailar, passively standing by and letting the atrocities go on. More than anything, Neitin wanted it all to stop. Free from the blood-haze, she was sure that Ekialde would see sense and return home, bringing the Lusetani back to their *mendi*, the mountains to the west that had sheltered them for generations. *'If achieving that goal means trusting a stranger, and one with reason to hate us . . .'*

Whatever the wisdom, Neitin wanted to believe in this woman. "You will swear again, beneath the stars, with all the appropriate rituals," she said. "If you betray us, my sisters will slice out your kidneys to feed their dogs." The woman nodded, with a slight smile that looked almost like approval. "And I will have your name."

"You ask much and little all at once, as befits a queen," the woman said, still smiling. "The people of my home know me as Sakarbik. What the stars call me is my own business."

"Sakarbik will do." Neitin turned on her heel and marched over to the man who seemed to be in charge of this knot of slaves. "That woman with the black hair and the markings on her arms. Untie her," Neitin commanded. "I lay claim to her."

"Lady . . ." the man said, his eyes rolling slightly. "These Cossetans are spoken for. There's a captain in Olissippo willing to pay top coin for them. I can't just—"

"You can and you will," Neitin snapped. "I am the wife of your *erre-gerra*, and you will obey me in his absence." Her sharp tone startled her son, who set up a cry, but that seemed to remind the man of who had given him an order: not just the *erregerra*'s wife, but the mother of his child. "I desire this woman for my service. Cut her bonds, and do it now."

Her fierceness did the trick; he cut the woman's bonds, then knotted the spare ends back together, securing those she had been tethered to. Neitin felt a pinch of shame, that of all this tribe, she had only chosen to spare one. *'But if I said, strike all their bonds, send them home, who would listen? And with their men dead, their village plundered, where could they go? They'd only be recaptured and sold anyway, by Tyrians or Aventans if not by us.'* Her position as *erregerra*'s wife only earned her so much, and Ekialde himself had marked the Cossetans as enemies. Looking at the drawn faces of the bound Cossetans, though, it was harder than ever for Neitin to understand why.

XI

STABIAE

Sandals dangling from her fingers, Latona cast a long shadow as she walked along the beach with the setting sun warming her back. Aulus had insisted she bring two lads along, to carry a shade and protect her skin, but she had left them behind, where the path down from the Vitellian villa met the sands. Merula, too, waited there, though with a disapproving scowl and folded arms. *'As though some great danger will swarm up out of the deep to claim me.'*

Latona needed to be alone—as alone as a lady of her station ever could be—and she needed to think.

The days since finding the remnants of Discordian ritual in the grove had had lingering effects. Restless nights with unsettling dreams—not nightmares, precisely, nothing so acute, but twisting whorls of light and half-heard voices that had her waking every hour. During the day, she twitched at every unexpected noise. She could hardly keep up conversation. Aula had commented on her preoccupation but had not pressed her on it. Perhaps the Discordian taint had affected her, too, though not as strongly. But then, Latona was the mage, and Latona had actually interacted with the miasma.

Walking alone helped to clear her head of the muck that seemed to have settled over it. Almost directly to the north rose the great hump of Mount Vesuvius. To the west, the brilliance of azure waters stretched to the horizon, turning to tourmaline foam here at the shore. Latona let the waves lap at her feet, her skirts tucked up in her belt to keep them from dragging through the wet sand. *'Venus was born from the sea, after all.'* Maybe treading in her waters strengthened the goddess's power inside Latona, scouring away the wretched Discordian influence.

Even with her mind clearer, though, her thoughts still dwelt on what she had seen and what she knew. *'Ocella banished the Discordians from the city . . . And what did we think happened? That they simply melted into nothingness?'* In truth, no one in Aven had given it much thought at all. Surviving the predations of the Dictator had absorbed most families' attention. If the strange cult was gone from under their noses, that had been good enough. One less thing to worry about. *'The men Ocella pro-scribed crept back after his death. Why would not the banished cultists?'*

At least one had made it as far as the Temple of Janus, after all. Small wonder others were making themselves known.

'But what could be done?' She could summon the Augian Commission, perhaps, the civil servants who ensured that Aventan citizens adhered to the *lex magiae,* those laws governing the use of magic. All men with talents to see magical signatures, they could both investigate and punish magical transgressions. Yet Latona misliked the idea. Too many of them had once been on Dictator Ocella's payroll, their sacred purpose turned sour as they acted as his hounds. Some had abdicated their positions after his death the previous year, but not all, and Latona was not sure she could trust those who remained. *'And who knows where else Rabirus might have allies? He found one in a temple . . . why not the Commission?'*

The thought of Lucretius Rabirus prickled Latona's skin, despite the warmth of the evening. Pinarius and Rabirus—both had menaced her, but Latona was not certain who troubled her more. Rabirus's cold gaze haunted her, his threats and his insinuations. She had managed to avoid Rabirus in the time between the fire and when he left for Baelonia, but she could only assume that he had been less than pleased to learn of her survival and his pet mage's downfall, even if he could not explain quite how it had happened. *'That he did not seek vengeance immediately hardly means he will fail to do so . . .'*

A sudden dizziness struck her, swelling like the rush of the tide. Spirit magic, rising unbidden from her stress and worry. *'Down, damn you, down.'* Latona stopped walking and concentrated on her surroundings, taking a moment to feel the sand grinding under her heels and shifting beneath the balls of her feet. *'Breathe.'* She forced the tension from her fingers, trying to quell the rising unease inside her chest.

'Strange . . .' Usually Spirit magic gone turbulent made her susceptible to the emotions of others, but she could not sense Merula and the others, so far down the beach. The energy suffusing her now was less focused yet more intense, seeming to wrap her from all around, as omnipresent as sunlight. *'What are you? Where are you coming from?'* But as soon as Latona reached for it with her own tendrils of magic, the sensation faded, leaving her with nothing more than a slightly aching head.

As she turned back toward the villa, her eyes scanned the wide waters. *'All may look calm, but there are storms on the sea, for sure.'*

When she returned to the path at the base of the hill, Merula tsked through her teeth as she repinned Latona's mantle into her hair. "You will be freckling, Domina."

"There are worse things, Merula." The fabric of the mantle stuck to Latona's skin, damp with sweat and the sea breeze, and it itched. She plucked it back off as soon as they were inside the villa.

She hardly had time to settle on a couch, though, before Aula rushed in and grabbed her hands, dragging her back up again. "Bona Dea, you're finally back!" Aula exclaimed.

"I wasn't gone that—"

"*I've* been out and about at the market," Aula rolled on, tugging Latona out into the back garden. Unlike the peristyle garden in their home in Aven, their garden in Stabiae was not hemmed in by walls, but opened out toward the cerulean expanse of Crater Bay. "It's starting to fill in properly, you know, as the season gets going." Summer heat had sunk over Truscum and was starting to drive the wealthy out of the city and to their summer estates, even though Junius was not yet over. And where the wealthy went, so too went those with goods to sell them. "I spoke to many of the merchants whose goods come from around the bay and the woods to the south." Her eyes gleamed with eagerness, as they ever did when Aula latched on to an intrigue. "There've been all sorts of strange tales. Crows behaving oddly, sudden storms, that sort of thing."

"It *is* nearly summer," Latona pointed out as Aula steered her along the paths of white pebbles that criss-crossed among the patches and hedgeways, meeting in the center around a burbling marble fountain. The pink oleander was not yet fully in bloom, but hyacinth and narcissus gave their colors to the garden. "Changeable weather isn't out of the ordinary."

"True." Aula's next words caught on her tongue a moment, until they reached the ambulation, a shaded avenue of packed earth between overhanging cypress and mulberry trees—the best place to have a conversation without fear of it being overheard. "The season hardly explains the story about a dog whelping a litter of snakes, or of a farmer's chickens who will only walk backward."

Latona's brow furrowed. Such things *were* troubling omens—if they could be verified. Many had occurred in Aven in the days before Ocella had claimed the city and his Dictatorship by force. Lightning strikes, dogs struck mute, frogs swarming up from the Tiber River, owls shrieking at midday, sparrows flying into temples and there dropping dead. The mages with prophetic gifts and the other augurs had been at their wits' end trying to keep track of all the ill omens. Other signs had been directed more to individuals than to the state. Their friend Maia Domitia's altar had begun to drip blood shortly before her husband's proscription and subsequent murder, and Proculus Crispinius swore that, at the very moment of dawn on the day the Dictator had brought up charges against his brother, every door and shutter in the house had banged open at once.

"The most consistent tale I've heard, though," Aula went on, "involves a plague of bad dreams."

"Bad dreams?"

"Not just bad—horrific. Haunting, really. It mostly seems to be afflicting farmers. Some of them on latifundia, others on smaller holdings, mostly between here and Pompeii."

Latona frowned. The latifundia were enormous agricultural estates, owned by patricians in the city but generally operated by local overseers. "Any of Father's tenants?"

"Not that I heard, but that doesn't mean none have been afflicted."

A new voice made Aula and Latona both jump. "Afflicted by what?" Alhena asked, striding forward from between two tree trunks.

"Alhena!" Aula exclaimed. "Darling, what are you—"

"Mus said she'd seen you drag Latona down here. Were you talking about the Discordians without me?" Reproach colored her voice.

"We—well, yes, pet, but it was only—"

Alhena scowled, her hands settling on her hips in a gesture that was very like Aula. "I cannot believe you would leave me out of whatever it is you're discussing. Even now?"

Aula's cheeks had pinked. "Dearest, we didn't want to trouble you—"

"I'm not a child." Alhena's irritation was directed at Aula, but Latona felt the cut. It was so easy, still, to think of Alhena as the baby of the family. Looking at her now, Latona could see bits of herself and her other siblings, there in the youngest of them: Aula's ivory skin; Gaius's long limbs and serious brow; Latona's unfashionably tip-tilted nose; then, that reddest of red hair, shockingly bright, all her own. She was a woman grown now; she had turned seventeen in Aprilis. It had been Alhena whose dreams had summoned Latona to Stabiae, Alhena sneaking texts from the temple libraries so that Latona could study, Alhena who brought Vibia to her rescue during the Aventine fire.

"You're absolutely right, dear one," Latona said. "I'm sorry."

"I understand you want to protect me," Alhena said, "but ignorance won't keep me safe."

Latona reached out to squeeze her hand. "We must get into a better habit of including you. We *will*."

"You'd best," Alhena said archly, "or I won't tell you what *I* found out."

By way of apology, Aula left Latona's side and went to loop her arm through Alhena's. "Very well, pet, I promise. I was only telling Latona that the countryfolk near here are complaining of a plague of bad dreams."

"That's no surprise to me," Alhena said, lifting her nose a touch. Her face had taken on a stubborn, superior set that Latona was actually glad to see; it reminded her more of the girl Alhena had been before the death of her betrothed had broken her heart, and it was preferable to the frantic waywardness her visions often induced. "A man came to the temple today, begging intercession from Proserpina, because his farm has been haunted by a fiend."

"A fiend?" Aula and Latona echoed in unison.

Alhena nodded tightly. "An evil shade has been terrorizing their nights. It invades their sleep and keeps them from rest. But then they wake, and see it still, looming in their houses. It has no respect for walls or doors, but comes and goes as it pleases."

"How long has this thing been troubling them?" Latona asked, at almost the same moment as Aula said, "Are they sure it is only one?"

"Ten days, the man said. And he only mentioned one."

Latona's fingers twisted in a loose lock of her hair. *'I have had a taste of this Discordian magic now. I know its character. If this fiend is a Discordian's doing, I might be able to dispel it. And I could see if it has the same signature as what we found in the grove.'* The heavy air pressed at her from the outside, and within, she felt the call to action.

"You want to go see, don't you?" Aula asked.

"I do," Latona confessed. "And if I can help, I should."

"It only visits them at night," Alhena said. "I'm not sure what Father will think of us wandering out into the countryside after dark."

"'Us?'" Aula echoed. "You can't really be thinking—"

"*You* can't be thinking I'll be left behind while you and Latona—"

"My honey, I have no intention of visiting strange farms in the middle of the night."

"But you'll let Latona—"

"I clearly have no control over Latona, as numerous events in the past year demonstrated—"

While they bickered, Latona continued to twine her hair around her finger, tugging gently on the lock. A year ago, she would have passed the problem along. Perhaps to some well-connected priest, if not the potentially duplicitous Augian Commission. A younger Latona would not have welcomed the challenge, and she would have shied away from the potential attention her interference might draw. *'No more. I can act, so I must. Juno requires this of me.'*

Juno, and herself.

As they strolled closer to the upper gardens, Aula and Alhena still trading arguments, the villa's steward appeared, trotting toward them. "Domina," he said, first to Aula, then in repetition to the other two sisters, "the Lady Vibia is arrived."

"Well," Aula sighed, her eyes casting briefly toward heaven, "what fine timing."

◇◇◇◇◇◇◇◇◇◇◇◇◇◇◇

Near Toletum

"I tell you, I do not like this, sister."

Neitin ignored Reilin's objections as they tramped out into the woods. Most of the brush had long since been cleared to feed the campfires, so their feet kicked up only ocher dust as they moved between the trees. In Neitin's arms, her son babbled happily to himself, oblivious to the tension between his mother and his aunt.

"It is *dangerous*," Reilin continued.

"Nonsense," Neitin replied. "There are no Aventans between here and the river."

"They are close enough! What if a scouting party managed to slip out of the gates? What if their reinforcements have arrived faster than we expected?"

"Then I expect they will have greater things on their minds than a few humble women passing through the forest." Neitin's chin was held stubbornly high.

She felt, rather than saw, Reilin's scowl. "And I do not like that you have left your husband out of this decision. He ought to know, ought to be here—"

Neitin cut her off with a derisive snort. "When has the naming of babes ever been the province of their fathers?"

Reilin swatted at a branch that had the nerve to brush against her. "Your child's father is no normal man."

Cheeks burning with irritation, Neitin stomped on. *Erregerra* her husband might be, god-chosen, but not a god himself. This near-worship of him that had afflicted so many of the Lusetani aggravated her. *'I loved him when he was just a handsome young warrior,'* Neitin thought. *'Would that he had never been more than that.'*

When they reached the riverbank, two figures already waited for them on the shore: one, the bearded form of Neitin's uncle Otiger. Neitin's own mother could not be there, but some of their family ought to be, so she had brought Reilin along, disapproving wench though she was, and she had begged the presence of her mother's brother. Along with him was the midwife who had helped Neitin to bring her son into the world. She had a right to witness his naming.

And there, too, was Sakarbik, the Cossetan magic-woman whom Neitin had claimed and given protection. Reilin's lips pressed into a thin line when she saw the dark-headed woman, but she held her tongue. Sakarbik had pledged herself to the boy's protection; she ought to be there for his naming.

There was a ritual for this, but not one guided by any magic-man or magic-woman. Otiger and Sakarbik alike would only observe. This was simpler stuff, the right of any mother. Neitin had earned the authority for this through blood and tears, and no one could gainsay that. It was the privilege of every Lusetanian who had given birth, reaching back through the centuries.

She stripped the swaddling clothes off of her son and stepped out of her doeskin slippers. As she waded into the shallow water at the river's edge, she felt a rush of gratitude that she had waited till midsummer for this naming; the process would have been unpleasant in the months immediately following the birth. Clutched to her breast, the boy wriggled and squawked. Recently, Neitin had begun to feel that he was trying to communicate with her. Words would be a long way off yet, of course, but his coos, burbles, and babbles seemed to carry a great deal of emotion. His little fist grabbed onto a lock of Neitin's chestnut hair as she waded knee-deep into the cool, gently running water. He wanted to touch *everything* these days; Neitin had had to stop wearing the gold hoop earrings that had been a wedding gift from Ekialde.

A few more months, and he would be crawling, then walking. *'Please, let the time not pass too swiftly . . .'* Neitin had brothers, back in the village that was her home. She remembered how soon they had left her mother's side, how early swords and slings had been placed in their hands. *'Not my son. Please, not mine.'*

It was a perfect day for the ritual. Oppressively hot, true, but Neitin took comfort in the bright glare of the sun overhead. Beyond the boughs of the trees, bobbing softly in the breeze, the sky was a pristine blue, unblemished by even the suggestion of a cloud. If Nabia was ever listening to her daughters, surely, her ears would be open on such a day.

"Gods of my people," Neitin said, as her son continued to chatter nonsensically, "I have passed through the gates of motherhood. I have paid the coin of blood." Her lips twitched slightly even as she said the words. Once, they had seemed innocuous. Her mother had warned her that women's lives were about blood, from green girlhood to the grave. But now, with the perverted use that Bailar made of that which gave life—

She shook her head. Here was no place for such intrusions. What mattered here, now, was the blood of life, not the blood of death.

"I bear my child in my arms," she continued, "and I would introduce him to you."

Closing her eyes briefly, Neitin took a moment to enjoy the feel of the natural world around her: the breeze that provided intermittent relief from the heat, the twittering of birds and the snap and flutter of leaves as they bounced from branch to branch, the low rumble of the brook as its waters rolled over rocks and logs. *'Someday, my son, we will follow this river to its source. I will show you the Endless Ocean and the city of Olissippo.'* Her mother's village was a little way upriver from that port. Neitin had visited, twice, in the company of her father and brothers, but it had always frightened her, so many people and so much noise. Perhaps her son would like it, though.

"As mother of this child," Neitin said, holding him up to the sun, "I name him: Matigentis." The root of the name meant "goodness." Neitin hoped it would be enough to protect him from the perfidies of the environment he had been born into. "I beg of you, gods who surround us, hear his name and know his face. Endovelicos, protect him as the sun rises and sets and rises again. Nabia, let him always find peace in your waters. Trebarunu, let him always find his way home." She swallowed over a lump in her throat before she made her final plea. "Bandue, look away from him, forget the sight of his face, let him never answer the call to your banner."

She wasn't looking at the others, but she felt their gazes on her in that moment. *'Well. Let them be scandalized. I will not give my son over to this madness, not if anything can be done to prevent it.'*

Matigentis's chubby legs waved in the air, and his head flopped to one side, his pale brown eyes searching for his mother. Neitin drew him back down to her chest as an anxious whimper started up. He quieted quickly, even as Neitin knelt down, slowly so as to keep her balance. The cool water soaked her tunic to the waist and her knees rubbed against the uneven riverbed. She brought Mati down to the surface of the water, just enough so that it wetted his back and legs. "He is yours to protect, Nabia," she whispered. These words were not part of the ritual, but Neitin felt them important to say. "Look after him well."

◇◇◇◇◇◇◇◇◇◇◇◇

CENTRAL IBERIA

Marching through shrubland with little tree cover had become a nuisance, and the men of the Tenth and the Fourteenth grumbled as they went along. The men of the Eighth, however, fresh from the rain-soaked hinterlands of Vendelicia, almost seemed to be enjoying it. "Damned hot," General Onidius commented. "But at least it's dry!"

Lack of water was rarely a boon to an army, however. The Aventans had few maps of the Iberian interior, but Sempronius knew what direction to head, and they had the stars to guide them. Unknown to anyone else, Sempronius was also using one of his gods-given blessings to find his way to the northernmost tributaries of the Tagus River.

Shadow ran strongest in him, but he had enough Water that, if he focused, he could always *find* water when he needed it. The talent had been of use to him during his tribunate campaigns in Numidia, and he found it valuable again now. Over such a great distance, the thread was thin, and concentrating on it gave him a headache—but by the summer solstice, his magical instincts led the legions to the Henarus River. This, he knew from the reports that Gaius Vitellius had sent to the Senate the year before, was the path that the vexillation had taken.

Here, the depredations of the rebel tribes were evident. The legions passed fields that should have been green with crops, orchards that should have been budding with fruit—dead, scorched, barren. *'Wasteful.'* Sempronius knew the strategy behind such tactics, but still, something inside him revolted at the squandering of good food.

Each morning, before the legions had fully broken camp, Sempronius sent cavalry detachments out scouting, with instructions to look for allies and enemies alike. Two days past the solstice, one such expedition paid off. Autronius Felix came galloping back to Sempronius at the head of his knot of scouts. "There's a town not far ahead," he reported, "and it looks friendly. We're in Arevaci territory now, or so our man from Tarraco says."

Sempronius nodded. The Arevaci had featured prominently in Young Vitellius's dispatches. "Show us the way, then."

◇◇◇◇◇◇◇◇◇◇◇◇◇

The town, which Sempronius learned was called Segontia, was the largest they had encountered since leaving Nedhena. Still small by Truscan standards, it nonetheless boasted a solid—and apparently newly reinforced—border fence, as well as signs of prosperity like fresh paint and decorative door-ornaments. The town guards had been alerted that the legions would be approaching, but still went wide-eyed when they saw the massive troop movement.

"Set the men to making camp," Sempronius instructed his tribunes as he dismounted outside the town's walls. "It's early yet, but we may as well spend a night here while we get the lay of the land. Felix, you're with me."

Quick conference with the town guards confirmed what Sempronius had pieced together from Vitellius's letters: Segontia was an Arevaci stronghold and, usually, one of its largest population centers. Now, however, it was a town of women, children, and the elderly, left with only enough of a garrison to fend off the Vettoni raiding parties. The bulk of their fighters, along with their chieftain and his wife, had gone south with the Aventan vexillation. "If you can crush the Lusetani and the Vettoni," one of the guards said in Tyrian, the only language they had enough of in common for conversation, "then do so, swiftly."

"I assure you," Sempronius replied, "that is my intention."

"Sir!" Onidius Praectus, rushing up from the gate. "Riders approaching!"

In a flash, Sempronius broke into a run toward the half-constructed camp. "Find Felix, tell him to get the pikes ready. Have the centurions sound the alarm—"

But the town's guard was at his heels. "Sir, I—Yes! I recognize that banner." Then he laughed. "And I recognize the riders, I believe! These are our people!" A slight frown overtook the joy of recognition. "But . . . not all of them."

"You're certain?" Sempronius asked.

"Yes, General. Those are Arevaci riders, no threat to you. I just don't understand . . ."

As his voice trailed off, Sempronius looked back to Onidius. "We don't need to sound an alarm, then, but have the centurions stand ready, in case our Arevaci friends here are fleeing from something." He shielded his eyes with one hand, peering at the riders as they drew closer.

It was a small party, as such things went: perhaps twenty riders. At their head was an unexpected sight: a tall woman whose skin was a far deeper brown than that of the Iberians who surrounded her, with her hair worn in a series of little knots all across her skull. Sempronius recognized the style, as would any of the officers and legionaries who had served in Numidia: men and women alike favored that style in the area near Cirte, the trading post which had served as Aven's main base during the wars of the previous decade. She was dressed, though, in Iberian style—and as she came closer, Sempronius saw that her tunic was shorter than most women would wear it, exposing long, muscular limbs.

She dismounted unceremoniously but with a lithe grace, before her horse had even come to a complete stop. One of the girls riding at her side caught the beast's reins. Her eyes flicked over the assembly briefly before she made straight toward Sempronius. She knew enough of Aventans, then, to identify the ranking officer.

Sempronius inclined his head respectfully as she approached, and she returned the gesture with brisk efficiency. "You must, I think, be General Sempronius Tarren."

"I am, honored lady," Sempronius said, and watched as relief drew some of the tension out of her shoulders.

"I am Hanath, wife of Bartasco, leader of the Arevaci." Sempronius recognized the names; Vitellius had mentioned both in his letters. "We have been besieged in Toletum with Tribune Gaius Vitellius. Thank the gods you are here."

Glancing over his shoulder, Sempronius saw that his command tent was still in the process of being erected. "It will be a little while before I can offer you shade and a place to sit, madam," he said, "but will you take some water and speak with me?"

She nodded briskly, then jerked her head toward the town. "May I lead you to my home?"

"I would be honored."

Corvinus, anticipating their needs, was already on hand with two skeins of water. Hanath took a long, deep quaff from hers, then dribbled a bit of the water over her face and the top of her head. "Forgive me, General," she said. "We have ridden hard."

"There is no need to explain," Sempronius said, gesturing at his own dusty clothing. "We're barely off the road ourselves." They started down the central street, Hanath marching purposefully and Sempronius lengthening his own stride to keep pace. Corvinus and one of the women who had ridden at Hanath's side fell into line behind them. "Tell me the news from Toletum."

"None good," she said. "The city is not starving yet, but the threat is there—and I worry for the winter, since they have not been able to plant."

There would be a need, then, to bring food up from the coast, once the city was recaptured. Sempronius made a mental note to tell his quartermaster to start working out a preliminary plan, to be adjusted once they saw just how bad the devastation of Toletum's farmland was—and how many citizens were left alive to be fed.

"We have been harried in a fashion that beggars belief," Hanath continued. "What the Lusetani are doing—dire magic is involved, General. And I worry it will get worse."

"Tribune Vitellius mentioned as much in his early letters, but we've had nothing from him in some time. Is he well?"

A slight smile touched Hanath's lips, lightening the severity of her expression. "He was when I left him, General. A good man, that. He has done honor to your people."

"His family will be glad to know of it."

"Here!" Hanath gestured to a house, one of the largest buildings lining the central square of Segontia. "Still standing, I see!" She tried the door, found it barred, and gave a barking laugh. "Glad to see my people have not been lax in securing the place." Raising a fist, she pounded hard, three times, on the door. "But if no one is home, we may as well have waited for your tent to be raised!" She turned, leaning her shoulder against the doorframe and folding her arms over her chest.

Sempronius could see now how well-toned her muscles were: he would not have mistaken her for a woman of indolence at first glance, but now he realized that she was a warrior indeed. A quick glance at the bow-wielding girl behind Hanath confirmed that she, too, was familiar with the arts of Mars. *'Or Bandue, I suppose.'* It was not as usual a practice among the Iberians as among the Tennic tribes north of Maritima and Albina, but it was no transgression, as it would have been in Aven or Athaecum.

"How many men have you here?" Hanath asked.

"Three legions," Sempronius answered. "Minus the cohorts of the Eighth that are already in Toletum. Near fourteen thousand fighting men, in all. More, if the legions from Gades join us." He did not mention how little faith he put in Rabirus's leadership to make any sort of difference in the tides of war. "Six hundred horse of our own. We had Lacetani cavalry with us until recently, and we were hoping to pick up some Edetani and Arevaci horse now that we're in your territory."

Hanath's eyes closed briefly, as if in prayer. "Fourteen thousand, plus horse. Yes. That should be enough." She rubbed her thumb over her fingertips. "Ekialde's numbers are difficult to ascertain. I do not believe we have ever seen the full force gathered. Even now, he holds the siege with his own Lusetani, but sends his allies out raiding. Sometimes they don't come back. Sometimes, they come back with new recruits. The allied tribes have less loyalty to him."

Sempronius filed that useful fact away. He had already seen what havoc the Vettoni were wreaking, and he had heard similar stories from other regions. A strong show of force from Aven might be enough to make those allies question if continuing to stand by the Lusetani was really worth it.

"I would estimate his full power to be at ten thousand men, but—" Hanath gestured broadly. "It could be as many as twenty, if he were able to assemble them all at the same time. If every supposed ally answered his call."

"Still no major challenge for three Aventan legions," Sempronius said. The numbers were not dissimilar to those they had faced in Numidia. "But the real trouble, we are given to understand—"

"Is not only from their blades," Hanath finished. "Yes, I will tell you all, incredible though it will seem."

Sempronius risked a small smile. "You may find, Lady Hanath, that I am capable of believing all manner of improbable things."

She snorted. "Good. We may all survive the longer for it." She glanced back at her attendant. "We have letters, by the way. Some are for you, General, but others should be sent back to Aven."

Sempronius nodded. "We shall send them immediately."

"The roads have stayed open that far?" Hanath asked, with an inquiringly arched eyebrow.

"I have other means," Sempronius said. "Birds, directed by one of our mages."

Hanath's liquid brown eyes opened wide. "Magnificent! It has been many years since I have seen such. I am glad you have them at your disposal. Perhaps we are not so alone as we have feared."

"Lady Hanath," Sempronius said, fixing her with his gaze, "the allies of Aven will never be abandoned. I pledge this to you on the spirits of my ancestors and on the duty I owe my gods." Then he let his expression soften a bit. "Though I do apologize that we have not been swifter in reaching your side."

Another snort. "General, as you might have guessed," Hanath gestured at herself, "I am not from Iberia. I grew up in Cirte. I have faith in Aven's duties to her allies and client states—but I also know something of how your people work. My father always said if there were six Aventans in a room, there were seven opinions."

Laughing half in surprise, Sempronius had to concede that point. "At least."

The door of Hanath's house at last opened, revealing a ruddy-haired boy of twelve or thirteen, who exclaimed something in Iberian. Hanath answered in kind. Sempronius could only pick up a few words, but she seemed to be reassuring her servant that she was, in fact, alive. The boy's eyes darted from her to Sempronius rapidly, and then he scurried off into the rear of the house, leaving the door open behind him.

"Come, General," Hanath said, gesturing for him to precede her into the house. "Let us sit and eat, like civilized people, and then—" She took a deep breath and released it in a slow sigh. Sempronius saw worry in her eyes, masked by her general demeanor of brisk determination. "Then, I shall tell you a ghost story."

XII

Vibia shivered, despite the warmth of the night. "I don't like this," she said, watching as gray clouds drifted high above them, obscuring the stars. The moon's light was a dim glow near the horizon, soon to slip under and disappear behind the pine trees that stood a short way in the distance.

"Nor I," said Latona. "But we did promise—"

"Yes, yes, I know." She sighed. She knew her duty perfectly well. Even though these were not, directly, her people—not tenants or clients belonging to her father or brother—she still felt a dual responsibility, as a patrician and as a mage. These people could not help themselves. They were too poor to get even the notice of their own landlords and patrons, and if there were any mages among them, Vibia had yet to see evidence of it. *'Some trifling Earth mage, perhaps, helping things grow without even knowing it, or a Fire mage keeping the hearth.'* Outside of the city, that could be the case with the weakly gifted. What a more trained eye might recognize as the gods' blessing might go unnoticed, thought only a quirk of nature or a peculiar talent. The nearest temple with any mages was ten miles away, back in Stabiae, or up toward the black-soil plains of Pompeii. *'This little village has no defenses.'*

And that made Vibia *angry*. These were little people, living little lives, and they should be allowed to do so. Little lives were the sinews of Aven's success. *'Someone is trifling with them because he thinks it won't matter, that he'll never be caught, that these people are so small that they don't matter.'* Vibia's assessment of worth was sharper and perhaps less compassionate than her brother's, but she still had a keen appreciation for everyone's place in the spectrum of humanity. *'Even the ordinary has its importance.'*

So she little needed Latona reminding her why they were standing in a dirt road—if one could even call it a road, an unpaved muddy track hardly big enough for one cart to rattle down—in the middle of the night, attended only by Latona's aggressive little maidservant, while a pair of burly slaves from the Vitellian villa waited a small distance away with their carriage. How Latona had managed to get their cooperation, Vibia had no idea; surely if Aulus Vitellius knew what they were up to, he would not approve. But Aulus was off in the nearby town of Salernum for the next few nights, and it was Aula who ran the household, in any case. Vibia presumed the men had been paid well for discretion. *'And it certainly isn't as though I was going to walk this far.'*

Latona had been all afire to set out for this nowhere-town the very night that Vibia had arrived in Stabiae, but Aula had convinced her to wait. Alhena had wanted to come too, and the girl had only been mollified by being persuaded that there were better ways to serve their needs. She had done much of their preliminary work, helping Latona and Vibia to make acquaintance with the afflicted farmers, but she would be spending the evening in prayer at the Temple of Proserpina in town. Aula and Latona were happy to have their little sister in a safer location, and Vibia had her own reasons for not wanting the girl close at hand. *'If she hasn't already realized how little I did to save her sister and how much was Sempronius's doing, well, all the better that she not witness my frail talent.'*

The town was too unimportant to even have a name; in truth, it was only a small collection of houses wedged between olive groves on one side and a muddy-looking field on the other. No market, no shops; these were people who either ate what they grew or surrendered it to their patron—a man Vibia did not know, but of whom she thought little, considering the state of disrepair his tenants' homes were in. *'If he checked in now and again, we might not have to be here now.'*

According to report, the fiend appeared at random. At least, so far as a group of uneducated villagers could figure out, it did. It had no particular path, did not appear in any particular house on any kind of pattern. All they had definitely been able to determine was that it never appeared when the sun was up. *'A reason to bless long summer days—and a reason for us to nip this problem in the bud, before they begin to dwindle, now that the solstice is past.'*

And so Latona and Vibia were standing in the center of what barely passed for a village, in the dead of the night, waiting for an apparition.

To Latona's credit, at least she didn't seek to fill the silence with chatter, as her elder sister doubtless would have. She paced back and forth across the little lane, from fencepost to fencepost, with a thousand thoughts flittering across her face. Vibia guessed that the Spirit mage was trying to use her empathic abilities to get a sense of the sleeping townsfolk, to pinpoint the trouble.

The half-moon slunk lower and lower in the sky, until at last its silver light fell beneath the tree line. Latona's slave-girl fidgeted. At first, Vibia thought she was merely trying to keep herself awake, but then she caught the look on the girl's face: alert as a dog on the hunt. A town like this was unlikely to attract bandits or other predators of a mundane nature, but the girl was poised as though she might have to fight off a horde any moment. Vibia felt a grudging respect for her dedication. *'She's all sharp edges, like shards of glass.'* A Fracture mage could understand that. Vibia had seen her many times before, of course; she was Latona's shadow as much as any other patrician lady's attendant was—though Vibia had not subjected her own to this particular adventure. She had never given the little Phrygian much thought. *'Perhaps that has been an oversight . . .'* Knowing more about the maid might reveal much about the mistress.

Just as Vibia was beginning to hope the peasants' stories were foolishness and no true indication of dark magic at work, a high-pitched whistle cut the air.

Merula whirled around, looking for a source, but the noise seemed as though it came from everywhere. Latona stopped in the dead center of the lane, and Vibia felt it: a tear in the world, somewhere, a rift through which a shade might pass. A chill went through her—not fear, but every magical sense she had shivering a warning.

"Do you feel—" Vibia started.

"The cold," Latona finished. "Unless it's about to storm—"

"It's not."

"—then there's no reason for that. And it's against the wind." Latona's head whipped about. "I can't tell from where . . ."

If the village had been large enough to have a crossroads, Vibia would have suggested moving there; such places attracted diversions of the natural order. That was why every major intersection in the City of Aven had its own well-tended shrine, to keep peace and hold the balance. But without such a focus . . .

"I know what might attract it," Vibia said. She scratched a quick X in the dirt with her foot, then looked over at Merula. "Girl, your knife." Merula blinked several times, in a way that Vibia might have called stupid, if not for the keen suspicion in her dark eyes. Vibia held out a hand imperiously. *"Now."*

Latona was, perhaps fortunately, too distracted to be curious. "Give it to her, Merula." Her fingers were kneading softly at the air, as though she were trying to find something. Vibia was grateful for that; it spared her explaining that she knew of the girl's knife-wielding habit because Sempronius had once shared the tidbit with her. Scowling, Merula lifted her tunic to the thigh and took out a blade she had strapped to it. With remarkable deftness, she flipped it in the air, caught the blade in her hand, and strode forward to offer it to Vibia, hilt-first.

As soon as she had it, Vibia held the blade aloft, trying to see its edge along what little starlight the sky provided. "Lord Janus and Lady Fortuna, look here," she said, when she caught the glint. She placed the toes of her left foot carefully at the center of the X she had drawn. "I call your powers to this place. I call your—"

A blast of wind nearly knocked her off her feet. The air had been hot and still when they arrived, and the initial chill had come on like that of a distant storm, but now it was as if a titan were blowing cold air directly down the village lane. *'If that's really all it took to catch the thing's attention . . .'*

Latona's expression had become a bit more frantic, and she came to stand at Vibia's side. A bitter gust tangled Vibia's skirts between her knees. Her mantle was wrapped securely around her body, but Latona's hung loose, only pinned into her hair, and she had to snatch at it to keep the wind from stealing it away.

After a moment, though, the air went still again, seeming to sit even heavier than before—but clammy now, a damp and unpleasant chill. Thinking perhaps she had failed to call down the appropriate attention, Vibia started to raise the knife to the starlight again, but before she could get a word out, the fiend appeared.

The shade manifested as if congealing out of the air. It didn't *come* from anywhere, but Vibia watched it piece itself together in front of them. At first, the form was blurry, like something seen through water. Then, it bobbed closer, and Vibia's breath froze in her throat as unbidden fear swelled within her.

'No.' She drew in air deeply, filling her lungs all the way down to her gut. *'It's tricking you. Don't let it.'* So much of fear was physical, the body trying to convince the mind to flee from a hazard. Vibia had to control her breath and blood in order to remain out of the fiend's influence.

Next to her, Latona swayed unsteadily. Concerned that the other woman was less prepared to steel herself against the shade's powers, particularly with Spirit's vulnerabilities to Fracture, Vibia reached over and gave her a pinch.

Latona scowled, but seemed more focused afterward. "What are you sensing from it?" she asked in a whisper.

"Definitely one of the *lemures*," Vibia said, in a tone that was not as centered and grounded as she would have liked. "Of what sort, I'm not—"

Suddenly, the shade's figure sharpened: no longer a vague human-like form; now it looked as much like a real, living man as something translucent and colorless could. Thick eyebrows, a tremendously prodigious nose, a thick-set scowl. *'Father?'* Again, she stamped down hard on the thought. *'Dammit, Vibia, focus. That's only what the damn thing wants you to think.'*

She glanced over at Latona, astonished to see there were tears glimmering on the younger woman's cheeks. *'Who is she seeing, I wonder?'*

But in that, the shade had given itself away. Now Vibia could put a name to it: an *umbra mortuora*, a shade that took the shape of the dead. No true spirits, not the actual dead drawn back into the living world, but cruel imitations. Through their insidious magic, the stronger of them could reach into a person's *anima* and decide what form would be most likely to unsettle. For Vibia, the father she chiefly remembered as a stern taskmaster was as good a guess as any. "Enough of that, you," she hissed. Next to her, Latona still had damp cheeks, but her hands were clenched into fists, and she was muttering beneath her breath. *'Good. Not overwhelmed by it, then.'*

As Latona kept muttering, the *umbra* began to lose its unsettling shape—and yet, at the same time, it grew brighter, a silver cloud against the darkness. Vibia reached out, trying to trace its path, but her own magic was too thin, too weak to pick up on the trail. Her teeth ground into each other in frustration at her inability to perform, but then Latona asked, "What are we dealing with?"

'I suppose I can, at least, provide information. That makes me not completely useless.' Vibia sighed. "It's an *umbra mortuora*. Nasty work. The magic that calls to it is particularly gruesome Fracture magic." She frowned, reaching for the right words. "You don't get an *umbra* without tearing a rent from the world of the living into the world of spirits. For some reason . . ." Since Latona's eyes were fixed on the fiend, Vibia risked glancing around the village. "Someone chose this place to make that tear."

"Someone chose . . . There would be a—a—"

"Something like what you described, remnants of a ritual, yes."

Nothing useful was coming to Vibia's sight, nothing to let her know where the fiend might have been summoned from or if any other mage was around, directing its actions.

"If we can find out where it's coming from—what called it here, or where the—the crack between the worlds is—" Latona's words were strained; Vibia suspected she was having difficulty focusing, but she admired the effort. "The locus, the . . ." Her throat worked; Vibia wondered if she was having trouble swallowing or if she was trying not to retch. She shook her head, golden curls bobbing. "I can't follow it, Vibia. I can feel the wrongness, but it's not my element. I can't follow its path." She looked over at Vibia; her green eyes seemed unnaturally bright against the darkness. "You have to find it, Vibia. Find the tear in the world."

A pit settled into Vibia's stomach; Latona had no idea what she was asking. Of course she didn't. For all she knew, Vibia was the one who had defeated Pinarius Scaeva in that warehouse. The one who had rescued her. Why wouldn't such a heroine be able to find the gap between the worlds that had let this thing through?

'Well. Why wouldn't you?' She knew the principle. Her powers were weak, but she was blessed by Janus and Fortuna nonetheless. If Vitellia Latona could cast into the ether and sense whatever it was that had her gazing about like the gods themselves were whispering in her ears, then surely Vibia could reach out and find that tear. Edges—if a Fracture mage knew nothing else, she knew about edges. And that's what this was, what she had to find: an edge where none should be. A gap in the natural world.

Sucking in a long breath, Vibia widened her stance until she was straddling the X she had drawn in the dirt. Whether or not that would help, she had no idea, but she figured it couldn't hurt. Fracture mages pulled power from boundaries—and she had no intention of sitting astride a nearby fence. "All right, you," she hissed at the fiend, who was starting to regain its shape. "Show me what made you."

Like a musician tuning a cithara, Vibia threaded her magic, thin though it was, seeking the point of harmony that might lead her to something useful. *'How did Sempronius always talk about it?'* For him, it always seemed like the elements lay down to do his bidding at the gentlest nudge. She was sure the truth was more complicated, but it had been so hard, when she first learned of her little brother's hidden talents, all those years ago. Vibia had struggled and grasped for all she had, and it felt barely enough to count as a blessing sometimes. Envy had threatened to devour her, and she had defeated it by devoting herself to Sempronius's cause, helping him to keep his secret. She had tried to learn theory from him, even if she couldn't practice. *'Use that now. He always says it's like the elements fall into place, clicking like a puzzle-box.'*

And as soon as she thought of it like that, something *did* fall into place—or, rather, Vibia could feel where it ought to, but would not. A jagged gap where there ought only to have been smooth night. "This way." Hesitantly at first, then with a greater sense of confidence, Vibia started down the path.

XIII

Latona's senses felt muddled, as though the *umbra* had clogged her ears and blurred her vision. She had to keep refocusing; the more heavily she relied on her Spirit magic, the easier it was to clear the sludgy sensations away.

A little more than halfway down the lane, Vibia jerked to a halt. The trail turned sharply off to the right, behind one of the peasants' huts. The sensation of pollution here was not as overpowering as it had been in the mountain grove, but it was similar: a roiling aversion, like smelling rotten meat and knowing, instinctively, not to eat it.

"It's near," Vibia said, gazing about. "Quite, quite near."

A frown pinched her features as she continued to search. Then Vibia led Latona and Merula around the side of the house, where a little orchard stood behind a droopy herb garden—an orchard hardly worth of the name, a spare half-dozen trees half-heartedly bearing pears. Vibia touched the trunk of the first she came to. "No. But close."

At the third tree, Vibia stopped and looked up. Latona followed her gaze. There, bound to a branch, was a little bundle: white cloth wrapped with black thread.

"Merula," Latona called. "Could you—"

"Yes, Domina." In a trice, Merula had grasped the lowest-hanging branch, braced a foot against the trunk, and hauled herself into the tree.

Vibia looked behind them. "It's following, the *umbra*," she said, "but it doesn't want to come too close to here, for some reason." Then she glanced up at Merula, already halfway up the tree. "My, she's a sprightly little thing, isn't she?"

Latona wasn't sure that Vibia had meant that as a compliment to Merula, but her head was too swamped with the Discordian taint to parse the comment. "Indeed . . ."

From above them, Merula made a disgusted noise. Then the bundle dropped out of the tree, landing at Latona's feet. Vibia took a step back. "That's definitely it."

"It certainly is." Now that they were close, Latona could feel it pulsing at her, that sense of utter *wrongness*, of disruption to the natural flow of the elements around her. "It's not quite like the last one, though. In the grove, we just had to clear away the offal, and then I was able to cleanse the area. This feels . . . different."

Vibia's lip was curled in distaste as she glared at the offending Discordian charm. "Just tossing it over the fence wouldn't do any good. We'll have to unravel its power." She glanced up, as though seeing something Latona couldn't. "Then, I think, cleansing. Though perhaps better to come back and do that by daylight." Vibia sighed, rubbing her forehead. "I think I know what to do. Just . . . keep near me, would you? In case it's worse than it looks." As Vibia bent down to the bundle on the ground, delicately keeping her knees off of the damp earth, Latona stood at her shoulder.

"Do you mind—" Latona started, then cleared her throat, suddenly uncomfortable. "I may be able to, ah, support you. With Spirit magic, that is."

Vibia looked over her shoulder at Latona, and for a moment Latona thought she saw annoyance in those dark eyes. But then they softened, and she nodded. "Yes. Anything that might help." So Latona laid her hand on Vibia's shoulder, drawing up the sensations of power and solidity and trying to channel them into Vibia.

"It may not like what we're about to do," Vibia warned, "and I really am not sure what that might mean. If it starts to get to you, just—slam it out. Remember that it lies."

◇◇◇◇◇◇◇◇◇◇◇◇◇◇◇

As soon as she touched the bundle, Vibia wanted to vomit. "Definitely Discordian," she said. "It has the reek . . ." Not exactly the same as that which she had encountered on Autronius Felix the previous summer, but close. A different worker, but a similar tool.

She hated to admit it, but Latona's presence *was* a comfort and a help. With the Spirit magic seeping into her, Vibia felt stronger, more capable, and she was able to grasp the bundle in her hand without flinching away from it. *'So long as I don't think about what's probably in it.'* It seemed to pulse back against her. In recognition of another Fracture mage? Or in defense against her intents?

'Unwind,' she thought, focusing her magic on whatever was inside the

bundle. *'Unbind. Fall apart.'* Vibia tried to probe gently, unsure of how it might respond to more force. The Discordian charm was like a shim, jammed into a crack in the world to keep it open—something broken, and then locked into place. The raggedness of it called out to her. Some Fracture mages would have felt the compulsion to widen the breach, to keep tearing at the world's fibers, but for Vibia, things ran differently. She had trained her mind to find such shredded edges in order to smooth them out, like a surgeon who had to know how a leg was broken in order to set it.

As Vibia probed, she could feel the shade losing form, but not power. The humid night felt cold and clammy. Latona was shivering slightly, though her hand stayed firmly on Vibia's shoulder. Through the fabric of her tunic and gown, Vibia could feel the heat of her, bolstering against the invasive chill—though at times almost uncomfortably warm, as though she were being slightly sunburnt where Latona's fingers touched her. *'Sweet Fortuna, does she run this hot all the time? Or only when performing magic?'*

As Vibia continued to work, a faint wailing started up behind them. "Don't turn," Vibia said. "That's what it wants." She furrowed her brow. It also wanted her to lose focus, which meant what she was doing was working. *'Unwind, unbind. This charm falls apart, and the jagged edges of the world will fit neatly back together again. Unwind, unbind, and send this shade back to Pluto's realm where it belongs.'*

The wailing grew louder, and a sudden breeze kicked up, blowing at the women's clothes. Merula had a dagger in her hands and was twirling it distractedly. *'As though that will do anything to a shade.'* But Vibia supposed she could not fault the girl her instinct to defend herself and her mistress. Latona's fingers pressed a little harder into Vibia's shoulder. *'I can do this. I am doing this.'* The charm was unknitting between her fingers, something within breaking loose and starting to rattle.

A high-pitched whistle split the air—no, not a whistle, a scream, the shade protesting its banishment. Vibia gasped as the bundle disintegrated in her hand, the fabric rotting a hundred years in an instant. She had only a brief glimpse of what lay within, bird bones and other viscera, before those, too, dissolved into dust. "Ugh." She held her hand out away from herself as she stood up. *'Why is it always me that ends up with poisonous magic on my hands?'*

Someone had come out of the nearest hut; Vibia recognized him as one of the villagers that Latona and Alhena had spoken to the day before.

'Bless him, he's got a scythe and everything.' The man had rushed out in his tunic and bare feet, gripping the farm implement like a weapon.

"Ladies!" he said, coming forward. "We heard such a cry—Are you well?"

"We are, I thank you." Latona regained her composure as easily as she might draw a mantle over her head—or did it only seem so? Unless Vibia missed her guess, Latona was putting out Spirit magic, a glamour of confidence, to try to calm the peasant. Vibia's Fracture magic could still sense her unease, bubbling below the surface. *'How often does she do that?'* Vibia made a promise to herself to keep a closer eye on the ambitious Vitellian at social events in the future. There might be much to learn about the undercurrents of her emotions.

"I think we've taken care of this problem, at least," Latona went on. "That particular shade shouldn't trouble you again." She glanced over at Vibia, who nodded tightly. "But you should be on the lookout. Someone planted a charm to draw it here. They may return and try again."

The villager's brow furrowed. "But . . . why would someone do such a thing?"

Vibia was at a loss to explain that, herself. What benefit could there be in frightening a village of two dozen peasant farmers?

"I don't know," Latona said—and there, Vibia felt the dichotomy between her words and her feelings again. Not a lie, not quite, but not the whole truth, either.

'She may not know,' Vibia thought, *'but she suspects.'*

Latona strode forward to the villager, smiling. "I am glad you came to the Temple of Proserpina with this information, so that we might know of it and address it. Rest assured that I will be doing everything in my power to figure out who sought to harm you and why."

"They—they will hear of this? In Aven?"

"Someone certainly will."

Again, the duality. *'What game is she playing at?'* But her smile was like the dawn breaking—a blast of genial energy, putting the villager at his ease.

"If anything else happens, you may send to me. I will be at the Vitellian villa in Stabiae for most of the summer, but if a message fails to find me there, our domus in Aven is well-known."

"Of course, Domina," the villager said, bowing his head. "If there is anyway we can repay—"

"Live good lives," Latona said. "Take care of your family. Be kind to your wife and children, your servants and slaves, and honor the gods. That is all the repayment I need."

'*Lady Bounty,*' Vibia thought, a bit sourly. It seemed to come so naturally to Latona, the grace and ease when interacting with these people. Vibia held them in no disdain, as some patricians did, but she never knew quite what to say to them.

"Your carriage is nearby?"

Latona nodded. "We left it up at the main road, with some of our men."

"Let my boys walk with you that far, please. It's so late . . ."

"We would welcome the company."

The villager's boys, lads of ten and twelve, trotted on either side of the ladies and Merula as they wound their way back up the dirt road toward the main road, where the carriage waited. They were quiet, awed, at first, but Latona drew them out with gentle questions, and soon they were telling tales of what the shade had done in the village over the past few nights. Nothing too dire or jeopardizing—sudden appearances in the night, wailing and crying and generally not allowing anyone to sleep— but Vibia could feel the frisson of fear running beneath the boys' bravado in relating their stories. Everyone knew such things *could* happen, but they weren't supposed to. If you lived rightly, if the priests performed the proper rituals, then shades and spirits were meant to stay in their place. For an adolescent boy, it might be exciting—but also an uncomfortable lesson that the world was not so safe a place as the innocence of youth might presume.

The ladies bundled themselves into the carriage, crawling in among the pillows and light blankets placed for their comfort. Latona offered to let Merula join them—without, Vibia noted, seeking *her* approval—but the girl preferred to sit outside, next to the driver. "Is she sweet on him?" Vibia asked yawningly, settling herself in.

Latona smiled. "I don't think so. But she had a fright this evening, whether she admits it or not, and she'll be wanting to work that out under less scrutiny."

Vibia tilted her head. "You understand her well, I take it?"

"I hope so," Latona said. "She and I . . . She's been with me ever since I left the Temple of Juno. I trust her with my life. There are many understandings between us."

Vibia nodded, though she still found it unusual. Her own servants were well-treated and well-fed, the freedmen and slaves alike paid well for their efforts, the slaves manumitted in due course. But she could not consider any of them her friends, as Latona plainly did her girl. But Vibia shrugged that off. All three Vitellian women seemed to have that oddity about them, unusually attached to their personal attendants. *'Perhaps it is a family tradition.'*

They rode in silence for a short time, but neither woman seemed likely to drop off to sleep. Vibia could hardly see Latona in the darkness of the curtained carriage, but the other woman was far too fidgety to have nodded off. After a bit, Vibia ventured the same question that the villager had asked, as much to see if Latona would give her the same answer as anything. "Why there?" she said. "This is Discordian magic, and it's not some over-talented but under-taught kid messing about. It has a purpose. It has *finesse*. So why target that poor little village?"

Latona drew in a deep breath, then let it out in a sigh. "I don't think they were targeted," she said. "I think they were practice." Words left unsaid hung in the air; Vibia could feel the tension of Latona feeling her way through the problem. No untruthfulness now, though, no skirting the issue at hand. "Pinarius Scaeva may have been acting alone, at Lucretius Rabirus's direction," Latona said after another moment had passed, speaking slowly, as though still piecing the thoughts together. Vibia waited patiently for her to assemble them. "But he did not learn his Discordian magic in isolation. Someone taught him. Someone planted that charm in the orchard. Someone left that carcass in the grove." The curtains wafted, and a thin beam of moonlight fell on Latona's face. Her thoughtful frown reminded Vibia of Sempronius, puzzling out some political tangle. "Someone taught Pinarius Scaeva, and someone learned from his haste."

"Learned to move more slowly?" Vibia said.

"But also learned that there are openings in the city . . . that Discordian magic has a path it may follow . . ."

"With the city still recovering from Ocella, that's not much of a surprise," Vibia agreed. "The temples are still putting themselves back together—"

"So many mages died during Ocella's reign . . ."

"—and so many of the powerful men who survived have now gone to Iberia."

"Someone is pressing an advantage, but delicately. Someone with more subtlety than Pinarius Scaeva had."

Vibia drummed her fingers against her lap. "Do you think this person is also taking orders from Lucretius Rabirus?"

"I don't know." The moonlight lit a wry smile on the younger woman's face. "Are Fracture mages typically given to taking orders from outside their own prerogatives?"

Vibia snorted. "A fair question," she said. "And my answer would be, any Fracture mage who has gone over to Discordia is unlikely to act for any but his own reasons."

"Or hers," Latona murmured. "We shouldn't assume."

"No," Vibia agreed. "Though everything I've encountered so far has had a masculine feel to it."

"Still . . ." Latona's voice was drifting far away, though Vibia did not think it was sleep finding her. Rather, she was descending into her own thoughts, and Vibia was content to let her. "We should not close our eyes to any possibilities . . . Men underestimate women enough as it is. We should not join in their error."

AESTAS

XIV

Vitellius's early letters had been insufficient warning.

Hanath had better prepared Sempronius, on that first evening in Segontia, and then during the march toward Toletum. Reading words written on paper was one thing; hearing a tale of ghastly hauntings from the lips of one who had seen them, quite another. But nothing compared to the specters themselves.

Sempronius's legions first encountered the *akdraugi* when they were, according to Hanath, yet a day's ride from Toletum. They struck as dusk fell, while the legionaries were still making camp. A sudden chill rolled through the air, and at first, Sempronius looked to the skies. Thunderstorms blasted the plateaus in central Iberia regularly during the summer, and the legion had had several drenchings since leaving Segontia. So he looked for lightning, wondering if his men would have enough time to finish pitching their tents for shelter.

But then he heard it—the high-pitched keening, impossibly loud, as though a funeral approached with hundreds of paid mourners shrieking grief to the heavens.

Sempronius rushed to the center of the camp. From there, he could look out all four sides at once, down the *via principalis* and the *via praetoria*. The wailing gave him no indication what direction the fiends might be approaching from. His guess was that they would come from the southwest, toward Toletum—but he would not allow such an assumption to leave his troops vulnerable. Even as the thought struck his mind, however, he felt it slipping away. A fog was closing in on the camp from the south, and Sempronius felt it infecting his mind as well, softening the keen blade of his wits.

'None of that from you,' he thought, pushing back against it. Sempronius knew how to clear soporific magic from his mind, thanks to his long working with Shadow. Sleep and dream magic had never been his particular strength, but he knew the theory behind them, and whatever effect the Iberian magic was trying to have, it felt kin to Aven's Shadow. He wiped away the cobwebs, assessing the best way to help his men do the same.

"General." Hanath had appeared at Sempronius's side and grabbed his arm. He saw several of the nearby soldiers startle, that a foreign woman should dare to touch an Aventan general without explicit permission, but Sempronius did not think this was the time to prize social niceties. "General, you must have your men form ranks, immediately. If the Lusetani behave here as they do at Toletum, they will attack while the *akdraugi* make you weak."

Sempronius nodded his understanding and gave the signal for the men to re-don their armor and form lines. Even as they did so, however, he wondered: *would* an attack come? If it did, might that be a sign that the forces surrounding Toletum were thinner? Or did the Lusetani have enough men to attack the city and the field at the same time?

As the legions formed up at the edge of camp, Sempronius sent an aide to tell the drummers and horn-blowers to strike up a tune. Hanath nodded approvingly; she had already told him of the bolstering counter-effect strong music seemed to have. Sempronius's aide brought him his own armor and strapped it onto him while he stood at the crossroads, dispatching further orders.

Fortunately, the legions operated with perfect precision in their camp-making, the same way every evening, and the terrain here was broad and flat enough to have presented no challenges for the engineering unit. As such, their earthwork ramparts were already complete, with stakes facing outward. A few moments earlier, and their defenses would have been weaker.

They weren't proper walls, though, such as Toletum had, and Sempronius wondered what difference that could make to the *akdraugi*. The fog was rolling closer, its silvery weight unsettlingly incongruent in their surroundings. Sempronius looked west, toward the setting sun, as though it might be able to help.

The *akdraugi* rolled over the camp like a wave. To his horror, Sempronius watched as the soldiers all around him buckled at the knees or stooped from the shoulders.

The hazy effect that the *akdraugi* had at a distance morphed as they suffused the camp. Instead of dazed and vaguely sleepy, Sempronius now felt drawn to them, like iron to a lodestone. Shapeless, formless things, all around him, and yet an urge was building in his chest, a strange, compulsive pressure, telling him he should reach out, fall into them, let himself be absorbed. The haunting draw reminded him of the maw that Pinarius Scaeva had created the previous year, when Sempronius had last been in Aven. He gritted his teeth, preparing himself to resist the siren call.

Yet even as he thought that, even as the fog drifted closer, Sempronius felt its hold on him lifting, his head clearing. He became aware of a warmth at his neck, at first almost unnoticeable, given how hot the day was already. But then it began to tingle softly, and when Sempronius glanced down, he noticed a faint red glow coming from beneath the collar of his cuirass. *'What in—The focale!'*

The glow was Fire magic, visible to his eyes only because of his own strand of Water talent, and it bore the coruscating signature of Vitellia Latona's work. *'Lady, once again, I owe you more than I fear I can repay.'*

Sempronius looked around. His camp aide was nearby; he grabbed the young man by the shoulder, giving him a firm shake. Only with difficulty did the lad drag his eyes away from the fog surrounding them. "Sir?"

"Bring my horse, then find Autronius Felix and tell him to mount up as well." If any man could stand solid against these fiends, he had to believe it would be Felix.

The aide never returned, but Felix did, already astride and leading Sempronius's horse along with him. Felix's eyes were as wide as all the soldiers', but he didn't look afraid; rather, a bit crazed. *'If these fiends reach into men's souls,'* Sempronius thought, *'they may find more than they counted on in Felix.'*

"I sent the lad to your tent," Felix said. His voice was too bright, too sharp, like wet blood on a whetted blade. "What are we doing?"

"Grab a torch," Sempronius said, "and ride." He jerked his head toward the faltering lines. "Behind the men. Stir up their courage. Say and do whatever is necessary. If the Lusetani charge in the midst of this miasma, we cannot break."

Felix nodded his understanding and, without waiting for any further instructions, charged off toward the eastern side of the camp. Sempronius swiftly mounted and rode toward the west.

The closer Sempronius rode to the boundary, the hotter the focale burned against his skin. Not uncomfortable, not yet, but he could feel its magic working on him, striving to keep his head clear against the onslaught of the *akdraugi*. But he trotted back and forth behind his men regardless, calling out the names of those he knew. That seemed to jolt them a bit, enough to help them ground themselves. From the other side of the camp, he heard something most unexpected: a song. A *bawdy* song.

He could have laughed. Felix had apparently stirred the men on the eastern side of camp to enough defiance of the fiends to combat darkness with profanity.

"You hear that, lads?" Sempronius bellowed to the men at his own lines. "Not going to let those cohorts show you up, are you?"

A few men on his own side took up the chanting song, and Sempronius rode to the northern end of the western line. It was pointless to peer into the distance; he couldn't see anything beyond the fog. He could only pray that the other two legions were comporting themselves similarly, that Generals Onidius and Calpurnius had listened to Hanath as carefully as he had.

One quarter of an hour passed, then another. Felix seemed to have no end of vulgar tunes to lead the men in singing. And then, the *akdraugi* began to fade.

At first, Sempronius didn't trust it. Surely, something else had to happen. But as the fog cleared and his scouts looked beyond the confines of the camp, it seemed that the threat had passed.

Sempronius met up with Hanath and Felix back in the middle of the camp. He had not yet given the order for the men to pull back from the ramparts, just in case.

"No fighters," Hanath said.

"They must not have wanted to pull them away from Toletum," Sempronius said. "So they sent their mages, to try to scare us off."

"Testing your mettle, General," Hanath agreed. "These were not even particularly strong *akdraugi*." Not, precisely, what Sempronius had hoped to hear. "Not so strong as reached the top of the Toletum walls, anyway. Those had more shape. They never looked quite like men, but close. Like men all blurred together, if you take my meaning."

"I doubt I could truly know without seeing them," Sempronius said. "I'm grateful for your assessment, however."

"Why such a weak showing, though?" Felix wondered. His eyes held traces of manic energy, but he, too, seemed to be calming down, if slowly.

"Testing us, as Hanath said," Sempronius offered, "or testing themselves. Or perhaps . . . perhaps they are farther away than they are from the walls of Toletum."

"It may have been a feint, of a sort," Hanath said. "Hoping you would move in another direction."

A slight growl escaped Sempronius. "Small chance of that." He nodded to his camp aide, who had staggered up, still bleary-eyed, but determined to do his duty. "Have the centurions sound the all-clear. Then send someone out to the other two camps. I want Onidius and Calpurnius to meet me here, to discuss what just happened." As the aide trotted off, Sempronius looked back to Hanath. "We should expect this to get stronger as we get closer to Toletum, then?"

She nodded. "I'm afraid so, General."

Sempronius's jaw tightened. "Then we shall have to come up with better ways to steel ourselves against it."

Once the horns sounded the all-clear, the legionaries went back to their duties—almost, but not quite, as if nothing had happened. They still moved with well-drilled efficiency, but Sempronius could see hesitation and wariness in their eyes. *'Good. Let them stay alert, now that we know what beyond mortal means we're up against.'*

Sempronius pinched the bridge of his nose between his thumb and forefinger. In the wake of the magical onslaught, he was suffering a headache not unlike a hangover, thick and weighty. He waved Felix back over. "Make sure camp is secure. Choose a few tents to take on an extra watch shift. We'll rotate so that different men are taking the extra duty each night, but from now on—"

Felix nodded. "More guards. I'll see it done."

"I'll be in my tent. I need to compose a letter to the Senate about this."

And he fully intended to do so, but Sempronius also wanted some time alone to contemplate what had just occurred. As Corvinus helped him out of his armor, he said, "Stand watch outside, please. I do not wish to be disturbed unless at great need, until Calpurnius and Onidius arrive."

"Understood, Dominus."

Once safely within his tent with the flaps closed, well away from the eyes of his troops, Sempronius all but collapsed onto his cot. Falling asleep would have been a simple matter, but he forced his eyes to remain open, staring up at the dark cloth ceiling and replaying the *akdraugi* attack in his mind.

The magic was foreign, and yet Sempronius could recognize it, like hearing a familiar song played on an unusual instrument. The tone would be different, the rhythm perhaps off, but it would still be recognizable, still have the same rises and falls, the same shape in the listener's mind. The shades felt thus to Sempronius. *'Lemures . . .'* he thought, though the Lusetani would hardly call them so. And they were not, quite, the dark spirits that haunted Aventans, shades hauled from the netherworld, but they were as like them as the Iberian deer were to their Truscan cousins. *'And, like deer, both can be hunted . . .'*

The trouble was, Sempronius wasn't sure how, given their current circumstances. Aventan *lemures* were not bound to any one element, but certainly a Shadow mage could have some influence over them. Would the Lusetani *akdraugi* be the same? And even if they were, could Sempronius risk trying to reach out to them?

Here was the downside to having brought useful noncombatant mages like Eustix and the healer-mages mixed in with the medics. However secure he felt in his abilities to hide his talents at home, in his own domain, he had fewer resources out here in the wild. Could he risk working such direct, combative magic underneath the noses of Air and Water mages, who might catch his signature? Worse still, could he dare reaching out to the fiends, not knowing how they might respond? The memory of Pinarius Scaeva's soul-devouring maw lingered in his memory, a temptation that had come too close to consuming him. Foreign magic, much stronger than that summoned by a single man, could have deleterious effects he would not be able to predict nor prepare for.

Sempronius rubbed his forehead irritably. No; he did not think he could risk so much, which left the problem still dancing before him.

He unknotted the focale from about his neck and threaded it thoughtfully through his fingers. *'Fire magic, clearly, has some effect.'* But this was the Fire that forged the shield, not the sword. *'Could it have offensive as well as defensive merit? Could it purge the akdraugi from a place?'*

There were no Spirit mages among his company, nor any of Light, the elements which instinct told him might most easily defeat these dark, soul-draining shades. Air might have some degree of success in dispelling them, perhaps, if it could redirect their rolling fogs, but Air mages attached to legions were trained as messengers, not as warriors of the psyche. *'Earth? Could Earth ground them somehow, hold them in place . . . or hedge them in?'* He would have to ask. There were Earth mages in Tarraco—though adequately describing the situation in a letter would be a challenge for his rhetorical skills.

Spirit would be best. At least, that was his guess, if they were at all like the *lemures* of Aven. Spirit might have the power to control them, or banish them, or break them to pieces. But who brought Spirit mages on campaign? No one in the annals of history going back to the age of kings. Sempronius was odd enough for bringing any mages at all beyond Eustix the bird-messenger. There were Fire-forgers in the major military towns, like Nedhena and Gades, but to drag them into the wild as part of the noncombatant contingent of a legion was unheard of. Sempronius had had to offer quite a bribe to convince a single Fire-forger to attach himself to the Tenth. *'But where I would even find a Spirit mage in this part of the world . . .'*

Of course, holding the focale in his hand, one candidate did come to mind: the finest Spirit mage he knew, a woman of incredible power and such a strong soul. He had no doubt that Vitellia Latona would be able to sort out these *akdraugi*, given time to examine them. To Aventans, bringing a woman on campaign would be even more unthinkable than dragging mages along, yet Sempronius knew that not all peoples believed as the Aventans did, particularly on the lands bordering the western half of the Middle Sea. *'Consider Hanath.'*

A smile pulled at his lips, picturing Latona positioned among the legion, perhaps riding alongside Hanath. Could she even ride? He had seen her ahorse once, clinging to Terentilla's back, though he could only vaguely remember it—that was the day he had been poisoned by an errant arrow, and delirium had already been setting in by the time that she and Terentilla had met up with the group of hunters in the woods. And it did not mean that she would be able to ride on her own. *'She could learn, though.'* That, he was sure of. Anything she put her mind to, she would excel at.

Well. He might not be able to summon her to the Iberian wilds, but he might be able to benefit from her knowledge nonetheless. "Corvinus, I need paper." He needed to send word back to the Senate as well, of course, now that he had firsthand experience with the Iberian magical attack—but with the letters he gave to the Air mage Eustix, he would include one for Vitellia Latona, and one for his sister. To their eyes alone would he entrust a more personal account of the terror, and in return, perhaps, he would receive some wisdom.

∞∞∞∞∞∞∞∞∞∞∞∞∞

CAMP OF LEGIO II, BAETIS RIVER, SOUTHERN IBERIA

Lucretius Rabirus had left Gades. No one could say he had emulated his predecessor and holed up inside the city, ignoring his duties to the rest of his province.

If he had not gone very *far* outside of Gades—well, why should he?

Baelonia's population was concentrated on the coast. His duty was to reassure the province of Aven's attention toward it, and he could reassure more citizens close to the capital than he could wandering in the wilderness. And it *did* make for an impressive show, three legions marching along the Baetis River. What Aventan citizen could fail to feel safe after witnessing such a display?

Rabirus had determined to take his legions up to Hispalis, the next major town on the Baetis River. A mongrel town, founded by one of the Iberian tribes, taken over by the Tyrians, and settled with Aventan veterans a hundred years earlier, at the end of the Tyrian wars—but it was better than nothing, Rabirus supposed, if only marginally. Governor Fimbrianus had assured him there were sensible men there, the agents of Aventan landowners who would be happy to discuss arrangements for feeding the legions defending their property against barbarian incursions. Better to supply from Hispalis than Gades, at least as long as they were in the field.

The first day's marching had Rabirus feeling better about this venture than he had since leaving Aven. The legions were orderly, the centurions swift with their discipline, and even the weather decided to cooperate, with the blazing Iberian sun settling itself behind clouds at midday. Only one annoyance marred his satisfaction: the chief of the Fourth Legion's engineers, pestering him as they made camp. "Sir, I must protest—" the weedy little man said, following behind in short but persistent strides as Rabirus went to the command tent for his own legion, the Second. "I really don't believe that to be a wise choice."

"What troubles you?" Rabirus asked. "The fresh water? The open field? The ease with which we've been able to sink the palisades and build the walls?" The trenches *had* been a bit watery in places, but that was to be expected on a riverbank, after all.

"The soil, sir, it suggests—"

"Make camp for the Fourth farther inland, then, if you will," Rabirus said, with a brisk wave of his hand. "The Second stays here. But tell the legate he'd better not dally in the morning! I'll expect his troops back in formation, *here*, at the river!" He went into his tent and did not invite the engineer to follow.

The shouts woke him in the middle of the night.

"Praetor! Praetor Rabirus, sir!"

Rabirus's slaves reacted first, one of them rushing to Rabirus's side with sandals, the other moving to open the tent flaps, admitting a pair of panicked-looking tribunes. For an instant, icy terror coursed through Rabirus's veins. Were they under attack? But from whom? None of the reports suggested any barbarians were raiding this far south. "What is it?" he said, swinging himself off his cot and scrubbing his light brown hair back from his face.

"Water, sir!" one of the tribunes barked. "That is—the camp is flooding, sir!"

"What?" Rabirus paused only long enough to sweep his crimson commander's cloak over his sleeping tunic before charging out to see what in Jupiter's name they were talking about.

Water was gushing into the camp, seeping in from beneath the southern and western gates. Some legionaries and their support servants were scrambling to pick up equipment and move tents, while others were attempting to dam the flood with sacks of sand or dirt. Some of the water had reached the stables, and the horses were shrieking their indignation, adding to the general din of men shouting orders and profanities.

The chief engineer attached to the Second Legion was older than the Fourth's, and apparently slower-witted as well. He stood, dumbfounded, in the midst of the chaos, startling visibly when Rabirus stalked up to him. "Explain yourself!"

"It's, uhm . . ." The engineer scrubbed at his head. "It's the tide, sir. It must've been low when we camped. I thought we were far enough upriver that it wouldn't matter, sir, or else I'd have—"

This was what the engineer from the Fourth had been trying to warn him about, Rabirus realized. And he hadn't listened. *'Well, if the man had made himself clear, rather than stammering and stuttering about it!'* Rabirus wouldn't have made camp on a damned tidal floodplain if he'd *known* about it.

"How much more should we expect it to rise?" Rabirus demanded. "How far back do we need to move?"

The engineer's shoulders moved helplessly. "I'm not sure . . . If we had local auxiliaries to ask . . ."

But Rabirus had contracted none yet. He had wanted this to be a thoroughly Aventan endeavor, relying as little upon the locals as possible. Even if they could be trusted not to betray the legions over to the rebel tribes, it looked ill, to request aid and support from those who had begged *your* protection in the first place, as though Aven could not provide for itself.

Rabirus resisted the urge to pinch the bridge of his nose. "Send a rider to the Fourth, wherever they've camped," he said to his tribunes. Little though he liked this tacit admission that the Fourth's engineer had had the right instinct, even if he'd done a poor job expressing his concerns, Rabirus couldn't let his camp be swamped. "Find out how far inland they saw fit to camp. We'll move a similar distance. Quickly!"

As the tribunes scrambled, Rabirus stalked back to his tent, deciding how to make the best of this disaster. The Second would be in no state to march by morning. Moving camp would take until dawn. Tomorrow would have to be a rest day. A scouting day, perhaps. Yes, that would suffice. Let the Fourth venture out and get a better lay of the land, so that the Second would have a day to recover themselves.

An inauspicious beginning. Rabirus would show no sign of consternation or fear, though. *'No weakness.'*

XV

Neitin watched, arms folded over her chest, as Bailar tapped ink into her husband's skin with a porcupine quill. Ink, he called it, but Neitin knew the truth of it. How *proud* Bailar was, to have blended the blood of fallen foes into the mixture. How he had prayed over it, how he had chanted, and what praises he had heaped upon Ekialde, for his willingness to submit himself not only to the pain of the markings, but the side effects of taking such powerful magic into his own body. There would be illness, Bailar warned. Fever, perhaps, and nightmares.

Had the Aventans not been so thoroughly penned up inside Toletum, Ekialde might not have risked it. As matters stood, he felt comfortable leaving Angeru in charge of the siege for a few days, while he came to the western camp for the ritual and recovery.

The whole affair made Neitin miserably unhappy. She hated that Ekialde was taking on this new commitment to Bailar's magic, but she could not wish for him to stay on the front lines of the siege. Ekialde bore the agony of the process with a face carved of stone, but Neitin was weeping freely. *'This cannot be undone. Every other step along the way, he might have backed off from. But this makes Bailar's foul magic a part of him, forever and ever.'*

This handsome young man, so strong, so promising, had once been hers to love. Every day, he felt farther away and less retrievable.

Sakarbik stood at her elbow, glaring daggers at Bailar. She had tried to persuade Neitin not to watch, but Neitin had insisted. "If he will consign his soul over to Bailar's demons, then he will do so in the face of my displeasure. I will not allow him to pretend I approve."

And so, since Neitin had insisted, so had Sakarbik. "If I'm to keep protecting you and the babe, I'll not let you stand alone in front of that man while he's working magic."

Every stab of the porcupine needle pierced Neitin's own heart.

<><><><><><><><><><>

"Rest," Bailar said, laying a hand on his nephew's head. "I must prepare more of the ink. One more bowl should be enough to finish the design."

For once, Ekialde was disinclined to argue. His back and shoulders were sore with a thousand pinpricks, and he could feel the magic suffusing through him. *'Like a river,'* he thought. *'But rivers belong to Nabia, and this is Bandue's work. Bandue's rivers, here in my blood.'*

He shivered. Was the fever coming upon him so soon?

Someone drew a blanket over him, soft summerweight wool, loosely woven. His wife's hands, he realized through the swiftly descending haze, and he reached up for one of them. "My love, my precious rabbit," he said, bringing her fingers to his for a kiss.

She knelt by his cot. So beautiful, his wife. Those warm brown eyes and gently curling hair, all the softness of her body. He had loved her the instant he saw her, when he first visited her father's village on a trade mission from his own father. He was a second son, not yet *erregerra*, but already a warrior who had proved himself. He had returned, again and again, presenting her with hides and meat and bands of gold, until her father was suitably impressed to allow them to marry.

'I wanted to make her smile. Not cry.'

He squeezed her fingers, little though he could manage the strength for even that much. Then he reached out and tapped the clay pendant that hung about her neck, a protective charm, made from his own blood. No enemy's blood there, only his own, his strength, to guard her and his son, when he could not be at their sides.

"You need water," she said. Her voice was yet thick with tears. "Can you prop yourself up enough for it?"

Moving his arms at all was agony, but, after a struggle, Ekialde managed to get his forearms underneath him, pushing himself up so that Neitin could hold a cup of water to his lips. He drank greedily. Perhaps it would help with the fever, with the pain.

Her fingers moved through his hair, stroking softly, and she hummed a little tune. Ekialde thought of a day, not long after they were married, a spring day when the last snows still lent a chilling crispness to the breeze that came down off the mountain. They had lain beside the riverbank, his head in her lap, as she hummed and sang.

Then the tent flap opened. Bailar had returned, and Neitin's fingers tightened briefly in Ekialde's hair. She let him go, helped him ease himself flat on the cot again, and then took up her position of vigil a few steps away, where she had waited all these long hours.

'For you, my love. And for our boy. I seek this glory for you.'

◇◇◇◇◇◇◇◇◇◇◇◇◇◇

Ekialde stayed in the magic-man's tent that night, ostensibly so that Bailar could guide any visions he might have—and so that one of the other magic-men, who had more talent in healing than in summoning and enchantments, would be close at hand. Neitin returned to her tent, which she now shared only with Sakarbik and Matigentis. Her sisters were in their own, close by, but Neitin had long since discovered there was no use talking to them about her misgivings. Two of them were madly in love with young men from Ekialde's war-band, and the third wanted to join it herself. They were utterly enthralled with their *erregerra* and everything he did. They had never for a moment questioned the wisdom of the war, nor of any course he trod to win it.

Sakarbik crooned a low lullaby to Matigentis while Neitin paced the room, brooding. "Is he beyond saving?" she wondered aloud.

Sakarbik proved her wisdom by not answering directly. "All men make choices, little wife, and most regret some of them. He makes his choices, and you make yours."

Neitin snorted. "I? What choices do I get to make? If I had my choice, we'd be back in our own village."

Sakarbik shot her a speaking glance, then turned her attention back to Mati. "There are still many choices for you, and what to do with this young lad is not least among them."

With a sigh, Neitin came to Sakarbik's side. "There is that." She stroked Mati's dark hair, soft as a duckling's feathers. "Bailar won't have you, my darling. He'll never touch you."

The tent flap rustled, and Neitin whipped around, terrified that her words might have accidentally summoned the wretched man into her presence. It was not Bailar, however, but her uncle Otiger who entered, looking somber. "Uncle," she said, striving to keep acid from her voice, "whatever are you doing here? Shouldn't you be with the others, praying that fiends and spirits consent to inhabit my husband?"

"I was with the star-readers," Otiger replied. A reminder that he always declined to participate in Bailar's rites. At least he would not participate directly. He cleaved to the older forms of magic, which might sometimes use the blood of animals, but never that of humans. Here, Bailar frowned on that as insufficiently committed, and so it was safer for him to keep his magic to that of the stars and trees.

Too, Bailar was quick to challenge anyone he saw as a threat. The previous year, when a few of the warriors had preferred Otiger's way to his own, Bailar had not been tardy in making his displeasure known. Otiger, ever a peacemaker, had chosen not to press him.

"And do the stars smile on this deed?" Neitin asked.

"Bailar chose his moment well," was all the explanation Otiger saw fit to give.

At that, Sakarbik made a derisive noise deep in her throat while she settled Mati down into his basket. She hardly ever spoke directly to any of the men of the Lusetani. Neitin didn't blame her. They had, after all, subjugated her village and her people. But she seemed particularly contemptuous of the magic-men, though she would never go into a great deal of detail as to why. Neitin got the sense she felt they had everything about magic dead backward.

"I have been asked," Otiger said, "to relay concern." He spoke with a deliberate slowness, the sort of tone used with invalids. The condescension of it made Neitin want to scream. "There is a worry that your reactions to Bailar's methods might be undermining the general effort."

"I should be astonished to learn that anyone in this camp paid the slightest attention to my opinion of Bailar and his methods." Neitin tossed her head. "I may be Ekialde's queen, but I'm little better than a broodmare where most of them are concerned. The warriors have no use for me, and the magic-men think me a nuisance. That, I believe, is the extent of the thought *anyone* here pays me."

Otiger's face was tight beneath his beard. Pained, almost, though Neitin couldn't imagine why. Then he eased himself down on a cot—a family privilege, even when one's niece was a queen. "Come sit, child."

Being called a child set the hairs on the back of Neitin's neck up, but she obliged.

"You remind me so much of your mother."

Whatever Neitin had been expecting, it hadn't been that. The frank change of focus punctured her indignation. "I miss her," she said. She hadn't seen her mother in a few years, not since leaving her home village to marry Ekialde. "But I don't see how I'm like her. Everyone respects her." Neitin's mother had always had a quiet dignity, fueled by a serenity that Neitin herself had never been able to master. When things were wrong, she could never just accept them. *'I am not like the river, for all I try, for all I honor divine Nabia. I cannot flow around an obstacle. I seem unable to do anything else but smack straight into it.'*

"Your mother's respect was well-earned," Otiger said. "You may not remember, as you were quite small at the time, but she did a great deal to soothe ruffled feathers between the villages in our homeland. She always had the right words, suited to appeal to the personality of each different chieftain or war-band leader. She kept skirmishes and raids from breaking into all-out warfare more than once."

Exasperated, Neitin slapped her hands into her lap. "There, you see? I certainly have never demonstrated that kind of skill."

Otiger reached over and took her hand in his. His fingers were rough-worn, a workman's hands. His magic was a craft as well as his calling. "You do not have the same gifts as your mother, perhaps," he said, "but you have the same stalwart spirit. You know the shape you want the world to have. And you have been sorely tested, I can see that. The gods have set you a far different challenge than your mother's. A harder one." He gave her a wry smile. "Knocking the heads of chieftains together is one thing. Wrangling magic-men is another, even at the best of times."

"And these are far from the best of times."

"They are unusual times, to be certain."

Another snort from Sakarbik, who was now sitting cross-legged on the rug beside Mati's basket, rocking him gently. She stared unabashedly at Otiger and Neitin, though Otiger paid her no mind.

"Whatever I may think of Bailar's methods," he went on, "they are . . . extraordinary. He has accomplished things that no magic-man in living memory has done."

"He has accomplished perfidies and abominations that no magic-man in living memory would dare," Neitin corrected. Otiger's head wagged in allowance. *Too* allowing, too complaisant. She had not begged him to join her so that he could be a peacemaker, but so that she would have an ally against Bailar. He had not turned out to be the pillar of strength she had hoped for.

"He has a great many people in awe," Otiger said. "Not all of those like him. Some are terribly afraid of him. And I think it gives them heart, to know that you are not."

Afraid of Bailar she was not. Afraid of his influence on Ekialde, certainly. "You think it gives them heart?" she echoed. "Why does no one say? Why does no one else stand up to him?"

"He *is* kin to your husband," Otiger reminded her, "and he has a great deal of power—"

"He would have less if everyone did not pay him such deference." Neitin pushed back to her feet, unable to remain still and sedate any longer. Across the room, Sakarbik was smirking. "He is kin to the *erregerra*, but you are kin to the *erregerra*'s wife. You could have power here, too, if you chose to grasp it. You say there are others who feel as I do? Tell them to refuse to obey his orders. By what right does he command you? He is no closer to the gods than you. He is not king of priests."

"You must admit, niece," Otiger said, "he is capable of greater magic than we, which may indicate that the gods—"

"Greater!" Had Neitin been outside, she would've spit on the dirt. "Is it greatness, to pervert what the gods give us into these horrors?" Infuriatingly, Otiger's shoulders moved in a slow shrug. Neitin's lip curled. "I was so glad when you joined us, uncle. I thought here, perhaps, would be someone to counter Bailar's perversion. What a disappointment you are." Part of her shrank back from these harsh words, but the blood thrumming in her veins, pulsing at her throat and wrists, reminded her that she was a daughter of a chieftain and the wife of the *erregerra*. Command was as much her right as Bailar's, surely. "You may as well return to my mother's side, for as much good as you're doing here. At least there, Bailar will not be able to use your blood to raise his wraiths, should an Aventan sword or Arevaci arrow strike you down."

She could hardly bear the sorrow on Otiger's face, so she turned her back on him, under the guise of bending to check on Mati. The insouciant glee sparking in Sakarbik's eyes pleased her no better.

The cot groaned as Otiger rose from it. He shuffled across the room, placing a hand on top of Neitin's head. "Whatever you may believe, darling niece, I have your best interests in mind. If you truly wish to send me away, then I will go, but I would sooner stay and watch over you."

Neitin bit back the sharpness that prompted her to point out what little good it had done her so far. She stroked her child's soft cheek, seeking comfort in his innocence. "Do as you please," she said thickly.

Once Otiger had left the tent, Sakarbik cleared her throat. She never needed prompting to do or say as she pleased. "I don't think your uncle is a bad man, little mother," she said, "and he says nice words. But it's actions that make us who we are. If a man wants to be good, he must act for good."

XVI

Stabiae

Rural though the people of the villages and farmlands surrounding Stabiae might have been, they still knew how to pass along gossip. As spring turned to summer, word got out that the Lady Latona, daughter to Censor Aulus Vitellius, and her friend from the city had banished an *umbra*—and then, it seemed, other villages became willing to admit their own problems. First slowly, then in a seeming flood, messages found their way to the Vitellian villa, asking if the ladies in residence would condescend to visit and sort out their preternatural problems.

In one location after another, they found more of the same: curses bound to the location, tearing open the world just enough to let *lemures* in. Sachets and curse tablets, befouled groves and mutilated carcasses. Some bore marks of decay, indicating they had been placed longer ago; others were relatively new. Even Vibia could not put names to all of the varieties of *lemures* that the unknown Discordians were raising. Some manifested as whistling mists or pervasive shadows. Others were *umbrae*, which Latona dreaded, never eager to face those specters with the shapes of the restless dead. The shape the *umbrae* chose to haunt her—but she slammed down on that thought every time it came to her, unwilling to give either face or name free access to her mind.

Troublingly, the newer ones were getting harder to dispel.

On the Ides of Quintilis, the ladies set out toward a latifundium where farmers had been reporting strange occurrences. Crops were doing something beyond spoiling: stalks of wheat turning black and flaky, olive trees gnarling and collapsing in on themselves, vines crisping away to nothing. So far, it was only in spots, dotted across the fields—but the farmers were, naturally, wracked with concern. This time of year, many crops were browning in the heat and dry weather, but nothing so natural had blighted these fields. Patches of charcoal-like stalks marred the neatly planted rows.

"It's as though a fire moved through," Latona said, examining one of the stalks. "Except it clearly didn't." Some sheaves were utterly untouched, while others looked like the crops of Pluto's realm.

Vibia knelt to the dirt, scraping at it with her fingers. She flicked her eyes up to Latona, then to the latifundium's overseer, hovering anxiously nearby. Latona took her meaning.

"I think we have the measure of the situation," she said, turning to the plebeian, "and we may best be able to speak to the gods and seek intercession in private."

"Of course, Domina." The overseer looked all too eager to put distance between himself and the cursed vegetation—or perhaps he just didn't like the way Merula was glaring at him.

Only once he was safely out of earshot did Vibia say, "Thank you. I thought it might concern him unnecessarily to know that his crops have been sown with grave dirt."

"Grave dirt?" Latona knelt beside her, placing her palm flat on the earth. She could feel the poison in the soil, but unlike Vibia, had no way to determine the components.

"Mm-hmm." Vibia was frowning, glaring at the dirt as though that might force it to reveal its secrets. "Mixed with some other unpleasant elements. Ground bones, certainly." Latona resisted the instinct to snatch her hand back; after all she and Vibia had seen, ground bones were no longer out of the realm of the ordinary. "Some other herbs and things, but . . ." She glanced around. "I wonder if it's the same in all the afflicted patches?"

"Only one way to find out."

The two mages began picking their way through the field, finding the spots of withered wheat, with Merula prowling warily around them, alert for any mundane threat. Even in the country, the heat by mid-Quintilis was nigh-insufferable, the air sitting heavily on the rolling Truscan hills. Latona dressed in a short tunic with a thin gown overtop, but she had not yet been able to convince Vibia to discard modesty and prestige in favor of comfort. As soon as they were out of sight of the latifundium's overseer and any other gawkers, Latona tucked the overgown up into her belt, exposing her calves to the wide world.

Vibia, still properly covered shoulder to heel in a tunic and gown of lightweight cloth, tsked audibly. "Honestly, you're getting as bad as Terentilla." Latona only grinned in response to that. "At least your hair is still up, I suppose."

"Too hot to have it down," Latona said. "I don't know how Tilla stands having it on her neck in this weather."

After about hundred paces, they found the next afflicted patch of grain. Vibia bent again, examining the soil. "Same mixture." Another hundred paces away, however, the stalks looked different. Not flaky and crisped black, but oozing a pitch-like substance. Merula made to prod at one with the tip of her knife, but Latona caught her wrist. A fourth patch had instead gone white, brittle as ice, shattering at a mere touch.

"They're experimenting," Latona thought aloud as they moved on in search of the next patch. "Searching for the perfect poison . . ."

"To what purpose?" Vibia asked. "Are the crops their real goal, or are they only testing their methods here?"

Either seemed plausible. If they had a curse that could level entire fields, they could leverage that to wield significant economic and political power. Destroying latifundia would harm not only the smaller cities of southern Truscum, but Aven itself, the heart that required so much of the surrounding country's lifeblood to keep beating. And that, Latona knew, could have a devastating effect on Aven's stability.

The alternative was that the poisons tested on plants might prove equally destructive to living creatures. *'Some assassination scheme?'* If the Optimates were behind it, their most obvious target—Sempronius Tarren—was also nearly impossible to reach, half a continent away in Iberia. *'But there are others.'* Galerius Orator, for one, the appealing and popular consul, or any of the men who looked to take his place. *'Or . . .'* A chill settled in Latona's stomach like a stone. *'Or the Discordians might be looking to eliminate inconvenient mages who are interfering in their affairs . . .'*

The sky seemed to be darkening, though it could be nowhere near sunset yet. What had begun the day as fluffy white clouds were turning dark and flat. "Think we should be heading back, Domina," Merula said. "Could be a storm, coming in off the water."

Latona glanced up, her nose crinkling. "I think you're right. I hate to leave the job unfinished, though."

"It might be the best thing, really," Vibia said. "Rainwater to wash away the grave dirt. I don't know how we'd manage cleansing this much territory ourselves."

"I'm exhausted just at the thought of it."

"Perhaps if—" Vibia halted abruptly. When she spoke, her voice was faster and even more clipped than usual. "Something's happening, Latona. I don't like it."

A low-pitched keening did not so much break the quiet as insinuate its way into it. Latona's arms prickled as every hair stood on end.

Something took shape before her eyes, rising up out of the soil. A wisp of smoke without fire, thin at first, then stronger and larger. It wound its way around a healthy stalk, embracing it like a lover—and then, before her eyes, the wheat turned first sickly pale, then charcoal gray, shriveling and curling like a singed hair.

It was being devoured.

Once the transformation was complete, the twining smoke-creature moved on to another stalk and began again, just as another sprang up on the other side of them. "These are different." Vibia's breath was shallow, almost panting. "Not the same feel. Not at all." She was blinking more than usual, her gaze shifting each time her eyelids fluttered closed. "It's not poison. The ground. It's not poison. It's food. Food for fiends." Her eyes had gone too wide, the whites shockingly visible around the dark irises. Vibia swayed, her shoulders sagging for a brief moment, before she snapped upright as though jerked by a hook. "Run!"

And Vibia bolted—but the wrong direction, further into the field rather than toward its border.

Merula reacted first, leaping after Vibia like a hound after a hare, and Latona followed, crashing through the grain. Latona skidded to a halt after a few paces, though, when one of these strange new *lemures* swooped right in front of her. She darted instead down a different column of grain, off to the right. Ahead, she could hear crunching and crashing: Vibia still running, Merula still in pursuit.

The grain scratched at Latona's bare arms and calves as she ran, and she hoped none of the pricks were enough to draw blood. If grave dirt could be made into food for fiends, the gods only knew what the blood of a Spirit mage might do for them. Pinarius Scaeva's words from the past year haunted her: *'Do you have any idea how delicious it is, to break and devour a power that radiant?'* Terror tightened in her chest, as it had when she found the first Discordian remnant with her sisters, but she could not allow it to trip her up.

After a moment, the sounds of the chase came to a halt. Had Vibia stopped running? Or had they gotten too far away to be heard?

Then, an opening in the press of vegetation, where the wheat stalks had been not just shriveled but shredded. Beyond were four of the spirits with nearly opaque forms, smoky and hovering, and Vibia Sempronia in the middle, looking less composed than Latona had ever seen her. Her sable hair had come half out of its pins and her mantle was dragging in the dirt. Her feet seemed mired in place, and as the four *lemures* bobbed around her, her upper body lurched toward them. Her jaw hung slack, and her eyes were not her own. On the far side of her stood Merula, legs and arms both splayed wide as though ready to grapple with Vibia—but she shuffled back and forth, unable to get through the *lemures*.

"Juno help me," Latona breathed, bending forward to rest her hands on her knees while she analyzed the situation. Whatever had woken here, it was far worse than the *umbrae* they had encountered before. Those were unsettling; this, horrifying.

Worse, she couldn't sense Vibia's emotions. There was nothing of *her* there, just a blank. Merula's energy, tense yet eager, crackled like the lightning that would soon break above them. But from Vibia, nothing, not even the low hum of energy she would have expected from an animal. It was as if Vibia had simply ceased to be present.

'They've been opening cracks between worlds and summoning demons through. What if this time, they're trying to take something back with them?'

Latona started forward, but when she drew nearer to Vibia and the demons, her whole body reeled as though she had been struck. The sensation was, unfortunately, not unfamiliar; Scaeva's magic had had a similar effect, as though able to physically repel her. She reached out with her magic instead, focusing her energy on just one of the fiends. *'Perhaps, if I can pluck their energy away from her, one at a time . . .'*

A tugging pain in her chest alerted her to her error, and a strange taste blossomed on her tongue, sour-sweet like an overripe citron, overpowering the cinnamon-spice of her own magic. *'The fiend's magic? Or could that be the signature of whatever Discordian summoned it?'*

Latona had no time to contemplate the thaumaturgy, however. Instead of being dispelled by her magic, the fiend had latched on to it, drawing her power out and seizing it, claiming it. For a moment, the hovering spirit glowed brighter, a color like the moon behind clouds.

This, too, Latona had felt before, when Scaeva attacked her. Then, it had been as a harpoon shot straight through her core, a wrenching pain, and she had not had the strength to take back control.

But Latona was not who she had been at the Aventine fires. She had thrown less of herself out to begin with, and so there was less for the fiend to sink its supernatural claws into. And this little fiend did not have the focused malevolence of Pinarius Scaeva. It tugged on her by instinct, not willpower. With effort, Latona was able to withdraw the tendril she had extended, pulling her magic back into herself.

One of the *lemures* descended upon Vibia. For a brief instant, its form merged with hers. Latona stepped forward again, only to again be sent reeling by the force of the Discordian magic.

By the time she straightened, Vibia had turned toward her. Her face was ashen as the embers of a long-cold hearth, and her head lolled as though her neck were hardly able to support it. Her dark eyes had gone entirely black. *'Not good, not good.'*

Some power emanated from Vibia's form now, but it was not Vibia. It didn't feel human at all, didn't have the symphony of energies that made each person unique. This was raw and hungry, a gaping pit of sensation and emotion, as though Pinarius Scaeva's maw had taken human form.

'Come on, Latona, think. 'Fire protects,' so the charm says. But you have no Fire here to draw upon!' She thought of the mages of legend, who could call flames to their fingertips, conjuring them out of nowhere, and she ached for such a power.

"The fiends hunger," Vibia said, in a voice that was not her own, far-away and ringing as though spoken through a metal tube. Latona's arms shivered, but she ground her heels into the dirt. "The fiends hunger," the thing that was not Vibia repeated, then, "and humanity is such a sweet dish. Sweeter ever than dirt and grain and trees. What life is here." The sickly smile that crawled over her face showed too many teeth. "What life there is in cities. In *your* city."

A blast of chilly air tore through the field, snapping and cracking the stalks of wheat. Latona wasn't sure if it was natural or an effect of the Discordian magic, until a roll of thunder pealed overhead. *'Please, please,'* she thought, *'let Vibia be right about rainwater dispelling this, because I have no idea what to do, Juno help me.'* Tears of frustration sprang to her eyes. *'I don't know what to do, I don't know what to do!'* What fools they had been, to try to take on such malice by themselves.

"We will devour you!" the fiend inside Vibia screamed, its sepulchral tone melding with the howls of its fellows in a harrowing cacophony. "Flesh is sweet and souls are sweeter and mages sweetest of all! We will have you, and your magic, and your strength will be ours!"

A flash of lightning cast the whole world into sudden, stark relief. Vibia's head snapped from side to side, and her fists clenched. *"No!"* she cried. Her eyes flung wide, the whites showing again. "Latona!"

Merula saw her opening. She hurled herself at the slender Fracture mage, hooking her arms behind Vibia's elbows and using that leverage to drag her away from the *lemures*.

Vibia fought with astonishing strength, the fiend within her struggling both against Merula and against Vibia's own attempts to wrest control of her body. She scratched and kicked, even tried to crane around and bite Merula. Yet though Merula was half a head shorter than Vibia, the Phrygian girl was much stronger than the Aventan woman and trained in the arts of combat. She knew how to use her solid musculature to advantage, and she ignored what blows Vibia was able to land.

"Drag her as far away as you can, Merula!" Latona shouted over the wind. She couldn't tell by looking at the ground how much of it might be sown with grave dirt, but she hoped they would soon step out of the fiends' reach. The fiends shrieked their displeasure, swooping toward Latona— but they could not seem to quite reach her. *'Are they repelled, as I am? Why aren't they possessing Merula? Is it only because Vibia is herself of Fracture that they have the opening?'* So many questions and no time to answer them.

Then, after another brilliant white flash and a crack of thunder that Latona felt in every bone, the heavens opened. A pelting rain poured down, cold and merciless. The shrieking of the *lemures* turned to a piercingly high whistle, and then they vanished. Vibia suddenly went limp, crashing to the earth and dragging Merula to a lurch.

"Let her go," Latona said, rushing to Vibia's side.

"It may be she is faking, Domina."

"No, she's out cold." Latona had felt it like the snap of a bow, the fiend leaving Vibia and her own *anima* recoiling into place. "Whatever was in her has lost its strength."

Latona went to her knees, clasping Vibia's pale, angular face between her hands. She gave Vibia's cheeks a little tap, and when that did not rouse her, called up Spirit magic. "Sweet Juno, restore her to herself. Blessed Juno, give me the strength to bring her back." These words she repeated, over and over, until the taste of cinnamon blossomed on her tongue.

When Vibia's eyes fluttered open, dark and watery and entirely her own, Latona almost sobbed in relief. Vibia coughed, then spoke, her voice creaking. "Latona. Latona, those things, I can't."

"Tell me later." Latona looked up. "I'm so sorry, but you have to get up." Vibia winced at the very thought, but she managed a weak nod. "Merula, help her. We have to get out of this field." She slipped her hand around Vibia's waist for support as Merula draped one of Vibia's arms over her shoulders and began to haul her up. "I'm sorry. I know you're exhausted, but I have no idea how far we may have to walk."

A sense of apprehension had hung over Alhena all day long. "The trouble is," she told Aula, as they strolled under the eaves of the peristyle garden, with rain cascading down into the pool in the center, "I never know what to make of it. Am I apprehensive because of my gifts? Because something's going to happen, and I don't know enough to make any use of the feeling? Or am I apprehensive because, well . . ." She made a vague gesture at herself. "Because it's just who I am?"

Aula jostled Alhena's shoulder affectionately. "Oh, my honey. You are much too hard on yourself, in either case. At least we know Gaius is safe! There's good news!" Letters had come for Aulus that afternoon, including a packet from Iberia. Seeing that one bore their brother's tribunal seal, Aula and Alhena had been unable to resist opening it. Waiting the long hours until Aulus returned from his work would have been torturous; they read enough to assure themselves that Gaius lived, if in dire circumstances.

"We know he was, several days ago," Alhena pointed out glumly. "Anything could have happened since that letter went out." She hugged her arms close to her chest. "I wish you would let me go with Latona and Vibia." It had become a familiar grumble. "It's broad daylight this time—well, it was when they left, anyway."

"And you see what good sense I have? They'll be soaked through if they haven't gotten back in the carriage yet."

Aula's fingers were ever in motion, always needing to touch something—her hair, her clothes, trailing through the water of a fountain, stroking the soft petal of a flower. Alhena walked tightly, folded in on herself. She envied her maidservant, Mus, for her slight stature. Alhena was unfashionably slender and glad for it. Without Aula's fertility-promising hips or Latona's graceful curves, she attracted less attention. But she just kept getting taller, and a tall girl with blazing red hair drew eyes wherever she went.

Aula plucked a white oleander flower and reached up to tuck it behind Alhena's ear. "Lovely."

Alhena smiled, despite the still-buzzing anxiety pulling at the edges of her mind. It was comforting, her big sister's belief that a bit of loveliness added to the world really could make things better. Alhena could never quite believe it herself, but Aula still did, with unquestioned constancy, even with the horrors she had herself witnessed. Cheering, that optimism could thrive, in the right sort of heart, no matter how it was challenged.

"Perhaps a change of scenery is what you need," Aula said.

"You just want me farther away from this Discordian problem."

Aula didn't bother to address the charge, so Alhena knew she was right. "The Ludi Athaeci are soon," Aula went on, as though Alhena hadn't spoken. "I imagine Father will want to go back to the city for them." Aula plucked another flower. This time she pulled the petals apart, tossing them behind her as she walked. "General Aufidius Strato is sponsoring, and he brought enough loot home from Albina to fund quite a spectacle." She cast the last few petals into the air above their heads. "And we shouldn't even have to worry about Father using it as an opportunity to husband-hunt, since so few eligible men will be in town."

Alhena frowned. "I don't know if I want to marry, anyway."

A tittering laugh escaped Aula. It was a little too high and brittle to have been born of amusement. Aula's laugh always gave her away, to anyone listening carefully, and so Alhena knew that her next words would be half-truth, half-not.

"'Want' doesn't have much to do with it, my darling! It's . . . what we do. A matter of duty." She rolled her eyes. "Look at our sister."

Alhena twisted her fingers together, eyes down on her toes. "Father wouldn't force me, though. Would he? If I really didn't want to? If I—if I wanted to stay in a temple, instead?"

This time, Aula paused before replying. "Marrying doesn't necessarily mean you can't serve in a temple."

Most of the temples didn't prohibit married men or women from serving; only a few of the gods required celibacy from their devotees. Certainly most of the High Priests and the men of the Pontifical College were married. But what man wanted to marry a woman who had to divide her time between her own home and a god's? Who would care to compete with that devotion?

"But no, pet," Aula went on. "I don't think Father would force you, if you didn't want to." She smiled sideways at Alhena. "You've always been his baby, after all. He wouldn't want to make you unhappy."

"He made Latona unhappy." The words were out before Alhena could catch them.

The mirth fell from Aula's face. She looked older, when grave concern entered her merry eyes. "Yes. And I suspect he's learned his lesson about that." She slipped an arm around Alhena's waist. "But even that, he did to keep Latona safe—or at least, he thought that would be the result. And he wants the same for you."

"Safe first, happy second?" Alhena sighed. "I suppose, if one must prioritize . . ."

"Happy is transient in any case, darling," Aula said. "Safety may be as well, but its loss can be fatal much swifter than the loss of happiness can be."

They walked a moment more, turning around the statue of Neptune at the end of the garden. "I don't want to be undutiful," Alhena said. "I would've married Tarpeius as he bid. I knew Tarpeius. There wasn't discomfort there. But the thought of another man just . . . leaves me cold."

"I'm sure he won't wed you to a stranger sight unseen. Some men might, but not Father."

Alhena frowned again, not sure how to explain what she meant to Aula. It wasn't only the unfamiliarity. Getting to know a man wouldn't make her feel any better about it, she was sure. A man, any man, would always be a foreign creature to her. Aula wouldn't mind doing her duty so much, though she'd doubtless find a way to have her pick of potential partners. But Aula liked men, was interested in them, found them charming. *'The ones who don't terrify me,'* Alhena thought, *'I just can't seem to summon that much interest in.'* She thought of Aula, flirting at parties with Autronius Felix, Publius Rufilius, the Domitiae brothers, and whoever else caught her eye, and giving all indications of enjoying their attentions. She thought of Latona, whose long-banked passions burned now with such a focus, for a man half a world away. *'I wonder if I'll ever feel that sort of . . . fascination with a man.'*

Her thoughts were broken by the sound of rapid footsteps, coming down the path from the house. Latona burst around a corner, pebbles skidding beneath her sandals. She was, as Aula had predicted, drenched. Her overgown was still looped into her belt, her skirts plastered to her thighs. Her hair had fallen nearly completely loose of its pins, hanging limply over her shoulders. What struck Alhena to the core, though, were her eyes, the emerald green fervent, just shy of wild.

"I think," Aula said, clutching Alhena's arm, "we may have discovered the source of your apprehension."

XVII

"We failed."

It had taken a cup and a half of wine before Latona could speak the words she didn't want to admit. She, Vibia, and Merula had all changed out of their sodden clothes and toweled off their hair as best they could, then settled onto couches to explain matters. Aula had called for dinner, but Latona had no appetite. She was only grateful that her father wasn't present, but taking his own meal with Appius Crispinius on the other side of Stabiae. She didn't think she had the strength left for any subterfuge.

"It was more than we were prepared for." Vibia's voice was still thin, lacking its usual briskness. Unlike Latona, though, she had plenty of stomach for her food, tucking into boiled eggs, sausage, and an entire dish of cherries.

'The fiend must have drained a great deal of strength from her,' Latona thought, *'and she needs to replenish herself.'* However enervated Latona's limbs, it was not enough to overcome the nauseated pit in her stomach.

"It's a latifundium, at least," Vibia continued, in between bites. "They've plenty of other fields to work. That one will yield nothing this season. Imagine if the poor wretches had to depend on it alone." She spat a cherry pit into her napkin. "Perhaps they can clear the other fields before more misfortune befalls them."

"Who owns that latifundium?" Aula asked. "We must find out and write him. Let him know it is no fault of the farmers."

"We should," Latona agreed. "But it isn't enough." It wouldn't make the grain grow, or the fiends depart. "What *can* we do?" She prodded moodily at a dish of currants and blackberries, persuading herself to take an interest in consuming them. "We couldn't fix the problem, so what *can* we do?"

"We send for priests of Ceres, to bless their fields," Vibia replied. "Tell them to sprinkle sacred water and pray that clears away the curse. I can't think what else." She rubbed at her forehead. "It may work. I still get the sense that this is all . . . experimental. I mean, why torment a bunch of poor farmers, chosen at what seems to be random?"

"I wonder if it *is* random," Aula said, her eyebrows arching signifi-cantly. "Another reason to find out who owns that land." They knew by now it was not targeted at Vitellian clients and tenants, but considering Lucretius Rabirus's willingness to contract with a Discordian, Latona could not help but suspect that other Popularists might be the focus of the curses.

"Could you get any sense of what they were planning?" Alhena asked.

Vibia shook her head. "Not from the *lemures*. They're not human, they don't think like humans, so they can't plan. But they have desires. They have intentions."

"Hungers," Latona said.

Vibia nodded. "Creatures of instinct, really. Tonight, they will have had a glut, and we may hope they will lie quiet for a while afterward. They are not men, to hunt for sport."

"Not on their own, perhaps," Aula said. "But they are driven by men, or women, who might."

They all fell silent, pensive, and then Latona felt a nudge on her leg. Vibia, still lying flat on her stomach, had reached over to prod her. "We did the best we could," she said, some of the accustomed sternness enter-ing her tone. Latona had never thought to find it comforting, but it left no room for self-pity or doubt. "It is no fault, no failing of ours, that what we faced was beyond our knowledge or capacity. We will try again, better prepared. That is the most anyone could expect."

It made sense. And Latona *was* grateful, that Vibia's forthrightness could cut through to unassailable facts, stripping away blame. *'But I still expected more of myself. And if the farmers did not expect, surely they hoped.'*

After a moment of uncomfortable quiet, Aula gestured for one of the nearby slaves. "Would you fetch me those letters that arrived from the city this afternoon? Thank you." She lifted her cup of wine. "Well, Vibia, I'm dreadfully sorry that we haven't been able to furnish you with a more relaxing vacation."

Vibia gave a soft snort. "I hope you won't take it amiss if I say that 'relaxing' is not, precisely, the word I would associate with the Vitelliae. I might not have known exactly what I was in for, but . . ." She seemed barely able to summon the energy for a shrug. "I knew I wasn't coming to Stabiae for a lark."

The slave returned with a small stack of letters. Aula took them all, flicked through, and withdrew one from the pile. "Perhaps this will bring you some comfort," she said, passing the paper over to Vibia.

Vibia's face softened from its accustomed angles. "From my brother?" she asked. As Vibia took the letter, Latona felt herself leaning forward as well, her heart suddenly a-flutter between her ribs. She had to school her expression into far milder interest than she felt.

Aula nodded. "Father's received enough of them that I can recognize the seal."

Vibia rose from her couch. "Ladies, I think I will retire."

"Of course," Aula cooed. "After the day you've had, I'm astonished either of you are still conscious."

Vibia locked eyes with Latona. "Get some rest," she said. "We'll get to the bottom of this. I vow it by Fortuna and Janus."

"By Juno and Venus," Latona promised. "Somehow."

Vibia's lips twitched slightly, and then she strode off to her chamber, letter clutched in her hand. Latona's heart gave a painful twinge. *'Don't be a fool,'* she told herself, swirling the wine in the bottom of her cup. She knew how often messages were passing from Iberia to Aven, thanks to the Air mage Sempronius had contracted, and she didn't expect a letter for her in every packet. It wasn't as though she wrote to *him* on a daily basis. She had only just alerted him to his sister's presence in Stabiae, and she had not dared commit more than the vaguest outline of their troubling discoveries to paper.

Still, the ache persisted. Knowing there were words he had written, here under her father's roof, but that they were not for her—

"Oh, don't look so forlorn," Aula said, rolling her eyes. "I didn't want to say it in front of Vibia, but you received a letter, too." Latona's hand was out before she was conscious of having told it to extend itself. Aula snorted. "It's in your room, you goose. Tucked beneath your jewelry box. You think I'd be flashing it about in front of her?" She snorted, popping a blackberry in her mouth. "Do give me a little credit. There's one from Gaius, too."

Latona bolted upright and started untangling her skirts. "You should have told me earlier."

"When, pray tell, was there time, in between you barreling home, drenched as a naiad, and—Vibia?" Aula looked down the colonnade, brow crinkled as Vibia skittered back into the room, looking cold and serious. "Is something wrong?"

The very word struck an icy bolt of horror through Latona's whole being. *'No. No, if the worst happened—It could not be—News of his death would not arrive in a letter with his own seal—'* But the terror seized her nonetheless.

"Read this," Vibia said, thrusting the letter in front of Latona with white fingers, "and tell me if these *akdraugi* don't sound familiar."

Latona looked where she pointed, about a third of the way down the paper. It took a moment for her eyes to focus past her dread, another for the written words to penetrate her spasmodic thoughts. "*Lemures,*" she breathed, looking up at Vibia with wide eyes. Alhena came half out of her seat, making as though to shift beside Latona to read the letter as well. She hesitated, though, until Vibia nodded her assent. "He's describing *lemures.*"

"In Iberia?" Aula asked. "How—?"

"It may not be exactly the same," Alhena ventured, as her pale eyes scanned the paper. "The wolves of Truscum are not the same as the wolves of Vendelicia or those of Phrygia."

"Yet all will hunt." After the tart retort, Vibia pinched the bridge of her nose. "Forgive me. It's only . . . My brother speaks of the Lusetanian devils in the same terms I would use to describe *lemures*, if I were some- one with no magic to help me discern their nature. The haunting sensa- tions, the mind-muddling—these are what we have witnessed, here."

But Latona shook her head slowly. "Like, and yet unlike. He reports that they roll in like a fog, and he gives no indication that they are an- chored to a particular place, to a rip between the worlds created by some charm. They seem to be summoned on the spot by the Lusetani mages."

"I grant those points. Related creatures, then—and perhaps they can be defeated in similar ways."

Latona's hands fell into her lap. "We've only half-figured out how to defeat our variety," she said heavily. "How are we to advise him what to do, half a world away? We can't send him a useful Fracture mage in the post."

"I will tell him what we *do* know," Vibia said, "and keep him apprised of further developments." Her brow was deeply knitted, her eyes focused distantly rather than at any of the Vitelliae. "Strange, that such similar spirits should arise, so far away . . ."

That pronouncement hung in the air like a storm cloud for a long moment, before Aula broke the silence with a thin sigh. "We live in tu- multuous times, I'm afraid." She rose from her couch and put a hand beneath Latona's arm, urging her up as well. "Come on, my dear. We'll all be the better for some sleep."

At first, Latona wasn't sure what had prompted this sudden concern for her somnolence, and then Aula's true aim dawned on her: to get

Latona away from Vibia, to examine her own letters. "Yes . . ." she said, allowing herself to be drawn up. "Vibia, please tell your brother . . . well, tell him whatever you deem useful. Tell him we are doing our best, here, and shall do whatever we can to help him—and the legions—out there."

"I'll think on what to tell him. And we'll . . ."

"We'll try again," Latona said, even as Aula continued to steer her away. "We'll learn, and we'll *win*. We have to." Vibia looked approximately as convinced as Latona felt, but that thin thread of surety was the best they were likely to achieve that night.

∞∞∞∞∞∞∞∞∞∞∞∞

As soon as they got into Latona's room, Aula nudged her ungently toward the table with her jewelry box. "Go on. I want to know what's in *your* letters."

Latona's face folded in a scowl as she took up the papers: one with Sempronius's falcon-in-flight seal, the other with the seal of a military tribune. "If you think I'm going to let you read—"

"Oh, I don't mean all of it. If I were that determined, I'd have popped the wax and resealed it."

"Aula, you are utterly impossible."

"She'd do it, too," Alhena intoned from the doorway. "I've seen her do it to Father's."

Aula's eyes narrowed at their younger sister. "Oh, do come in, if you must, and shut the door." Alhena did as bid, but that didn't stop Aula from complaining, "Subterfuge was much easier to achieve when you were too small to be included."

"You'll just have to get a bit cleverer about it then, I suppose," Alhena retorted, unflustered. For Latona, she had a softer tongue. "What do your letters say?"

"I haven't had the chance to read them!"

"If you're too nervous—" Aula began, her fingers twitching toward the papers.

Latona snatched them away from her. "No, *thank* you, I rather think my wits, enfeebled though they are, are up to the task." She sat on the edge of her bed and looked between the two letters, feeling a twinge of sororal guilt when she decided to open Sempronius's first. '*Sorry, Gaius.*' For the moment it was enough to know that he was alive and well enough to send a message. A woman in love had to be afforded some indulgence in her priorities. Latona tried to ignore her sisters' eyes on her, avid and anxious, as her eyes flew over Sempronius's words.

He had evidently written in some haste, for the penmanship was even worse than usual.

'My friend, Vitellia Latona,

'I have written before, inquiring of your thaumaturgical studies. I must ask again now, with a more personal interest in the answer.'

She read swiftly, knowing there would be time to savor each turn of phrase later—once she had satisfied her sisters' curiosity. "He tells me the same story as he told Vibia, only—" Toward the end, a note of optimism, and one which made Latona draw in her breath sharply.

"What?" Aula asked. "Latona, what is it?"

Latona pressed her fingertips to her lips, allowing herself a moment to revel in the warmth that spread through her whole body, finally chasing away the damp chill of the dousing rain. *'I saved him,'* she thought, and nearly laughed with pride. *'My magic. I did that.'*

"Err, Latona?" Alhena said, with a note of concern. "It's gotten rather . . . brighter in here."

Latona's fingers fluttered unconcernedly. "They'll be fine." The little flames in the lamps had responded to her emotions without her intending it, yes, but they weren't out of control. "It's—it's good news. Of a sort. It would seem that—" She coughed lightly, mastering the sudden giddiness. "I gave him a gift, before he went to Iberia. A focale I'd woven, like I did for Gaius." She glanced at the other letter. "He may have a similar tale."

Aula's face sharpened in understanding. "One with—" She gestured around at the bright lamps. "With your magic in it?"

Nodding, Latona continued. "He thinks the protective charm works against these *akdraugi*." The unfamiliar word had a sour taste, and Latona thought of the signature of the Discordian curses. "It kept him from falling under their sway. He could feel it, warm on his skin . . ." Her fingertips touched her own throat, aching to once again feel his heat. Her eyes lingered on his closing words.

'Lady Latona, I must tender my deepest gratitude to you, though doing so in words and across so many miles hardly feels adequate.

Mars and Jupiter willing, I shall return to Aven and be able to make a better job of it—though I'm not sure all my holdings have enough fruit to fill as many baskets as would be required to honor your talent and generosity.'

She had to laugh. Fruit had indeed been his gift when she had saved his life once before. An appropriate gift from a single man to a married woman, nothing that would raise eyebrows—though he had brought the baskets himself, and Herennius had taken umbrage at that.

'So perhaps I shall have to dare something more fitting. Until then, know that you are in my thoughts—and if you have any insights as to the nature of these *akdraugi*, write back in all haste. Many lives may have cause to praise your name, if you can help us defeat this challenge.

'I remain,
'Your devoted friend,
'V. Sempronius Tarren'

Stronger words than he had dared to use before. Because he had written in such haste, not choosing his words carefully? But no, that hardly seemed like Sempronius. Even when impulse took him, there was always swift calculation attending it. So what had been his purpose? *'He would know I would notice.'*

Latona folded the letter and placed it firmly under the jewelry box again, though she knew Aula's fingers would be itching for it. *'I did that. I helped him.'* After the utter failure of the day, she had needed that boost, a reminder of the strength she could summon. *'I just need the right approach . . . I have to find it. I have to do more to assist the legions, if I can't find the right answer here. To protect Sempronius, and my brother, and all the men of Aven and their allies who are facing these terrors.'* She drummed briefly on top of the lacquered wood, painted with images of Venus's doves, then took up her brother's letter.

He was a less oratorical writer than Sempronius, more sparing in his descriptions. "It seems these *akdraugi* have been as responsible for besieging Toletum as the living Lusetani," she said, with sudden hollowness in her chest. Gaius's letter she had no compunction about handing over to Aula and Alhena for perusal. "I need to write them both back, though I don't know what to tell them." Aventan magic could only do so much good in such circumstances, with Mars forbidding its use as a weapon of war. Protection, though, was the domain of Fire. "I should be weaving more. If it can help the legions, protect them against their own breed of fiends—" She started, as though to head to her loom despite the late hour and her own exhaustion, then halted mid-step. "But how can I do that and still tend to the Discordian threat here? There aren't enough hours in the day!"

Aula rolled her eyes. "You can't outfit three legions on your own, anyway, not if you wove every hour of daylight from now till the Saturnalia." Seeing the suddenly mulish expression on Latona's face, she hastened to add, "That was *not* a challenge!"

Latona blew out air through her nose in irritation, but after a moment's consideration, she sat back down.

"Your challenge is in Truscum, not Iberia," Alhena said. Aula's and Latona's heads both snapped toward her, for her voice had taken on the vague echo that meant a thread of Time magic was in it. But she shook her head. "I'm not seeing anything. Not now, I mean. I just . . . I just know. You have helped them both. You will help them again, in the future, in other ways. But for now, the gods want your focus at home." She gave her head a little shake, and her eyes cleared.

Latona's hands pressed tight into her blanket. A bitter tonic—but she trusted her sister's intuition. "Very well," she said. "But I want some red-dyed wool all the same. I've been a fool." She pinched the bridge of her nose. An embarrassment, not to have thought of it sooner, but it was such a military thing, so far removed from the domestic mural of her life. "We should be wearing these charms ourselves, and *that* much, I can certainly accomplish."

"Armor of our own," Aula said. "Yes. That should help even the odds."

XVIII

CITY OF AVEN

Consul Galerius Orator had braced himself for a tumultuous year in office, considering the turmoil that had preceded the elections. Yet, so far, it had passed relatively peacefully. Oh, busily, to be sure. The backlog of issues needing the attention of the Senate and Assemblies was immense. Dictator Ocella had hoarded the public treasury, unwilling to release funds for anything he deemed insufficiently critical. As such, many repairs to public buildings had been overlooked, many legal disputes had been left unresolved, many records and registrations had fallen into chaos. Galerius's first major initiative was overseeing an internal census of Aven's municipal employees, determining what they had done in the past several years and where resources might need to be reallocated.

'Not,' he thought with a wry smile, *'the sort of measure which gets a man into the annals of history.'*

Such had never been Galerius's aim. He wanted to serve, and if a pedestrian task was what the Fates demanded of him, then he would complete it with all the diligence and careful attention of his nature.

As for the Senate, strife there had limited itself to a manageable level of bickering and squabbling. Arrius Buteo, the aging champion of the Optimates, would stand up at any opportunity and decry the many degradations of the modern state, but he mostly seemed interested in hearing his strident voice echo through the Curia chamber. *'Perhaps losing the consulship hit the Optimates harder than I had imagined.'* Galerius himself was a moderate, and he would have entertained whatever legislation had passed in front of him, at least in theory. No matter should be beyond debate. But his co-consul, Aufidius Strato, was a military man with a forbidding glower. He did not suffer fools—and he had made plainly clear that he considered Buteo a fool of the grandest caliber. He would not look favorably if Buteo left off ostentation and actually moved to putting forward legislation.

The thing was, *no one* seemed to want to introduce much new legislation for debate in the Senate and consideration by the Assemblies.

Galerius didn't mind; it gave him more time to focus on setting the state back to order. But it did seem odd, that following the first elections after the death of a Dictator, the Senate had grown timid.

When he opined on this to his wife, Marcia Tullia, she gave a small smile. "Well. It *is* summer. Half the Senate is in Stabiae or Baiae, if they're not overseas. And of course, the Iberian war has neatly removed two pillars of the opposing factions from the city for the whole year. Small wonder you've a quieter time of it inside the Curia."

And that was true. Without Sempronius Tarren and Lucretius Rabirus going for each other's throats in the Curia, the other Optimates and Popularists appeared content to snipe informally only, without dragging the law into it.

Not that the gentlemen in question had gone unheard from. From hundreds of miles away, they made their voices known. Throughout the spring and early summer, the Senate of Aven had been subjected to a regular torrent of letters from Sempronius, chronicling everything from new villages dotting the rivers to the consumption of grain by the legions. Rabirus had gotten a later start and was not so thorough a correspondent as Sempronius, but he had not allowed his rival's volley of paper arrows to go unchallenged; his own messages spoke of the quiet mood in Gades, the peaceful attitude of the nearby tribes, every letter constructed to make Sempronius's look like warmongering hysteria.

In the hottest part of the summer, it was rare that the Senate could scrape together a proper quorum. As such, Galerius had withheld his latest news for a few days. He had informed Strato, who agreed that the report was grievous enough to warrant waiting for a market day, when more senators would travel back to the city for business.

Not everyone returned, but the Curia was closer to its usual capacity than it had been since mid-Junius. The rows of wooden benches were filled with men in their striped tunics and togas, and the mages of the Augian Commission stood on the floor near the consuls' chairs, ever alert to violations of the *lex leges magiae*. Galerius rose, signaling his intent to speak rather than open the floor for commentary and debate. He had a boy with him, a public slave, bearing a basket full of scrolls and papers.

"Venerable fathers," Galerius said, pitching his voice above the few men still chatting. "Well met. I hope we shall be able to conclude our business swiftly."

A general favorable muttering answered him. Quite apart from the desire many men had to get to their business or to parties, the Curia was stifling. Aven had dubiously enjoyed half a month of unrelenting sun-shine. Summers in Aven were always dry and hot, but this Quintilis seemed to have taken a particularly scorching turn. Everyone would be glad to leave the stuffy chamber and be able to change into less formal clothing.

"I have received another letter from the honored praetor, Sempronius Tarren." Galerius had, in fact, received three in the time it had taken to assemble a quorum, but he thought a bit of conflation no true deception. "I believe it bears a full reading—"

Unsurprisingly, Arrius Buteo voiced immediate objection. "Must we endure another of these self-aggrandizing tales?" he sneered. "We have heard enough from sly Sempronius. We know every mile he has tread since leaving Liguria! And how many talents of silver he has paid out as wages, how much grain he has carted up from Tarraco, how many times it has *rained* in Iberia since the spring. I am only surprised that he has not quantified the shits taken by the auxiliary horses!"

"Give him time," muttered Decimus Gratianus, another of the prom-inent Optimates, whom Galerius and Strato had beaten out for the con-suls' chairs the previous December.

"I am aware," Galerius said, leveling his gaze at Buteo, "that some of you believe these accounts to be excessive in their detail. I assure you, I would not waste your time with excrement, equine or otherwise." This parry earned Galerius a few approving shouts and claps from the Popu-larists and moderates. Buteo looked about to say something else, but Licinius Cornicen—ever among the most practical of the Optimates—leaned down from his bench to place a hand on the older man's shoulder and hiss in his ear. Buteo settled, his mouth closed, though he did not look pleased about it. "I only wish," Galerius continued, "that all of our number were here to bear witness to these words—but I have no doubt that the news will spread to them swiftly. Indeed, all of Aven will know the general shape of it soon, but we, reverend fathers, ought to be in full possession of the facts before we step out into the world."

Galerius turned to the boy standing behind him, took the top letter off of the pile, and began to read.

"'Reverend Fathers of the Senate, I regret that I must write you with ill news and dark tidings. I have brought the Eighth, Tenth, and Four-teenth legions near to Toletum, but our journey has been more arduous than expected—not due to any normal toil, nor even due to pitched bat-tle. No, what we have faced on our journey south has been trouble of another kind: metaphysical and magical. And I fear that what we have encountered is nothing to what those cohorts trapped inside Toletum have suffered.'"

A few of the senators began murmuring to each other at that, some curiously, some dismissively. Galerius wished that Aulus Vitellius were among those present. It had been his son, after all, who had first warned the Senate that dark magic was afoot in Iberia, and his son who was now leading the men trapped behind Toletum's walls. But the censor was serving Aven in another capacity, tending to the electoral and tax rolls in southern Truscum, and Galerius did not think the news could wait long enough for him to return.

Galerius read on. Sempronius told a harrowing tale, to be sure, of fiends raised on the battlefield. That alone was enough to shake some of the men present from their skeptical disdain. Raising spirits was one thing, by itself; the priests of Aven had been known to do so on occasion, though rarely in recent history. *Lemures* could trouble citizens who were not diligent in their respects to their household gods, and everyone was a little tense on the days that the *mundus* was open, in case any malevolent spirits should decide to walk abroad in the city. But such things were rare. *Lemures* never appeared in large numbers, certainly never enough to overwhelm an army, and the very idea that they would be called upon in combat was anathema to Aventan thinking. To Athaecan and Tyrian, too, for that matter. Their gods did not allow it. The Iberian gods, it seemed, were untroubled by the need to keep magic and warcraft separate.

With his keen rhetorical eye, Galerius appreciated how Sempronius told his story. While Sempronius's speeches in the Curia were elegantly constructed, and while his missives from the field had been perhaps excessively detailed, in this account, he resisted embellishment. He also kept himself out of it, presenting the tale dispassionately, an observer rather than a participant. Not only would that undercut accusations of sensationalism, it also avoided placing Sempronius in a position where he looked weak or afraid.

"'These *akdraugi*, as the Iberians call them, do not behave quite as our *lemures*,'" Galerius finished, "'but I must think they have some similar origin. We believe they have been responsible not only for fatigue but for deaths inside Toletum. I have put our best military minds alongside the expertise of our Iberian allies to find a way to defeat them without incurring terrible losses. I intend soon to write to you of victory.'"

And that was Sempronius all over: speaking his intentions for men and gods alike to hear, then willing them into existence.

"'I remain, reverend fathers, your dutiful servant, Praetor Vibius Sempronius Tarren.'" Galerius let the scroll slide closed, then passed it back to the public slave behind him. He gazed over the assembly, taking in the faces: concerned, astonished, aghast, skeptical.

And, in Arrius Buteo, vindicated.

All too aware of what chaos he was about to unleash, Galerius said, "I open the floor for discussion," and eased back into the consul's chair.

◇◇◇◇◇◇◇◇◇◇◇◇

The tales of haunting Lusetanian fiends were not new to Marcus Autronius, sitting next to his father on one of the uppermost benches in the Curia. They were neither of them important: Gnaeus, a man whose mercantile forbears had given him just enough wealth to drag the family into the senatorial class; Marcus, an Earth mage who could never look to any higher office than that of a simple senator, thanks to the *lex cantatia Augiae*. But Marcus's brother Felix was Sempronius Tarren's right hand, and though Felix was generally a poor correspondent, the encounter with the *akdraugi* had moved him to some eloquence—or, at least, effusiveness. Sempronius's account gave Marcus a clearer idea of what had actually happened.

Buteo was on his feet. "Well, this just proves it! He's unfit for command! Fiends and hauntings—these are children's stories!"

Galerius gave Buteo a severe look. "Can you really dismiss the account of a fellow senator—a praetor—so easily?"

"Of that man? Of course!" Buteo's hawkish face was as unyielding as ever, but around him, Marcus observed that the other Optimates looked less certain. Restless unease had crept into the Curia. The story Sempronius Tarren told was unusual and unlikely—but not impossible. They would have preferred that it be impossible, that he had written of some catastrophe out of the age of legends: Iberian mages summoning burning rain or tornadoes, or turning themselves into monsters with fangs and horns. Such fantasies would have been easier to dismiss. This story had the smack of truth about it. All men knew the danger of the *lemures* and other spirits, and what Sempronius described did not seem far apart from their world—not nearly enough for comfort.

"He has included, also, the sworn testimony of Generals Onidius and Calpurnius, as well as Tribune Autronius Felix," Galerius said, lifting another three scrolls from his pile. "Do you doubt them, as well? Do you call them liars, or mad?"

"It is possible for those who are not mad themselves to be taken in by those who are. And it is *certainly* possible for good men to be deceived— inveigled, *beguiled* by a silver-tongued trickster!"

"If he were lying," Quintus Terentius broke in, "it would be an awfully bold lie, considering every man of his legions could speak the truth about it once the campaign is over." In Sempronius's absence and with Aulus Vitellius seeing to his censorial duties, Terentius had stepped up as the most prominent speaker for the Popularist faction. "If he were mad, surely Onidius and Calpurnius would have relieved him of command by now. And I feel I must point out that this report concurs with everything that young Gaius Vitellius has written during his vexillation."

"Young Vitellius," Buteo spat, "has been spinning such fables for a year. His word is no more to be trusted than Sempronius's."

"Be reasonable, friend." This interjection came from Licinius Corni- cen, among the more sensible members of the Optimate faction. "The reports are in accord. Logic would indicate that—"

"I don't care," Buteo said, his thick eyebrows knitted together in a scowl. "He's conjured these fables to keep us from questioning whether we should extend command. What has Praetor Sempronius to show for his efforts in Iberia, besides this endless deluge of papyrus? Months he has been on campaign, and he has hardly done more than dispatch a few mea- sly raiding parties!" Buteo gave a thin laugh. "How much easier, to blame fiends and shadows, rather than admitting he provoked this conflict—"

"Now, that's unfair," Cornicen said. "We had reports of trouble long before—"

But Buteo was hearing no objections. "It was *he* who drove us into this war, and now he finds himself embarrassed. When *I* was on campaign—"

"Yes, do remind me," Terentius drawled, leaning forward on his bench, "in which rugged hinterland did you serve your years as a military tribune, friend? Ephesus, wasn't it?" Buteo's face grew florid as snickering pattered through the ranks of the senators. "I expect you ventured so far as Smyrna, didn't you? Why, that might have taken as much as three days! Did you get pebbles in your shoes?"

Buteo spluttered and grumbled his displeasure, but it was Gratianus who stood next. "A proposal, august fathers—" he said, raising a hand to call for order. Marcus couldn't see Gratianus's face from his seat, but he *did* see Galerius's pale eyebrows arch in tolerant bemusement and Strato's brow knit in irritation. The consuls had been allowing a fair bit of disorder, but Gratianus was overstepping by behaving as though he had any authority.

"By all means, Decimus Gratianus," Galerius said. He did not seem to raise his voice, but he had a pitch that commanded attention nonetheless. A way of re-establishing his authority without losing his dignity. "Let us hear your suggestion."

Gratianus's shoulders straightened. "We ought to refer these reports to the Pontifical College, before we do anything else." He glanced around; there were a few pontiffs in the Senate, but not many. The pontiffs were usually, though not always, mages, and an ambitious man would get further in their college than trying to scale the *cursus honorum*, the upper ranks of which would always be denied him. "They are better suited than we to determine the truth of these stories. If indeed there are such apparitions spawning in Iberia, the mages among them may have insights as to their nature, and the College's annals and records may have information about previous encounters with them." His hand circled in the air. "From the Tyrian Wars, perhaps. And they may have advice we can pass to those in the field. If they determine there can be no veracity in the tales, however, then it will be our duty to determine what is to be done with a commander who would spin falsehoods."

It was a good idea. *'Damn it.'* The last thing the Popularists needed was an Optimate—one who would likely be a candidate for the consulship again this year—looking steady and reasonable while the Popularists reacted to frenzied tales of eldritch horrors. Yet Marcus couldn't help but be impressed by the balanced nature of what Decimus Gratianus proposed. The Earth of his nature admired that which was solid, measured, slow-paced. He wasn't like his wild younger brother, always racing from one thrill to the next.

Galerius called for a vote, and the proposal passed easily. Most of the Popularists—including Marcus and his father, and even the Terentiae—moved to the right in favor of the measure, though many did so while grumbling about unnecessary delays. They could hardly stand against a course of action that might lend pontifical weight to Sempronius's words, though. Gratianus had neatly trapped them into an accord.

'*How many pontiffs are in his pocket, though? Or Buteo's, or Rabirus's?*' And then, because Marcus was not a naive man, the thought followed: '*Or Sempronius's, for that matter?*'

Perhaps that would be worth looking into. As the Senate moved on to discussing a building request from the master of the Aventine docks, Marcus picked up the wax tablet he typically brought with him to the Curia for note-taking and began to compose a letter to Sempronius Tarren. If he was swift in copying it over to paper, he might be able to get it to Galerius Orator that afternoon—and then perhaps Marcia Tullia would send it with her next bird-borne packet.

SPLINTER THE THIRD

No one knew better than a Fracture mage how impossible a thing a plan was. "It won't work how they think," Corinna whispered to the floor. She hardly saw the images, laid out in neatly placed tiles. She saw the grout in between, the white lines between glossy vermilion and shining cerulean. She saw the chipped edges, the missing square. "It may get them what they want, maybe, maybe, but it won't work how they think."

Such an easy thing to break, a plan. So simple to warp.

A battle plan could go awry with one wrong-footed horse, one frightened man, one dull blade.

She should have *known*, really. Off she had fled, to work her little wonders, but it hadn't gone as *planned*. Something—someone—had intervened. She'd nearly been found. She'd had to move, out of isolation and back into the crowded, hustling, noisy world. Were there more broken things, here? Or simply a different kind? Corinna couldn't decide. Her work was harder in some ways here, easier in others.

All a plan was, really, was the desire of mortals to feel like they had some control. "But we never do." She ran her fingers over the bump where a tile had been cracked but mortared into place anyway.

The touch of Discordia was everywhere, why did so few understand? Corinna knew it instinctively. "Silly men, silly women," she said, shaking her head in dismay.

XIX

Three legions waited on the edge of the woods a few miles from Toletum.

The path through the forest was blocked, Sempronius's forces had discovered, not by a fighting force, but by a cluster of men in robes of blue and green, nearly blending in to the trees. "Magic-men," one scout reported, riding back. "Twenty or so. I don't see signs of any warriors with them. Not immediately near them, at least."

"They remained safe on their side of the forest," Sempronius said, "and sent these men out to prevent our passage through."

Sempronius considered. He had three legions at his back, lined up in the ocher dust of the Iberian plateau. The river lay immediately to their east, perhaps a hundred paces away. Before them, a line of trees, which Lady Hanath assured him was scarce more than a mile thick. On the other side of that, the walls of Toletum—and the Lusetani horde besieging the city. In theory, his action now would be simple: cross the forest, thus pinning the Lusetani between the walls and the advancing army, and then crush their foes. That was the way breaking a siege *worked*.

Sempronius did not believe it would be so straightforward this time.

The mages were not there for no reason, and if Ekialde had not sent warriors to reinforce them, he clearly believed that, whatever they were doing, it would be enough to stymie the legions' progress.

Sempronius worked his jaw. There was no true way to know what the Lusetani magic-men would do, what havoc they could wreak, without marching against them and meeting their defense. But to do so was to stride boldly into a trap. An unsubtle stratagem, but still a difficult one for a commander to work his way around without offering up some sort of victory to his opponent.

It galled him, to know that Toletum was so close, yet to be rendered unable to charge to its immediate relief.

"Tell the centurions to make camp," he told Felix. "I want to see what these magic-men will do. Then return to my tent, once it's up." He looked to Corvinus. "Fetch Onidius, Calpurnius, and the Lady Hanath. I want to discuss a plan of attack before we do anything else."

A sense of unease filled the camp, like the air before a thunderstorm. The legionaries went about their work as though looking over their shoulders, wondering when the magic-men would send their mysterious fog or some other uncanny horror. Yet through the early evening, nothing happened.

Hanath was the last to join the group in Sempronius's tent. She and a group of riders had been testing the boundaries of the forest, seeing how close they could get before the Lusetani magic-men appeared.

"Lady Hanath," he said, gesturing her to where he, Felix, Onidius, Calpurnius, and Corvinus were gathered around a table, "if you would be so good as to join us." Impatience was written in her features, and Sempronius felt a pinch of sympathy for her. It could not have been easy, to leave her husband behind in a city besieged by demons. "We've been compiling the information from our scouting detachments to try to create some semblance of a map, but I imagine you have even better information."

"I shall try, General," she said, and took the stylus that Corvinus proffered to her. With Hanath's adjustments, the map took greater shape. The Tagus River wriggled back and forth through the terrain like a Gorgon's hair, and Toletum sat nestled at the southernmost end of a particularly deep bend. The Aventan legions had approached from almost due east, at first, then had hugged the river as it cut suddenly south. Crossing the river was one option, though not an ideal one. The riverbanks were so steep that they would have to backtrack before they could find a good crossing, and then likely come across much further west—perhaps surrounded by the Lusetani.

"The city here," Sempronius said, thinking aloud. He pointed to the deepest part of the Tagus's curling bend. "The Lusetani here, out of arrow range."

"The Lusetani *warriors* there," Hanath corrected. "They have a larger camp downriver."

Sempronius arched an eyebrow. "Noncombatants?"

"Many, we believe," Hanath said, "though I have not seen for myself to confirm." Sempronius flicked his eyes to Onidius, then Felix, and they nodded their understanding. Scouts would need to be sent westward. "They have brought civilians along with them. Women who do not fight, older men, their star-readers and other magic-men. Slaves, both those they had already and those they have taken from other tribes." She scowled, no doubt at the idea that there would be Arevaci held in Luse-tani fetters. "And, we believe, it is from this larger camp that Ekialde dispatches his raiders."

"How far downriver?"

One lean shoulder lifted in a shrug. "At least this far," she said, point-ing to another place where the Tagus careened south, then west again, sluicing almost at right angles through the rocky terrain. "But perhaps farther."

Sempronius nodded. "All right. Toletum. The field of battle. The Lusetani warriors, encamped. Then, this stretch of forest, and us in the middle of it. Lady Hanath, does this forest stretch all the way to where the river cuts north again?" She nodded, and Sempronius smiled. "We might be able to turn that to our advantage. They have blocked our passage here, but what if we divert their attention?" His fingers sketched out his plan on the map. "I want to send the Eighth and the Fourteenth north, back into the hills."

Onidius arched an eyebrow. "Away from the river? We'll run out of water fast, especially in this heat."

"You can carry enough with you for what I have planned. I don't want to send you far—just enough so that the Lusetani won't immediately know where you're going. Onidius and the Eighth should continue all the way to the far side of the peninsula, along the Tagus again. Calpurnius and the Fourteenth will cut back down the middle of the peninsula here." A grim smile crept onto his face. "Let's see if Ekialde has enough of these damned magic-men to raise fiends against three separate forces." He sighed. "I wish I had an Air mage to attach to each legion, but we'll have to make do with horse couriers. We must stay in communication—every attack, magical or otherwise, all three of us need to know about."

Calpurnius nodded agreement, but Onidius looked concerned. "How long do you intend that we hold these positions?"

"Long enough to garner the information we need to attack," Sempro-nius answered. "Their numbers, their patterns of magical interference, how often they send for reinforcements from their western camp—and you'll be in the best position to determine that, Onidius. We'll coordinate when we have a better sense of their movements." He looked up, out past his tent flaps, as though he could gaze down the *via praetoria*, beyond the forest, to the walls of Toletum itself. "I wish I could get word to Tribune Vitellius to let him know that we're here, let alone what we plan, but I don't want to risk the bird getting shot down."

"Maybe if we can distract them sufficiently?" Felix offered. The grin that crept over his face was not quite the same as the one that charmed hearts across Aven's seven hills, but it had a confident appeal of its own. "They tried a feint on us with those damned spirits. Let's show them a feint of our own."

Sempronius smiled, glad to see Felix thinking strategically. "I like it." He looked to Onidius and Calpurnius. "Let's make one big push before we split our forces. It will give us the chance to test their strength, but we'll back off swiftly. I'll send Eustix with Lady Hanath and the cavalry, to get as close as they can."

But Hanath was shaking her head. "He has too many men on the lookout. We tried to get birds out during skirmishes—just ordinary pigeons, of course, not driven by your magic-men—but Ekialde always kept archers ready." She spun the map to look at it more closely. "If we were to ford the river with the messenger—here, perhaps." Her dark finger jabbed at a point a little ways back from their present position, where the bluffs on the riverbanks had not been as high. "Then we could release the bird from the other side of the river, close to the city, *here*." She looked up at Sempronius through her eyelashes. "The Lusetani would not see it coming."

"One message now, to give them hope and to tell Vitellius to be on the lookout," Sempronius said, "and another, if you can manage to cross the river again at the appropriate time, to coordinate the attack." He rubbed at his chin with the back of one hand. "Though I grant that may be more difficult, perhaps impossible."

"We shall do it if we can, General," Hanath said, with a decisive nod. "Tribune Vitellius has been stalwart and brave. He has endured much that he did not expect since arriving in Iberia. He deserves as much aid as you can give, as quickly as you can give it."

◇◇◇◇◇◇◇◇◇◇◇◇◇◇

As dawn broke over the Tagus River, Hanath and a cavalry unit had doubled back to the ford and crossed to the southern side, taking a wide route to avoid coming within eyesight of any Lusetani or Vettoni scouts. He had given her a mixed group—her own Arevaci along with the cavalry attached to the Fourteenth legion—and then redistributed portions of the Eighth and Tenth cavalry over to the Fourteenth. A sweating Eustix was nestled in their midst, with two trained birds clinging to his shoulders and two copies of Sempronius's message tucked in a saddlebag. *'At least the man knows how to ride,'* Sempronius thought, though being able to keep a seat and being able to keep up with Hanath's thunderous pace might prove different skills.

As soon as the sun was up, intense heat began baking the plateau. Many of these men would be unfazed; anyone who had served in Numidia had learned how to handle wearing full armor no matter how relentless the heat. Sempronius worried most about the Eighth, men who had spent their service in the northern territories. He hoped they had sufficiently acclimated during their journey south.

Fourteen thousand men in full battle array. An impressive sight anywhere, but the blazing sunlight cast a gleam on all those helmets and plates, and though the breeze blasted like an oven, it also set their banners to snapping, their crimson and gold streaking the morning light.

His commanders knew their role: attack, see what the Lusetani magic-men would do, and then, when the *akdraugi* became unbearable, retreat. He wanted it to look as chaotic as possible, as though the encounter terrified his men into breaking ranks and fleeing for the hills. The scouts reported that there were still no Lusetani warriors in close range, so their retreat should not be vulnerable—but the magic-men would report back to their war-king, and perhaps then, when they engaged in true combat, the Lusetani would underestimate the Aventans.

Sempronius only hoped that, whatever the Lusetani magic-men had in store, the disordered retreat would *remain* no more than an act.

He nodded to Felix, who in turn gave the centurions their orders. At a series of sharp whistles, up and down the lines, fourteen thousand men began to march in unison. It shook the earth beneath them, and their armor clashed and banged in a strange symphony.

The Lusetani magic-men were not slow in responding. Wherever they were, hidden behind the tree line, they soon had the bright day turning gray around the legions. The heat of high summer dropped in an instant to a clammy chill, and the same fog that they had encountered before rolled out of the forest, its advance curling like a wave hitting shore.

As Sempronius watched, the mist both thickened and darkened, swiftly turning from wispy light gray to a smoky shadow. Then it began to coalesce, taking sharp, angular forms. The *akdraugi* did not quite have the shapes of men, nor beasts, but they had their own cohesion, jagged and haunting. It confirmed one of Sempronius's theories. *'They are stronger, here, closer to the men who summoned them.'* His mind worked swiftly, trying to dismiss or consider other variables, even as the legions contin-ued to march. *'What else . . . Could they be taking power from the trees, like the Tennic tribes in the north do? The wind is at their back, perhaps enabling them to move faster. We are the same distance from the river. It's broad daylight, so they need not only act in darkness—but the moon still moves. It's just past new now. It was waning gibbous when we first encoun-tered them.'*

These matters fascinated him intellectually as much as they were im-portant to him for strategic purposes. *'I would know more about your magic, Iberia. May your gods and mine give me the chance to learn.'*

◇◇◇◇◇◇◇◇◇◇◇◇◇

INSIDE TOLETUM

Vitellius felt like he knew every street and sidepath in Toletum by now—to say nothing of every citizen, at least by face, if not by name. He walked, every day, every night, from one end of the city to the other, from the haunted walls in the north to the riverside bluffs in the south, in the hopes that it might help him feel less useless.

Rarely did it make much of a difference.

Toletum was large by Iberian standards, but walking it end to end was like walking from the Forum to the Campus Martius at home, only a section of the larger city. Some days, Toletum's walls felt like they were closing in on him in reproach for his failure to dispel the Lusetani. *'I was sent south to learn what was happening here,'* he thought, glaring at the western wall with the rising sun already baking his back. *'And I suppose I've done that . . . But what sort of Aventan commander lets himself be net-ted like a hind bayed in by hounds?'*

He raised both hands to the back of his neck, then scrubbed them through his gingery hair—too long, but standards did slip under siege. He knew, really, that this was no fault of his, that no Aventan legion could have entered this realm prepared for what the Lusetani had un-leashed. But he was Gaius Vitellius, son of an ancient patrician family, and he had his pride. He should have known better. Should have figured *something* out by now, some escape or stratagem.

"Vitellius!"

At Mennenius's shout, Vitellius broke into a panicked run. The *ak-draugi* usually attacked at dusk or in the night, but they had come in full daylight before. Vitellius suspected the Lusetani magic-men knew how much more easily terrors could creep into the human heart in the dead of night and typically pressed that psychic advantage—but they released the *akdraugi* even under the brightest sun, too, just to prove that they could, that daylight was no safeguard against the demons.

But as he drew nearer, he saw that Mennenius's face was not alarmed, but grinning broadly. He had something in each hand—scrolls.

"Vitellius! We've had birds—They came up over the south wall—"

Eyes wide with a hope he dared not voice, Vitellius grabbed for the scrolls. His heart leapt to see a seal that he recognized: a falcon in flight rendered in black wax, the seal of Sempronius Tarren, from whom he had received correspondence the previous year. "Dear sweet Mercury," he exhaled as he tore the seal open and unfurled the scroll as rapidly as he could, "let this message be what we need to hear."

The letter was short, and though it was not quite in code, it was terse enough to have likely stymied any Truscan-reading foes, should it have fallen into their hands.

"VIII, X, XIV N. Fenced by *lemures*. Lady H well. Be alert. V. Semp."

A half-strangled laugh escaped Vitellius. "They're here." He closed his eyes, whispering prayers of thanks to Mars and Mercury and Jupiter, all together. "The gods have smiled on us at last, Mennenius. Sempronius Tarren is here with three legions—and our own Eighth is among them. Where's Bartasco?"

"Here, Tribune." The Iberian had also come running at Mennenius's shout.

Vitellius grasped Bartasco's shoulder. "I told you they would come. I told you Aven would not abandon us. And—" He showed the letter to Bartasco, even though he knew the man could not read Truscan script. "Your wife is with our general. She's well!"

Bartasco's hand landed heavily on Vitellius's shoulder in return, and tears sprang to the man's eyes. "Thank the gods," he breathed, sagging with gratitude.

Vitellius's breath was coming hard with excitement—with the sense that *now,* finally, their stalemate might be broken. He tore open the second letter, in case it had different tidings, but found an identical message. Sempronius was no fool: of course he would have sent more than one bird, in case one didn't make it. But *two* had gotten through. Heartening, that.

"He says they're fenced in by *lemures.* He must mean the *akdraugi*." He looked to Mennenius. "The birds came from the south?" Mennenius nodded. Vitellius bit his lower lip, thinking. "He doesn't mention the Fourth out of Gades. And that 'N'—he must mean they've approached from the north. But managed to dispatch a message from the south . . . We might be able to send a message back. If they used an Air mage—the bird might know to find her master again."

He looked at the pigeon's suspiciously intelligent face. Not one of the fat birds common to the streets of Aven, thieving scraps and waddling their way through life. This bird was lean and keen, its beady eyes focused intently on Vitellius. *'Creepy,'* he thought, *'but useful.'*

"Mennenius, get the packet of letters in my room, quick. We'll divide them between the birds, just in case, but if we're fast enough, they might be able to travel the same route of safety they took to get to us."

◇◇◇◇◇◇◇◇◇◇◇◇◇

As they had on the march south from Segontia, the *akdraugi* hit the assembled men like fog rolling over a riverbank. At first only a gray haze, they coalesced into phantasmal shapes—not human, never fully distinct from one another, never holding the same form for very long. "Hold lines!" Sempronius Tarren bellowed, and the centurions echoed the order.

All around him, fear began to take over his men: controlled fear, disciplined soldiers that they were, but fear nonetheless. Pallid cheeks, trembling hands, bewildered eyes. The *akdraugi* could not harm them directly, at least not in such ways as soldiers typically understood harm. But Sempronius could see the effect that the spirits had on their resolve, their courage, their very souls.

Sempronius shared their apprehension, but he felt no gut-chilling fear. What he felt was more like . . . desire. The Shadow of his nature ached, like calling to like.

The focale around his throat burned, like hot sunlight on his neck, searing through the compulsion. No longer the gentle tingle he had felt at his first encounter with the fiends; here, so close to the Lusetani magic-men, it had to work harder to counter the *akdraugi's* effect.

The even beat of the legionaries' footsteps faltered; the rhythmic clank of swords and armor turned gradually more cacophonous. Men were staggering, the neat and practiced rows softening into an amorphous mob. *'We may not have to feign much of the chaos of our retreat . . .'* Sempronius thought.

The occasional pained groan, utterly human and in stark contrast to the wailing of the *akdraugi*, began to join in wretched harmony with the other noises of the march. Some of the men were doubling over, clutching their heads; a few had wrenched their helmets off and were rubbing furiously at their ears. Sempronius could only wonder at their agony; he felt still the draw of the *akdraugi*, the chill of their presence on his limbs, but the nigh-searing warmth of the focale around his neck continued to stave off the worst of the effects.

"Enough."

With luck, the feint had held the Lusetani's attention sufficiently to allow Hanath and her riders safe passage. Sempronius could no longer force his men to endure torment, and he did not want to risk giving the Lusetani warriors enough time to cross the forest to them.

He whistled the command to break off the forward march and hoped that Hanath and good news would meet him back at the camp.

XX

STABIAE

In the days that followed their ordeal in the wheat field, Latona braced herself for more of the same. But there was nothing. Even the *umbrae* she and Vibia had spent so much time unbinding seemed to have disappeared. Aula had gone on her usual rounds of gossip and heard nothing, either in the marketplace or in other ladies' receiving rooms. Merula had done the same among Stabiae's public slaves, the dockworkers, and the laborers bringing goods to the market. No one reported any more trouble.

Not that Latona was sorry for it, but the sudden shift set her ill at ease. Her mind refused to settle to reading or weaving. Every time she heard a door open or close, she was sure it was someone coming to summon their help—but it never was. She asked Alhena, too frequently, if Proserpina had granted her visions of anything explaining the sudden vacuity of trouble, but Alhena only shook her head.

By the fifth day before the Kalends of Sextilis, she was nearly frantic with anxious energy—so much so that Vibia had chased her out of her own villa. "You're driving me mad with your pacing and fretting," the other woman had snapped. "If you can't sit still like a civilized woman, then go do *something* with that overactive girl of yours until you've exerted these nerves out of yourself."

So Latona went, down to the beach beneath the Vitellian villa. While Merula raced sprints up and down the wet sand, Latona walked, thoughts in tumult, with cerulean waters lapping at her toes. No gown trailed in the surf today; she had put on one of her bathing costumes, fabric wrapped firmly around her breasts and wound about her hips, leaving exposed a great deal more skin than would be appropriate anywhere except a beach or a gymnasium. The fashion was still relatively new: Aula had embraced it immediately, but Alhena still preferred a short, belted shift at the seaside. Latona hadn't been sure, at first, ever wary of being seen as too racy, but the sensation of sunlight on nearly every inch of her body was too delicious to pass up. The warmth restored her more than any amount of pacing inside the villa had done.

'I will need that,' she thought, as Merula bounded past her, heels kicking up a spray of sand. *'This is not over. Whatever was going on here, it's not done.'* Latona didn't have Alhena's precognition, but something of her Spirit had tangled with the Fracture magic, and that resonance continued to thrum a low warning in her heart. *'It's not over, and my gods are not done with me.'* She just wished they would be more forthcoming with their expectations. *'How in mercy's name am I supposed to live up to their plans if I can't figure out what it is they want?'*

Juno was everywhere. She governed so many aspects of Aventan life, especially for its women. She was in the triclinium and the bedchamber, the nursery and the kitchen. Here on the shore, with sea foam clinging to her ankles and eagerness for action heating her blood, it was Venus she called out for in her mind. *'Lady Venus, make me strong enough for whatever will come.'*

Fire came in so many forms. The flame that forged iron into a sword— or a shield. The quiet hearth, the raging blaze, the flickering ember. But it lived inside people, too, in the spark of inspiration, the flair of creativity, and, more literally, in the blood that fueled the limbs. *'Make me stalwart, make me unflinching, make of me a shield against the troubles that plague my people.'*

She felt the goddess's hands on her, every time she used her magic, but Latona had never known what it was to hear the deity's voice—neither Venus's nor Juno's. She ground the ball of one foot into the sand, feeling it squelch, until her toe came into contact with a buried shell. Sighing, Latona looked up, across the waters. The sun was falling, and its scattered light set a glossy sheen on the softly bobbing waves. Every so often, the water would sparkle as though dripping diamonds, as swiftly there as gone.

'I will follow a path, if you can show one to me. Or, I can keep blundering about blindly and hope that I careen into the correct course of action.' Latona's lips twisted at the corner. *'But I don't think that method is working out quite so well as we might wish.'*

She looked down at her feet, where white foam frothed around her ankles. Somewhere above her, a gull cawed. Somewhere behind her, the Discordians plotted. And somewhere far across the water, hundreds of miles across the Middle Sea, her lover tried to rescue her brother from doom and defend Aven's interests against an onslaught.

'What a tangle.'

◇◇◇◇◇◇◇◇◇◇◇◇◇◇

When Latona returned to the villa, she found herself in the mood to ex-
periment. Aulus was out on business, Aula had gone to the market and
Alhena to the temple, and Vibia had, according to her attendant, gone to
bed with a headache, complaining of the stifling heat. Latona had the
garden to herself. She settled down between wilting hyacinths and nar-
cissi, with a small bronze lamp, ornamented with leaping dolphins, on
the table beside her couch.

The first thing every Fire mage learned was how to bank a flame. A
safety precaution, more than anything else. Then came more detailed
work: controlling a flame's size or its heat. Many mages learned how to
charm a hypocaust system to hold a desirable warmth, or an oven.

Latona thought she could do more, though she wasn't positive to what
end. For the past year, ever since Dictator Ocella's death invited her to
loosen her strangling grip on her powers, fires had been particularly re-
sponsive to her—alarmingly so, in some cases. She was becoming more
aware of the connection, and some days felt as though the flames were
calling out to her, asking her to come play.

A dangerous prospect, perhaps. But enticing.

Latona's fingers curled and pulled as though molding clay. The physical motion had no actual effect on the fire, and of course she kept far
enough away not to burn herself, but Latona felt the action helped her to
focus her mental energies. She took the leaping, flickering wisps and
curled them first one direction, cupping them toward her hand, then
pushed them out the other way. Again and again, undulating like a wave.
Then she pulled her fingers back, folding them into her lap, spinning her
magic with her mind alone.

A tingling warmth spread over Latona's skin, but in pleasure, not
warning. As she nudged the flame into different shapes, the ever-tense
muscles in her shoulders and back seemed to ease. A sense of rightness
flowed in her blood. It called to mind the golden bliss she had felt in Sempronius's arms, with all the gifts of Venus breathing in her. The memory
brought a warm blush to her cheeks, and the flames burned brighter, but
did not lose their carefully managed shape.

'I should weave,' she thought, 'with this power dancing through me.'

Before she could get up to move to her loom, however, Aula came into
the garden with more than her usual bustle. "Juno's mercy, where have
you been?"

Latona blinked in confusion. "Here." She wasn't sure for how long, but she was certain she'd returned to the villa before Aula had. "Where else were you looking?" Frowning, she channeled her magic back in the proper direction. She'd had a decent spiral going before Aula's interruption, but distraction had caused the shape to falter. The world would not always provide her with peaceful sanctuary. She had to learn not to lose control even if chaos burst around her.

"Well, you weren't in your room *or* the bath *or* the sitting room, and all Vibia would say is that you were being 'supremely irritating' and so she sent you away."

Latona rubbed her thumb against the tips of her first two fingers, thinking of the flame like a bit of wool that needed threading. A gentle twist, slow and easy, so as not to pull it apart. "Yes, I'm afraid I was getting on her nerves. So I went for a walk."

"Well, you should've *told* someone." Aula did not, as Latona expected, fling herself onto a chaise. Instead, she paced alongside Latona's couch, hands on her hips. "You get into quite enough trouble without disappearing without a word."

"I told Helva," Latona said lightly. "Did you ask her?"

"Well, *no*, and I couldn't find Merula, either."

"She wanted more exercise, so I told her to do as she pleased until dinner. She's probably wrestling with the stable boys."

"You encourage that?" Aula asked, aghast. "What if someone gets hurt?"

"Merula will be fine, I'm sure."

"Of course she will, I'm worried about the stable boys."

Latona snorted softly. Then, she smiled; she had re-established the gently swirling spiral, even through conversation. "Aula, come look at this."

A rustle of fabric as Aula came near, leaning toward the table. A moment of silence, then: "Latona, that's beautiful." Aula's voice was softer than usual, holding a hint of awe. "How are you doing that? Well, I mean, obviously with your magic, but—"

"Rubellia showed me some tricks before we left Aven." Latona gave her finger a slow twirl, and the helix of flame spun in place. Then she released the energy, and with a slight *whuff*, the flame sank back into its natural form. Latona's back fell against her cushions, and she rubbed at the center of her forehead. "I can't hold it very long yet, but I'm making progress."

"I should say." Aula laughed. "Keep this up, and you can perform feats of spectacle during the public games."

Latona rolled her eyes. Some mages did perform during the games, but they were usually gladiators and illusionists—rarely women, and never patricians. "So what had you all a-froth to find me?"

"The games, actually. Or, rather, our need to go to them."

Latona quirked an eyebrow. Many of those who had left Aven for the summer would return for the Ludi Athaeci, held at the Ides of Sextilis. Latona had not intended to do so unless Herennius forced the matter, however—but then, she had also thought that the Discordian troubles would still be keeping her busy. "Does Father intend that we do so?"

"He said something about it, yes," Aula said, finally settling down next to Latona, the sky-blue linen of her gown poofing out around her. "I think we should go, and not return to Stabiae for the rest of the summer."

More concerning and confusing. "You really want to stay in the city, as hot as it's been?"

Aula gave her a wry smile. "Well, it means we'd be in the city for your birthday, for one thing." Her expression rapidly turned serious again. "But no, I've been thinking about it, and I believe we must." At the sound of footsteps, both women looked up. Vibia had come down into the garden. "Oh, good," Aula said, and actually seemed to mean it. "You should hear this, too."

Vibia's brow creased. "Hear what?"

"She thinks we should go back to Aven before the Ludi Athaeci," Latona said, "and stay there."

Vibia was quiet, considering, a moment. "I don't know that we've finished what we meant to do here," she said at last, "but I don't know that we haven't, either. Things have gone so quiet, but—"

"That's what concerns me," Aula broke in. Vibia scowled at the interruption, but Aula, either unnoticing or uncaring, barreled on. "The general assumption in Stabiae is that the trouble—all of it, fiends and hauntings and spoiled grain and all—was caused by some young miscreants, or else some mage who didn't yet know his power." She flicked her eyes meaningfully to Vibia. "You felt its power. Do you believe it to be the work of an inexperienced or foolish mage?"

Vibia shook her head, dark curls bobbing. "Certainly not. Everything we encountered here was not only intentional, but malicious."

"So why have they stopped?" Aula shrugged theatrically. "You didn't catch them. We'd have heard if anyone else had. Logic dictates, then, that they haven't *stopped*."

"You think they've moved." Latona passed a hand over her brow. "Back to Aven." She remembered the words the fiend had spoken through Vibia: *'What life there is in cities. In your city.'*

"Wouldn't you?" Aula asked. "Imagine yourself a devotee of Discordia, sworn to create strife and hostility. We're about to enter the last third of the year."

"The elections," Latona breathed. "You think they mean to interfere?"

"I don't know. But it seems a possible explanation for why activity here has suddenly ceased."

Latona pulled her hair over her shoulder and began combing through it with her fingers. "You may be right . . . But, oh, if we left here only for the madness to start up again . . ."

"We could always come back, after the games, if needed," Vibia said.

"How would we know if we needed to?" Latona countered.

"Someone would write us," Aula said. "I'll leave word with the villa staff." She leaned in, speaking not so softly that Vibia could not hear, but words clearly intended for Latona alone. "And you can't keep on like this in any case, my darling. We've been lucky to have Father so distracted with his work, but sooner or later, he's going to notice you disappearing at odd hours. Or someone will tell him. And your husband—" She could not seem to frame suitable words regarding Herennius, instead pulling a face that spoke volumes.

Latona diverted the consideration. "Taius Mella must be missing you," she said to Vibia, hoping the pang of envy stayed out of her voice.

Vibia's thin lips gave the hint of a smile. "And I him, to be sure." She gave a little cough. "It will also be easier to receive news from my brother in Aven."

Latona nodded. Though messages sent with an Air mage's birds traveled faster than those going by boat, Sempronius's packets went directly to Aven and had to be dispersed from there; he could not spare a second bird to flap about all of Truscum seeking out other recipients. Vibia had sent her reply to Sempronius by way of his clerk, Djadi, in the city—as had Latona, little though Vibia knew of it. If Djadi had received letters in return, they had not yet made their way down the Via Appia to Stabiae.

Latona curled a lock of hair around her middle finger and gave it a tug. She did not want to doubt her sister's analysis of the situation, but she feared to leave a job half done. Still, in Aven it would be easier to seek counsel from other mages—Ama Rubellia, or Marcia Tullia. *'And if Aula's right, if the Discordians are moving in Aven, we will be needed there even more than here.'* Aven, with so many people crowded together, so many potential points of friction, would be so much more susceptible to a Discordian's manipulation. They had gotten a taste of that the previous year, but the idea of a concentrated attack filled Latona with horror.

She released her hair and gave a tight nod. "Very well. Home for the games. And then . . . then we'll see."

XXI

They were still, perhaps, a day or so from Hispalis, or so the scouts claimed. Rabirus sighed, pawing through his trunk at the end of another interminable day, searching for a long-sleeved tunic. Intolerable as the heat was, his arms could take no more abuse. Between the biting flies that seemed to prefer his flesh to any legionary's and the relentless sun baking his flesh, his skin felt pocked and peeling all over. The lid of the trunk rattled when he slammed it shut. "Misery . . ." he muttered. That was what he'd had, since leaving Aven. Different breeds of misery.

Once he had changed into a fresh tunic, Rabirus opened the flaps of his tent. Only a moment later, the lanky senior tribune of the Fourth Legion entered, saluted, and awaited Rabirus's acknowledgment. Rabirus was not too swift with it; it was always best that military inferiors believed you had matters of great consequence on your mind, so Rabirus shifted a few papers on his desk before saying, "At ease, tribune."

"Sir."

The man in question was Cominius Pavo, the son of one of Dictator Ocella's advisers. The elder Cominius had not kept himself in favor, and Ocella had eventually had him executed, but the younger members of the family had been obsequious enough to spare themselves. Cominius Pavo had served his first campaign in Phrygia and earned a reputation as a dependable officer. Rabirus hoped that dependability would translate into loyalty. "What news?"

"Letters from Corduba, sir," Pavo said. Then his throat worked. "And, ah, from Praetor Sempronius."

Rabirus scowled. He'd had a spate of messages waiting for him when he arrived in Gades. All were addressed to him, not to Governor Fimbrianus, even though Sempronius knew damn good and well that Rabirus had not left Aven until spring. An irritating, presumptuous reproach. Each one indicated that a copy had been sent to the Senate in Aven as well, and most of it was damned tedious. Since entering Iberia, Sempronius had detailed every troop movement and skirmish in exacting specification—or so it was meant to seem. Rabirus suspected embellishment. Surely the Eighth, Tenth, and Fourteenth legions had not been so beleaguered as their general claimed.

"Tell me, then," Rabirus said, waving a hand irritably as he settled himself into his chair. "But don't read the damn thing out loud. My head aches already without having to suffer through General Sempronius's overblown rhetoric."

Pavo nodded, broke the seal on the letter, and scanned it a moment before speaking. "He wishes to advise you—and the Senate—of the magical situation, as it seems to stand, with the Iberians."

Rabirus sat forward in spite of himself; he had felt sure the rumors of dark blood magic were exaggerations, fabrications that the Vitellian boy had spun in order to support the Senate's move toward war. What he had heard in Gades, though, had him wondering what the truth was. Not that he thought truth was what he was likely to hear from Sempronius Tarren.

"He . . . he says he has encountered the Lusetani and their allies in battle several times since the start of summer. His progress from Tarraco to Segontia went reasonably well, but from Segontia to Toletum, his legions were slowed by . . . strange and mystical encounters." Pavo's face expressed a minor war of its own, not sure whether to believe the words he spoke. "The Lusetani are summoning spirits, similar to what we would call *lemures*. They have what he describes as a draining effect on the troops. A mist descends that muddles their minds and saps them of strength."

That followed the stories that Fimbrianus had told him back in Gades, but Rabirus gave no physical sign of acknowledgment. "What else?"

Pavo's eyes skipped down the paper. "There's a great deal of detail on the spirits, sir. You may wish to see for yourself . . ." But at Rabirus's pointedly unmoved expression, Pavo cleared his throat and continued. "He has made his way within a few miles of Toletum, but cannot reach the city. The barbarians—mostly Lusetani, he says, though some Vettoni are filling out their ranks as well—have effectively blocked the only land approach."

Rabirus's lip curled. "Then he's not the military man he claims to be. The fool should have the capacity to break a siege, particularly one engaged by barbarians who hardly know what to do with a wall when they encounter it."

"He . . . acknowledges that." The tribune's eyebrows furrowed. "He details two main difficulties: the infrequency of communication with the garrison in Toletum, and further magical interference."

An inelegant snort escaped Rabirus. "Likely story. Blame his incompetence on barbarian magic."

"Something about their magic is hindering their approach. He has men working on finding a way to break it, he says, and scouts looking for an alternate approach. They used an Air mage to get a single message in and out of the city, but apparently there was some risk in doing so, and he cannot venture the birds regularly. He suggests that if we were to make our way to Toletum, we might be of assistance in approaching from across the river . . ." Seeing the expression clouding Rabirus's face, Pavo trailed off.

"What news from Corduba?" Rabirus asked. Corduba was the largest inland settlement in Baelonia, another six days' travel upriver. A mining town, with as muddled a population as every other settlement of notable size in Iberia. *'Weakness on the Tyrians' part,'* he thought, *'not to have held themselves aloof from the locals. And further weakness on the Aventan traders who followed.'*

Pavo shuffled the papers. "They beg for aid, sir, from their praetor. They are not besieged, like Toletum, but they are raided. Their workers are kidnapped as they go to the lead mines and stone quarries. The city council fears that the Lusetani are selling them as slaves, to their allies in the north and west."

A troubling proposition, if any of those kidnapped were Aventans. If the captives were taken to the port town of Olissippo at the mouth of the Tagus, there was no telling where they might end up. The traders there had contacts all across the Middle Sea, and even northward to the western coast of Armorica and the wild isles beyond. What the Iberians did with their own people was their own business, but if they had dared to trade in Aventan flesh, that insult could not go unanswered—little though Rabirus wanted to be responsible for answering it.

The young tribune still hovering in front of him cleared his throat. "Sir, if I may . . . I would not want this to be taken as criticism of your strategy, merely as my duty to keep you informed of the mood and inclination of your troops."

Instinctively, Rabirus's eyes narrowed. Plucky initiative was not a characteristic he valued in a military subordinate. "Go on," he said, with ice enough in his voice to counter the insufferable Iberian heat.

Pavo either didn't notice or was determined enough to sally on anyway. "I am confident in your strategy to remain south of Praetor Sempronius's fight," he said. "With so many unknown variables, particularly.

Until we know more, better to keep our distance and not endanger any more legions in what may be folly."

Rabirus stared. "What a keen military mind you have, tribune," he drawled. He was beginning to re-evaluate his hopes for the young man. What sort of tribune thought his senior officer needed *his* approval?

"Corduba, though, may have given us an advantageous opening," Pavo went on, undeterred by Rabirus's cool demeanor. "The men are eager for a fight. The men of the Fourth, mostly, more than any others. They feel the loss of their missing cohort. The prefect of the Fourth . . . Well, he's not a man with your wisdom, sir. All he knows is that his men are fighting, somewhere, and he's not a part of it. The rest of the legion takes their cue from him, you know. They would all rather be fighting. It is, after all, their job."

"Their job," Rabirus interjected, "is to obey my orders."

"Indeed, sir, of course," Pavo said, his cheeks coloring. "All I mean to say is . . . They would be grateful, sir, for orders that took them into battle. I think they'd like to feel of use. Clearing out the bandits from around Corduba, redeeming some citizens from captivity—well, that would be just the thing, sir. Without involving them in the Cantabrian campaign."

"As it happens," Rabirus said, "I had intended to check in with our friends in Corduba, after we reached Hispalis. That they have sent a message merely expedites matters." He forced himself to smile. "I'm glad your instincts are so well-honed, tribune."

Pavo's face twitched with uncertainty, but he nodded. "Shall I make your intentions known to the prefects, sir?"

"No. There's no need for them to look so many days down the line." Rabirus wagged an admonishing finger in Pavo's direction. "And you shouldn't let them bully you into giving up the information. Your subordinates will trust in strength. If you scurry to answer their whims, they will not respect you." He lifted his chin. "We'll inform them once we've reached Hispalis. And then, yes. Let us find someone for them to fight."

∞∞∞∞∞∞∞∞∞∞∞

CAMP OF LEGIO X EQUESTRIS, NEAR TOLETUM

"In any other situation," Sempronius said, rubbing at his forehead irritably, "this would be the end of the siege. We have the enemy pinned between town walls and an advancing army. Our forces far outnumber theirs. And yet we cannot touch them."

Neither Felix, standing to his right, nor Corvinus, on his left, had anything to say. They had, as Quintilis waned into Sextilis, tried any number of stratagems, coordinating attacks between the three prongs of their force. Nothing had worked. One legion could advance, but another would have to retreat. Thus far, Sempronius had been correct, that the Lusetani magic-men could not field enough of their fiends to counter all three components of the Aventan forces at once. They were agile in their deployments, however, capable of shifting focus once their opponents were sufficiently overcome by perfidious magic, so that no legion could gain enough of a sustained advantage to press on through the forest.

It was small comfort that it seemed the only power capable of breaking the famous discipline of the Aventan legions was a phalanx of unholy spirits dredged from the netherworld.

Sempronius had faced magic in battle before. The Numidians used drums to invoke the warrior spirit into their armies, and the strongest of their mages could summon sandstorms, ideal for driving off a foe or covering a retreat. But such measures were temporary, and could be overcome. Too, Sempronius had read every military history there was to read in the libraries of Aven. He knew the stories of magic used in battle by cultures whose magic was governed differently than the elements used by the Aventans, Athaecans, and Tyrians. The enchanted arrows of the Scythians, the bard-mages of the Tennic tribes, the fearsome sorcerers of Parthia, all had their catalog. Yet even in those, there was nothing like this—nothing to halt an army in its tracks through spiritual force alone.

To be mired in unseen mud, unable to advance . . .

'*Maddening.*' Sempronius had never before encountered a problem that neither his mind nor his magic could find an answer to. '*And I haven't yet,*' he thought, setting his jaw stubbornly. '*Just because I haven't found the answer as of this morning doesn't mean I never will.*'

The most recent packet of letters from Aven had included one from the Lady Latona. Two, in fact; one was for her brother, should they ever reach the poor soul, but Sempronius was reluctant to risk sending Eustix's birds across the Lusetani lines.

Latona's words had been carefully chosen, as always, nothing that might get either of them in trouble were the missive intercepted. Sempronius's Shadow magic could feel certain threads in them: the fear of discovery, the deceit of not saying quite what she meant, the mingling of frustrated hopes and painful worry. Modestly she accepted his praise for the magic in the focale she had woven; effusively she wrote all she could tell him of the protective effects of Fire magic. It had confirmed his guesses, in part, and given him some nuance to talk over with the sole Fire-forger attached to the Tenth Legion. The man was no weaver, of course, but he was going to try crafting some amulets. Sempronius had written to the magistrates of the coastal cities, too, to see if there were any Fire mages among their citizenry with the talent to do as Latona had done.

'I hope, yet I doubt.' Latona was extraordinary, more powerful than she knew. A less gifted mage might be able to re-create her efforts, with enough time, but time was a resource running ever shorter.

The letter had also turned his mind toward the one thing left he hadn't tried. Had feared to try, if he were to be honest with himself. Summoning his gods-given gifts inside the commander's tent veered too close to the edge of perhaps the one prohibition he had never yet flouted, the decree of Mars separating the affairs of war from those of magic. His whole life, Sempronius had defied man's law. Defying a god—and one whose favor he needed—was another matter.

'But would this flout Mars's will? He commands there be no magic on the field of battle, and here, now, no such fight is engaged.'

He thought on it a long while, as he, Felix, and Corvinus watched the sun dip low, drenching the sky in bloody red light. Then, at last, he made up his mind. Boldness had ever been his friend.

"Felix," Sempronius said, "go and see if there are any new messages from the other two camps, if you would."

"Sir." Felix jogged off after a perfunctory salute.

After he was out of earshot, Sempronius said to Corvinus, "Bring a bowl of water to my tent—the darkest bowl you can put your hands on." Corvinus nodded, understanding. "And inform the guards that no one is to be allowed in or even near my tent. Tell them—tell them I am seeking counsel of the gods." It wasn't, strictly speaking, untrue. "I must not be disturbed, even at direst need, short of the Lusetani launching an assault on our ramparts. Anything less than that, they must take to Felix."

"At once, Dominus."

∞∞∞∞∞∞∞∞∞∞∞

Sempronius stared down at the surface of the water. Corvinus had brought him a clay bowl painted black on the inside, making the liquid within as dark as possible. Still, he yearned for the flawless surface of his favorite tool, the obsidian mirror nestled in the base of a trunk back in his home in Aven. That was far too precious to risk on campaign, so he had to make do. Shadow was stronger in him than Water, but the talent for scrying was still in him—if more a challenge to access, without his preferred instrument.

A stiff breeze rustled his tent, brushing the fabric against the dusty earth. Beyond that, the muffled noises of the camp, laughter and grumbling and the clank of armor. Sempronius ignored it all. Dulling his senses did not come easily, not to a man so primed to notice the world around him and assess threats and opportunities alike, but slowly, he framed his mind to the purpose. The ambient sounds of the camp faded away. So too did the oppressive heat of the night, the humid air plastering his tunic to his skin, the flicker of the only lamp left lit.

"I call upon Pluto, Lord of the Underworld; I call upon Nox, Lady of Night; I call upon Neptune, Master of the Seas; I call upon Lympha, Reader of Souls." He whispered his invocations, refusing to allow any hint of trepidation to enter his voice. However strange it felt, calling upon them in such circumstances, he had to steel himself to the task, or the gods would not heed his call. "Governors of Shadow and of Water, I, Vibius Sempronius Tarren, entreat you. Look here, gods; look here and answer me."

Slowly, the magic rolled to him, out of the dark corners of his tent, up from the bowl of water before him. In it, Sempronius felt the touch of the gods' hands, the weight upon his shoulders that had been with him since childhood. He knew what they wanted of him: to protect their people, their nation of Aven, and to put it on the course to a glorious destiny. So they had showed him before, many times, and one such vision had led him to Iberia. As they had shown him the way before, he had faith they would do so again.

"I am stymied," he confessed. "I seek guidance, if I am to do your will in this land. Gods who have blessed me, show me the path I must take."

The surface of the water rippled, as though it had been struck by a pebble. Then it clouded over, growing milky-white in delicate whorls. The gods were listening—but for long moments, it seemed as though they had nothing they wished to say. The very idea tightened Sempronius's breath inside his chest. Frustration? Or panic? He didn't care to examine the feeling too closely; he far preferred to push through it toward more productive energy.

"*Please*, blessed lords and ladies," he said. "My soul is yours to command. I seek to satisfy your will in all things. My life is bent to your desire. But against these fiends, I know not what power to call. Mars forbids our magic against theirs. Swords and shields are of no use." He worked his jaw a moment. "If I cannot defeat them, then Aven's glory dies here, in the Iberian dust. Our enemies will scent our blood and attack. Our allies will think us a painted banner with no strength behind it. Show me the way out of this net, and I swear to you, I shall make Aven the center of a federation of nations such as the world has never seen."

It was the Aventan way: to implore the gods, but to remind them, too, what use you were to them.

Sempronius hardly dared to breathe as the swirling mist on the surface of the water continued to shift and flow. The gods were listening; he *knew* it, he could feel their presence with him, their gaze like a hot sun on the back of his neck. Why would they watch and listen and yet deny him the advantage that knowledge would provide? '*Am I being tested? Have I something left to prove to them?*'

When the clouds on the surface of the water began to coalesce into an image, Sempronius's shoulders sagged with relief. He bent closer to the bowl, eager to inspect the divine message.

Yet instead of the usual flurry of images cascading upon each other, only one would present itself. A spear, with blood on the tip.

Sempronius stared at it, waiting patiently in case another message should come. Stubbornly, only the spear remained, glistening on the surface of the water. A spear, and nothing else. No background to give him a sense of time or place. No hands holding it. No wound made by it. Nothing else to lead him to a path. Just a spear.

A spear of Numidian design, Sempronius realized.

He sat up, spine straight, with a shock of realization. "Lady Hanath."

But why? He had included the formidable woman on his war councils, had taken her advice, had listened to all the information she could provide about the Lusetanian magic. '*What am I missing? If she is the key to this, somehow . . . then what shape is the lock?*'

XXII

Latona would have appreciated more time to re-acclimate herself to the city—and to her husband—before making a public appearance, but the night after the Vitelliae returned to Aven, she received an invitation to a dinner party thrown by Galerius Orator and his wife Marcia Tullia. Herennius accepted for them both before Latona even knew about it. *'Perhaps just to prove to anyone in town that his wife has not, in fact, abandoned him,'* she thought as Merula plaited her hair into a coronet. A simple style for a formal dinner, but it was too hot to contemplate letting her curtain of hair hang down her back. She pulled a few tendrils out to frame her face.

When she joined Herennius in the atrium, he looked her up and down, frowning. "Is that new?"

Latona had chosen a soft, grassy green gown and a contrasting currant-colored mantle for the occasion. In deference to the heat, she was wearing the lightest-weight sleeveless tunic she owned and had draped her gown loosely over her curves. "It is," she said. "I had it commissioned before I went to Stabiae, and it was delivered in my absence." When Herennius continued to glower at her, she added, "It wasn't costly, if that's what you're worried about."

"It's a bit . . . daring. Don't you think?"

"Everyone's fashion turns daring when the heat rises," Latona quipped. Herennius himself was in a short-sleeved tunic of a similar color to her mantle, which Latona found unexpectedly irritating, and a loosely wrapped orange cenatoria instead of a formal toga.

"Galerius has invited moderates as well as Popularists tonight, you know," Herennius added.

"I'm sure we all feel summer's burden the same, no matter our politics." Latona gestured to the door. "Shall we?"

The receiving line at the Galerian domus was not long, and they were soon inside, where Latona was almost weak-kneed with relief to see her father and sisters. Aula was in a gown of bright sky blue, with her mantle closer to sapphire and her gown even more loosely belted than Latona's.

Alhena was in lavender, modestly tucked and folded despite the clinging heat. "Latona! There you are. How lovely all my girls look!" Aulus proclaimed, kissing her cheek. Then he shook Herennius's hand. "I'm glad you're with us tonight, or I should be even more desperately outnumbered."

"Another reason to look forward to the war ending, sir," Herennius said. "Your son will be able to help us match things up."

"Except that Gaius will need a wife once he gets back," Aula tossed back, grinning. "And, Father, if you'd like any suggestions on that front, I have had some thoughts on the matter—"

Aulus waggled a finger at her. "I'd rather hear that you were sounding out new husbands for yourself." Aula rolled her eyes theatrically, prompting Aulus to add, as if it were a concession, "Or for Alhena!"

Latona felt a surge of anxiety from her younger sister, so she clapped her hands delicately. "Shall we see who else is about?"

Aula took the hint, linking her arm through Alhena's and steering them toward the garden. "Leave us to our gossip, gentlemen, and go make yourselves useful debating some terribly important policy or other," she chirped over her shoulder.

Latona caught a glimpse of Herennius's scowl before they swanned off; likely he couldn't decide whether or not Aula had just delivered him a veiled insult.

"Maia Domitia should be around here somewhere," Aula went on, "speaking of husband-hunting. She thinks if she can find a suitable match before her brothers get home from Iberia, they'll just accept her choice rather than trying to influence her."

"I imagine she's right," Latona said, scanning the crowd for their friend's glossy dark hair. "Maius and Septimus just want her safely wed." Maia's first husband had been one of Ocella's victims, leaving her with two small daughters, near Lucia's age, to care for. "I doubt they'll be too particular about it—though who she thinks there is to choose from with most of the Popularists out of town, I'm not certain."

"I doubt she'd mind an older fellow, past his military service, if he offered money and comfort enough," Aula said. Out of the corner of her eye, Latona saw her sister grin. "She's not as wantonly lustful a creature as I am, after all. And a man who already has an heir secured might not mind that she comes with two daughters attached. But she might also be sounding out some fathers on their sons' behalves."

"Well, if nothing else, we should give her our support."

As Herennius had predicted, the crowd at the Galerian domus was more mixed than the Vitelliae's usual cohort of liberal-minded friends. Aula squeezed Latona's elbow, groaning. "Oh, gods, don't look now."

"I don't know why you say that, when your intention is clearly that I do so." Near one of the trellises sat a knot of Optimate wives. Willowy Memmia was wife to Arrius Buteo's ally Gratianus, while stocky Gratiana was his elder sister. With them was Glaucanis, pale as milk and prettily rounded, the wife of Lucretius Rabirus. Seeing them, Latona stifled a groan. "Juno's mercy . . ."

"I thought the advantage of Decimus Gratianus losing his bid for the consulship last year," Aula grumbled, "would be that we wouldn't have to endure him and his womenfolk on social occasions."

"Our world is too small for that," Latona said, "and evidently Galerius and Marcia are making a conciliatory effort."

"What are you two whispering about?" Alhena asked, plucking Aula's sleeve.

"Mean cats," Aula replied.

"Come on," Latona said, trying to affect a cheerful countenance. "I'm sure Marcia has more sense than to have seated any of us next to them, at the least."

◇◇◇◇◇◇◇◇◇◇◇◇

Marcia's hostessing skills were all that Latona had anticipated. Latona found herself sharing a couch with a member of the Pontifical College and Rufilius Albinicus, the famed general past his campaigning years but nonetheless full of opinions about the Iberian venture. Across the room, Aulus had been placed next to Marcia herself, no doubt a recognition of his censorial office, while Aula was between an older senator and one of this year's aediles—both men of moderate political inclinations, unlikely to provoke the sharp side of Aula's tongue. Alhena was less conspicuously placed, sitting with Crispinilla and one of the younger Fabiae daughters at a lower table. Latona silently thanked Marcia for her kindness in making that concession to Alhena's shyness.

Thanks to Marcia's careful tending of the seating chart, the meal itself passed with only pleasantries. *'The advantage to so many Popularists being out of town—and the number of Optimates who followed them—is that it leaves enough moderates left to serve as a buffer,'* Latona thought as the tables were cleared away. Some of the assembly might depart now that the meal was finished, but Marcia had arranged musical entertainment and opened plenty of amphorae of wine for those who wished to stay and mingle. A glance at her husband let Latona know that they wouldn't be going home anytime soon: Herennius was with her father, both deep in conversation with several of the men who owned immense latifundia in Umbria, those giant farms which were, in theory, subject to regulation by the censors. Aulus was no doubt giving them a piece of his mind based on his observations around Crater Bay, but Latona wondered whose side her husband would come down on. Economic interests tended to surmount ethical quandaries in his mind.

Aula darted up to her side, a goblet of wine in each hand. She passed one to Latona, taking a deep swig from the other. "Caecilia says her husband is going to stand for consul this year."

"Quintus Terentius? Truly?"

"So she says, and I expect she'd know better than anyone."

The Terentiae were an ancient family, with roots going back to the days of the kings, but many of the Optimates viewed them as unacceptably odd. They were well-traveled and had a habit of making marriages outside the usual bounds of Aventan society; Terentius's mother had some connection to the Palmyrean royal family, and other generations had married nobles from Athaecum and even Numidia. Terentius himself had chosen an Aventan bride, had two sons dutifully preparing themselves for the *cursus honorum,* and one of his daughters was a Vestal Virgin, as unimpeachably Aventan as you could get. The other, though, was Latona's friend Terentilla, an Earth mage who had been allowed to take after her patroness, the goddess Diana, and run rather wild. Openminded and, in the eyes of many, far too permissive, the Terentiae were of the Popularist faction, but Terentius had never before evinced much ladder-scaling ambition.

"Well, good," Latona said. "I was wondering who would step up for the Popularists."

Aula took another drag of her wine, glancing about the room. "I'm going to go find Maia. She was sitting next to Old Crispinia during dinner and looked to be having a merry time, so perhaps she has some amusing story to pass on. Are you coming?"

"In a moment," Latona said. "I want to look at the new frescoes Marcia had painted." She gestured at the walls lining the peristyle garden. "Rubellia saw them earlier this summer and said they're lovely."

Aula tittered. "I never thought Marcia Tullia, of all people, would succumb to modern trends in interior design." She tweaked one of Latona's curls. "All right, my honey, come find me and Maia when you're done admiring."

◇◇◇◇◇◇◇◇◇◇◇◇◇◇◇◇◇◇

Marcia's new frescoes combined the traditional narrative pictures with the new fashion for suggested architectural elements, with columns and arches giving the impression that any onlooker was watching the scene within through a window. *'Or perhaps on a stage,'* Latona thought, strolling along the colonnade at the far side of the garden, taking in the quiet elegance of the paintings. Appropriately, the scenes were those from the life of the hero Ulysses—beloved by Minerva, aided by Mercury, the gods who governed the element of Air and who had blessed both Marcia and her adolescent son. In one, Ulysses was outwitting the cyclops Polyphemus; in another, Mercury offered him the magical herb that helped him resist Circe's charms.

Latona wondered if the painter was one of the mages of the city who specialized in such artistry, a Light mage with a keen eye for color, perhaps, or an Earth or Water mage who could manipulate the subtle interplay of dyes and pigments. Certainly Marcia could afford to engage the services of one so talented.

As Latona meandered, contemplating the delicate brushstrokes in a rendering of Minerva drawing down a mist to disguise Ulysses's passage, she was halted by the sound of her own name—not called out to her, but spoken in a scandalized whisper.

"Vitellia Latona? You can't be serious."

"Now, Memmia, you *know* how little I like to speak ill of anyone, it's just that—"

"Glaucanis, you're being tedious. Spit it out, if you have something to say."

Latona halted in her steps. Memmia, Glaucanis, and Gratiana, on the other side of the trellis—obscured from her sight, and she from theirs, by the thick weft of ivy and flowers that covered the wooden structure. Talking about *her.* Latona's cheeks flushed. *'Why? What in Juno's name for?'*

"Well, you know I'm not one for gossip," Glaucanis began, in the conspiratorial tone only perfected by veteran gossips, "but everyone who was at Ocella's court knows what she got up to, even if they're all too polite to mention it now. It wasn't only her magical gifts he was interested in—though of course he put those to use as well, had her reading emotions and reporting to him if anyone was acting shifty. *Quite* the little spy."

Latona's fists clenched so hard that her nails pressed painfully into her palms. The unfairness of the accusation set a fire in her heart. The Dictator had commanded the use of her gifts that way, true—and she had given as little as she could get away with. She had spent so much effort convincing him that her powers were cripplingly weak that she had started to believe it herself.

"Anyway," Glaucanis went on, "her real talents weren't those on public display, if you take my meaning."

"Is that fair?" Memmia's voice was wavery, and Latona was absurdly grateful to her for it. "She's hardly the only one to have fallen prey to the Dictator's, uhm, unsavory proclivities."

Glaucanis, on the other hand, Latona could happily have slapped. "Oh, she wasn't prey, my lamb. Everyone thinks it's her sister who's got the ambition in the family, but mark my words, Lady Latona is the one who sets her sights the highest. And having had a taste of sitting in power's lap once, who's to say she wouldn't like to try it again?"

Latona was mildly worried her nails might've been drawing blood from her palm now, but the pain was welcome, a distraction that might keep her from losing control of her magic and setting half the room ablaze. The flicker of a dozen lamps reached for her, eager to respond to her heightened emotions, and only wrenching control over her Fire magic kept them from flaring.

'*How dare she? How dare she?*' Latona had bartered herself for Aula's safety, and Lucia's, while the blood of Aula's husband was still pooling on the floor. '*All I did, I did for them, while Glaucanis lapped up the benefits of having a husband whose hands were filthy with doing the Dictator's bidding.*' The accusation would have been insult enough coming from another woman. From Glaucanis Lucretiae, the hypocrisy was maddening.

Gratiana snorted, sounding very like her brother. "Much good may it do her to try her wiles on our current consuls. Galerius is uxorious, and Aufidius Strato wouldn't notice a naked woman in front of him unless she had battle plans painted on her tits."

"Gratiana!" Memmia squeaked in objection.

"Well! He wouldn't."

"I'm just saying she bears watching, is all," Glaucanis said, her voice falsely light. "It's not as though Galerius and Aufidius are the only men of consequence that she might set her sights on."

Latona's rage gave way to sudden fear. If Glaucanis mentioned Sempronius . . . *'No. She can't know anything. We were—'* But the thought caught in her mind like a rabbit in a snare. They *hadn't* been careful. Much though Latona tried to blame it on the Saturnalian revels or years of pent-up deprivation, she knew what choice she had made: to cast caution aside right along with her gown. *'And Sempronius made that choice too, even knowing what a scandal could cost us both.'* For him, demolition of his political aims; for her, utter ruin among society and the subsequent havoc wreaked upon her father's and brother's careers. Together, perhaps, the utter devastation of the Popularist cause, the abandonment of their shared dream of Aven-that-could-be.

At the time, it had felt not a mistake, but an imperative, a marker placed for them on a course set by the gods. *'A glory, a sublime gift of a moment.'* Harder to hold on to that feeling, separated from her partner in transgression by months and so many miles.

Tangled in that unpleasant contemplation, Latona waited to see if Glaucanis was about to link her name to Sempronius's. Surely, if anyone had a vested interest in spreading such a juicy morsel of news, it would be the wife of Sempronius's great enemy. Who else could profit so much from the discovery of Popularist imprudence and ignominy? But to her great relief, Glaucanis seemed to have nothing else to offer, for it was Memmia who spoke next.

"I still think you're being unfair. That provincial husband of hers would put her off if she really behaved as you say."

Latona held in a sigh. There was the reminder she'd been searching for, of why *she* hadn't yet put off *Herennius*. A husband, no matter how boorish, was a shield against the spear-thrust of many-tongued Rumor.

"True." Glaucanis drew out the word in a sing-song. "After all, it's not as though she's given him any children to be grateful for."

The temporary relief of finding her secret safe was replaced with the painfully blunt impact of that undeniable truth. Glaucanis might have only had one son to her name, but she had that, at least. Latona, favored one of Venus and Juno though she might be, had no children and a husband she could barely tolerate sharing a roof with. *'What a mockery.'* The multi-fold unfairness of it—unsuccessful in a marriage that she did not even want, publicly judged for that failure, barred by custom and circumstance from reaching for true happiness—roiled inside her like bile, sour and poisonous.

A wicked impulse struck Latona. She could take what she felt now—the shame, the revulsion, the mute fury—and turn it back around on the gossips. She could flood them with those negative emotions, then amplify those feelings until they wept. She could turn their own hearts against them. They would be humiliated and have no idea why.

Latona crinkled her nose, surprised at herself. *'I'm not sure what's worse, if that was my own idea or the result of some Discordian taint lingering on my soul.'*

Instead, she lifted her chin and smoothed out the soft linen folds of her gown. *'I don't need to abuse Juno's gifts to make them feel ashamed of themselves.'*

Beaming brightly, Latona took the long way around the trellis, so that they would not know she had been eavesdropping. Then she strode to the couch adjacent to theirs and dropped elegantly onto it. "Ladies," she said, "good cheer. What a fine pair of flautists Marcia's hired this evening, don't you think?" Memmia turned as red as the couch cushions, Gratiana fiddled anxiously with her earrings, and Glaucanis looked as though she had swallowed a frog. *'And if any of you choke on your shame, I shan't be sorry.'*

Latona stayed, tormenting them with pleasantly nugatory conversation, until someone else caught her eye: Salonius Decur, a member of the Augian Commission. Not one who had given her cause for concern in the past—he had never been part of Ocella's court, that she could recall, nor did he have strong family ties to any of the Dictator's creatures—and so, perhaps, he was someone she could speak to. "Do excuse me, ladies," she said, rising from the couch and trying not to give outward sign of her satisfaction at how close Memmia appeared to apoplexy. "Have such a pleasant evening."

XXIII

Alhena had officially reached the point of the evening where she stood against a wall next to some over-achieving shrubbery, not sure if she more hoped to be or not be noticed. It never took long after a social meal for this to happen. Alhena could manage perfectly well through dinner, since the seating provided her with conversational partners, but as soon as people began to mingle, she lost her tongue. She'd never managed the art of striking up an unsolicited dialogue or of gliding into a conversation and inserting herself effortlessly into the discourse. *'Why is it so easy for Aula and Latona?'* Miserably, she slouched against a pillar, wishing that at least one of the boys with wine would wander past and not mistake her for an exceptionally well-painted statue.

"Hoy, Alhena!" a cheerful voice called. A grinning Terentilla approached and shouldered her playfully. "Who're you hiding from back here?"

"I'm not hiding." Feeling awkward, Alhena smoothed out the front of her gown. "As if a girl with my hair who's taller than half the men in the room *could* hide," she grumbled.

Tilla laughed. "You do seem to have grown even since spring. Don't sound so cross about it. Fortune smiled on you! Everyone thought I'd be as tall as my stately sister, but I've stopped a bit short."

"Have you?" Alhena cocked her head. Tilla was nearly her height and far more muscular. She was wearing a plum-colored Athaecan-style gown tonight, knotted up over one shoulder and belted beneath her breasts, and her raven hair was in a simple plait that hung limply over her shoulder. "I think she just looks taller because of how she has to wear her hair." The Vestal Virgins had a traditional style, wound with cords and piled into a cone on top of their heads.

Tilla gave another bright laugh, and Alhena found herself blushing, pleased to be thought amusing by someone with as much personality as Tilla. "You know, you may be right! I'm going to tell myself so, anyway, to soothe my bruised ego. I—" She broke off, reaching out to snag two cups of wine from a passing platter. Pressing one into Alhena's hands, she resumed, "Well, *I'm* hiding from my father. He's been trying to introduce to me to young men." Tilla rolled her eyes. Alhena noticed how long and dark her eyelashes were, though she doubted Tilla used kohl or burnt cork on them as Aula did. "What a bore."

"Mine, too," Alhena said. Aulus *hadn't* made any efforts in that direction so far, not really, but it gave her something to talk about. He *would*, Alhena knew, because he'd started joking about it. "Aula's trying to hold him off for both of us until more suitable candidates return from Iberia."

"Yes, I can't say I care much for the selection available tonight." Tilla snorted into her cup. "But honestly, who would choose one at all if we didn't have to?"

Alhena blinked a few times, startled that Tilla would put it so bluntly. *'Well, if anyone would . . .'*

"I mean, men are decent enough in their ways," Tilla went on, with the air of one making a gracious allowance, "but I confess, I find it a bit hard to imagine yoking myself to one." She jostled Alhena with her shoulder again. A little of the wine sloshed out of Alhena's cup onto her fingers, and she took a quick sip to lower the level in the cup before Tilla's exuberance caused further upset. "Least you've got your sisters for examples, eh? Quinta's no use at all to me in that regard!"

"I do . . ." Alhena said, carefully. "Aula enjoyed being married, I think. As far as I remember, anyway." A bit of color came to her cheeks; she'd been too young to be privy to conversations on the advantages of wedded bliss when Aula had first wed, but she'd heard plenty enough in the years since. "But she enjoys the independence of widowhood, too." Latona, she declined to comment on; marriage had done her no favors thus far, but Alhena suspected a different choice of bridegroom might alter Latona's opinions considerably. "But you—" Alhena ducked her head. "I mean, with your magic—if you pledged yourself to Diana—" Attaching herself to a temple wouldn't get Alhena out of marital entanglements, as Proserpina demanded no celibacy from her devotees, but the acolytes of Diana were another story.

Tilla gazed up at the ceiling, wagging her head back and forth. "I could. Papa wouldn't prevent me, I'm sure." Her lips curled in a mischievous grin. "In fact, it'd be just the right sort of eccentric for our family, to have *two* daughters pledged to virgin goddesses, wouldn't it? And it's not as though he hasn't got the boys to give him grandchildren to dandle about." She rolled her shoulders. "But no. Tempting though the thought has always been, I'm afraid I'm terribly afflicted with a sense of duty to my family. So if Papa thinks it best that I wed, then wed I shall." She shrugged, as though it were merely an inconvenience. "I figure if I don't put up too much fuss, he'll be more likely to pick someone who will let me do as I please."

"It's an idea . . ." Alhena mused. Latona was transparently happier the more her husband left her to her own devices.

Tilla shifted her wine to one hand and slipped the other around Alhena's waist. "Come on," she said, those deep dark eyes sparkling with mischief. "You're too lovely to stay hidden behind a column all night, even if we don't want any courtship thrust in our direction. Maia Domitia got our lady host's permission to start up a friendly game of dice in the garden."

"Oh," Alhena said. "It's Aula that's the gambler. I don't even know how to—"

"I'll teach you!" Tilla's fingers tightened warmly around Alhena's waist, and Alhena felt then she'd agree to just about anything, if it meant staying in Tilla's company a while longer.

◇◇◇◇◇◇◇◇◇◇◇◇

"Commissioner Salonius," Latona said, approaching the portly man with her best charming smile. She could use no *actual* charm, of course; like all members of the Commission, Salonius was a mage with a highly developed talent for sensing the elements at work. *'Is he Light or Air?'* she tried to recall. Not Water, she thought, and she would've known if his talent were in Spirit. *'No matter, really.'* Whatever the origin of his blessing, if she attempted to use Spirit to influence him, he would smell it out immediately.

"Lady Latona," Salonius said, inclining his head toward her. "Well-met. You and your sisters make quite the pretty party, if you don't mind my saying."

"I don't," Latona said, "and my sister Aula would mind even less, I suspect." She deliberately used a bright tone that bordered on indulgence; men in positions of authority like his, she found, liked women who were just short of simpering. Not so insipid as to annoy, not so sharp as to threaten. A fine line, but one which Latona had learned to trace with exacting precision.

"You've been summering with your family in . . . Pompeii, is it?"

"Stabiae," Latona said. She noticed that Salonius's cup was nearing empty, and she gestured for a nearby server to refill it.

"Yes, Stabiae, that's right—Oh, very good, thank you, m'dear. Your father's doing work with the census?"

"Indeed. He's been visiting some towns in the area that had discrepancies."

"Good, good." Salonius shuffled his weight, his gaze starting to wander.

Unwilling to surrender his attention so swiftly, Latona rushed on. "Commissioner, I encountered some strange occurrences—strange *magical* occurrences—in Stabiae that I should like your opinion on." As anticipated, that snapped his focus back to her. "My sisters and I came across a gruesome display in the forest, an animal sacrifice with a malevolent feel to it, and soon thereafter—" In brisk terms, Latona outlined their discoveries of the *lemures*.

She didn't get far, though, before Salonius waved a hand. "These peasants see fiends and frights everywhere. Probably they were looking at a low crop yield, eh? And some unhappy landlords? Well, what better than to blame it on spirits?"

Latona's heart sank. *'That is not an encouraging attitude.'* Nevertheless, she tried again. "But Commissioner, I *saw* them. I visited the people who were haunted, and—"

Salonius's nose twitched. "Now then, Lady Latona, let me ask you— This farm, was it in good condition?"

"I—" Latona blinked, not sure what that had to do with anything. "Well, the first one we visited was an orchard in a very small town. I'm not an expert on such things, but it looked to be poor soil. Of course it was early summer then, and there hadn't been much rain—"

"Yes, yes." Salonius nodded, as though her words had somehow confirmed something in his mind. "If the peasants were so neglectful of their fields—"

"Orchards," Latona cut in, annoyance growing.

"Orchards, then. If they were neglectful of their duty in one regard, I mean to say, it follows that they may well be neglectful of their duties to their household gods as well." He circled his hand in front of his chest, affecting the lecturing air of a *magister*. "It's often so, you know, where there isn't a firm overseer or landlord. People get lazy, they forget to do the proper rituals."

"Commissioner, I saw no sign of—"

"Early summer, you said it was? So that would be just after the Lemuria! Well, that explains it, my dear, surely these peasants simply failed to—"

"Commissioner!" Latona said, rather louder than she had intended. "It was *Discordian* magic, I *felt* it."

That brought Salonius's pontificating to an abrupt halt.

Latona took a breath, steadying her voice. "And it was not only in one place, but in many. This was done *to* the farmers, not something they brought upon themselves."

Salonius's brow creased. "Lady Latona, I am compelled to ask how you would know to identify Discordian magic upon encountering it?"

'Damn.' Latona didn't want to draw attention to Vibia, not with how poorly the conversation was going, so she chose her words delicately. "My Spirit magic recognized its inverse. The inimical element. But I have felt the magic of Janus and Fortuna, and this . . . this was not it."

"My dear," Salonius said, with the sort of smile that parents used on small children when they were on the verge of running out of patience with juvenile antics, "don't you think it's possible you've . . . misinterpreted something? I mean, Discordian magic being practiced on some little farms around Crater Bay? What possible purpose would that serve?"

Latona could scarcely speak around the tightness in her jaw. "That is precisely what I was trying to figure out, Commissioner—what I hoped you would be able to help with."

Salonius rubbed at his brow with a sigh. "I can send someone down there to look into it, but I'm sure we'll find it's just as I've said. Was there anything else?"

Only with effort did Latona keep her face placid. Another skill she had learned in Ocella's court and longed to abandon. But she would get nothing more out of Salonius Decur, she could see that now. *'Why was I foolish enough to try?'* But it wasn't foolish. The Augian Commission was precisely who she *should* have been able to take this to. *'They are, after all, only men.'* They had men's prejudices. "No, Commissioner," she said, once she trusted her tongue to sound sweet and deferential again. "Nothing else."

Salonius's shoulders dropped almost imperceptibly. Evidently he was relieved that she was not determined to pursue the matter any further. "There, there, you mustn't feel bad about it. Even if they were just the product of poorly tended altars, no doubt the *lemures* gave you a fright. It's the heat, you know," he added, patting her shoulder paternally. "And all that sun, down there at the shore. Inflames the brain, yes. And women are so much more susceptible to such things, you really *must* take care."

Latona had to look down, under the guise of nodding in bashful agreement, so that Salonius would not see the rage in her eyes. *'I will not set Marcia's lovely sitting room on fire. I will not. Whatever the provocation . . .'* Another steadying breath, and for the second time that night, she peeled her magic away from the flames in the room. How eager they were, to dance at her command. "You're so good to be concerned, Commissioner," she said.

She didn't think he could have disappointed her any more, but then, with another condescending pat, he said, "Ah, look. Here's your husband."

◇◇◇◇◇◇◇◇◇◇◇◇◇◇◇

Salonius did not go directly home after the Galerian dinner party. He made his farewells, to his hosts and friends alike, and sauntered northward. Around him were four attendants, each bearing two torches; two walked before him, and two behind, casting a wide circle of light around their party. Instead of crossing to the east of the Subura, however, he continued straight past it to the low slope of the Quirinal Hill.

He knocked at the door of a modest domus, but one whose furnishings and artwork spoke of ancient wealth. The door-slave greeted him first with a scowl for the late hour, but his expression melted into concern when he recognized the caller. "Commissioner Salonius, sir. What brings you to—"

"I need your master. Quick." As he stepped in the door, he told his attendants, "Stay here. Remain vigilant."

Salonius paced in the receiving room, uneasy in the shadows cast by the single flickering lamp the slave had lit for him. In a moment, he was joined by a tall man dressed only in a roughspun sleeping tunic, his fair hair near as bright as the flame. He was younger than Salonius, but held himself with such dignity that it was impossible not to show him deference. Durmius Argus, a mage of Spirit and his fellow Commissioner.

"Durmius, my friend." The air hung heavy and damp, even inside the well-appointed house. "We have a problem."

XXIV

The ground to the south of the camp was soaked with blood, staining the ocher dirt a deeper shade of brown. So it would stay, until some summer storm came to wash it clean—and even then, Ekialde suspected, the earth itself would remember, in its bones, what had been done here.

Bailar had explained it all, and it made perfect sense to Ekialde. They could only summon so many *akdraugi*. This, they had known. Even with the magic-men Bailar had accumulated from the allied tribes, there was a limit on what they could safely pull across from the world of the dead. So now, with the new Aventan legions arriving and surrounding the peninsula on which Toletum stood, they had to change tactics. *Akdraugi*, more mobile and easily deployed, had been the correct choice to assault the legions in the field. And now, for the city, they had to call on a manifestation that was harder to summon, but capable of working long after the men whose lives paid for its power had bled their last. A pestilence, Bailar promised, though he confessed he did not know how it would present itself. No one had worked this magic in many generations, after all. Bailar was an innovator and a visionary.

Bailar thought this sacrifice would work better if it harnessed the power of Aventan blood, turning it against its own people. Unfortunately, Aventan prisoners were hard to come by. The legions had quickly learned to disengage from battle when the *akdraugi* raged, and when they did fight, in their tight lines, behind their shield walls, they presented little opportunity for the Lusetani to carve a few hostages away from the whole.

'*They have a coward's way of fighting,*' Ekialde thought. How was a man to earn glory and honor in such a fashion, if he could never stand apart from the throng? '*An offense to Bandue, surely. How does their own war-god stand for it?*' Yet it was, he had to admit, frustratingly effective.

With no Aventans on hand for the sacrifice, Ekialde sent instead for prisoners that the Vettoni had taken from the enemy tribes. '*They invited this death,*' Ekialde told himself. '*They are traitors. They had the opportunity to join with us, and instead chose allegiance to a foreign power and the gifts it promised them.*' Another voice in his head, which sounded a lot like Neitin's, told him that many men and women would prefer peace and wealth to war and uncertainty. That voice spoke to him less often these days; he could not allow it to seed doubt or shame. He had to be stalwart, focused. *'I am erregerra, beloved of Bandue. He blesses the course I have chosen. To doubt myself is to doubt him, and to doubt him is sacrilege.'*

Three score men and women were stripped naked, bound with rope, and flung to their knees, there in the bloodstained dirt, where others had met a similar fate to summon the *akdraugi*. Never so many at once, though. Bailar assured him the quantity was necessary. From one mass sacrifice, the magic-men would be able to call up the pestilential power more than once, if Bailar chose their days correctly. Ekialde did not understand the reasons; that was for the star-readers to ascertain. All Ekialde needed to know was what must be done, what was necessary for victory.

'What Neitin would think of this . . .'

Ekialde had not returned to the larger camp around the riverbend, where his queen and the noncombatants waited, since the day after Bailar had marked his skin. He told himself that his presence on the siege line was necessary, all the more so now that Aventan reinforcements had arrived. Their western force had not quite cut off contact between the two Lusetani camps, particularly not since the magic-men could summon distracting *akdraugi* to cover transit—but still, it was a risk, and should the *erregerra* risk himself so? His capture would mean the end of the entire endeavor. The Vettoni and other allies would disband immediately, and even the Lusetani would take such ill fortune as a sign that Bandue had withdrawn his protection.

Ekialde told himself all of this, but deep in his heart, he knew that it was also simpler to avoid his wife's displeasure than to suffer it.

If only he could make her understand. *Why* couldn't she understand? All his warriors did, all the men and women who had left their homes in order to protect them, to drive the Aventans out of Iberia. *'Everything I do—even these darker magics—this is all for you, my darling rabbit, and for our son. For all Lusetani sons and daughters, that they never know what it is to walk beneath a yoke.'*

And so, when Bailar looked to him for confirmation, he nodded. Just once, solid and sure.

For this deed, Bailar had trusted only his own associates, the magic-men of the Lusetani who had been with them since the beginning, not the allies. There were not enough of them to slit all the throats at once. Some of the sacrifices struggled; others merely wept. Bronze blades, specially consecrated by Bailar, neatly parted flesh, and in a moment, it was done.

It didn't smell like a battlefield. No sweat, no leather, no tang of adrenaline. Just the pungent metallic reek of so much life-force spilled out in such a short time. As Bailar lifted his hands, beginning the ritual, the unharnessed power of all that blood buzzed along the lines and whorls inked into Ekialde's skin, the markings which gave him strength and kept Bandue's eye securely fixed upon him.

"Thank you for your deaths," he said to the corpses. "May they bring the Lusetani bountiful life."

◇◇◇◇◇◇◇◇◇◇◇◇◇◇

INSIDE TOLETUM

"You would think," Mennenius said, watching as the legionaries on guard switched stations, guided by the precision of the centurions' whistles, "that we would get used to this."

Vitellius nodded. It had been nearly two months since the first Lusetani attack on Toletum, longer since Mennenius had first encountered the *akdraugi* out in the wilds. The legions went through their duties as they always had, as they always would, and yet Vitellius knew, to a man, none of them had become inured to the haunting effect. Each night, just as at the start, Vitellius had to rotate his guards rapidly as soon as the haunting mist rose over the walls, guarding against any weak spots forming. It was a sort of planning he felt sure no other commander had had to wrangle with. No arrow-hail had ever taken out guardsmen so swiftly as the *akdraugi* brought men to their knees.

'At least fewer of them die from this sort of assault.' Fewer, but not none. The toll mounted as the summer dragged on, both legionaries and townsfolk succumbing to the *anima*-devouring power of the *akdraugi*. *'Haunted to death.'* It was how Mennenius had described it, when he staggered in from the forest; Vitellius had yet to find a better way to describe it.

While the men moved into position, Vitellius asked Mennenius for updates from the rest of the city. He had delegated many civic responsibilities to his friend, including the task of liaising with Toletum's own council. There was simply too much to keep track of for Vitellius to have sole governance of it all: not only the rationing, but keeping track of production within the city as well. They could not reach the greater fields, but the city still had gardens. Mennenius dutifully recorded yields and investigated any accusations of hoarding or theft.

Too, the Lusetani had not entirely been able to keep Vitellius from reaping the advantage of the river. The city's position, cut into such a deep bend of the Tagus, was their advantage, as was the Lusetani's lack of discipline. Fish were the bulwark standing between Toletum and utter disaster.

Yet even these broader considerations melted away as the sun set. The scope of Vitellius's world narrowed in the fading light. He might as well have been adrift on the Endless Ocean, with no domain past the confines of a single ship. The world outside Toletum's walls became as foreign as the broad seas, as unreachable as Olympus. All Vitellius could do was try to hold those walls and safeguard the souls within them, to the best of his ability.

Just as every other night, they waited for the gates of Tartarus to open.

∞∞∞∞∞∞∞∞∞∞

OUTSIDE TOLETUM

Bailar's hands were brown with the muddled dirt and liquid; his bare feet were tinted crimson. "We do this for our blessed *erregerra*, my brothers," he said to the other magic-men as they trailed behind him. "Remember that, and feel divinity's blessing upon you. We, beloved of Endovelicos, are privileged to reach into the shadow realm, where we may fetch weapons for Bandue's service."

They formed a crescent at the edge of the forest, facing Toletum and its walls. Others, they had left behind, on the far side of the forest, to keep Aven's impressive legions at bay. But this, Bailar knew he had to do for himself, and he had selected the bravest of his fellows to join him. Each bore a sacred instrument, wet with the blood of the sacrificed prisoners: knives and needles, rods and rings. On each end of the crescent stood a man with a bone flute. At Bailar's signal, they began a low and mournful tune.

Bailar rubbed his thumbs against his middle fingers, feeling the blood moving against his skin. It had begun to crust beneath his fingernails, but there was enough of it on his hands to stay warm and damp a while yet. *'A sacred thing, this, the blood of death.'* Strength lived in it, the power of the gods that beat in every heart, and too, the strength necessary to take it from another. Blood given freely had its uses, but blood *taken*, blood *commanded*—that, Bailar had come to believe, was the most potent of all.

A cloud passed over the stars. Bailar began his invocation, calling out to Endovelicos in the gods' secret language.

All around him, the living world dimmed. The color leeched out, and even the darkness grew blurry, as though a silver veil had been drawn over it. When first Bailar had encountered this, many years earlier, it had terrified him. He thought he was dying, crossing into the land of the dead. When sense returned to him, he realized he had been but on the threshold, walking a shrouded path—a place where he could touch what lay beyond without truly traveling through to it.

Was it so for the other magic-men? Bailar did not know. Perhaps they saw something different, or perhaps they saw nothing at all. *'Every man dies his own death. No one can tell us how it feels or what it looks like. Perhaps this is the same.'*

No matter. So long as the magic worked, Bailar cared little what his fellows experienced. He knew he walked a path trod by Endovelicos himself.

As Bailar reached deep, deep into the shadows around him, wonders and terrors alike pricked at his blood. So many things he might stretch for, might seek to drag across into the sunlit world—but Bailar was chief of the magic-men not only for his strength, but for his wisdom. He knew not to try to grasp that which would slip through his fingers.

'Yet, yet . . .' he thought, the words a low hum in his heart. *'I do not have the power yet. That does not mean I never will.'*

◇◇◇◇◇◇◇◇◇◇◇◇◇

INSIDE TOLETUM

The mist rose, but this time, there were no accompanying demons. No eldritch howls, no demonic faces. The men looked about, confused. After a moment, a few began to relax, but the cannier among them tensed further, as Vitellius did, suspecting some sort of trap. "Hold positions!" he bellowed, and the centurions' whistles carried the order down the wall on both sides.

And so they waited, in the dark and the damp, while nothing happened.

After a few minutes, Tribune Mennenius jogged to the base of the ladder beneath Vitellius. "Nothing on the riverside," he reported. Recently, Vitellius had become concerned that the Lusetani might try to mount an attack up the steep cliff, despite the disadvantage of the terrain. "Not even the mist."

As Mennenius gazed up at the wispy clouds cresting the ramparts, a stab of regret guilted Vitellius. He tried to keep his friend away from the Lusetani fiends. They had affected him so badly that first time, out in the wilds. He knew Mennenius still had nightmares about it. Too many nights, he witnessed Mennenius wake in the tribunes' quarters, drenched in sweat and gasping for air, crying out to the gods to spare him. So, the centurions told him, did some of the legionaries who had been with him. Those were the men he was most reluctant to put atop the battlements at night, the men he always saw relieved of duty first.

'Your pity is a weakness,' he told himself, 'and it denigrates them as much as it shames you.' And yet, he could not bring himself to force them into contact with the horrors of the *akdraugi* any more often than was necessary. 'You'll never be fit for real command if you can't harden yourself.'

Half of him said there was no place for softness, during a siege. The other half said he should exercise compassion wherever he could, since they were likely to see so little of it handed down to them by fate.

"Stay below," he told his friend. The *akdraugi* rarely affected those in the center of the city as strongly as those on the walls. "Make sure reinforcements are ready to ascend."

The gibbous moon slunk across the sky, its light blurry and scattered behind the haze of the Lusetani-summoned mist. Vitellius could practically feel the entire city of Toletum holding its breath, waiting to see what fresh hell the Lusetani would unleash. But there were no *akdraugi*, no howling fiends, no maddening sounds—and no attack, no warriors scaling the walls.

Gradually, Vitellius noticed a strange odor in the air: not unpleasant, but strange. Not damp, as he might have expected in a mist. It lacked the green boskiness he remembered from the Vendelician border, that utter vitality that infused every breath, reminding a man that everything surrounding him was alive and growing and greedy. An uncanny feeling, sometimes, but he had come to understand why the Tennic peoples thought it holy. Yet this was different—not earthy, nor smoky. Instead it had an almost metallic tang—

'Blood,' Vitellius realized, and took a horrified step back, as though that would somehow protect his nose from the odor. The mist smelled of blood.

Vitellius had long known that the Lusetani used blood in their rites. The Arevaci magic-men had confirmed as much from the start, though they eschewed the practice themselves, so thoroughly that they could explain little of how it worked. The mist had never carried this scent before, and Vitellius shuddered to think what that might mean. As he scanned the ramparts, crinkled noses and confused expressions indicated that some of his men were noticing it, too. The focale around his neck grew warm and itched, the Fire magic woven into it recognizing a threat and rising to defend.

Still no *akdraugi* appeared, but through the mists, the Lusetani charged, criss-crossing the plains surrounding the town to avoid the defensive ditches, then pitching themselves against the walls. Fewer had ladders than in past assaults, and Vitellius marveled at the strength of those warriors who could haul themselves up by jamming pick-axes into whatever crevices they could find in Toletum's walls.

Whatever questions Vitellius had about the strange turn in the Lusetani magic fell to the back of his mind as he commanded the fighting men. This came easily, now, and without the *akdraugi*, the legionaries were able to fight with their customary vigor. If the mist surrounding them was eerie, well, these were men trained in the forests of Vendelicia. Fogs and clouds couldn't spook them. The Lusetani warriors swiftly realized their foes were at full strength, not weakened by the *akdraugi*, and broke off their attack.

Nonetheless, only when the black sky began to give way to the glowing blue of pre-dawn did Vitellius feel comfortable giving the order for the men to stand down. As the sun rose over the eastern bend of the Tagus River, the mist began to burn off, as though it were a normal morning fog. Only then did the warmth in Vitellius's focale begin to fade.

Vitellius sent the legionaries to their long-overdue beds, summoning replacement guards for the walls from the ranks of the rested auxiliaries, but he himself continued pacing the ramparts. The tension of the night would not leave his body.

When he finally came down from the walls, Mennenius was waiting for him. "Still nothing?" he asked.

"Nothing," Vitellius said. "I ought to be glad."

"But you can't shake the feeling that there's something we're not seeing?"

Vitellius nodded. "Why would the Lusetani change their attack pattern after so long? There must be some strategy behind it, but in Mars's name, I can't figure out what it is." He didn't have enough information, that was the trouble, and he had no idea how to get it.

"Maybe they're tiring," Mennenius suggested. "Maybe something we're doing has—has broken their magic?" He looked out toward the wall, as though he could see through it and beyond the Lusetani encampment, past the forest and up the river, to wherever their reinforcements were approaching from. "Maybe the other legions have broken them, somehow?"

The entire affair rubbed Vitellius the wrong way. Before Mennenius could say another word, Vitellius swung himself up onto one of the ladders and scaled it, joining Centurion Calix at the middle of the north wall. Mennenius followed. Calix saluted briefly, then shook his head at the retreating Lusetani. "That was . . . odd, sir."

"Deliberately so, I think," Vitellius said. "Did it seem you, Calix, as though their heart wasn't really in it?"

Calix nodded. "That was a smaller force than they usually send against us—and we haven't killed *that* many of them during their assaults."

Vitellius rubbed his chin. He was in need of a shave, but they had all let a few niceties slip since barricading their gates. "They may have met with some other calamity," he said, reasoning out loud more to himself than to Calix or Mennenius. "They may have been attacked from the far side, by our legions. The Vettoni allies may have deserted the Lusetani. The Lusetani themselves might be fracturing." He raised his eyes to Calix. "But you don't think so, either, do you?"

"No, sir, I don't. They gave up far too easily. This was a feint." Calix frowned, and Vitellius got the sense he was watching the battle a second time in his mind's eye. "In another situation, I would say it was meant to lure us—but they must know we're not going to leave the city. We haven't even sent a sortie out in quite some time." With Hanath and the bulk of the cavalry already out of the city, they had few horses and horsemen left behind. Vitellius hadn't wanted to risk them on pointless sallies. "And the—the *things*." Many of the Aventans would not use the word *akdraugi*, as though that might summon more of the fiends or grant them extra strength. "Where were they? Why send a mist without the demons behind it?"

"We could ask the Arevaci magic-men," Mennenius suggested. "They may have some idea."

Vitellius sighed. "Every instinct I have is telling me this is some kind of trick, but I'll be damned if I can figure out what it is."

"We'll keep a good watch, sir," Calix said. "If those bastards try anything else, we'll be alert to it."

Vitellius clapped him on the shoulder. "Set someone else to it. *You* need rest." As Calix saluted and left them, Vitellius looked pointedly at Mennenius. "You, too."

"No more than you," Mennenius said, dropping his voice. "The men may think you're immune to these *akdraugi*, Gaius, but you and I know you're not. If they get into your head, if they fell you—" The concern in Mennenius's voice was not only tactical, not merely the worry of what would befall the cohorts without their primary commander; it was the compassion of a friend.

"I know," Vitellius answered softly. "I will rest. I promise. I just . . ." He shrugged. "I need a walk first. A lap of the walls will do me good."

Mennenius frowned, but nodded in acquiescence. "Wake me when you come in, then."

He walked until nearly dawn, first on the walls, then back and forth through the city, from the main square to his headquarters and back again, until the ceaseless repetition of his feet finally quieted his unsettled mind enough to allow him to sleep. He passed Bartasco several times along the way; the Arevaci leader was as worried for his people as Vitellius was for the legionaries and spent as many nights in wakeful apprehension. In mutual understanding, they merely nodded as they passed, each man leaving the other to his contemplation. There would be time to strategize later.

In the glowing morning light, Vitellius made good on his promise, waking Mennenius and flinging himself down on his bed, finally having walked himself to exhaustion, if not to restfulness. The sun was scarce any higher in the sky, however, when pounding on his door had him hurtling out of bed again. Even as he went to the door, he was looping his sword-belt around his waist. "What is it?" he asked, even before the door was open enough to see who was on the other side.

Mennenius was there, but not alone. With him were two other men he recognized: an Aventan medic and one of the healers native to Toletum. "Gaius," Mennenius said, "we have a problem."

∞∞∞∞∞∞∞∞∞∞∞

"Keep your distance," the Aventan medic advised as he pulled open the door. "We don't know what caused this . . ."

Two legionaries lay on pallets in the healer's back room. Their wheat-colored tunics were drenched through with sweat. One man was moaning, rolling from shoulder to shoulder on the cot; the other lay still, his eyes wide and staring up at the ceiling, his arms limp at his sides.

Sudden illness of any kind was bad enough. A fever sweeping through the camp now could be disastrous. But when the medic swung a lantern into the room, illuminating the men's faces more clearly, Vitellius sucked in a horrified breath. He clamped a hand over his nose and mouth, backing away from the door frame.

Spots. Red spots and purplish blotches, all over their faces and beginning to crawl down their necks and shoulders.

Plague.

Vitellius thought of his focale, which had burned with his sister's magic all through the night. Fire magic could purge poisons and illness. *'Thank you, Venus and Vulcan, for your protection. Thank you, Latona.'*

The medic let the door swing closed, leaving the legionaries alone with their misery once more. Vitellius staggered backward a few more steps, nearly colliding with Mennenius. "What—how—" He turned a stricken gaze to the medic, then to the Iberian healer. "Tell me this isn't as bad as it looks. Tell me it isn't—it isn't—" He could not bring himself to say the word aloud.

"It does bear similarities to the red plague that visited Aven some years ago," the Aventan medic said. Vitellius's shoulders sagged. "But it is not precisely the same. There may be . . ." His voice squeaked with desperate hope. "There may be easier remedies. Or perhaps it is less . . . less . . ." Helplessly, he looked to his Iberian colleague.

The Iberian healer made a feeble gesture with both hands. "I cannot say what this is. We shall treat it as best we can. The fever is the greatest danger, it would seem."

Vitellius rubbed at his forehead with the heel of one hand. "How? How did this happen? There hasn't been unusual illness in the city since we got here, so why now?"

"They were both on duty last night." Mennenius's voice, just behind him. "During the Lusetani attack." A pause. "They were on the walls when that mist rose up."

XXV

City of Aven

The days of the Ludi Athaeci were the hottest of the summer.

For the heat itself, Vatinius Obir didn't mind. He knew heat, from his hometown of Walili, which the Aventans called Volubilis. Knew cold, too, for as a youth he had visited the great mountains that rose up beyond the cedar forests south of that place. Weather never troubled Obir much, for it was simply dealt with, to his thinking. Put more clothing on, or take off as much as you could manage without offending anyone. Easy.

What troubled Obir about this heat was that it seemed to be driving the city mad.

"Explain yourselves." He folded his arms across his chest, glaring at the men who stood across from him: an assortment of boys and men, all sporting bruises and scrapes. When no one immediately ventured a narrative, Obir settled his weight back against the edge of his desk. "Explain yourselves *now*, before I have cause to grow angry."

"It was only a tussle," said one, who divested himself of his sullen attitude at an arch of Obir's eyebrow. Standing up straighter, he went on, "With the boys at the Volscian Gate."

At least they had not caused a ruckus with their neighbors on the Esquiline Hill. Some of the collegia in the city were brutes who preyed upon their neighborhoods, beating payments out of shopkeepers and artisans in exchange for dubious protection against other thieves. Obir disdained such practices—and furthermore, his patron Sempronius Tarren had forbidden them. Obir's men kept order in their neighborhood, settled disputes between their own, and dealt abrupt justice to outsiders who tried to muscle in. The Esquiline had flourished for a decade as a result, and Obir found his neighbors quite as generous in their security as they would've been in fear. It would have been an indignity and a hassle, if his lads had caused trouble in their own territory.

"We were just scouting out, I swear it, captain. We'd heard about someone giving trouble to our fullers on the corner there, you know, by the—"

"I know where our fullers are, yes. Stop stalling."

The youth's shoulders hunched uncomfortably. "Well, the Volscian boys were there, and they . . ." He rubbed at his creased brow. "They were . . ."

"Yes?" Obir spread his hands. "I will be disappointed if you lose your tongue so soon after finding it."

"That's the trouble, sir." This, from another of the lads, wiping at his bloody nose. "We can't quite recall what started it."

"You can't recall?" Obir looked from him to the others. "Did they knock your heads about that badly?"

"They're telling the truth." A new voice, accented more heavily than Obir's, but with a different flavor: one that spoke of dark northern forests and a swift-flowing river, rather than arid foothills and red earth. Ebredus, Tennic-blond and tall as one of the trees he worshipped. He was scarred all over and marked with ink as well, but Obir saw a fresh gash upon his cheek.

"Don't tell me you were part of this!" Obir expected better; Ebredus was a man his own age, and like him, had come to Aven by way of a legion's auxiliary service. He didn't have citizenship, like Obir, but he had made his home in the city nonetheless. "Did all of you leave your good sense in bed when you rose this morning?"

"I cannot explain it, captain," Ebredus said. His face was stoic as ever, but his pale eyes held a hint of shame. "I would swear to you that no harm was meant, on either side. We stepped off the curb, and then . . . then we were fighting. They must have said something."

"We stopped when the priest of Concordia came!" one of the younger boys exclaimed, as though it were some sort of defense for having brawled to begin with. "You know the one, the Air mage from the temple on the other side of the Clivus Patricus—"

"Enough."

The boy's words pricked a reminder at the back of Obir's mind: another day, when men had come to blows and could not be stopped, except by magical intervention. Nothing more had come of it then, so far as Obir knew. '*But this . . .*'

For now, order had to be maintained. "Now look," Obir said, straightening to his full height. He had the advantage of everyone in the room except Ebredus in that regard. "The city's crowded for the games. Lots of visitors, lots of traders, lots of chance for trouble. But people need to feel safe here, yes? When the Subura scares them off—" One of the boys spat on the floor at the mention of their rivals. "—then I want them spending their coin on the Esquiline. But they're not gonna do that if they see you ugly brutes brawling in the streets, eh?" He gave the nearest boy a slight cuff. "So go make yourselves useful. Find the travelers, hustle them into our inns and taverns. Make sure Ferinna and her girls and boys get good custom. And if you can't do your jobs without bloodying yourselves up, might be you'll find yourselves cleaning out the latrines for the whole neighborhood."

They dispersed, with hangdog expressions and mumbled apologies. Ebredus in particular ducked his head and tugged at his forelock. "Will not happen again, captain."

"It better not!" Obir growled, though his thoughts were more of a prayer than a command. *'Let this be only an oddity. These hot days madden the blood, and no surprise if the fool boys were too embarrassed to tell me what started the fight. No surprise if they broke it off when they saw a priest.'*

Still, the memory discomfited him. The previous year, he and his boys had been the ones breaking up a fight—in the Forum, of all places, during the campaign season. Autronius Felix and some of his friends, supporters of Sempronius Tarren, had scuffled with men loyal to Sempronius's opponent. They had fought like men possessed, all of them, and only halted when Felix's brother, an Earth mage, cast his magic into the ground around them. Sempronius had hauled Felix off for answers, but if he had ever gotten any, Obir knew nothing of it. He had wrangled the other Popularist fighters to their homes—with the help of his brother, Nisso, who had died not long after, defending Sempronius against an assassination attempt.

It had been Nisso who had first learned of that fight, in fact, when the Lady Latona's maidservant burst into the collegium's tavern, seeking aid. *'How funny they looked.'* Nisso had been taller even than Ebredus, and the girl Merula scarcely came up to his chest, for all her ferocity. *'A bantam facing off against a stork.'*

The memory put a pang in Obir's chest. Nearly nine months now, he had led the collegium without his brother at his side, and there was no day he did not feel the loss. Obir trusted his men, and the women who worked for the collegium, too. Some had fought alongside him in Numidia; others had been on the Esquiline even before he'd taken control of the collegium from its previous captain and had assisted in that struggle. But none were his brother. None had shared hearth-space with him all his life, and none knew his mind so well. If there were trouble brewing in the city, Obir would need a strong partner at his side, but it was hard to learn to trust anyone as he had trusted Nisso.

'Oh, brother, would that you were here.' But as soon as he thought the words, he cast his eyes to the earth and made a quick sign with his right hand. Calling upon the dead in such a way could disturb their spirits. *'And that's the last damn thing we need now.'*

◇◇◇◇◇◇◇◇◇◇◇◇◇◇

On the morning the games began, the city went quiet everywhere except the Circus Maximus, with all attention streaming there. The Circus could hold a quarter of the city's population, and many of those denied admission would be thronging around the stadium, peering in through the tunnels to catch a glimpse, or simply waiting to hear news of victors and wonders. Inside and out, they drank and ate and cheered.

Things were calmer on the far side of the Forum, beneath the shady greens in the garden behind the Temple of Venus. There, Latona sought the counsel of the High Priestess, Ama Rubellia.

Venus had done well by her chosen votary; Rubellia had amply rolling curves and glossy dark hair, with warm brown skin that fairly glowed in the summer sunlight. Well into her thirties, Rubellia exuded not only sensuality, but a quiet self-confidence that Latona had long envied. If Rubellia had ever felt anything less than certain of her place in the world and the gods' plans for her, Latona had never seen sign of it.

Latona had written Rubellia from Stabiae, but there had been so much she had feared to commit to paper. As the two women sat beneath myrtles and oleander, with a bowl of iced wine and a vermilion dish of pine nuts between them, Latona filled her friend in on the full story, from Alhena's summons to the fiends that had nearly felled Vibia. Rubellia's lovely face grew grave as the tale went on, but she never interrupted. Only when Latona had finished telling her of Salonius's utter dismissal at the Galerian dinner did Rubellia release a tense sigh and speak. "Well, my dear, I won't say you were wrong to try and find support from that quarter, but neither will I say your initial instincts against trusting the Commission were ill-founded." She shook her head, long carnelian-and-gold earrings jangling. "Ocella used them as a tool for harassing and hunting his enemies, but he was not the first. Their order has long strayed from its noble purpose. They expect to know what advantage is in it for them, what payments will be forthcoming, before they deign to stir themselves."

"The name of the Augian Commission still inspires fear and good behavior among mages, but it seems their enforcement has become . . . selective." Latona's eyes went skyward. "I knew Ocella had corrupted some of them, but I did not think to find the rest so feckless. And if we are on our own to deal with this menace . . ."

Rubellia's well-shaped eyebrows arched. "On our own?" Her laughter always rang as clear as bells, even in dire circumstances. "Latona, dear one, there are more than three hundred mages in the city. Fewer who have talent strong enough to combat the forces of Discordia, I'll grant you—"

"*Far* fewer," Latona said. "And I say that not to disparage a man or woman among them, but sweet Juno, Vibia and I barely got past the last trap they laid, even with the benefit of education and preparation."

"So we must educate and prepare others."

Latona thought of the Cantrinalia ritual, the sacred power of so many mages joined together, warm and glowing. What a thing it would be, to harness that fellowship toward a worthy cause! But Latona doubted it could be done as easily as imagined. "Commissioner Salonius made it clear he thought I was addled. Others will think the same."

"Some others. Not all."

"All the same, I can't say I'm eager to gain a reputation as a madwoman on top of everything else." Latona grabbed a few pine nuts and rolled them in her fingers, remembering what others already said of her. '*A barren harlot. An ambitious conniver. A little spy.*' She pinched one nut between thumb and forefinger till the shell popped and the soft seed popped out. "And even if I could lay my vanity aside enough for that—"

"It's not vanity."

"—it wouldn't help in persuading anyone."

"Likely not," Rubellia agreed. "So we must start with those we *can* convince, and have them keep alert for any trouble in the city like those you had in Stabiae."

"Rallying our friends may not be enough. The power of those things, when they had Vibia . . ."

Rubellia gave a smile that spoke of total confidence. "Then we must also make ourselves stronger."

◇◇◇◇◇◇◇◇◇◇◇◇

Merula was missing the first day of the games, but she didn't much mind. The atmosphere outside the Circus Maximus was as lively as within the stands, and the first day was less interesting than the second would be. It mattered little that, as a slave, she could not get into the stadium on her own to see today's hunts and races; tomorrow, she would accompany the domina to see the theatrical presentations and the gladiatorial matches.

Still, the domina had given her coin and told Merula to go enjoy herself for a few hours, while she sat in the Temple of Venus with the priestess, so enjoy herself Merula would. She wandered through the crowded streets surrounding the Circus, snagged a hot sausage and a handful of cracked nuts from a thermopolium, and wondered if any fights would break out during the racing. The four teams—Reds, Whites, Greens, and Blues—had ardent supporters, all, and none of them took losses lightly. A bit of rowdiness would not go amiss, so long as she got back to the domina before she needed to be collected for supper.

As she rounded the curve at the northern edge of the valley, she caught sight of a man she knew, amid a knot of others, some of whom looked vaguely familiar: Vatinius Obir, with the men and women of his collegium. They had claimed a segment of the low wall between the street and the stadium, and were sitting on it, straddling it, leaning upon it as they quaffed from clay cups and passed around bags of snacks. *'I could be having worse company,'* Merula decided and trotted over to them.

"—So the professor says, 'Damn fool! He's gone and woken up the bald man instead of me!'" Whatever Obir's joke had been, it had evidently been very funny, judging by the guffawing laughter the others devolved into. Obir's dark eyes widened in recognition when he saw Merula. "Oh-ho! Careful, boys!" he cried, affecting an oversized expression of terror. "Here comes a she-hawk who will tear your ears off soon as look at you!"

"As if I could be reaching yours," Merula said, pointedly looking up at him. Even sitting against the low wall, he towered over her.

This earned another boisterous laugh. "What can we be doing for you, little hawk?" His brow creased slightly. "Where is your mistress, eh?"

"You are not knowing?" she retorted, folding her arms over her chest. Lady Aula had told her about Praetor Sempronius's plans to guard the domina with his pet collegium. She had wanted to dismiss the notion, taking offense at the implication that she could not keep her lady safe— but there was sense in having more eyes and ears alert for peril, and the men of the Esquiline had proved useful enough in the past.

"We do not follow her every step," Obir said, unruffled. "Our reach rarely extends below the Forum."

Merula rolled her eyes. "Perhaps you should be showing me these boys who are trailing my domina, so I am not accidentally slitting any of their throats."

Obir obliged her, pointing out a few of the younger men with them. "You must come by the collegium sometime to meet the rest of the boys." He grinned. "Some are even smaller than you, little hawk!" Her scowl had no appreciable effect, and Obir continued in the same jocular vein. "So, I must assume you're off-duty! Come and drink with us. The Blues took the first two races, so we are toasting their glory."

"My family supports the Reds," Merula said, but she held out a hand for a cup anyway.

"And if they win," said a rosy-cheeked young man to Obir's right, "we'll toast their glory, too. Anyone but the damned Greens, really." This prompted a rousing chorus of insults and invectives against the Green faction. Merula only shrugged and drank her wine.

"Not interested in the races?" Obir asked.

"I am preferring the fights. Tomorrow, Dimo the Thessalan will be taking all challengers, and Tryphona of Cynosoura has returned from Chrysos just to fight Fair Ariadne." Merula heard the breathless eagerness in her own voice and scuffed her heel in the dirt. "Or so they say."

"Ahhhh," Obir said, crossing one foot over the other. "So who do you favor?"

"Tryphona," Merula said without hesitation. "Ariadne's magnificent, yes, but Tryphona's been the champion across three provinces. It'll be a fight worth the watching, though."

"Think anyone can take down Dimo?" asked another of Obir's men, a squat older fellow. This set off a lively conversation, all the collegium chiming in to agree with Merula's assessments, or argue with her. They discussed the advantages of different styles, *retiarus* with net and *secutor* with trident, round-shielded *hoplomachus* or the more heavily armored *murmillo*. Merula allowed herself to be persuaded into putting some money on the strength of her opinions, and she expected to earn a tidy profit off the bets. She was rarely wrong when it came to judging fighters.

Once that excitement faded, and the conversation turned to other matters, Merula took another cup of wine and watched Obir with his fellows. He was always at the center, though not always the focus of whatever happened. The others rotated around him even as they talked to one another, while Obir stayed planted. Though he laughed and joked and drank with the rest of them, his eyes often went above their heads, taking the measure of the area. *'Watching for threats.'* Merula approved.

"Is your face always this serious?" he asked, when he noticed her observing him. "Or do you have something on your mind?"

Merula considered a long moment, assessing Obir with an unblinking gaze. She did not know how far to trust this man. He had an easy openness about him. No doubt many spilled secrets without even realizing it, looking into his broad smile. *'You may even be a good man, Vatinius Obir. You are trusted by Sempronius Tarren.'* Merula reserved more judgment on the praetor than did her mistress, but she grudgingly admitted that Sempronius had some fine qualities. If he was leading the domina onto treacherous roads, well, the domina was all too willing to accompany him. *'But what am I knowing of you?'* A man who could hold a crossroads collegium did not do so through good temper alone. He had to have strength. Cunning was even better. A willingness to commit violence when necessary. A cool enough head to manage the violent inclinations of others. Traits both encouraging and dangerous.

"We have not had an easy summer," she said at last. "There has been trouble in Stabiae."

Obir cocked an eyebrow. "Do you think it followed you here?"

"Domina, she worries *we* were on *its* heels. So tell me, Vatinius Obir, who is having so many ears and eyes north of the Forum—Have you noticed anything strange going on in the city lately?"

He had. Merula knew a feint from a true strike, and she knew the flicker of fear that preceded Obir's tight laugh. "Stranger than usual, you mean?" he said, shrugging broad shoulders.

Merula refused to join in his laughter or do anything else to put him at his ease. She fixed him with a hard stare, hoping he had sense enough to know she was serious. "You will be letting me know, if you do," she said. "Your patron, he would be wanting you to alert the Lady Latona, I am thinking." She passed her cup back to him. "I shall be seeing you tomorrow after the fights, to collect my winnings."

XXVI

Camp of Legio II, Outside Corduba, Southern Iberia

Ever and always, they came too late.

The prominent citizens of Corduba, rather than welcoming Rabirus and his legions with effusive gratitude, met them with exasperation. They drew no distinction between Rabirus and the coward Fimbrianus, whom they had futilely petitioned for help a year earlier. Even the town's Aventan citizens had no sympathy for Rabirus, but only wanted to squawk at him about how they had been forced to shut down some of their mines and quarries for lack of workers.

'They're as bad as the damn flies, buzzing and stinging at every opportunity.' Rabirus's skin was still red welts all over, as the biting insects had followed him all the way up the Baetis. A single night in the city, though, was enough to cure him of any expectation of respite. After listening to hours of complaints, he had taken the finest accommodations on offer— and found himself a feast for fleas.

So Rabirus had set out again, in search of the kidnapping brigands. To no avail, as it turned out. They had found deserted camps, but never the bandits. For days on end, the Second and Fourth legions had chased themselves in a circle, up and down the hills that looped the city. They had fought no one, redeemed no prisoners from captivity, done nothing except exercise their legs quite thoroughly. All the while, Rabirus had to pretend this was precisely what he intended, ignoring the sidelong skepticism of the centurions.

'I just need a win.' The sun was slipping beneath the horizon, casting the trees ringing the legionary camp in a shade of deep green-blue. Soon the heat would vanish, and if the gods were good, no storm would follow. The evening chill would force another change of tunic, however; the sweat-drenched one would become intolerable in cooler air. *'Just one win, and I can proceed from there. Please, gods of my people, look to me here in this foreign land.'* Jupiter, Mars, and the rest had to have some presence, even here. The Aventans in Corduba had not neglected their worship so

far as to jeopardize that. *'Where I am, my gods will find me. Please, divine ones, bring me a victory.'*

Rabirus dug a fresh tunic out of his trunk, changed, and had just sat down to a disappointing supper of overbaked bread, stringy hare, and olive oil considerably inferior than he would have expected in a region so replete with the stuff, when one of the junior tribunes came to his tent, begging leave to admit a pair of scouts. "It's good news, sir," the tribune rushed to assure him. "They've found something."

"Send them in, then." It wasn't as though his supper were too magnificent to bear interruption.

A pair of scouts entered: both looked to be mid-career men, one with dark hair and olive skin, the other ruddier of complexion. Both saluted, though one was crisper about it than the other, who seemed impatient to get the formality over with.

"You may speak," Rabirus said, easing back in his chair.

"Sir," said the darker man, who had given the finer salute. He gave his name, which Rabirus promptly forgot, and his rank in the Second Legion. "We've found a village, a few miles past the last abandoned camp. Deeper in the hills, a rough path. Maybe two hundred people there."

Rabirus lifted an eyebrow. "Lusetani?"

The scout from the Second shook his head. "Not this far east. But one of their allies—"

The other scout interrupted, face red with frustration. "Sir, I have to protest—"

The man from the Second glared at his fellow. "We've been over this."

"And I remain unconvinced." He turned toward Rabirus. "Sir, I'm with the Fourth. Been here for six years. Before Governor Fimbrianus pulled us into Gades, we spent a lot of time in this region. There are Counei, yes, who are allied to the Lusetani and who may have been raiding the Corduban mines and quarries. But there are also Tartessi."

So many tribes, dizzying to keep up with. "And to whom are they allied?" Rabirus asked. "Have they joined forces with the Arevaci?"

The scout hesitated. "Sir, you must understand, our information is old. Governor Fimbrianus pulled us back to Gades long before allegiances settled among the tribes. But we have absolutely nothing to indicate that they are aiding the Lusetani."

"No more than that they are aiding *us*," said the scout from the Second. "At best, they have ignored Aven's calls to assemble as auxiliary forces, but *if* these people are Tartessi—and I'm not convinced they are, sir, not at all—then they have been negligent in that. Rather than answering the call and joining the defense of Toletum, they've holed up here in the south—"

"Like we did?" the man from the Fourth snapped. Righteous anger flashed in the scout's eyes—a dangerous heat that needed cooling. "Nothing we saw suggested that they've been involved with the kidnappings—"

"Just because we didn't see it doesn't mean—"

"I've heard enough," Rabirus cut in. "I think it likely that these are Counei, if they have not felt the need to barricade themselves against threats. But if they are Tartessi, then they have forfeited Aven's protection by failing to uphold their duties toward mutual defense."

"Sir—!" the man from the Fourth started, but Rabirus held up a hand.

"You are dismissed. Return to your camp and tell your tribune I wish to speak with him."

The scout's jaw worked for a moment. Would this man—not even an officer, merely a ranking soldier, no doubt some conscript from the landless Head Count—dare to challenge a praetor? But legionary training went deep. After a moment, he saluted and left the tent without another word.

Rabirus looked to the other scout. "I thank you for your information," he said. "Find Cominius Pavo, and we'll begin discussing the assault."

◇◇◇◇◇◇◇◇◇◇◇◇◇◇◇◇

TAGUS RIVER, CENTRAL IBERIA

Sakarbik was glaring at the sunset.

There was no other word for it, though Neitin could not imagine what reason she would have for such a thing. But every night out of the past six, the Cossetan woman had left their tent when the sun's light began to muffle itself in the trees that surrounded their camp. She went to the western border of the camp, ignoring the suspicious glances cast her way, and she leveled a glowering stare sunward, not moving until the last glimpse of golden light had disappeared. Then she turned around, beneath a bruise-colored sky, and returned to the tent.

"That's a strange slave you claimed for yourself," Neitin's sister Ditalce said, as Sakarbik kept her twilight vigil.

Ditalce was sitting on the ground near a campfire, with her knees bent up and Matigentis dandled in her lap. He could sit up by himself now, though only for a moment at a time. They seemed to have made a game of it between themselves, where Mati would bend up toward Ditalce, then she would poke his nose, and he would fall back against her legs, laughing. Neitin thought it the only sweet sound in this hateful wilderness.

"Reilin and Irrin think she's going to slit your throat someday," Ditalce continued, conversationally and without raising her gaze from Mati. "Or Mati's. Or both."

"She's not slitting any throats," Neitin replied. "She has sworn oaths."

Reilin would have snorted and Irrin given a haughty sigh, but Ditalce only shrugged. "She's still strange."

"She's a magic-woman. She's allowed to be strange."

Ditalce considered a moment. "She gave Mati this, yes?" She touched a charm tied to the boy's tunic: a rock from the river, with a hole worn through it.

"She did." Sakarbik had searched for days to find it, then woven the cord for it out of strips of doeskin.

"And you let her?"

"I did." Neitin scowled at her sister. "What concerns you?"

Ditalce shrugged. "I would not have thought Bailar would have approved."

He hadn't. He said it smacked of foreign practices, of Tyrian or even cursed Aventan influence, to use a charm to draw the goddess's eye. Sakarbik had sniffed, saying that the protection of the good river was superior to that of stolen blood. Neitin agreed and had told Bailar once again that no part of her son was his to influence. Bailar had departed, vowing to take this up with Ekialde, but neither man had visited the camp since that argument.

Before Neitin could remind her sister how little she cared what Bailar approved or disapproved of, however, Sakarbik's twilight vigil came to an end, and the Cossetan woman stalked back toward them from the edge of camp.

Ditalce was no fledgling warrior, like their sister Reilin, but she had her own bravery. Her eyes followed Sakarbik rather than shying away, and when the woman drew near, she raised her voice. "What do you do out there, every night?"

"Seek wisdom," Sakarbik replied, voice sharp as an arrow's flight. "You might try it sometime."

Ditalce was not cowed by the rebuke. "And does the sun share his wisdom with you? Are you his pillow-confidante, as he takes to his nightly rest?"

Sakarbik blew air out through her nostrils. "Who said the sun had anything to do with it?" she sneered. "It's the light I'm trying to get to talk to me."

"How is the sun different from its light?" Neitin asked, bewildered. But Sakarbik had already sauntered on.

"I told you," Ditalce said, returning her attention to Matigentis, babbling blissfully in his incomprehension. "That's a strange woman."

However much Neitin had decided to trust the Cossetan magic-woman, she could not disagree with that assessment.

◇◇◇◇◇◇◇◇◇◇◇◇◇◇

CITY OF AVEN

In the Senate, Arrius Buteo continued to beat his drum against Sempronius Tarren and all the praetor stood for. There were only a handful of senators remaining to hear him, however. Even Consul Aufidius Strato had pleaded off after the Ludi Athaeci were over, frankly declaring that another day of listening to Buteo's bleating would tempt him toward violence. Strato went to the seaside, along with half the senatorial families in the city, and Galerius was left to listen to Buteo pontificate, at least on such days as they could scrape together enough of a quorum to convene.

Marcus Autronius was there to listen, too. The Autroniae had no country home to retreat to—though Marcus's mother was begging his father to purchase one in fashionable Baiae, and Marcus suspected that Gnaeus would give in one of these years. The family was well-off enough to bear the expense, and Gnaeus could never long deny his wife her indulgences. *'She'd be so proud to have a villa to welcome our friends to, rather than waiting around every summer hoping for an invitation to someone else's.'*

Buteo had a talent for turning everything back toward his condemnation of the war in Iberia and the man he blamed for it, though Galerius put in a valiant effort at steering senatorial conversation toward other matters. Grain distribution, aqueduct repairs, fights in the Subura, there was nothing Buteo couldn't, somehow, pin on Sempronius Tarren.

The opinions of the Pontifical College had come in during the Ludi, with the effect that almost no one had paid attention to them, and in any case, their assessment of the Lusetanian *akdraugi* was mixed. *'Not entirely unexpected,'* Marcus thought, *'considering the Optimates managed to befriend or bribe as many of them as we did.'* From the evidence presented to them, the best the pontifical collegium could assert was that such things were, perhaps, possible. Half the men had asserted their belief in Sempronius's and Gaius Vitellius's accounts, and half had expressed skepticism, stating that mass manifestations of spirits had not been seen in centuries at the least, maybe not since the days of the legendary heroes. Ulysses, perhaps, might have encountered them, but surely no Aventan ever had or ever would.

Against their denial, new letters arrived every few days. There had even been one from Gaius Vitellius, smuggled out from besieged Toletum. The Optimates spat upon them all, but many of the people of Aven were more willing to believe. Marcus had seen to it that the newsreaders received some of Sempronius's messages and read them out in the Forum on market days, when the most people would be in the streets. He wanted them to hear what their legions were up against, and to judge for themselves. And the people were perfectly willing to believe in the perfidious magics of foreign foes.

Buteo and the Optimates had their adherents as well, though, many of whom felt the best defense against such horrors was to be nowhere near them—people who would happily abandon Iberia to its fate, never mind the damage such a withdrawal would do, both to Aventan trade and to the civilians who had asked Aven's aid. No, those men's cares and concerns were much closer to home. Some of them, Marcus suspected, would live and die without ever setting foot outside Aven's walls. *'And they have not the imagination to realize that what happens without can affect their lives within.'* Depressing, to realize how many people not only lived lives so small and incurious, but actively preferred to stay that way, rejecting anything that might jeopardize their precious ignorance.

As the election season drew nearer, Buteo's rants had taken on a pointed focus. "I think it is time—long past time, in truth!" he bellowed, "—to begin questioning whether or not we should extend the command of a man who has demonstrated such paltry success in the field! What has Praetor Sempronius to show for his efforts in Iberia, besides an endless deluge of papyrus? Months he has been on campaign, and when the sluggard *finally* reached his province—"

"Have a care," intoned Rufilius Albinicus, who had spent most of his career along the border of the northern provinces, "when criticizing the speed of someone crossing half the bloody world." A good deal of appreciative murmuring followed Albinicus's proclamation; he had won fame and glory for subduing the Tennic tribes in Albina, earning him his *cognomen*. His word on matters of war was generally taken as sound, even more than Strato's. "Iberia is vast, far more than Albina, and has no proper roads. A wise man would not move so swiftly that he outpaced his supply lines."

Buteo, however, was insensible to the bull's horns being lowered in his direction. "When finally he reached Cantabria, did he settle in to the capital to govern? No, he took his legions to the heart of wild country—"

"As the Centuriate Assembly charged him to do!" Quintus Terentius snapped. "Gods above, the Lusetani are besieging Toletum, not Tarraco."

Decimus Gratianus picked up Buteo's thread, however. "My honored friend Buteo's point is worth examining, reverend fathers. In a few months, we will be electing new officials—new praetors, who may want to take on provinces themselves, rather than oversee the law courts. Cantabria would not be an option to them if we extend Sempronius Tarren to a propraetorial command."

"Nor," said Rufilius Albinicus, his gaze steely, "by that reasoning, would Baelonia. And I see far more reason to extend Sempronius's command than Lucretius Rabirus's, considering Rabirus could not even be troubled to remove himself *to* his province until half the year had passed."

Galerius cleared his throat before speaking. "Arrius Buteo, what you propose is a matter for the Centuriate Assembly, not for the Senate. The power to extend a general's command lies with them."

"The Senate is empowered to issue instructions to elected officers and to make recommendations to the Centur—"

Galerius's expression remained mild. "My friend Buteo, if you wish to propose such a recommendation, we can debate the matter. However, I would suggest you first consider the likely reactions of the Tribunes of the Plebs to such a maneuver."

'*Just try it,*' Marcus thought. As one of said Tribunes, he would not hesitate to use his veto to keep Buteo from undermining Sempronius's command.

"While you contemplate that," Galerius continued, "I suggest we move on to other matters."

Buteo sat down, but his pinched lips and narrow eyes promised that the issue was far from settled.

◇◇◇◇◇◇◇◇◇◇◇◇◇◇

"Blessed Jupiter, that man can talk," Gnaeus Autronius said to his son when they left the stuffy chamber a short while later. "Oh, good gods, Helios is in full force again today, I see, and still no damned breeze."

"It seems we can't blame Buteo for *all* the hot air," Marcus said, squinting in the blazing light. They stood in a narrow block of shade beside a column. The sun beyond was so bright that it seemed to wash out all the color of the Forum, leeching saturation from the gorgeous reds, blues, and greens of statues and walls.

"What a fool that man is," Quintus Terentius grumbled, coming up beside them. "Intransigence for the sake of intransigence."

Gnaeus blinked a few times, startled by Terentius's sudden company. The Terentiae, for all their eccentricities, weren't often associated with plebeian backbenchers like the Autroniae. Certainly Gnaeus would never have approached the father of a Vestal Virgin of his own volition. Marcus had a stronger measure of Terentius, however, having encountered him at several dinner parties thrown by Popularist friends, and he was very fond of Terentius's younger daughter Terentilla. Her Earth was more wild-spirited than his, but he still felt a certain elemental kinship with the girl. As such, he had less trouble than Gnaeus in finding his tongue. "He thinks he's doing battle for the sake of the Republic, I take it. In his head, Sempronius Tarren represents the dissolution of order and law and the *mos maiorum* and probably the gods themselves. So anything which opposes Sempronius must, therefore, be right and good."

"I think you've the right of it, irrational though it is." Terentius scratched at his shoulder and shrugged the weight of his toga into a different position, looking quite like he'd like to tear the cumbersome fabric off right there in the Forum. "Marcus, Gnaeus, I assume you must correspond with young Felix, yes?"

"Yes, as frequently as we can," Marcus replied, since his father was still gaping at Terentius's informality with them. "Though he's not much of a correspondent. Sempronius's letters have been much more, ah, thorough."

Terentius arched an eyebrow. "Have you had some from Sempronius that we haven't heard in the Senate?"

"A few. He's had ideas for my tribunate, though I've only been able to introduce a few of the less ambitious measures."

"Ah!" Terentius snapped his fingers. "Some of those urban renewal projects, I suspect, have his mark upon them? Not to cast aspersions on your own legal mind, of course."

Marcus took no offense. "He's been a great help, especially when it comes to framing things in a suitable way. My legal mind isn't as creative as Sempronius's."

Terentius laughed. "That's one way of putting it, I suppose. Nimble as an Abydosian dancing-girl, that man's wits." He flapped a hand. "Anyway—I wanted to ask, because I'm thinking of standing for consul."

Marcus's chest expanded with what he belatedly realized was relief. "Forgive my saying so, Terentius, but thank Jupiter. I was wondering who the Popularists would be able to scrape up this year."

"Consider me sufficiently raked, then," Terentius said. "I'd like as much information as I can get about what's going on in Iberia—and not only from Sempronius, thorough though his reports are. Not everyone's willing to take them at face value, and if I'm to take the consulship, I'll need to win over a great many men who aren't already on his side. I've got Rufilius Albinicus passing along what his son has to say about it, but you know what Publius is like. I'm sure he's far more focused on those Iberian warrior-maids in the auxiliaries than he is on battle plans."

Marcus suppressed a grin. Publius Rufilius, often called Young Apollo, was too handsome for his own good and an incorrigible flirt. "I'm not sure Felix is much better in that regard," he confessed. Felix's most loquacious letters so far had been in praise of the girls he'd met in Nedhena—just as, during his Numidian campaign, they had been about girls in Cirte and Volubilis.

"Now, be fair," Gnaeus said, coming to the defense of his younger son, "I don't want Quintus Terentius thinking my son a frivol. Felix has a good head on his shoulders, for all that he does like a good revel. And he's as military-minded as you could ask for."

"So I've heard," Terentius said. "And it's his perspective I'd like. I think it might win over quite a few of the equestrians—enough to over-come whatever senators are won over by Buteo and any news that comes in from Praetor Rabirus."

Marcus nodded. "It's a solid strategy. I'd be happy to pass word along."

"Good, good!" Terentius stuck out his hand to shake first with

Gnaeus, then Marcus. "Do stop by my domus anytime. North slope of the Palatine, blue door with the bronze sun emblem over it. In fact, come to dinner—no, not tonight, I'm promised to Appius Crispinius tonight—tomorrow, then."

"You're most generous," Gnaeus said, eyes wide.

"Bring your wives, of course. Caecilia would love to chat with them, and Tilla will be around. We'll have a fine little party." Terentius mopped sweat from his face with his forearm, then peered off across the Forum. "And speaking of Caecilia, she'll have my head if I don't bathe before dinner—not that it makes much of a difference in this damned heat. I'll be sweat-soaked again before I make it home." He clapped Marcus's arm, then sauntered off. "See you tomorrow!"

Gnaeus stared after him. "Juno's tits."

Marcus gave his father a wry smile. "Better not use that sort of language in front of our new friend's Vestal daughter."

XXVII

Latona's twenty-third birthday fell shortly after the Ides of Sextilis, and she marked the occasion with a small family dinner at her home with Herennius on the Caelian Hill. Aulus presented her with a new strand of pearls, and Aula gave her earrings to match. From Alhena, there was a book of Athaecan poetry, meticulously copied out in Alhena's own neat script. "And Lucia says she's going to make honey cakes for you the next time you come over," Aula said. "She's obsessed with the kitchens lately, of all things!"

"You went through that phase, too," Aulus reminded her.

"I only wanted to steal snacks," Aula said. "Lucia actually seems to care how they're made."

Even Herennius had done well, gifting her with a wooden box of polished cedar, carved with images of Juno presiding over Aventan rituals as women beseeched her favor. Within were several skeins of soft red wool. The brilliant color could only have come from kermes dye, not the cheaper madder that produced less saturated hues.

"From my sheep—our sheep—in Liguria," Herennius explained. "Your father said you were doing a lot of weaving lately. For your brother, I expect?"

Latona declined to contradict him, particularly within earshot of her father. Some of this wool would doubtless be put to that purpose, though she had no idea when such a package might be able to reach her brother. The rest . . . *'I could make a full mantle for myself, at least. Maybe one for Vibia . . . I wonder if the Fire magic would work as well on her, or if her own magic would interfere with its protective power . . .'*

Latona found herself thinking more about that than about the conversation at supper. No Discordian magic had surfaced in the city yet, at least not that the Vitelliae had been made aware of, but Latona felt ever more certain that something was coming. She'd had a kind note from Vibia that morning, offering birthday felicitations, but also conveying Vibia's similar sense of concern. *'The thunderclouds are gathering, even if the storm hasn't broken. I only wish I knew where the lightning will strike first.'*

The sense of swelling pressure made idleness intolerable, and so Latona had spent part of nearly every day since returning to Aven with Rubellia, practicing Fire and Spirit magic alike, or coming up with plans for approaching the other mages in the city who might be able to help when the Discordians did strike. *'I should have invited Rubellia tonight. And Vibia.'* But looking outside of the family would have encouraged Aula to make a full party of it. *'Perhaps soon we should do just that . . . some night when Father's out of town, or at dinner with a client . . . We could invite Terentilla, too. Maybe even sound out Marcia Tullia . . .'*

"Latona?"

It was Aula's sharp nudge, more than her father's voice, that brought Latona back to her senses.

Aulus frowned at her from the couch he was sharing with Herennius as he reached for a helping of turbot. "My dear, are you quite well? You seemed far away."

Latona affected a smile. "I'm sorry, Father, I don't mean to be poor company, particularly on my birthday. I'm afraid I stayed out too long in the sun with Ama Rubellia, and it gave me a bit of a headache."

"Ah. And have you taken something for it?" Aulus wagged a finger at her. "Always too proud for remedies, you." He gestured to Merula, waiting at the edge of the room. "Have someone brew up a tincture of yarrow and vervain for the Lady Latona, please. As swiftly as possible." He smiled indulgently. "I cherish the witty voices of all my daughters, so I shall selfishly require her to recover her health as quick as can be."

Latona laughed, and it was more genuine than her earlier smile. If she could forget the looming Discordian peril, if she could pretend for a moment that she really did only have a headache, then it all seemed so normal, so typical of her family. *'My father does love me,'* she thought, tearing off a piece of soft bread and dipping it into a little tray of honey. *'He may not understand me, but he does love me.'*

A too-familiar grumble brought her mood back down, though. "You really shouldn't spend so much time out in the sun," Herennius said. "You're freckled enough as it is."

Latona's fingers clenched around the bread; the honey dripped onto her fingers. *'So swiftly, he can mangle things.'*

Aula saved her from a tart response. "Heavens, Herennius!" she chirped. "If you think Latona freckles, you ought to see what happens when Alhena and I venture from beneath the shade. Spots all over, like one of those Cyrenaican creatures they bring over for the games."

Alhena gave a shy giggle. "I've always thought a bit of sun looks charming on Latona, anyway. You and I just look like we've turned bright coral."

"Gaius must be freckles all over out there in Iberia," Aula said, "though he's more of Latona's complexion."

"Did you know," Herennius said, spearing a cut of venison sausage on a knife's point, "that the men of Athaecum keep their women indoors entirely?" He circled the meat in the air. "The proper women, at least, the nobles and mercantile classes. They are protected at all times."

"Juno's mercy," Aula said. She looked to be barely suppressing an eye-roll. "What a lonely life that seems."

"The Athaecans say," Herennius went on, "that it preserves dignity, to the detriment of no one and the benefit of all."

"The Athaecan *men* say that." This time, the pushback came from little Alhena, and Herennius's eyebrows shot up nearly to his hairline in surprise. Her bright blue eyes were fixed on the dish of pears in front of her couch, and her jaw was tight. "I don't suppose you would know what the Athaecan *women* say about it."

Latona could have kissed her for the sudden burst of courage. Aulus shifted on his cushions, clearly uncomfortable with the turn the conversation had taken. "Yes, well," he said, "the folk all over Athaeca did develop some strange ways over the centuries. Comes of not having a proper central government as we've had here in Truscum. Each city-state governed itself for so long, you know, in relative isolation, so they had time to grow idiosyncrasies."

"Yes," Latona said, wiping her fingers on her napkin with more force than was strictly necessary. "I've always rather admired the women of Cynosoura, who govern the city when the men are off at war."

"Their fashion is certainly quite liberated!" Aula chimed in. "Don't the citizens of Athaecum call them the 'thigh-showers,' because they leave their gowns open and unpinned on the side?"

"They do," Aulus warily confirmed. His eyes were darting among his daughters, as though he could not decide which one of them needed reining in the fastest.

"What a delight that fashion might be to bring to Aven," Aula said, beaming. "It would save a bit on the seamstress bills, too, I should think."

"Not to mention how very pleasant that must feel in hot weather," Latona added, raising her eyes to her husband and fixing him with a pointed stare, "when a lady goes out walking in strong sunlight."

Frowning, Herennius edged forward on his couch. "Now—"

"I hear," Aula's voice had a dangerously icy thread in it, "that the ladies of Cynosoura are even allowed to divorce their husbands for reasons of sexual dissatisfaction."

Herennius went florid, crushing his napkin in his fist. Aulus dropped his turbot in shock. "Aula, I'm not sure that's appropriate conversation for—"

She shot her father a dazzling smile. "I'm sorry, Father. I thought we were sharing curious cultural tidbits from across the sea." Aula, too, turned to stare at Herennius. "Weren't we? I'm *sure* that's all that Herennius meant by sharing his story about the women of Athaecum."

Herennius wasn't even trying to maintain composure any longer; he was outright glaring at Aula and Latona both. Only Aulus, clearing his throat loudly, broke the three of them out of their ocular impasse. "Alhena," he said, with more than a little desperation in his voice, "tell us about that poem I saw you working on this afternoon."

Alhena chanced looking up at her sisters before speaking. "Well, it's a translation, really. Of—of Pescion's tribute to the seasons."

"Could you recite a little?" Aulus asked. His eyes, the brilliant green that Aula and Latona had both inherited, were wide with anxious desperation. "Please?"

Alhena obliged, launching into a lyrical tribute to summer. Aulus relaxed, mollified by the change in focus, and Aula returned to her dinner in seeming grace. Only someone who knew her well would see the pique still riding high, evidenced by the economy of her gestures and the slight pinch around her lips, and Herennius certainly did not have that nuanced perception.

Latona could not resume eating quite yet. Her own fury was still stoked hot, even if the embers were carefully concealed beneath a polished cover. *'Make yourself a statue,'* she thought. It had been her habit in Ocella's court, to keep emotion from betraying her. She was weary of resorting to the tactic, born in terror and bred in soul-shattering desolation. To steady herself, she focused on every lamp in the room in turn, feeling their flicker, wick by wick. They wanted to flare, and Latona wanted to let them, but she turned her mind instead to control. *'Quiet, my friends, quiet and cool.'*

Herennius, too, was still in a temper. She could feel it sparking in him, the acidity of self-importance, the heat of a bruised ego, the nauseating drain of resentment and doubt.

A good, dutiful wife would do everything in her power to soothe and reassure him. Latona was sorely tempted to use her magic to leave him stewing in an inescapable morass of negative emotions.

She found herself thinking of what Sempronius Tarren had said to her, many months ago. *'The pigeon knows he has no right to love an eagle.'* And what a pigeon of a man her husband was, always pecking at crumbs, not a creature who could ever think to soar to grander heights. *'A pigeon, but a pigeon whose very inconsequence gives you a shield.'* Glaucanis Lucretiae's words at the Galerian dinner party had reminded her: Latona had to think of her reputation, too easily painted in lustful scarlet and ambitious purple, and of her father's and brother's careers. Staying shackled to Herennius protected her from accusations of imprudence, which would reflect poorly on her family.

'Someday, though,' she thought, *'even that will not be enough to be worth it. Someday he will push me too far.'* Behind that, another thought, surprising her as it surfaced. *'Someday, I will have power and prestige enough that such rumors cannot damage me or mine.'*

Heat was building in her palms—a warning sign she had not experienced in a while. Her magic, reacting to her high emotions, ached to leap into action. Again, she could feel the life in every flame in the room, torches and lamps begging her to call them to a more combustible destiny. *'Stop that,'* she thought, as much at herself as at the flames. *'We don't need to incinerate anything tonight.'* She glanced briefly at Herennius. *'No matter the provocation.'*

<hr />

The sun had been down for hours, but a hot blanket of air still sat on the city. Sweat crawled down Vatinius Obir's back and curled around the underside of his knees as he sat in the tavern that served as headquarters for his crossroads collegium, waiting for trouble.

Three nights in a row, it seemed, there had been trouble. Three mornings, now, he had received word of it, up and down the Esquiline. Rumor had it that similar unrest had fomented in the Subura, the valley to the southwest of their hill, but the Suburan collegia and those of the Esquiline were not on good terms. They shared neither confidences nor concerns. Still, Rumor had many tongues, and some of those had whispered in Obir's ears.

And so he waited.

'Not so different from guard duty, really.' He had served such a purpose in the legions, from time to time. Staying awake when one had a job to do was merely a matter of will—and Obir would never let it be said that his will had failed him.

The tavern itself was quiet: a few of his men drinking after their shifts, a few talking in low voices. Ferinna's girls had already made a pass through and taken two visitors away for entertainment. Ebredus sat beneath the window, his feet kicked up on a bench. His eyes were closed, but Obir knew he was not sleeping; his hands were folded tightly behind his head. A traveler had told him a tale earlier in the evening, and likely he was repeating it to himself, committing it to memory so that he could make a song of it later. Songs were sacred things to the Tennic people Ebredus came from, and potentially magical. Obir knew when to let him alone to his contemplative work.

Shortly after the water clock showed the third hour of the night had passed, Obir heard thumping footsteps rapidly approaching the door.

"Captain!" One of the boys, still a year or two away from manhood, Esquiline born and bred, burst through the door. All heads snapped toward him, except for one man who was too deep in his cup to notice. "It's happening again. The insula above the apothecary!"

Obir was already on his feet. Ebredus as well, snapping out of his meditation, but Obir waved a hand at him. "Stay here, in case there's more trouble!" But he grabbed his whistle off its peg as he pelted out the door, blowing out a summons: two short blasts, then a long. *'On me,'* the signal demanded, a military order that Obir had instilled in all his employees. Two young men loitering outside scrambled to their feet, and others would follow.

It was one of the larger insulae in the neighborhood, five stories high, with a wine shop, a shoemaker, and an apothecary on the ground floor. Obir knew the place well, and its people. Like most insulae, it was home to a variety of citizens: well-to-do merchants and even an equestrian on the lower floors; artisans in the middle; laboring freedmen and women or newcomers to the city and their families crowded into the smallest apartments at the top of the building.

He heard the shrieking as he rounded the corner. A crowd had gathered in front of the building—some of them tenants who had already fled, others who had come out from other buildings to gawk. "Is it fire?" someone shouted as Obir dashed by.

"No!" he called back, praying it wasn't a lie. Fire was a greater terror than any other in the city.

Or so he thought, until he raced into the atrium at the center of the insula.

XXVIII

Few lamps were lit at this late hour, and the moon was not in the right position to shine down through the opening in the roof. The air inside the insula had a strange chill, entirely at odds with the stifling summer heat and uncomfortable on Obir's sweat-damp skin. *'This is not natural,'* he thought, as the ice crept down his spine and knotted somewhere in his gut. *'Not at all.'*

A pair of women were huddled at the bottom of the stairs that led to the upper apartments. One was petting the other's hair, murmuring soft words, but at Obir's approach, her head dragged up. "They're upstairs! They're on every floor!"

"They?" Obir questioned, but the woman's lower lip trembled, and she shook her head, curling back in toward her companion. "Go, go on, get out of the building." Obir gave her a slight nudge as he went to the stairs. "Go to the collegium tavern, you'll be safe there." He stopped on the first landing but waved the men behind him to continue upward. "Check all the apartments, get everyone out, take them to the tavern if they have nowhere else to go." He went to the nearest door, beyond which he could hear a low keening mixed with hysterical sobs.

Obir had seen much in his nearly forty years, wonders and terrors, mundane and magical. He had seen a wildcat kill a viper, right at the foot of his bed; he had been in the midst of a battle when enemy mages called up a sandstorm; he had seen men die, in howling agony and in silent despair. Nothing had prepared him for the scene inside that apartment.

A man was on his knees in the middle of the room, with a woman behind him, clutching a hiccupping toddler to her chest. The man's hands were outstretched toward a hovering gray shape, like smoke made of silver. It was almost human in form and size, but indistinct. From where Obir stood, its features were like an image in a cheap and badly polished mirror, sometimes dark and sharp; sometimes distorted and blurred. "Please . . ." the kneeling man begged. "I have honored your memory . . . all the rites . . . your tomb . . ."

Obir averted his eyes from the shade and stepped up behind the woman as quickly as he dared, not wanting to alarm her more than was necessary. Still, she shuddered when he placed a hand on her shoulder. "Come, madam," he said, when she turned tearful eyes to him. "Come, out of here. You'll be safe outside."

"Wh-what did we do?" she blubbered, even as she allowed Obir to lift her to her feet and guide her toward the door. "W-We're g-good people!"

"I have no doubt, madam. Go on downstairs." At the door, he heard footsteps on the landings above, some padding rapidly down the steps. Obir turned back to the man and the specter within the apartment. "Good man, come away."

"Why have you returned?" the man howled, but not at Obir. All his attention remained fixed on the silvery-gray mass swishing through the room. "Why?"

Obir laid his hand on the man's arm, more firmly than he had with the woman. "It will not answer you," he said, and once again had to hope he wasn't lying. "Come away from there. We will send for a priest and—"

"But why is he here?" The man finally looked at Obir. Tears tracked down his pallid face, and his eyes were wild with terror. "We did everything properly! Why would he not be at rest?"

"I do not know who you mean, my friend," Obir said, starting to pull on his arm. "But if you come—"

"Her father!" he shouted, flapping a hand at the shade. "Dead six months, and now here? Why?" He sucked in a wet breath. "His restless shade has returned. Don't you see?"

Against his better judgment, Obir looked up at the specter. At first, he saw only the amorphous features he had before, man-shaped but vague. Then, as a heavy coldness settled in Obir's gut, the shape solidified, stretching taller—taller even than Obir, with long limbs and hair in tight knots. To Obir's eyes, it appeared not as the weeping woman's father, nor any other Truscan-born soul, but instead as someone he knew as well as he had ever known himself.

His brother Nisso, as he had been in life. But no, not as in life. Nisso had had a cheerful spirit. Never had he looked so dour, so mournful. His eyes had never shown such despair. Never, except in those last moments, when he had watched Death's approach, blood and viscera spilling from the gash in his stomach.

Obir hardly heard the sobbing man now. The shade of his brother did not speak, but Obir felt as though he heard him anyway, asking why, why

Obir had let this happen, why he had not done more to save him. Utter anguish swelled in Obir's chest, a sorrow that had lived at the bottom of his heart for many months and now rose like bile, expanding as though it might choke him.

"I am so sorry, brother." Obir's hand moved of its own volition, reaching out toward the shade. Obir liked to think himself strong, a man carved of oak, but gazing upon the image of his brother, he felt every crack, every flaw in his soul. Every weakness, every failure. "So sorry . . ."

Dimly, he heard the other man being dragged from the room, less gently than might be. Then someone seized *him*, rough hands gripping above his elbows. "Sorry 'bout this, captain." Obir did not fight it; he allowed himself to be led, but his eyes lingered on his brother's smoky shade until he had been hauled out onto the landing.

◇◇◇◇◇◇◇◇◇◇◇◇

Obir took a moment in the atrium to gather himself, splashing water on his face. His men had done well, clearing the building. Some six or seven shades had manifested, it seemed, and from the scattered cries and nervous chatter he overhead, everyone had seen the dead. Some recently departed, others long gone. Often members of the same family saw the same shade, but not always. Some, as with Obir and the man he had tried to help, looked upon the same smoky substance and witnessed entirely different shapes.

'Dark mysteries.'

As soon as he stepped out, a fleshy woman with glossy dark hair set upon him: the mistress of the building. "What has happened here, captain?" Her tone was half-begging, half-demanding.

"I do not know yet. But I vow to you, I will find out." He repeated that, louder, for the benefit of the gathered crowd, then added, "Those of you who do not have somewhere to go, come with me to the collegium tavern. We will care for you there." It would be somewhat crowded, but perhaps that would be for the best. Comfort could be found in a trial shared.

As the herd started moving, either dispersing into nearby homes or trudging along to the tavern, Obir found one of his boys, a russet-haired youth of sixteen, and caught him by the elbow.

"In the morning," he said to the lad, "send to the house of Aulus Vitellius—and to the house of Numerius Herennius. Tell the Lady Aula

Prima that Vatinius Obir would impose upon the assistance she offered, that her family would stand in place of my patron's."

"And at the house of Numerius Herennius?"

Obir's gaze went skyward for a moment, searching out a friendly star. "Tell the girl Merula that she was right, damn her, and to bring her mistress as soon as may be."

∞∞∞∞∞∞∞∞∞∞

CAMP OF LEGIO X EQUESTRIS, OUTSIDE TOLETUM

"General!" Hanath dismounted before her horse had come to a complete stop, swinging easily down to the ground and into a brisk stride toward Sempronius.

He had been walking the perimeter of the camp, speaking to the centurions, getting a sense of the men's moods. There had been deaths attributed to the Lusetani magic, men who had been too deeply affected by the demons and who let terror and melancholy consume them. Many cohorts were growing restless, needing action. It strained the nerves, being so close to an enemy but not able to strike them. Harrowing though their skirmishes were when the *akdraugi* manifested, though, they were not fearful. Confidence in their leaders had not yet waned—but Sempronius knew he was running short on time.

He'd sent patrols further afield, searching for allies to the south and east. More cavalry could be helpful, but more importantly, he wanted the opinion of every friendly magic-man they could find from Toletum to the coast. If the Lusetani had revived ancient magics, perhaps *someone* in another tribe at least knew enough of their methods to determine how to counter them. Hanath often joined the patrols, since she knew many of the local chieftains, by reputation if not directly.

She always reported to Sempronius promptly, but her haste and stony expression concerned him. "What is it, Lady Hanath?"

Her dark eyes glanced left and right, and Sempronius immediately turned to fall into stride beside her, angling toward the command tent. "Send for Felix," he called to one of the junior tribunes as they passed.

Once they had gathered in the tent, Hanath shared her bad news. "It seems your fellow praetor has finally bestirred himself to action," she said, acid lacing her tone. "He has responded to the people of Corduba, who have long implored the legion in Gades for protection against brigands and slave-traders."

Felix's brow furrowed. "The Lusetani haven't struck that far south. Not since digging in here, at least."

"Not Lusetani," Hanath said, shaking her head. "Counei, perhaps, or others, not allied with the Lusetani but merely taking advantage of the chaos."

The very chaos Aven was supposed to be quelling into peaceful prosperity. Sempronius felt the needle, even if Hanath had not intended it.

She continued. "Praetor Rabirus, in search of the raiders, found a village. A Tartessi village." Her lips pressed thin; there was a shine on her cheeks, and the muscles in her throat looked tight with the effort of speaking carefully. "The people of Corduba have had no complaint with the Tartessi, but that did not seem to matter to the praetor. He attacked without warning, and when he had won his cheap and unjust victory, he let his men fall to rapine and pillage. They were not our enemies, but Rabirus treated them as he would the Lusetani."

Sempronius and Felix were both silent a moment. Felix exploded first. "That damned viper!" he snarled. "May all the fires of Tartarus and all the tortures Pluto can invent be insufficient for him, the sun-blasted worm—"

First cold, then heat ran through Sempronius's blood. Pillage happened in all warfare, of course. The legions considered spoils part of their fair pay. Sempronius had never thought sacking towns to be the wisest course, even in the defeat of legitimate enemies. His natural abhorrence for waste rose up at the notion. When the time came, he intended to deal as fairly as he could with the Lusetani, without risking the ire of the legions or his Iberian allies. That Rabirus would have deliberately attacked an unaffiliated town, when they were in such sore need of local assistance . . . *'Did the man not know what he was doing, or did he simply not care?'*

As Felix began pacing, still swearing with his usual creative force, Sempronius looked Hanath straight in the eyes. "How many dead?"

"Half the village, it sounds like. The other half raped or brutalized. Their fighters were taken unaware and swiftly dispatched. Some few escaped and raised the alert in neighboring towns. Others they believe taken as slaves and sent to Corduba, or maybe all the way back to Gades."

"Who is 'they'?" Sempronius asked, voice low. "Who told you this sorry tale?"

Hanath settled back, crossing her arms. "Other Tartessi, who are heading this way to avenge their kin."

"This way?" Felix asked. "Why not—"

"Oh, no doubt some will set their sights on Rabirus's forces," Hanath said, her voice faster and her accent slightly thicker in her anger. "The foolish ones, and no doubt Rabirus's legions will cut them down like so much barley. But many are heading north, crossing the plateau from the Baetis to the Tagus, intending to join their strength with the Lusetani." She flicked her fingers. "Rabirus did not seem to mind which Iberians he slaughtered, so they do not mind which Aventans they kill."

Sempronius released a breath in a slow hiss. "I cannot undo the evil Rabirus has done. I will make what amends I can, when opportunity arises." Hanath's silence conveyed what such a vow would be worth, to those who had lost all. "How long before the Tartessi reach us?"

Hanath calculated. "Twelve days if they are swift and the weather favors them. But they will have to cross two mountains, or else cut wide to the east, and cross the Anas River."

"And get to this side of the Tagus, as well." He passed a hand over his brow. The gods had not yet seen fit to help him puzzle his way out of the trap he was in. He moved to his desk and braced both hands against it, bending over the map. "It has become even more essential that we break this siege. We can't let the Tartessi come around and hit us from behind. If we can break and scatter the Lusetani before they arrive, then I might stand a chance at reasoning with them."

"It would show their faith in the strength of the Lusetani less well placed, at least," Felix said, scuffing irritably at the ground.

Sempronius raised his eyes to Hanath again. "I cannot thank you for the nature of this news, Lady Hanath, but I am grateful to you for bringing it to me. I am sorry that Praetor Rabirus is . . . the man that he is."

Hanath's fingertips drummed against her bicep. "It would have been too much to expect all Aventan generals to be as you and Gaius Vitellius," she said. "War makes monsters of many men. I have seen this more than once, in other lands. Do not fear that the Arevaci will be so foolish as to forsake you for another man's errors—but it comes to me, General, that we have also not discussed how things will be, between Aven and Iberia, once this war is won."

Sempronius nodded solemnly. "I know. I know, and we will, I promise you." He had thought much on it, when his mind had not been churning over their impasse. Aven would owe much to their Iberian allies—and not all of Aven would want to be gracious in repaying that debt. He had plans for their recompense, and he was trying to lay the groundwork in his messages to Marcus Autronius and other friends, but he could not be sure of success. Not yet. "When we have redeemed your husband and the rest of Toletum, we shall have a lengthy discussion."

He received a tight nod in acknowledgment. "First, we have a battle to win. Somehow."

CITY OF AVEN

"*My* husband believes me when I say I have a religious duty to fulfill, even in the dead of night," Vibia said, fluffing her crimson mantle back from her shoulders. "And Ama Rubellia, I presume, may come and go as she pleases. But what on earth did you tell Herennius?"

"He thinks I'm at my father's," Latona said, bending to adjust her sandal. "And my father, of course, thinks I'm at home. Anyway, it's not the dead of night."

"Yet."

"Yet." The three mages had convened at the tavern of the Esquiline collegium just before sunset. Sextilis was winding to a close, but the sun still lingered long hours, and the air remained hot and thick even as its light faded away. All three had dressed as simply as possible.

Latona had only had time to finish one mantle so far. It hadn't needed to be crimson, really; Latona could have woven the charms out of wool dyed any color. It felt *right*, though, to choose the same red that the men of the legions wore, the same red protecting her brother and her lover in far-off Iberia. By common agreement, Vibia had donned it for this evening, saying, "We'll all be better off if this works and you don't have to try and pull me out of the abyss in addition to fending off whatever fiends are plaguing these people."

When dark fell, Vatinius Obir and a cordon of his men escorted the ladies to the afflicted insula. Vibia and Rubellia had both arrived with maids, but they remained in the tavern. Rubellia's girl, born on the Esquiline herself, accepted this cheerfully, but Vibia's attendant sat stiff and uncomfortable in the corner. Merula, of course, had refused to be left behind, for all that she seemed to get along with the collegium brethren just fine.

As they walked down the street, Latona felt kinship with her brother, for she felt as though she had encountered a town under siege. She had never heard an Aventan street so quiet. The usual noises of the city echoed from far off, but here, the only sounds were the footfalls of the mages and their guarding cordon, the rustle of the ladies' dresses, the soft brush of leather on leather from the men who had put on cuirasses or greaves. No use against ethereal enemies, of course, but Latona understood the instinct.

All the houses that had shutters for their windows had closed them up tight, and those that didn't had hung sheets or burlap sacks over the openings, as though that might keep the demons out. Everywhere Latona looked, she saw charms and bundles of herbs hung from the lintels.

"They're not just scared," Rubellia said, glancing around at the closed-off houses. "They're *pulsing* with terror. I can feel it from every house."

Latona could, too, little spikes of white-hot fear emanating from each building they passed. "The Discordians attacked one insula and terrorized an entire neighborhood."

"It wasn't the first," Obir said, his voice a low rumble. "At least, I don't believe so. We heard rumors from the Subura, from elsewhere on the Esquiline. But this is the first place my men actually witnessed the—the creatures."

"Not creatures," Vibia corrected. "Spirits. Fiends. *Lemures.*"

Obir muttered in what Latona assumed was Maureti, though from his intonation, she was not sure if it was prayer or curse.

They drew up before an insula four stories tall. The shops on the first floor were closed up tight, but the door with its peeling blue paint stood slightly ajar. "We will check the building, ladies," Obir said, "though I do not think anyone is inside. And then, I hope—" His throat worked; anguish and embarrassment both leaked out of him, pressing at Latona's primed empathy.

"You need not stay within," Latona said. Instinct urged her to comfort him, but it would have been beyond the bounds of propriety to lay a hand on his shoulder. *'We're pushing the limits and our luck far enough in that regard for one night.'* Instead, she directed soothing energy his way, hoping it would convince him that there was nothing to be ashamed of.

Two of Obir's men stayed with the mages, while the rest cleared the building. "We will be just outside," Obir assured her, as they prepared themselves to go in. "You need only call for us if—if we can be of any service." His lips quirked up on one side, an acknowledgment of what little good cudgels and fists were likely to be against what they faced.

Rubellia held herself more tightly than usual, but that was her only outward sign of fear. Vibia was fussing again with her mantle; she affected an unconcerned air, but Latona could sense her apprehension. *'Small wonder, after what happened the last time.'* Vibia had complained about the hour, the neighborhood, the short notice, the weather—but she had come, without hesitation. *'I owe her for this.'*

Inside, the terrible quiet stretched around them. The walls muted what little noise had been audible in the street. Latona shivered, unnerved by the near-silence, such a foreign thing in her life.

They took a few minutes to wander the insula, looking for any obvious signs of Discordian presence. Latona did no more than glance inside the apartments; it felt a wretched intrusion, even if they had been invited to work their magic here, to peer into the tenants' lives. Overturned chairs, spilled oil, a discarded doll—many signs suggested that the inhabitants had fled the night before and not returned since. Merula did not share Latona's hesitance, meandering freely through the rooms, performing a far more thorough inspection.

The women returned to the atrium. Assuming the Discordian was not a tenant, then that, the public area of the building, was the most likely spot for the curse charm to have been hidden. "Though I suppose it could be in one of the shops," Vibia mused.

"If we track it there, we can have Obir force a door for us," Latona replied.

They sat on benches near the triangular pool in the center of the building, waiting. Occasionally, one of them would speak, but Latona was hardly aware of the words she either heard *or* said, and she doubted the others were better off. *'Just noise, to remind ourselves that we're here. Noise, to stave off the silence.'*

All four stood up at once when a cold wind gusted up, biting like a December ice storm. The *wrongness* of the Fracture magic hit Latona more severely than it had in the past, summoning the old fear rising inside her ribcage. Vibia, too, shuddered as the world tore open somewhere near them. *'Juno preserve me, give me strength, guide me.'*

Not one, but three *umbrae mortuorae* manifested in the shadows of the atrium. They came not out of the water, but as if from beyond it, without causing so much as a ripple: silvery smoke rising without a flame. "One for each of us," Vibia murmured. Merula coughed pointedly from her position near the door. "Each of the *mages*," Vibia corrected, rolling her eyes.

Already, the fiends were taking shape, bobbing closer to the women. A howling noise rose from them, and Rubellia's lower lip wobbled. Latona had told her what to expect, both in sight and sensation, but nothing short of encountering the fiends could have prepared her. Vibia, on the other hand, mostly looked annoyed. Latona was glad for that; it meant the mantle was working its protections.

These *umbrae* were stronger than those they had encountered in Stabiae—though not, thankfully, so terrible as the possessing fiends they had encountered in the wheat field. In Stabiae, she and Vibia had gotten good at finding the charms and cutting them to shreds before the *umbrae* grew too vigorous, but here, with three of such intensity to deal with, Latona's fortitude was taxed. Their shapes grew more defined, losing their smoky blur and appearing more as their stolen shades would have done in life. The threat of it had a thin strain of panic vibrating in Latona's chest. *'No, no, I do not want to see . . .'* She pushed her Spirit magic at them, but couldn't seem to target all three at the same time. As one weakened, another would grow stronger.

Shades of the restless dead, the *umbrae mortuorae* were. Not the actual spirits returned from Pluto's realm. That was another kind of spirit, immutable. The *umbrae* took whatever shape they thought would be most unsettling. And there was one dead man in Latona's memory for whom "unsettling" was a grievous understatement. She averted her eyes, whenever one of the damned things darted before her, but tears sprang up anyway. She didn't feel fear, in the face of this fiend. He was dead and burned, almost a year past. What need for fear? But shame, yes, that rose like bile in her throat, and fury burned in her heart.

'Focus. You cannot let him—No! It's not him, it's them, these wretched things, and you cannot let them get to you.' Fists tight at her sides, Latona concentrated on the taste of cinnamon on her tongue, blossoming from her Spirit magic. *'Let Juno's gift be all your world, if that's what it takes.'*

Vibia found three charms, each concealed beneath loose stones at one corner of the central pool. She tsked loudly. "Smart," she murmured.

"Smart?" Rubellia echoed. Her cheeks were wet; she had been using her own empathic magic to help Vibia, or trying to, but the *umbrae* were much to adjust to in a single night. Her eyes kept straying back to the cloudy shapes. Latona wondered whose specter haunted her.

"The water," Vibia said, even as she dug the point of a knife into one of the charms. "Water's a conduit between worlds." Physically, her bronze blade shredded a bundle of cloth, bones, and other unpleasant ingredients; magically, the blade's edge formed a focus for Vibia's power, channeling it into the breach the charm had torn between the worlds. "Makes it easier to pass from one to the next—Blessed Fortuna, this thing feels like it's on fire." She pushed the crimson mantle away from her brow with the back of one hand.

"Good." Latona's voice sounded like it was coming from somewhere outside of her. "It's working—and working hard."

As Vibia sliced through and unraveled one charm after another, Latona sent her bolstering energy, as much as she had the strength to summon. Between that and the mantle, Vibia hardly seemed affected by the *umbrae* at all; she'd scarcely spared them a glance. Latona, by contrast, knew she was pouring so much into Vibia that she was leaving herself open to assault. She focused on Vibia's pale hands, her fingers working so fast, splinters of bronze magic jolting off of them with every deft motion. *'Faster, Vibia, faster.'*

An ache went through Latona, an ache she remembered, an ache of hopelessness, of suppressing all that she was in the desperation to avoid future pain. *'Not looking at the thing doesn't mean it has no power.'* And as Vibia hacked at the last of the three charms, the other *umbrae* faded away, but the final specter lashed out, sinking its claws into whatever heart it could reach.

'Fine. Let it be me.'

Latona raised her head to look at the thing. Its seeming-mouth was closed, but it emitted a keening noise nonetheless. *'Here I am, then. Feast on me, in your death throes.'* Tears were streaming down her cheeks now, and a tremor had entered her hands, but she could still taste cinnamon, and a golden sheen had settled over her vision: her own magic, surrounding and protecting her. *'Take what you want from me, if it keeps you from tormenting anyone else. You're merely a shadow. I lived through the reality, and I'm still here.'*

Vibia gave a little cry of satisfaction as the last charm finally unraveled, magically as well as physically, and before Latona's eyes, the face of Horatius Ocella, Dictator of Aven, broke apart and faded into the night.

XXIX

None of the women spoke much as a visibly relieved Vatinius Obir led the way back to the Esquiline tavern. Vibia had pity for Rubellia, whose emotional nature seemed to have taken the encounter poorly. Latona, too, looked more shaken than usual. *'What effort did she expend, in shielding me?'* The fiery heat in the enchanted mantle had cooled, but it had worked in the moment better than Vibia could have hoped, even if the sensation was uncomfortably like standing in the door of a blazing oven. Her head had remained clear and focused, despite the *umbrae* prodding at her. *'Let us hope it works as well if we encounter fiends of the other sort again.'*

They retrieved their waiting maidservants. Rubellia's girl had to be roused from sleep, but Vibia's had been a-frizzle with worry. "It was bad enough in the country, Domina, but *here*?"

"You should come back to the temple with me," Rubellia said to Latona, "since neither your husband nor your father will expect you till morning." Latona nodded weakly. Rubellia's lips worked soundlessly a moment, then she passed a hand over her eyes. "I—I do not think I can speak of this now."

"Who would want to," Vibia intoned, "with night's blanket still on us?"

"But we should discuss it—and what to do next." Her brow furrowed in sorrow and concern. "If this is happening elsewhere in the city . . ."

"Come to my father's house at the third hour," Latona said. "The men will be at the Curia by then, and the gods know Aula has sufficient control over the household that none of our people will carry tales, if they overhear us." Thus agreed, they prepared to depart the Esquiline, well-flanked by Obir's people.

"I have no poet's tongue with which to express my gratitude, ladies," Obir said as he saw them off, "but please know how deeply I appreciate your assistance." He glanced down the still-quiet street. "This is my home. To have it invaded and feel unable to protect it—" He shook his head. "A wretched thing."

"You must call on us again," Latona said, "if this problem continues to rear its head in your neighborhood."

"I will, thank you, Lady Latona." The man's eyes twinkled a touch conspiratorially. "Though my esteemed patron may not thank me for inviting you into danger. I'm not sure that's what he meant when he asked me to keep an eye on you."

Vibia's eyes cut toward Latona. *'Sempronius asked them to—? Hm.'*

For the first time since leaving the insula, Latona's face registered something other than weariness. Obir's words had brought a sly smile to her lips and a crinkle at the corner of her eyes. "Oh," she murmured to Obir, "he might surprise you." Even more maddening than Latona's guileful secrecy was the chuff of laughter that escaped Rubellia.

Vibia looked from one woman to the other with a creased brow. *'Now what do they know that I don't?'*

◇◇◇◇◇◇◇◇◇◇◇◇

The next morning, surrounded by the verdant foliage of the Vitellian peristyle garden, Vibia took the lead in explaining the night's activities to Alhena and Aula—who would, it seemed, not be left out, never mind that she had no magical gifts to draw on. *'Be fair, Vibia,'* she told herself. *'Aula was, after all, the first to realize the Discordians would be moving their power back to the city.'*

When Vibia was done, Aula asked, "And Vatinius Obir thinks this is happening in the Subura as well?"

"So he said," Rubellia replied. "And elsewhere on the Esquiline, out-side of his neighborhood."

"They're attacking poor citizens here, as they did in Stabiae," Alhena said.

Latona rubbed at the bridge of her nose, then raked a hand through her loose curls. There were dark circles under her eyes, and she was dressed in a plain tunic and a loose gown, with no cosmetics and unstyled hair, as though she had barely dragged herself out of bed in time for this meeting. The previous night had taken more of a toll than any of their excursions in Stabiae had. *'Poor thing,'* Vibia thought, and surprised herself with it. Pity was not an emotion she often felt for anyone, much less for Vitellia Latona, whom she had so long watched with a wary eye. To be sure, this woman was not the creature that Rumor's many tongues wagged of, conniving and guileful.

"We're going to have to move forward with convincing others to assist us," Latona said. "People with clients all over the city—the Subura, the Aventine docks, the neighborhoods across the river."

"Should be asking in the slave quarters, too, Domina." Merula had, till then, been so quiet that Vibia had almost forgotten she was there, sitting aside with Alhena's Cantabrian attendant. "Where the public slaves are housed, and any of the warehouses that have large quarters." One shoulder lifted and dropped. "If they are attacking those who cannot be defending themselves, who will not be speaking out—"

"You're absolutely right," Latona said, dropping her chin onto her hand. "I'm ashamed I didn't think of that."

"The public slaves would draw too much notice," Aula said. "Many of them are secure enough that they'd have no problem raising a fuss to the priests and augurs." Most of Aven's publicly owned slaves worked for the temples and administrative buildings, clustered in or near the Forum.

"I agree," Rubellia said. "It would be a bigger risk for the Discordians to target them. But the warehouses, yes, and perhaps any of the guilds who have large numbers of slaves in their employ—the builders, for example."

"Builders . . ." Latona's face creased in thought for a moment, then her eyes darted to Vibia. "What do you know about the progress on your brother's temple, over on the Aventine?"

"Only that it is progressing, so far as I know." Vibia caught the thread of her thought. "You think the slaves and freedmen building there may be affected?"

"It's worth looking into. The Discordians targeted Sempronius's dealings before. They may do so again."

A small part of Vibia was annoyed that Latona evinced such care for Sempronius's projects, but she knew the greater part of that irritation was with herself, for not having considered it first. *'If he did have to take an interest in a married, scandal-prone Spirit mage with a penchant for attracting chaos . . . well, at least she's a conscientious and detail-oriented one.'*

Latona drummed her fingers thoughtfully against her leg. "We need to know how far the Discordians are spreading their malice. It'll take us forever to track it all down ourselves, and even if we could, it isn't as though we'll have Vatinius Obir's men to accompany us everywhere. We have to find help."

"It's not that I disagree," Vibia said, "but even if we rally our friends, we'll still be running ourselves ragged if we try to solve this one problem at a time. The Discordian power is growing, and I've had about enough of reacting to whatever they throw at us. We need to go on the offensive and make it impossible for them to dig their claws into this city."

"They must have a center somewhere . . ." Alhena mused. "A—a base of operations."

"Like a legionary camp," Rubellia offered, with a small smile.

"Perhaps. If we can find that . . ."

Aula clapped her hands together. "One piece at a time, then. Let's each of us commit to dragging in at least one other conscript within the next few days. You three find mages; I'll find someone whose husband or brother has an enormous client base. We'll cast as wide a net as we can and see what Discordian fish we catch."

"That seems sensible." Vibia was already thinking of who she could trust enough to sound out.

Latona, Alhena, and Rubellia murmured their agreement as well. Rubellia looked thoughtful, and Latona still wan and exhausted. Alhena was blushing, Vibia assumed at the very idea of gathering the temerity to broach the subject with someone outside this room. Aula's gaze landed on Latona, and her next words were less officious. "There's something you're not saying, isn't there? About the *umbrae*?"

Vibia had always thought Aula Vitellia to be a frivol and rather feather-brained, but this long ordeal had shown her that the cheerful woman was cannier than she appeared—particularly where her sisters were concerned.

Latona's shoulders moved in a too-casual shrug; a lie of the body, for Vibia's Fracture magic could sense the shiver trembling underneath. "As Vibia said, these seemed more potent than what we've encountered before. They took shape more easily."

Rubellia nodded, sadness coming over her features. "It chose well, too. The fiend decided to show me the face of someone I failed, back when I was just an acolyte. When the red plague struck the city—well, Vibia may remember, but the rest of you would've been too young." Vibia did remember; Alhena wouldn't even have been born yet. "It was every man to his post—and every woman, too, and even girls of twelve. Every mage in the city with even the slightest healing power, every soul blessed by Light, Water, or Fire, we were all called to serve." Rubellia told the story smoothly but with distance in her voice, a pain long since passed but never quite made peaceable. "Fire has a great power to purge, but I was so young, not strong enough. And a woman who put her trust in me died, when I could not cleanse the contagion from her. Looking on the fiend with her shape, I didn't just see *her*. I remembered every bit of that failure, and felt its shame and regret tenfold."

"It wasn't your fault," Alhena said.

Rubellia smiled and reached out to cup Alhena's cheek. "I know, sweet girl. I did everything I could, for all that I was young and inexperienced. A great many died even in surer hands. The finest healers in the city couldn't save everyone." Her thumb rubbed gently over Alhena's pale skin, and then she eased back in her chair, folding both hands in her lap. "What the mind knows and what the heart feels are different animals. The *umbrae* give power to the heart's most painful instincts."

"That's a good way of putting it," Vibia said, as she took a small knife and began peeling a pear. "I wonder why they choose my father, for me. He was a stern man, with very high expectations for his children, so it's a bit unsettling, but not a horror. Why he'd be among the restless dead for an *umbra* to steal his shape, I can't imagine. He always seemed satisfied enough with his life."

"But he died before you and Sempronius were fully grown," Alhena said, with quiet insight. "Before he knew what lives you would make for yourselves. I . . ." She kicked her feet a little, scuffing against the packed earth beneath their benches. "I don't mean to speak for you, of course. But I know I worry what my mother would think of me. How she would judge me." Her head sank, hair hanging in curtains on either side of her pale face. "I was so little when she . . ." Alhena's voice trailed off, and Aula leaned over to kiss her on the temple.

"She'd be very proud and pleased of you, my love. But I take your meaning. We must always wonder what the beloved dead would say to us now, if they could. All the more if they were taken from us too soon." Aula cast a slightly rueful look across at Vibia. "I must confess a certain relief not to be afflicted with magical gifts that would call upon me to confront these spirits. As much as I would love to see my husband again, I do not think I would care for the version of him they showed me."

Latona's eyes were glassy, and she had gone still. Unnatural, on the woman who seemed to always be in restless motion. Vibia wasn't the only one who had noticed. Empathetic Rubellia cocked her head. "Latona, is something wrong?"

Latona managed a weak smile. "It's foolish, to be so unsettled just talking about the *umbrae*. But I must confess, those we encountered last night were . . ." She closed her eyes briefly, then shook her head. "The effects have lingered, I find."

"We should stop talking about it, then," Alhena said.

"No." Latona's fingers flexed, then curled tight into the sea-green fabric of her gown. "I'm sure I'll feel better after a bath, but in the meantime . . . Naming a thing that frightens you . . . It makes it less frightening, doesn't it? You bring a nightmare into the daylight, and it ceases to have power." She spoke with more hope than conviction.

"It's Ocella," Aula said, her voice more somber than was its usual wont. "Isn't it?"

Latona nodded tightly. "As he was at Capraia."

The very rumor that had made Vibia skeptical of Latona in the beginning. Dictator Ocella hadn't summoned stunningly beautiful young women to his court for the pleasure of their conversation, after all, and Latona was then a mage of untested power. *'Whose gifts did he want more, Juno's or Venus's?'* Had he more sought to satisfy his lust for ambition or for the flesh? Vitellia Latona would have been an irresistible prize in either case. A Spirit mage of noble birth, politically connected to every man whose support he needed and every man he hated. A Fire mage with hair of gold and flawless sun-browned skin, sensuality written in every ample curve of her body. *'Gods. She was eighteen when he pounced on her. Only a year married.'*

Vibia had heard the rumors, and she had worried about their implications for her brother's growing attachment to the woman, but she had never actually thought about what the truth behind them had done to Latona.

"He had that way of looking at you," Latona said, so softly that she sounded unlike herself. Where was the strident minx Vibia had once thought Latona? Or the bold defender she had come to expect? She found she would prefer the sly smiles, the half-mad confidence that had sent Latona trekking through muddy fields with her skirts hiked up around her knees. Seeing Latona like this, hearing the hollowness of her soul in her voice, it rattled Vibia. Her own emotions tangled: fury on Latona's behalf, revulsion at the tale, poignant shame that the woman she had trusted so little was placing so much faith in her, to speak of these things.

Latona went on: "A way of looking at you like you were something to eat. He could feign affability, and did, quite often, but his eyes gave him away. They were so cold. None of his smiles ever touched them, not truly. You never saw a spark of joy there."

She said "you," Vibia realized, not "I." Vibia picked up on the careful grammar because it was a break, a rift—a way for Latona to keep herself at a distance from what had happened to her.

Aula slipped down the couch, looping her arms around her sister. Latona leaned her head on Aula's shoulder, letting her hair be petted, but her hands were still tight fists in her lap. Across the table, Alhena stared, wide-eyed. *'Well,'* Vibia reasoned, *'she was far too young to have known the full truth. Aulus kept her well-hidden in those years, as I recall.'* The redheaded girl looked as though she wanted to go to her sisters, to share in their sorrow, but felt she had no right to do so. Rubellia must have sensed her distress, for she reached out and took the girl's hand comfortingly.

"Anyway," Latona said, in a forcedly brighter tone, clearly trying to shrug off the specters of the past, "that's what the *umbrae* look like to me. Horatius Ocella, stretching out his hand. So I'm especially fortunate that Vibia has the power to dispel the wretched things."

Vibia nodded and murmured something about being glad as well, but what she thought was: *'Sempronius was right to chide me.'*

Before he left for Iberia, Vibia had tried to warn her beloved brother away from Latona, worried by the rumors about her, especially those that said she'd developed a taste for powerful men. She feared her brother growing close to someone so brazen and immodest. Sempronius had corrected her in no uncertain terms, insisting that Latona had been Ocella's victim as much as any man he had proscribed and exiled.

'More than most,' Vibia realized now. *'They might have lost property in the proscriptions, but the ones that got away with their lives lost nothing they couldn't replace. What he took from Latona . . .'*

Vibia set her chin firmly. "Well. All the more reason for us to put an end to this Discordian threat. None of us need reminding of our darkest days."

SPLINTER THE FOURTH

Such satisfaction, in opening a door, and such pain, when it slammed closed.

"I've worked so hard," Corinna lamented to the dormice before her. Easily procured, filched from the kitchens. Why should such sweet little things be eaten, when they could serve such a grander purpose, fueling her efforts? Her bronze knife moved swiftly, splitting fur from flesh. "I have been dutiful. I have opened so many cracks in the world."

Prideful, perhaps, but she felt she had earned it. The first few rips, there in the countryside, had scarcely survived a few moments before closing again. In winter, she had started, thinking the bleakness would be her benefit. But her skill had not been swift enough, and when spring came, the whole world fought her every effort. Growth hated a breach; it sought to plug all holes, mend all wounds.

"I conquered it, though," she said, plucking sinews between her slender fingers. "I created gaps and held them open. For a time."

And then *someone* had begun undoing her work. So soon, too soon! Corinna had thought she would be safe in the country, and her fellow disciples had agreed. In Aven, there were so many mages living close together. Someone would have noticed her efforts before she'd had a chance to perfect her technique. In isolation, she had not expected anyone capable of countering her magic to discover her rites.

But someone *had*.

When Corinna could no longer evade her rival, she fled back to the city. She had learned enough, anyway, and her talents were needed. She returned to Aven and taught her fellows what she had learned. None of them were as deft as she had become with the charms yet. Some still flinched from what was necessary, and Corinna laughed at them. "If I'm not squeamish, I don't see why they should be," she said, rolling a tiny wet skull thoughtfully in her palm. But enough of them had the idea of it by now. They had been able to open so many doors! Across the hills and valleys of Aven, bronze doors giving passage between the worlds!

And then someone closed them *again*.

"I will find them," she vowed, tying together the charm that would unlock a new door. On the Aventine, perhaps, this one. Or deep in a crowded market. "I will find who keeps closing my doors, and they will wish they had not interfered."

XXX

TOLETUM

Slowly, with reluctant fingers, Vitellius unknotted the focale at his throat.

He disliked taking it off even for a moment these days, but it needed washing, or else it would chafe and leave his skin open to infection. That was not something Vitellius could risk, not now, not with disease stalking through the city on the heels of ill-blown winds. His sister's charms seemed powerful, but he could not be certain that they were infallible: not here, so far from home and the weaver's hands. Best not to tempt Fortuna.

For fifteen days now, Vitellius had been losing men to a swift, wasting illness. The vexillation's medic claimed this was like no other plague he had ever seen, and so far as Vitellius was concerned, that confirmed his suspicions. Whatever wretched magic the Lusetani were working now, it was no longer going after the souls of his men, but their bodies.

Once, he might have been glad for that, might have thought it an easier battle to win. But he couldn't fight the little red spots that appeared without warning on a soldier's skin, nor the fatigue and fevered shaking that followed. No sword could strike them down, no strategy outwit them. Within days, all the afflicted man's strength would seem to be stripped away, his muscles dwindling as though he had starved for a month.

'And we're all thin enough as it is,' Vitellius thought. His rationing had thus far kept the city from starvation, but by a slender margin. Meat had been a luxury in Quintilis, and even then it was best not to question its origins; in September, it was impossible to find. Even fish had become hard to acquire. There were still men brave or desperate enough to leave the dubious safety of the city walls and creep down the cliffside to the waters of the Tagus, daring Lusetani raiders to find them, but lately their catches had been meager.

The only boon was that the disease did not appear to pass from man to man. If it had, Vitellius thought the entire city would have perished by now. No, it came with the strange Lusetani-summoned mists.

After the first men fell ill, Vitellius had wanted to order all his men off the walls and behind barred doors—but the Lusetani warriors were still out there. They didn't seem to fear the plague-mist. They might have some immunity-granting charm, like Vitellius's. *'Or perhaps the king of blood doesn't mind sacrificing a few dozen of his own in the name of his cause.'* And standing on the walls when the mist rose was not a certain death sentence. One man might fall desperately ill and be dead the next day, while the guards on either side of him remained hale. *'No pattern, no reason to it.'* Vitellius wanted to tear his hair out.

With no idea how the curse chose whom to strike down, Vitellius set the legionaries and townspeople alike to finding some sort of protection. Most legionaries carried something of the sort with them, carved amulets or tokens made of twisted reeds. The water Vitellius washed his focale in now was no mere well-water, but infused with a variety of herbs and tree barks.

All the men of the legion had been ordered to wash their focales similarly, and to tie the red neck-scarves over their noses and mouths when the mists rose. Good water against bad air. Solid logic, supported by the theory of the humours, all the medics agreed. Was it helping to slow the spread of the disease? Vitellius had no idea, no proof. But he couldn't just do *nothing* while this Lusetani curse ravaged his ranks.

Vitellius had overseen the preparation of the tinctures himself, summoning the Aventan medics and Iberian magic-men alike to put their heads to the task. He had even taken the advice of one of his centurions, whose brother, a mage of Light and a healer, was pledged to the service of Apollo. The centurion knew little of his brother's art, but he could remember a few remedies that his brother had given him over the years. Vitellius was willing to try anything.

Alder wood and angelica flowers, juniper and vine, crushed together and made into a tincture. *'Thank the gods that Toletum had a few healers who were well-supplied before the siege started, and that we planted in those empty lots.'* Even as it stood, Vitellius was worried their supplies would run short. *'Those supplies, like everything else . . .'*

A pang of guilt throbbed inside him as he rubbed dirt from his focale with his thumb. For all his efforts, no other man had protection like this. *'And who am I to keep it for myself?'* But the answer came swiftly. He was the senior tribune of the Eighth Legion, the leader of this vexillation. And a leader had to keep himself safe if he was to have any hope of protecting his men. A cold calculation, but a necessary one.

He wished Bartasco would stay inside and well away from the evil mists, but the burly Arevaci chieftain would not hear a word of such suggestions. Instead, he strode forth as boldly as could be, looking to hearten his own men and the Aventan legionaries alike, as though he could defy the plague through sheer force of personality. Mennenius, too, dutifully carried out his tasks, though Vitellius tried to keep him away from the walls. More than once, Vitellius had been tempted to swap his focale for his friend's, to give Mennenius that extra defense. *'And what stopped you?'* He reasoned with himself that he could not be sure the enchanted garment would work on another man: it had been made by his sister, for *him.*

A darker awareness whispered that this was merely a rationalization, that the truth lay in his own fear and selfishness. *'Gods help me to know the right path. I am doing the best I can.'*

Vitellius wrung the focale out, water dribbling back into the bowl. He didn't re-tie the scarf while it was wet, but he did drape it over the back of his neck. September had dawned with no less blasting heat than Sextilis, and the cooling effect was pleasant: a single spot of relief in the increasing agonies of the siege. *'Heat and hunger and terror of the night were all quite enough to be getting on with. Plague on top of it . . .'* Only the knowledge that the legions were out there, trying to break the siege, was keeping general pessimism to a manageable level. *'But it's been so long with no sign of progress . . .'*

The door opened, and Vitellius shook his head, trying to clear morose thoughts from his mind as he turned to face the centurion who entered. He could not feign Bartasco's resolute buoyancy, but he would show strength and stalwartness nonetheless.

"Sir." The centurion saluted. Vitellius had not allowed them to get sloppy about such things, even under the stress of siege and strange magic. Lax discipline could incline men toward mutiny and riot. An Aventan legion adhered to form, no matter the circumstances. Vitellius nodded his acknowledgment. "Sir, more men have fallen ill, and—" His voice hitched slightly.

Bad news, then. Not that any sentence beginning that way was likely to turn out well. Not that he expected any other sort of news, at this point. "How many?"

"Nine since this morning, sir. And—"

Vitellius frowned, wondering what could be so dire that the centurion hesitated to frame his words. "Out with it, centurion."

"The new sick men, sir. Tribune Mennenius is among them."

CAMP OF LEGIO X EQUESTRIS, OUTSIDE TOLETUM

The Tartessi were across the Anas River and, by the scouts' reports, advancing swiftly.

"The weather, it seems, has been favoring them." Sempronius glared at the map, as though that might change the distance between the Anas and the Tagus. He wished he had a mage with him who could read the winds and tell him if a helpful sandstorm might whip up on the plateau and stymie the Tartessi's progress. Eustix had no such talent, however; he had been blessed with the Air of the birds, not the weather. All Sempronius could do was guess and rely on luck. *'And Fortuna has not been smiling upon me thus far.'*

"They will likely travel just north of us and cross the river here," Hanath said, gesturing. "The same point my riders used when we needed to swing south of Toletum."

"We cannot still be here when they cross. We must either be inside Toletum before they reach the river, or well away from this place."

Fleeing was one option, abhorrent though it would be to suffer such an ignominious defeat. But Sempronius could not stomach the notion of leaving the cohorts inside Toletum and the town's citizens to the predations of the Lusetani—nor was he at all certain that Hanath would agree to such an abandonment, with her husband and so many of their people still inside the walls. He could not risk losing the Arevaci cavalry, nor the loyalty of the Arevaci themselves.

"We have to act. We are out of other options." Sempronius's hand clutched hard around the edge of his desk. "The only thing worse than breaking ourselves against the Lusetani would be having the Tartessi fall upon us *while* we break ourselves against the Lusetani."

"We could try to get a bird into the city, to let them know what we intend," Hanath suggested. "Perhaps, if we can distract the Lusetani enough, Tribune Vitellius and my husband could evacuate. Cross the river to the south, get somewhere safe."

Sempronius nodded, considering. A town of a few thousand, likely weakened by hunger, desperate from long months of living under siege. *'Not to mention the effect of the akdraugi . . .'* Demoralizing enough on first encounter, their effect accumulated over time, and the cohorts inside Toletum had been afflicted far longer than the legions north of the forest.

"The idea is not without merit," he said, "but I feel it's too much of a risk. The Lusetani could fall upon them as they tried to cross, or they might run straight into the Tartessi on the other side."

He straightened. Hanath's posture was as firm and resolute as always, but the deep blue color beneath her eyes spoke of her weariness. They were *all* weary. *'And waiting any longer won't make us less so.'*

"Send messengers to Calpurnius and Onidius. We attack on the morrow, in full force. Another messenger will follow an hour from now with the battle plan—or as much of one as we can create, taking the *akdraugi* into account. Any legion targeted by the fiends should focus on taking out the magic-men. If we can break their magic, we can break through their lines. *That*, I am sure of."

⸗⸗⸗⸗⸗⸗⸗⸗⸗⸗⸗⸗⸗

CITY OF AVEN

If a party could be made out of something, Aula Vitellia would make a party of it. She needed to speak with Maia Domitia about the Discordian matter but had determined to do so only after having Maia—and a few others—over for a fine dinner. "We're asking something unusual and potentially perilous of her," Aula had justified. "The least we can do is feed the woman first. And anyway, I haven't seen her since she returned from Baiae. It'd be terribly awkward to spring all of this on her without preamble."

Latona arrived early to help Aula prepare, already dressed in her finery, a soft lavender gown over a crimson tunic, fastened with pearl-studded brooches. Her hair had been artfully arranged with pearls threaded around her crown, the strand that her father had given her for her birthday, with the matching earrings from Aula. A well-put-together outfit always helped Latona feel better prepared to face the world.

She needed that. As reports and rumors grew of strange occurrences all over the city, her nerves felt raw. Only twice had she been able to slip out of her husband's house and meet up with Vibia at the Esquiline Collegium. All the other cries for help had gone unanswered. That she could not have answered them all even if she had unencumbered liberty was not much of a balm. *'Vibia's right, and you know it. You have to kill this hydra at the heart, not keep lopping off heads and hoping they stop re-growing.'* But her heart ached, and her magic grew hot and restless in her blood.

'Well. At least I can use some of the energy this evening.' A fete was always good fodder for practicing her empathic talents, both reading and projecting. Aula certainly never complained if she used her skill to make sure everyone had a pleasant time.

Aula, still occupied with preparatory details, had not yet achieved her own desired affect of elegant carelessness by the time Latona arrived and found her in the peristyle garden. Her hair hung low in a frizzy knot, and she was still wearing a loose tunic and gown that Latona was quite certain she would never allow anyone other than the household to see her in. "I think we need to try adding a few more lamps along that wall," she said to the girls who were hanging decorations, fluttering a hand toward the eastern side. "The trellises have grown more ivy since last year, so the usual sconces aren't giving us enough light."

"Yes, Domina."

"The tri-nozzled ones, I think, every few strides." Her nose crinkled impishly as she cut her eyes over to Latona. "Wouldn't want anyone taking to the dark corners for illicit assignations."

Scowling faintly, Latona pinched the underside of her sister's arm, but before either of them could say anything else, Lucia came barreling into the room. "Mama, Mama—Oh! Hello, Aunt Lala. Mama, Gera says I have to go to bed early tonight, which means I must eat early, which means I must have my bath now, and I don't want to!"

Tucking her skirts under her knees, Aula bent down to be on eye level with her daughter. "Now, darling, we talked about this earlier, don't you remember? You don't have to go to sleep. I'll tell Gera to leave a lamp lit, and you can play with your kitten and your new dolls or practice writing on your wax tablet. But we're having quite a lot of people over."

"For a party." Lucia gave a sigh with the long-suffering air that only a six-year-old could manage. "A party you're having *without* me."

"I know, poor pet, it's monstrously unfair," Aula agreed. "But that's why you must learn those letters and do as Gera says, and before you know it, you'll be grown enough to come to all the parties."

"Aunt Alhena used to have to do the same, you know," Latona said, "when she was small but your mama and I were already grown."

"Aunt Alhena doesn't *like* parties," Lucia said, in a more astute observation than Latona would have expected from so young a child. "I do!" She flung herself on the nearest couch, which was high enough that she had to take a little leap in order to make her dramatic pronouncement.

"I like to lie on couches and eat food and tell stories, just like you, Mama!"

Latona couldn't help laughing. "She has you exact, Aula."

Aula narrowed her eyes up at Latona. "Careful, or you and I shall go pinch for pinch," she said, then turned back to Lucia. "I'm afraid we'll be up much, much too late for you, little love. But I tell you what: would you like to stay up long enough to say hello to Lady Maia when she arrives?"

Lucia swung her shoulders from side to side, considering. "Will Neria and Nerilla be there?"

"No, my darling, this is an adults' party. But—" Aula continued, cutting off Lucia's pout. "If you think you can do it nicely, like a little lady, you can ask her if they may come over tomorrow."

Lucia bounced up from the couch excitedly. "Oh! Oh, yes, I can! Lady Maia's always so nice to me, so I should be quite nice to her. Especially if it means Neria and Nerilla can come to play."

"Very well. You may stay up until she arrives, *if* you go with Gera and have your bath now, and don't give her another bit of trouble."

"I will!" Then Lucia got a very Aula-ish spark in her eyes. She pressed her lips together thinly before asking, "But may I run 'round the garden *three* times first?"

Aula petted her hair, standing up. "Very well. Thrice 'round the garden, then straight to Gera!" As Lucia shot off, Aula shook her head. "Why she wants to run around the garden is anyone's guess, but nothing wrong with a bit of exercise, and if it gets her to her bath faster . . ."

"Do you remember what it was like to have that much energy?" Latona watched as Lucia darted in and out of a line of potted plants, clearly taking a wide interpretation of "three times around the garden."

Aula settled her hands on her hips. "I do. I wonder where it all went?"

"I think you've still got plenty. You just focus it differently now."

"Ha! True. When you're all limbs and instinct, it's hard to know what else to do with it but run and run."

"Such long legs she's got," Latona said, watching as Lucia rounded the end of the garden and started charging back toward them. "It's a marvel how much she's grown since spring."

"Yes, well, she's at that age—Lucia, be careful!"

But the girl turned too swiftly, knocking over a table and spilling its contents onto the rugs beneath them—including a pair of blazing oil lamps, which a servant had put down while arranging a hook to hang them on. Aula shouted for help, and Latona dove to her knees, stretching out a hand—

The bronze lamps hit the rugs and tumbled, spilling hot oil everywhere. But the flames never touched the fabric.

They had, instead, leapt to Latona's outstretched fingers.

Latona, Aula, and Lucia all stared, transfixed by the gently waving flames dancing along Latona's skin. She felt the heat of them, but no pain; they seemed to be having no effect on her flesh. Her magic had formed some sort of protective barrier.

"Latona?" Aula's voice was high-pitched to the point of squeaking. "How are you—"

"I don't know."

"B-Because—"

"If I think about it too hard," Latona said, shaping each word warily and eyeing her own hand as though it were a venomous snake, "I'm afraid it may stop." She gave her hand an experimental roll, cupping her fingers. The flames tumbled down into her palm. "Can someone bring me a fresh lamp, please? I'm not sure how to extinguish this . . ."

One of the servants brought a lamp forward, but she hesitated a few steps away from Latona.

Latona flicked her eyes up. "It's all right," she said softly. "I've got control of it. It's not going to leap up at you."

Swallowing, the girl came close enough to set the lamp down in front of Latona, then skittered back. Latona watched the light flickering in her palm a moment longer, then put her hand alongside the lamp. *'Back where you belong.'* With a thought, she nudged the flames along, reaching for the same magic she had learned to use to shape a blaze. She felt them start to leave before she saw them move, a strange, dragging sensation, followed by a snap of release as the fire threaded itself onto the wick of the lamp. It burned over-hot for a moment, but Latona coaxed it down.

With delicate precision, Latona set the lamp on the nearest table that Lucia hadn't overturned. She glanced at the girl, standing stock-still a few paces away. "You're all right, little bee?" Lucia nodded dumbly, her blue eyes stretched wide. "The oil didn't splash you?" Her head wagged side to side. "Good."

Latona sat back on her heels, carefully placing her hands in her lap. Then she met her sister's eyes. There were tears in them, and Aula's pretty rosebud lips hung agape.

"So," Latona said. "That's new."

XXXI

The next day, Alhena sat at the loom in the garden. She wasn't supposed to weave alone—and, technically, she wasn't. Aula napped on a long couch, and Lucia was nearby, playing a game of *tali* with herself, tossing knucklebones in the air and trying to catch them on the back of her hand. Her efforts were somewhat impeded by her little brown kitten, who thought the knucklebones were provided entirely for *his* amusement. At the other end of the garden, an artist and his apprentice were painting a new fresco. Mus sat close at hand, working on some mending.

'Plenty of witnesses,' Alhena thought, *'if something should happen. Plenty of people to pull me out of a pit.'*

Repetitive movements could, for some Time mages, prompt prophecy. It was easy to fall into a trance state, when one's hands formed the same motions so often that one's mind could drift away, but Alhena wondered if there weren't more to it. Perhaps performing the same movements over and over again was almost like halting time, or trapping it, and that created the magical power.

Alhena's hands moved swiftly, drawing the heddle rod to her breast, pushing the weft bobbin through the rows of soft blue wool, then drawing the next rod forward and pushing the bobbin again. She was getting to be a better weaver than Latona, who tended to be more utilitarian about the task. Latona didn't hate weaving the way Aula did, but for her, it was a means to an end—a way to bleed off her excess power, or the only way to create the necessary enchanted garment. For Alhena, the action itself was the purpose, and her fingers had grown deft with much practice.

Weaving, she thought, might be of some use, if she could convince her magic to take her into a vision. Her sisters needed information, and Alhena desperately wanted to give it to them. *'And Latona might need it more than ever . . .'*

Alhena had not seen her sister's feat the night before. Aula had moved swiftly, swearing all the witnesses on the souls of their ancestors to utmost secrecy. Even little Lucia had been lectured until she was more afraid of her mother's wrath than she had been to see her aunt holding a fistful of flames. Alhena had only gotten the full story after their dinner guests had departed. *'This time, at least they told me as soon as they could.'* She could find some comfort in knowing they had not kept it a secret from her, even as they tried to do so from Aulus.

Alhena had to admit, too, that she was avoiding her responsibility to find them a new ally. Aula had laid the groundwork for sounding out well-connected Maia Domitia, she knew, and Latona was aiming for Davina of the bath-houses, who as a mage of Water might be able to see charms or curses at work—and who, as a plebeian whose work catered to high and low alike, would be well-placed to hear rumors from across the Seven Hills.

Alhena knew who she intended to ask for aid, and she would do so. She *would.* She just needed a little more time to work up the nerve. *'Tilla wouldn't need the time, if she was the one trying to ask you something,'* she thought, as she paused to beat up the weft, tightening the fabric's weave. *'Tilla's not scared of anything.'*

At some point, her father came into the garden, though Alhena only glanced at him through peripheral vision. The threads hummed beneath her fingers; magic was beginning to build. This was the progress she'd been working toward—to be able to call the visions to herself, rather than being at their mercy to show up whenever they wished, with no forewarning.

She did notice, though, that Aulus was still dressed in the toga of his censorial office, with two thick purple stripes as borders, so he must have spent the morning on official matters, and likely intended to return to them later in the day, if he had not troubled to change into something less cumbersome. Lucia immediately set upon her grandfather, begging him into playing a few rounds of *tali* with her, while Aula stirred enough to ask how his day had been.

"Full of tangles, I'm afraid," Aulus replied, but his voice held satisfaction, not frustration. "Oh, it's easier than it would have been two generations ago—yes, darling, very good!—but the tax rolls are still a mess. So many men undervalue their estates in order to shirk their responsibilities."

Aula had questions for him about the particulars, which Alhena only half-heard. Something about a trio of tax-dodging equestrian brothers. Far more Aula's domain than Alhena's, gossip and politics. *'It's good to see Father so well-contented, though.'* The office of censor sat well on him, and he looked the part: a solid and hale man, sharp-eyed and direct, authoritative yet fair, with just enough gray streaking his sandy hair to lend him the weight of *dignitas*.

"But the ones I'm most concerned about," he said, "are those who are actually entitled to *more* than they're taking. Some of the poorest farmers haven't the faintest idea what their rights are. I met a man today, wealthy enough for the Third Class, mind you, who didn't know where or when he should turn up to vote." The rattle of knucklebones, followed by Lucia's giggles. Aulus had evidently thrown quite poorly. "The Senate and Assemblies really must come up with a better system for communicating with . . ."

As her sister and father chatted, Alhena's mind wandered until she hardly heard them any longer, nor the clatter of the knucklebones or Lucia heckling her grandfather's lack of dexterity. The noises faded to the back of her awareness, as though she had a blanket over her head. Alhena moved to beat up the weft again, but her hands drew back covered in blood. *'Oh dear.'*

Strangely, no fear welled in her chest, no alarm whatsoever, and no pain. The blood simply *was*. Alhena looked past her hands, and saw that the loom had disappeared, and along with it, the frescoed garden wall. She sat not on a carved bench, but on ocher earth.

A city rose up in the distance beyond her. Much smaller than Aven. A single hill, if that, not seven, with low walls that looked a patchwork of brick, timber, and earth. As Alhena watched, with ongoing peculiar calm, a tide rose out of the dirt and lapped at those walls. Not water, she realized, but thick red blood.

She came back to her true surroundings with a short cry. *'I lost it!'* she thought. *'But you had it,'* came a second thought, swift on the heels of the first. *'You opened the door and ushered the vision in, rather than forcing it to break the barrier down.'*

Alhena became dimly aware that Aula and Aulus were both at her side, Aula having seized her hands and squeezed them. "What's wrong, my honey?" Aula asked, voice tight with concern. "Did you—"

"Yes. I'm sorry, I didn't mean to frighten anyone." A flash of bright blonde hair caught her eye, and she saw Lucia, standing a little further away, hugging her kitten to her chest. "I'm all right. I am. But something's happening. Or already happened. Or is about to . . ." She shook her head. "Hard to say."

Tentatively, Aulus reached out to stroke her shoulder. "Do you need anything?" he asked, so much more at a loss than when discussing the vagaries of citizenship rolls. "Water, or—"

"No, thank you, Father." Alhena offered him a weak smile. "I'm just . . . not sure what to make of it. I-I saw a tide of blood, lapping all around the walls of . . . well, I think it must have been Toletum." Aula's fingers pressed hers even harder. "But I don't feel nearly so frightened as that image would suggest." She looked up to her father. The last traces of the magic were fading, the threads pulling away from her. "If anything, I feel . . . heartened. By blood." Her nose crinkled. "Odd."

◇◇◇◇◇◇◇◇◇◇◇◇◇

LUSETANI CAMP, NEAR TOLETUM

Bailar swept a great circle around the pit of ashes in the center of the camp. They only lit the fires when absolutely necessary, for cooking or for rituals, hot as the waning days of summer had stayed. Most of the warriors wore as little clothing as they could get away with. Ekialde wondered how the magic-men in their dust-dragging robes didn't faint in the swelter. Perhaps the gods helped to cool them.

A cluster of magic-men waited behind Bailar. With Ekialde were some half-dozen of the best of his war-band, along with a few of the leaders of the Vettoni and other allied tribes. Such a sense of drama, Bailar had, but Ekialde had learned to read the currents of power. That drama was part of why the other magic-men deferred to him, why the Lusetani people believed in his capability. As Ekialde's golden circlet and leopard-skin cape communicated his status, so Bailar's flourishes did his. Ekialde waited patiently, arms folded over his chest, feet wide and strong against the earth, until finally Bailar came to a rest before him.

"Blessed *erregerra*. The star-readers agree: now is the time to strike."

Bailar's confident smile as he spoke gave Ekialde heart. The *akdraugi* had held off the Aventan legions, true, and by now the plague would be ravaging the men inside Toletum, but however effective these magics were as military tactics, they were not the same as fighting. The chosen king of Bandue, the god of war, could not comfortably sit in camp and await victory; he had to *take* it.

Bailar gestured back at his fellow magic-men. "They have had visions, several of them. A tide of blood, circling their damned city. It is a sign that our magic is strong enough to prevail against all foes."

"Good. Good." Ekialde heard murmuring from his war-band and the chieftains, but he did not turn his head to look at any of them.

"We can summon a greater force of *akdraugi* against the legions than we ever have before," Bailar continued. "I have trained the Vettoni magic-men to assist us. There are enough of us now to send *akdraugi* to all three of their camps at the same time—enough to subdue them utterly. And once we have done that, our warriors will be able to cut them to pieces."

"When shall we begin?"

"Far be it from me to suggest such nuances of military strategy," Bailar said, "but it is the dark of the moon tonight. I can perform the necessary preparatory rites tonight, which will give us all tremendous strength. We can make the sacrifice at dawn, and attack the legions thereafter."

"Then Bandue and Endovelicos shall give us strength," Ekialde said, "and we shall prevail."

XXXII

Sempronius was not sure what sort of an omen it was, that the Lusetani had decided to launch a full-scale attack the same morning that the legions had intended the same thing. Good, he supposed. They had not been taken unawares, at least. The men of the Tenth Legion, along the eastern bend of the river, were well settled into their lines and had nearly reached the forest before the wave of the *akdraugi* hit.

Their power was worse than ever, and even with the focale working its heated magic around his throat, Sempronius felt his head swimming with their effect. It was almost like inebriation, the muddle of something sickening and yet seductive, a poison that begged Sempronius to partake of more.

'*Shut it out . . .*'

All elements had their dangers, their detractions, and for those of Shadow, the temptation to use their powers for ruthless, selfish gain often presented itself. To sink into darkness, to embrace the deepest, unrelenting secrets of the universe and use them for personal advantage—that was what Sempronius guarded against, all the more so because he kept his gifts a secret from the rest of the world. The gods had entrusted him with power and thus far had given their tacit consent to his violation of Aven's laws; he could not repay their generosity by misusing those gifts. He had to be severe with himself, circumspect in how far he would allow himself to go. The soul-devouring maw that Pinarius Scaeva had summoned, the day of the Aventine fires, would have been an incredible source of power. So would the *akdraugi*—a way to leash death itself, to command powers that could harrow any man's soul—but it would come at far too high a price. It would demand nothing less than his own soul in repayment.

And so he turned his mind away from the eldritch call of the *akdraugi*. He had to focus, had to keep his men in command. But how could any man be expected to hold formation with fiends battering away inside his head? Even for Sempronius, the struggle was nauseating. The battle between his own magical instincts, the lure of the *akdraugi*, their enervating effect on his limbs, the defensive power of his charmed focale, and his own sheer determined grit was likely to swiftly exhaust him.

On they came, the Lusetani warriors, thundering through the forest behind their magic-men, then pouring out around them and charging across the field. The roar of their battle cries was faint at first but swelled like the tide as they grew closer.

For the first time in his life, Sempronius felt real fear in a battle. Was that valid, or another trick of the *akdraugi*, subtle enough to slip by the protection of Latona's gift? Never before had he doubted the ability of the legions to prevail. Never before had failure seemed a possibility. Not in Numidia, with arrows raining down under the cover of a sandstorm; not in Thessala, fighting between crumbling crags; not in Albina, facing woad-stained warriors and the haunting echoes of their battle-harps. So long as Aventan legions were in control of themselves, with a competent commander, they would win. Failure came only from lack of discipline or the fault of a foolish leader. That fact had underpinned Sempronius's entire military life.

'*Was I a fool, then, to think we could overcome this?*' The physical enemy had not yet come within javelin range, and yet the legionaries were trembling. Their shields ought to present a solid wall for the Lusetani to break themselves against, but it quivered.

'*Think, damn you! Think your way out of this, or we're going to get slaughtered.*'

Then Sempronius caught sight of Hanath and the rest of her auxiliary cavalry unit. She was wheeling her horse around, her sharp face displaying not fiend-stricken horror, but something between confusion and frustration. She yelled, losing her temper and leaning over to cuff another rider in the head. '*Well, she hasn't lost control of her senses.*'

He looked at the rest of the cavalry. Many of them were having trouble keeping their seats. Men swayed in the saddle, clutching desperately at the reins with hands that hardly seemed to obey their owners' commands. Others were bent over, their foreheads nearly touching their horses' necks. The horses themselves were spooked, though none had yet bolted. Sempronius supposed animals used to the cacophony and carnage of battle were hardy beasts. Most of the riders were in no position to mount a charge.

Most. Not all. And after another moment, Sempronius realized what all of the unafflicted riders had in common.

He gave his own horse a kick, spurring him toward the knot of cavalry. The world careened wildly around him as he rode, the surrounding trees and hills seeming to tilt and gyrate as though on multiple axes, a nausea-inducing whorl. Hanath assisted him by grabbing his horse's reins as he grew near. "General," she said, her clipped consonants all the sharper for her perplexity. "What's going on? And what do you wish of us?"

"For you to save us, Lady Hanath," he said. He gestured broadly at the men reeling and retching around them. "You and your maids." Finding the words had become a challenge. Between the influence of the *akdraugi*, the responding tug of his own magic, and the bright-burning Fire magic of the focale around his neck, Sempronius felt as though his entire vocabulary had flown out of his muddled head—or at least been wrapped in heavy, wet wool, difficult to peel away to find what he needed. "Women . . . unaffected." It wasn't all the women, he noticed—but it was many of them.

It was enough; Hanath took his meaning. At first, she looked around, confused. Then a broad grin broke out on Hanath's face, her dark eyes sparking with glee. "Fools," she chuckled, shaking her head as she looked across the plateau at the knot of Lusetanian magic-men. "What utter fools." Then she laughed, and her head cut back over to Sempronius. "I shall explain why later, General. You wish the girls and me to ride over and neutralize the threat?" she asked, and Sempronius confirmed the order with a nod. "Understood!" She called out the names of those women who were capable of riding. "On me, girls!" she bellowed, hoisting her spear—the spear the gods had shown Sempronius, the spear that might prove their salvation.

Hanath knew her business. She led her riders around the left flank of the approaching hoard of Lusetani warriors. As they thundered across the field, charging the unsuspecting magic-men in an ululating herd, Sempronius, to his shame, slid from his own saddle, barely managing to ground his feet beneath him. He leaned against his horse, grateful for the beast's patience with him, since his knees did not seem entirely equal to holding up his weight. '*What an indignity . . .*' For that, as much as for the military maneuver, Sempronius was eager to see these Lusetani magic-men brought low.

Felix, leading his horse rather than riding it, staggered up to him. "Did Hanath . . . go rogue . . . ?" Evidently Felix was suffering the same tongue-tied bewilderment as Sempronius. "Where're they . . . what're . . . why . . ."

Sempronius shook his head—then immediately wished he hadn't, as the pain was blinding. "My orders," he managed to say. "Women . . . unaffected . . ." Felix nodded, though whether that was in understanding of what Sempronius said or just in agreement that talking was too difficult, Sempronius could not say. Together, they watched through the dust kicked up by the horses' hooves. Some of the Arevaci used spears, like Hanath; others had bows and arrows, which they could fire with astonishing accuracy while still a-horse.

The Lusetani warriors were closer now, but hard to see through the haze of *akdraugi*. Still, a javelin volley might slow them, even if it wasn't well-aimed. "*Pila* at the ready," he said, as loudly as he could manage—more for the benefit of the horn-bearers than the fighting men themselves. Somehow, enough of the horn-bearers cleared their heads to sound the call. "Loose *pila!*" Sempronius said a moment later. How well it worked—how many of the legionaries even had the strength to hurl their javelins—he could not tell.

The hoofbeats of the cavalry were no longer audible, not with the *akdraugi* howling around the legion. Had Hanath and her women reached the magic-men? Sempronius could only hope. He could not hear the whiz of arrows, nor the wet thunks of spearheads embedding themselves in chest cavities, nor the agony of the dying, but he prayed for them. *'Father Mars, look here and save us.'*

At that moment, the first of the Lusetani warriors, howling their battle-rage, crashed into the front lines of the Tenth Legion. Some of the legionaries were less affected by the *akdraugi*, able at least to hold their shields in defense or to make a few jabs with their short swords. Some— but not enough, not to hold the lines.

Sempronius turned suddenly, despite that the action nearly sent him reeling, and seized the shoulder of one of the standard-bearers. "If our lines falter," he growled, "you take the eagles and ride for the coast as though the Furies themselves were at your heels. You hear me?" The young man's eyes were unfocused, tracking the *akdraugi* swirling around them. Sempronius shook him, hard. The standard-bearer swallowed, dragging his gaze to his commander. "Tell me you understand! Those Lusetani devils will not capture our eagles, you understand?"

"I do, sir. I-I will do my best, sir."

It would have to suffice.

◇◇◇◇◇◇◇◇◇◇◇◇◇◇◇◇

'Bandue, you honor us with the blood of our enemies!' Ekialde had been impressed, at first, when he saw the great lines of the Aventan legions.

He had chosen to lead the attack against the camp along the western curve of the river. Bailar was with the magic-men of the middle prong, so that he could move east or west if it was necessary. Each group of magic-men had hauled along a dozen Cossetan prisoners to supply the blood for their rites, and if all had gone as smoothly in the east and center prongs as it had here in the west, then Bandue would know much glory this day.

What music, the crash of metal, the split of wood, the crack of bone! What beauty, to see a blade flashing in the fading light before it came down and sank into flesh! Ekialde could feel his god with him, strengthening his arms, setting his blood to racing. This, *this* was what he was meant for, not plotting sieges from the safety of a camp. His uncle's specters were a boon, to be sure, they provided a sound military advantage—but he had tired of letting spirits of blood and ether do his work for him.

The Aventans were valiant foes, no mistaking. Ekialde would grant them that much honor. Even with the *akdraugi* harrowing their blood, they tried to hold their lines. Men who could not stand crouched behind their shields, cursing in frustration but not weeping in despair.

They broke, eventually. Of course they broke. They were mortal men, however well-trained, and mortal men could only expect so much of themselves.

First they fell back to their camp, and then they abandoned it, running for the high hills with whatever they could carry. Their legs found strength in the retreat, as it took them farther away from the *akdraugi*. Ekialde considered ordering the magic-men to come forward, so that the *akdraugi* could follow the Aventans, allowing them no rest nor safety. But he knew that, however strong tonight's summons, the *akdraugi* could not remain on the earth indefinitely, nor so far from the magic-men. Better to let the Aventans have their ignominious retreat and finish them off another day, when there was no danger that the *akdraugi* would weaken mid-charge.

Ekialde stooped over the body of one fallen man, not quite dead yet, but clearly gasping his last. Ekialde smeared his hand over the man's wounds, coating his fingers in blood and viscera. He thrust his fist up toward the sky, roaring, a wordless offering to Bandue in thanks for the great favor he had shown the Lusetani this day.

XXXIII

Just when Sempronius was thinking that his men could no longer stand the onslaught, that he would have to figure out how to retreat—miserable word!—with minimal damages, the *akdraugi* began to dissipate. As the mist grew suddenly thin, Sempronius risked reaching out with his own Shadow magic to get a sense of them. The *akdraugi* were crumbling apart, dissolving back into the shadows from whence they had come. Or, rather, dissolving back into nothing—or back into the veils between the worlds. Sempronius was yet unsure precisely how similar the *akdraugi* were to the *lemures*. The magic-men of the Lusetani seemed to be able to conjure them at will, anywhere. *Lemures* needed a specific gateway to come through, like the *mundus* in front of the Temple of Janus in the City of Aven. A powerful enough mage might cut through elsewhere, but it still had to be a fixed point. The *akdraugi* seemed to form out of the air itself.

Wherever they had come from and however they got on the field of battle, they were leaving now, and their absence cheered the Aventans as much as it alarmed the Lusetani. As the legions surged, one of the Iberians, a bulky bearded man with an animal-skin cloak, fell beneath an Aventan sword. The battle went to utter chaos after that. Bereft of their *akdraugi* comrades and an apparent commander, the Lusetani warriors panicked and broke off their attack.

Sempronius wanted to press the advantage, to chase them down—but his own troops were slow in recovering. Many who had been at the front were wounded, and the rest were still muddle-headed and trying to shake lethargy from their limbs. So he gave the instruction to reform lines and march back to camp, and as horns and whistles carried the order across the battlefield, Sempronius could feel no pride, only profound relief.

◇◇◇◇◇◇◇◇◇◇◇◇◇

The sun was midway down in the sky before Hanath returned. Sempronius had shucked off his heavy armor, trying to set the camp to rights. Those men left in one piece were reinforcing the ramparts and administering to the wounded and the dead. Many had reported the effects of dehydration, as though the *akdraugi* had been draining them of that vital life force. *'How much metaphysical truth might lie in that?'* Sempronius wondered. *'Another thaumaturgical mystery to reserve for peacetime exploration.'*

Hanath and her fellow riders looked like proper Amazons, all strength and valor and ruthlessness. Their bloody blades and empty quivers would perhaps convince some of the Aventan men who had doubted the wisdom of having women among the auxiliaries. Hanath's long limbs were spattered with blood, and she had a wild look in her dark eyes, not unlike that which he often saw in Felix's. "All dead or fled!" she announced, and spat at the ground. "There were too few of us to follow them all, but they ran like rabbits when they realized their magic could not touch us."

Sempronius felt no pity for the dead. For all they might look like priests, these were not unarmed men. The Lusetani had made combatants of their mages, then failed to protect them through conventional means. They were no innocents; their deaths were deserved. "I am glad to hear it," he said. "Settle your horses and your people, and let's convene in my tent. Someone find Felix. And Corvinus. I think they were both assisting the medics."

Within a few moments, the necessary staff had been gathered in the command tent. Hanath gratefully took a towel and a bowl of water from Sempronius and began sponging off the blood caked to her skin while they talked. Corvinus brought forward wine, and Sempronius poured for all four of them. "All right, Lady Hanath," Sempronius said, setting her cup beside the bowl of water. "You said you would explain. Why did the *akdraugi* not affect you and some of your ladies today, when they have before?"

A somewhat rueful grin crept onto Hanath's face as she slapped the towel down and took up the wine. "It is the simplest thing in the world, General," she said. "We are bleeding!"

Sempronius furrowed his brow, perplexed. "But none of you were wounded before the battle," he said. "None of you are—"

Realization dawned, prompted as much by Hanath's barely suppressed glee as by his own reasoning faculties.

"Oh." He blinked a few times, unsure how to respond to this information. "You mean you're—That is, at least some of you are—"

Unable to contain her amusement any longer, Hanath's grin broke into outright laughter. "You are, I think, as surprised as the Lusetani!"

Sempronius was not a man much given to blushing, but he could feel his cheeks heating. It was ridiculous, of course. There was nothing shameful about it, particularly not if it was an advantage he could harvest, but it was an arena of life with which he had little knowledge or experience. None, really. His wife Aebutia, dead these past eight years, had always been most discreet about her biological necessities, and certainly Vibia had never shared such intimacies while they were growing up. As such, Sempronius found himself uncomfortably at a loss for any language with which to discuss the matter.

"What?" Felix, a man with neither wife nor sisters, asked. "I still don't understand."

Hanath was laughing harder now, too hard to speak, so Sempronius found himself awkwardly trying to explain to his junior officer. "Lady Hanath means that she and some of her maids are . . . currently experiencing the effects of the moon's cycle upon their bodies." Felix's expression remained blank. Sempronius grasped for a less circumspect yet still tactful explanation, but discovered he could come up with nothing that wasn't couched in metaphor.

Hanath finally took pity on him, with her customary bluntness. "We are bleeding from our nethers, Tribune," she said, still grinning as she watched for the effect this information would have on Felix.

"Oh," Felix said, echoing Sempronius's initial perplexed reaction. Then, "*Oh*! Oh. That's . . . Er." He rubbed at his forehead. "I would've thought that would've been inconvenient to riding a horse . . ."

Hanath cracked up again, leaving Sempronius to try to restore some dignity to the conversation. "So I take it," he said, in as unflappable a voice as he could summon, "this somehow worked as a counter-charm to the Lusetani magic."

Straightening, Hanath nodded. "I am sorry," she said, though her continued grin and the mirth in her voice did not indicate that she was, in fact, at all sorry for Sempronius's and Felix's discomfort. "I know that many peoples of the Middle Sea have prohibitions against speaking of such things in mixed company."

"Not a prohibition, exactly," Sempronius said. "More a . . . custom." His face contorted slightly as he tried to picture any of his fellow senators having this conversation. "A rather intransigent custom. Such things are the domain of women, in our consideration. A religious mystery, really. Men prefer not to . . . trespass upon it."

Hanath waved a hand. "Yes, you Aventans do like your neat lines dividing up the world, whether or not they align with reality. As though moon-bleeding and child-bearing were all that makes a woman." Her voice turned more analytical and serious. "I think it is not to do with who bleeds from where, but with the magic of life triumphing over the magic of death. The Lusetani are using blood magic—and a form with which the Arevaci have little knowledge. But that is not the only sort of blood magic there is. Not all blood is stolen through violence. The Iberians consider moon-bleeding to be sacred, in itself, and it can be used for magical purpose." Her strong shoulders moved in considering shrug. "My people have similar customs, though you may never have encountered them while in Numidia. We can ask the Arevaci magic-men you have here to confirm, but to me, this seems sensible."

Once Sempronius could detach himself a bit from the awkwardness of the specifics, he could contemplate the thaumaturgy more carefully. Hanath was right; it *did* make sense. Just as Aventan magic had inimical elements, opposites with the power to counterbalance or even negate each other, Iberian magic must have similar forms of internal balance. That at least one of them should rest on the difference between a life-giving force and a life-draining one reminded him of some of the philosophies of the Abydosians. *'It might be a worthy project, to catalog the commonalities between such things across the peoples of the Middle Sea.'*

Harnessing that magic of life for his own purposes, though, was something Sempronius could fix his purpose to in the here and now.

"So, if this temporary immunity is tied to your, ah, internal functionings," Sempronius said, moving from the abstract to the practicalities, "how can we . . . That is to say, is there some way to . . . ?" Again, however, his knowledge failed him.

Hanath took up the line of his thought anyway. "You want to know if we can make strategy of this?" She paced a bit, tapping her thumb against her lower lip. "Perhaps . . . I never noticed the effect in Toletum. Tribune Vitellius preferred to keep us off the walls, so we rarely took the brunt of the *akdraugi* attacks to begin with."

"And it, ah, it doesn't seem to affect all of you at once," Sempronius observed.

Hanath shook her head. "No. In nature's courses, there would never be enough of us rendered immune at one time to neutralize all the Lusetani magic-men. We would be too vulnerable to other attack, and they could slip our pursuit, as they did today." Felix made a noise of disappointment, but Sempronius sensed Hanath's mind was still calculating possible advantage. "But there may be a way. There are herbs which can bring on bleeding. If we could find enough to supply every woman in the camp, all at once . . ." She wagged her head in consideration. "We would have to act swiftly thereafter, and we could not do it again, at least not for many months. A little of the herbal mixture brings on bleeding, but much of it poisons."

"But it might give us advantage enough to break the siege, at least," Sempronius said, "if we knew we could safely send your ladies out ahead of us—to make an end of the rest of the magic-men, then have the legions follow swiftly behind—"

Hanath's grin had changed, no longer prompted by hilarity, but by the slightly bloodthirsty glee he had seen before. "Yes, General," she said. "That, I think, might work. Without the *akdraugi*, you could engage the Lusetani warriors and," her lip curled, "cut them to pieces."

"How quickly can you get the herbs?" Sempronius asked. "The Tartessi may be—"

"Yes, we do not have much time." Hanath's brow creased. "I will send riders tonight across the river, to find the nearest villages. They should have what we need. So, two days, perhaps three."

The flap of the command tent snapped open. "Sir! Messengers from the Eighth and Fourteenth, sir!"

"In, in," Sempronius said, gesturing hurriedly.

Sempronius's burgeoning confidence was challenged by the sight of the bedraggled men who entered. Their faces, wan with care, bespoke horrors, and they looked as though they could hardly remain upright— yet when Sempronius bid them to sit, neither would. It was something, at least, if they had pride enough left for that. "Corvinus, bring water," Sempronius said. "Which of you is from the Fourteenth?"

"I, sir."

"Tell me what happened."

"General Calpurnius is dead, I regret to report," the first messenger said, "along with many others. It was . . . it was a right mess of a battle, if you'll forgive my saying, sir. Never got so much as a javelin volley off. Only half the legion was in formation when the Lusetani reached us. General Calpurnius ordered a retreat almost immediately, but we suffered heavy losses before we were able to pull back out of range of the *akdraugi*. Once we did, the Lusetani broke off their attack."

"Gods forbid they face us on equal terms," Felix growled, fire in his eyes.

"Indeed," Sempronius said grimly. "Who has command of the Four-teenth now?"

"Legate Severus." The messenger swallowed hard. "Sir, I want to make sure—That is, when you report this battle, say that General Cal-purnius died well. Had he not been determined to help cover our retreat, he might have lived. He fell with sword in hand and should be honored as such."

Sempronius nodded. "I shall inform the Senate and his family of his courage. Take water and a fresh horse. Tell Legate Severus to bring what-ever remains of the Fourteenth here." Sempronius was not eager to dis-cover just how abysmal the losses were, but delay would not make them less. "And the Eighth?" he asked, looking to the other messenger.

"General Onidius escaped with minor wounds," the second man re-ported, "but we had to abandon our camp. The eagles and standards are secure, but I must assume that our camp was thoroughly looted. Our losses were severe, but not, I gather, as bad as the Fourteenth's." He did not sound proud of that. Many legionaries would have thought it better to die than to run.

"I cannot thank you for ill tidings," Sempronius said, "but I honor you for your valor. The same message to Onidius—bring the Eighth and cut back this way." He turned to Corvinus. "A wax tablet. I want to have the battle plan sketched out before Onidius and Severus arrive. Felix, go find Eustix and tell him to ready a bird; I'll have a letter for the Senate tonight as well."

Corvinus waited until Felix and the messengers were out of the tent before asking, "And what will you be telling Onidius and Severus when they arrive?"

Sempronius rotated a crack out of his wrist. "That we have a plan for true victory, at last."

<hr/>

LUSETANI CAMP, NEAR TOLETUM

"What happened?" Ekialde demanded, thrusting off his buckler and casting it to the ground. He had arrived back at his war-camp, flush with victory, the markings on his skin singing with Bandue's brimming power—only to learn of the disaster that had befallen the easternmost prong of his forces. A dozen magic-men cut down by a cavalry force. The warriors there driven off without inflicting bloody ruin upon their foes. Ekialde needed answers, and perhaps fortunately, Bailar was waiting for him in his tent. "What in Bandue's name happened?"

"I don't know."

Hearing those words from his uncle stopped Ekialde mid-pace. He rounded on Bailar, not sure if he was more terrified or furious. "You don't *know*?" he asked. "How is that possible?" Before Bailar could answer, Ekialde jabbed a finger toward the entrance of the tent. "The magic-men there were Vettoni, not Lusetani, but that was your magic they were using. Your summoning charms. Were they too weak for this endeavor? Were you faulty in teaching them?"

"No," Bailar replied, swift pride in his voice. "No, they have performed this rite before. They have been beside us as we tormented the men inside the city. They knew what they were doing."

"If it was neither their incompetence nor yours," Ekialde said, "then what under Endovelicos's blessed sky happened?"

"I don't know."

"Don't *tell* me that," Ekialde snapped, but he could hear the note of pleading behind the fury. If Bailar's powers failed him, all could be lost. He had come to rely so much upon his uncle's magic. *'Too much, perhaps.'* He thought of his wife, how she had warned him, and for the first time, he worried that perhaps Bailar would lead to exactly the ruin she feared. "Tell me how you will fix it. Tell me how you will ensure it will never happen again."

Silence. Bailar had no ready answer, no slick words to assuage Ekialde's worries. His proud chin had a downward cast to it, his brows drawn together in thought. "The stars were favorable. The omens were so clear."

"Are you sure," Ekialde snapped, "that you were reading them correctly?"

He sank heavily onto his bed, suddenly desperately missing his wife. He had not seen her, nor their son, in too long. It was too dangerous for him to travel to the western camp, and certainly too much a risk to bring them here. Neitin's voice soothed him, even when she was cross. *'I have valued her too little, in listening only to Bailar's counsel.'*

XXXIV

"It was just instinct," Latona told Rubellia. "And I can't seem to replicate it."

They had met at the Temple of Venus every day that Latona could manage to get away, since the night that she had caught fire in her palm. All the practice had been for naught, however. Try as she might, Latona had not been able to grasp the flames like that again. She could, with focus, touch fire without burning, though even that had resulted in a few blisters before she got the hang of it. Yet all her efforts could not convince the flames to leap back to her fingers and dance along her skin.

"You're being too hard on yourself," Rubellia said, bestowing one of her typically warm smiles on Latona. "I say, without humility or aggrandizement, that there are likely few people in all of Truscum who know more about the history of Fire mages than I do. What you did—it's unheard of in centuries. Since the founding of Aven, possibly. An astonishing feat."

"What good is that if I can't do it again?" Latona grumbled wordlessly, rubbing her hands through her curls. "I've read and re-read every text Alhena has purloined from the Temple of Saturn for me, and none of them are any help, either."

"I'm not surprised. You're in rather uncharted territory, my dear."

"But there has to be something *some*where!" Latona spoke more out of desperate hope than true belief. "Who knows what texts might be lurking in the temples of Athaecum or the Great Library of Chrysos?"

"You should go someday," Rubellia suggested.

"Ha! I think I stretch my luck with Father and Herennius quite enough as it is. I can't imagine them letting me go jaunting off across the Middle Sea."

Rubellia's head bobbed in acknowledgment. "Perhaps not—but who knows what the future holds? One or the other of them may take a foreign posting, someday."

"That would be something." Latona grabbed Rubellia's hand and pulled her down to sit on the couch, then leaned her head on her friend's shoulder. "Thank you for all your help, Rubellia, truly."

"I'm happy to be of what service I can. I feel little enough use fighting the Discordians directly." Rubellia put an arm around Latona. "I don't think I have warrior's mettle in me the way you and Vibia do."

A barking laugh escaped Latona. "What a way to put it!" But even as long-accustomed instinct told her to demure, a small burst of pride blossomed in her heart. Women were not meant to have such ambitious desires, not meant to take joy in acclaim, but Latona could not deny the pleasure she felt in such praise. And not only on her own behalf—Vibia had shown more grit, more tenacity, more dedication to the cause than she had anticipated, and Latona admired her for it. *'I have been unfair, in my assessment of her. All her spikiness is the product of magnificent self-governance. She holds herself to such a high standard, and she has been willing to dig into this right up to the elbows.'*

Rubellia kissed her temple. "What else are you, my dear, if not warriors? Mars wouldn't have magic on a battlefield, but we're not in his dominion here."

"So we're magical gladiatrices, then?" Latona had to grin; Merula would appreciate the comparison.

"Of a kind." Rubellia sighed in mock-despair. "What I am, is a teacher. I've always known that. It's the best thing for a High Priestess to be, in my opinion. But I confess, in this, you've outstripped my ability to teach you."

"I still need you," Latona said, softly. "Uncharted territories or not, I've a great deal to learn about navigating it all."

Rubellia nudged Latona's head up from her shoulder, then cupped Latona's face in her hands. "You'll learn it, my dear, one way or another. I'm most worried about you burning yourself out in the meantime." She rubbed a thumb under Latona's eyes, where Latona knew there were dark circles. "How many times since the Kalends have you and Vibia gone out a-hunting?"

"Four," Latona confessed. She wished it had been more, but between her husband, safety concerns, and Vibia's spare rations of patience, that was impossible. "But, Rubellia, there's so much to do."

Their expanding network of eyes and ears had brought in harrowing tale after harrowing tale. From the Quirinal to the Aventine, the Discordians had clearly been hard at work. Most were *umbrae*, which only appeared and thus could only be traced at night—when Latona and Vibia were least likely to be able to hunt them. They had found, too, more traces of the curse-powder that set men to fighting in the streets. Vibia thought it seemed weaker than that which had afflicted Autronius Felix in the Forum the previous year; Aula, analyzing it from a political rather than magical bent, called it "subtler," and that was concerning, for it bespoke a long-term plan, not merely one designed to excite an immediate uproar.

"There is much to do," Rubellia agreed. "More than you could do by yourself if you had every hour of every day in which to do it."

"We can't put a stop to it until we find the Discordians at the heart of it," Latona said, more argument in her tone than she typically used with Ama Rubellia, "and we can't find the Discordians if we don't hunt down—"

"There are other avenues." Rubellia's voice, by contrast, was silk over steel. She was so kind by nature, so loving, but Fire's strength was in her, too. "Your sister is a prophetess; Proserpina may reveal many truths to her." Her full lips curled in a smile. "And if not, then wit and work will have to suffice. But remember, magic takes a great deal of energy. Spirit magic more than most! You'll do no one any good if you work yourself into weariness."

∞∞∞∞∞∞∞∞∞∞

As Latona departed the Temple of Venus, she saw a familiar face leaving the goddess's cell: tall, lovely Maia Domitia with her dark curls and big eyes. She smiled and raised a hand in salutation when she saw Latona. "Any news?" Maia asked in a low voice, when they drew near enough together.

"Not today."

"Fortuna bless us," Maia sighed. "I was going to call on your sister. Are you headed that way?" Latona nodded, and together they started toward the Palatine.

They walked together under a brilliantly blue sky. Maia pulled her mantle around her shoulders, but Latona nudged hers back, a lavender fall over her bright hair, so that she could feel the sun on her arms. She wanted to soak up as much of it as she could before summer ended. *'And freckles be damned.'*

"I expect you were visiting Rubellia on magical matters," Maia said as they crossed the Forum toward the southern side of the city.

"I was," Latona said. She had not told anyone outside the household about her newfound ability, excepting Rubellia, so she said, "Practicing empathy. That's rooted in both Fire and Spirit, you know. And Rubellia has more expertise with it than anyone else in Truscum."

Maia grinned sideways at her. "She's quite a marvel, isn't she? Does it—does the empathy help with the—the *matter*?"

Latona didn't question Aula's decision to trust Maia Domitia with their campaign against the Discordians. Maia was as well-connected an ally as they could hope for, and she had a good head on her shoulders. So far, though, she seemed fluttery and ill at ease with the whole concept. *'I suppose I can't blame her. She's not a mage nor related to any. No wonder she's a bit . . . out of her depth.'* So Latona nodded. "It does. It helps us find where there's trouble, and I can use that skill to bolster Vibia and keep her steady when she's unraveling a charm."

Latona could tell Maia didn't fully understand, but she was clearly listening carefully anyway. "Well, your reason for being at the Temple was nobler than mine," Maia said.

"And what were you up to?"

"Asking the Lady Venus for help in sorting out my marital future." With a sigh, Maia cast her eyes skyward. "I've got a few prospects, but none bring enough to the table to impress my brothers." A slight smirk. "Or me, for that matter." Maia huffed slightly, blowing loose hair away from her face. "Sometimes, I swear, I wish my husband hadn't been so damned honorable and had just taken the bribe Ocella offered. He'd still be alive, we'd have a fine piece of property near Crater Bay, and it's not as though I'd be any worse off."

Latona blinked several times and came to a sudden halt beside a juniper bush, not sure she had understood properly. "Maia—" she began, delicately, and then, as Maia stopped and turned to face her, found she had no idea what to say. Familiar coldness rose in her chest, the paralytic fear that froze all the fire of her nature in her blood. "Maia, do you— When you say taken the bribe—"

"Oh!" Maia laughed in a way that Latona knew all too well—a breezy disregard that bespoke past pains, aching beneath. "I'm sorry, I thought for sure Aula would have told you, the way her tongue runs on."

"Aula seems an incurable gossip, I know," Latona said, "but you'd be astonished what secrets she can keep, when they matter to someone she cares about."

Maia smiled. "You're right. That was ungenerous of me. I just assumed . . . Well, you're not just anyone she'd be telling tales to.

Everyone knows how close you two are. And particularly with what . . ."
Her hand made a circling gesture as her typically perky voice tripped
over itself. "Er. That is. I mean to say . . ." The affected effervescence
drained away, her shoulders drooping as she looked down at the uneven
gray stones beneath their feet. "Dis take me. I'm sorry, Latona, I don't
know any gentle way of putting it, and I'm afraid I'm prattling. You and
I . . . We weren't on Capraia at the same time, but . . ."

Latona sucked her breath in sharply. There had been rumors about
Maia and Dictator Ocella, if fewer and quieter than those about Latona,
and Latona had never known how much to credit them—and she was
certainly in no position to judge, whatever the truth turned out to be.
"Oh, Maia," Latona sighed, reaching out for the other woman's hand.
"I'm so sorry, my dear."

Maia pressed Latona's hand gratefully, but then withdrew it, waving
dismissively. "I've long since stopped being troubled by it. Or so I tell
myself, at least, and most of the time it's true. It's why my brothers had to
leave, you know. They were plotting to murder Ocella for it, and I had to
beg them to leave the city so they wouldn't suffer my husband's fate."

"And he suffered because . . . I always thought it was purely political."

Maia shook her head. "Not purely." A snort. "Nothing pure about it.
Ocella offered him—not directly, of course, but through one of his
creatures—a fine estate taken off of some dead senator or other, down
near Baiae." She sighed. "But he refused and let his throat get cut, the
blessed fool, and Ocella had me anyway."

Latona didn't know what to do. She wanted to embrace Maia; she
wanted to run away, as though that would leave behind the hated memories surfacing again now.

After a moment, Maia smiled and looped her arm through Latona's,
and they continued walking. "Anyway, I'm afraid I liked my husband well
enough that it's hard to imagine allowing myself to be matched to a total
dullard for the second. I'd like someone willing to be a good father to
Neria and Nerilla, and it's ever so hard to find someone willing to take
on daughters. Well, Aula could tell you—"

∞∞∞∞∞∞∞∞∞∞∞∞

Amber and glass beads, jasper and carnelian, lapis the color of the sky
and topaz bright as the sun. Aula picked thoughtfully over them all, testing their weight, passing them to Helva for second opinions of their

quality. She was of a mind to get Lucia some jewelry for her next birthday. Nothing *too* fancy or expensive, of course, but something that would make her feel a bit more grown-up on the occasions she was allowed to wear it. Lucia had mooned over her aunt's pearls at Latona's birthday, and Latona had let the girl play with them a bit. *'She's too young for those yet, though,'* Aula thought as her eyes roved over strands of brilliant white, burnished gold, soft pink, and inky blue-black.

There was gold and silver a-plenty, too, molded into all sorts of shapes, from acorns and leaves to the heads of lions, panthers, snakes, and other creatures. "I wonder if we'll start seeing western styles again, once the Iberian war is over," Aula said, running her thumb over the curves of a wolf-headed bracelet. "You remember after the Albine wars? All those heavy necklaces. I don't care for them."

From the market, Aula, Helva, and their retinue walked down into the Forum. Few days passed when Aula was in the city and did not at least wander through. Sometimes, it was no more than a leisurely stroll, but usually, there would be something worth hearing, from a newsreader if not from a speaker at the Rostra.

Arrius Buteo held the vaunted position atop the speaking platform when Aula first grew close enough to hear. One of his usual tirades, she assumed—but he seemed to have gathered more of a crowd than usual. "The problem with so many of our friends racing off to Iberia," Aula commented to Helva, "is that it cedes ground here to the Optimates." And an election was coming, just three months away.

Aula planted herself a short distance from the Rostra, but directly in Buteo's line of sight. A bit forward, perhaps—the area was no longer forbidden to women, but it was not usual for them to linger there. Doing so was, at least in the minds of the Optimates, a sign of imprudence and unwomanly ambition, but Aula didn't care. *'Let him see me. My menfolk may not be here, but he should damn well know the Popularist cause is not abandoned in their absence.'*

Buteo's theme this day was of a moralizing nature. "Our men are either warmongering brutes, ambitious and covetous—and yes, yes, you know of whom I speak!—or else they are slothful, wasteful creatures, dressing themselves in silk and eating honeyed dormice like Parthian potentates!"

"Mercy," Aula murmured to Helva, "I wish I knew what parties *he's* been going to." Helva blew air out through her nostrils, as much of a laugh as Aula was likely to get from her in public.

"Can such men be expected to lead a great nation?" Buteo went on. "Can they be thought to demonstrate purity of mind and true piety of the heart? And our women! Our women have not the steely virtue of their mothers and grandmothers, but paint their faces and strumpet themselves! They do not keep to the home, they neglect their children's education and the proper oversight of their households, in favor of walking the streets and inserting themselves into public affairs!" Aula didn't think she imagined the glare that Buteo sent in *her* direction. "How sad for our nation, when we cannot even count on feminine constancy to guide us!"

Buteo continued in this vein for another few minutes, and Aula was on the verge of leaving, suspecting he would begin repeating himself, when he handed the Rostra over to another man: Decimus Gratianus, who had been beaten out for the consulship the previous year. To Aula's shock, he began by addressing the *lemures* which had troubled the Subura and the Esquiline.

Not in so many words. He referred to "recent trouble in our city's humblest neighborhoods" and to "distressing circumstances." He did not speak the name of the *lemures* here in the Forum. He said nothing, in fact, that could have drawn accusations of histrionics or sensationalism upon him.

'How many people even know what he's talking about?' Aula glanced at the faces around her. *'Or do they think he's speaking of . . . of fights and poverty, perfectly mundane ills?'* The words could cut either way—vague yet pointed, if you knew what to listen for.

"I have heard some say," Gratianus went on, "that these people have somehow brought these visitations down upon themselves. That they must be deficient in some way, must have neglected their household shrines or in some other way offended." His head wagged with an affectation of sadness. "Good citizens, I will not say such things. The afflicted households and insulae are no more the cause of the ill than the rest of us. They are merely the first to be struck, as the gods cast judgment on the city."

"Oh, he's good," Aula murmured to Helva. "Better than Buteo, to be certain." And that worried her.

"We have all erred, my friends and neighbors! We have all erred. When omens such as these manifest, we must read in them the gods' displeasure. And then we must ask: what have we done, to cause such wrath? Good citizens, I can tell you."

"Of course you can," Aula muttered, shifting her weight to one hip and folding her arms over her chest.

"Aven has strayed from its sacred course! We have become a profligate people, seduced by luxury and an easy life! As Aeneas wandered the oceans in search of a home, we now wander in a moral desert, lost even to our own best interests. Would not our grandsires, the noble twins Romulus and Remus, be ashamed to look upon us now, to see how much we have diluted the traditions they set down?"

'Why, Gratianus, I hadn't realized what a clever eel you are.' Aula could feel her upper lip curling in distaste. Invoking Aeneas, Romulus, and Remus, talking about diluted traditions, decrying luxury and vice—all were ways of blaming foreign influence. As the Optimates painted the scene, Aven was all things good and righteous; eastern indulgences and western barbarians brought her low. And from that line of thinking, how easy to blame those traders who came and went from the city, peddling their degradations and bleeding Aven not only of its wealth but of its virtue, or the families who came seeking Aven's promised safety and made themselves at home, setting poor examples for their neighbors and infecting upright Aventan tradition with lesser customs. How easy to blame those who didn't belong. *'Never mind that Aeneas was a stranger here himself, or that Romulus and Remus founded Aven in the company of thieves, brigands, and whores.'*

Another thought struck her. *'We know the Discordians are targeting the less-wealthy districts of Aven. I wonder if they're also targeting the places where more immigrants live.'* They had thought the Discordians were simply picking on those least likely to defend themselves or have the ability to call for aid, but what if there was a deeper purpose?

Gratianus continued: "We must think, good citizens, my good friends, on all the gifts the gods have given us: this magnificent city, surrounded by good earth, nurtured by a bounteous river. We must make choices that honor these gifts, choices that show us to be as the gods wish us: dutiful, morally upright, prudent, and dignified. I am certain you will all remember this in the months to come, as you hear from those of us who seek positions of public trust."

As he stepped down, making room for some weak-chinned aspiring quaestor, Aula turned away, pointing herself back toward the Palatine Hill. "Helva, I need you to make a list for me."

"Of course, Domina."

"Every Popularist senator left in the city. Those not on campaign or serving as magistrates elsewhere, I mean. If they've just been in Baiae for the summer, I want their names." The promise of autumn was entering the air, in occasional crisp breezes that disjointed the humidity, and even the most resolute of the vacationing patricians would be closing up their villas and returning to Aven at the end of September. "We need them out *here*, speaking against Buteo and his ilk. I must see who I can convince." She wasn't trying to get her father elected this time around; censors held their office for five years. That left her attention open to influence their allies toward other goals.

"Of course, Domina. I'll have that for you after supper."

"Thank you, Helva," Aula said. *'And if I must write their speeches myself, then so be it.'*

◇◇◇◇◇◇◇◇◇◇◇◇◇◇◇

The little park behind the Temple of Tellus was as close to wilderness as one could get inside Aven, and so it was one of Terentilla's regular haunts. She and Alhena sat beneath the thick branches of a myrtle tree a short distance from the main path. Their attendants sat nearby; Mus was plucking flowers and weaving them into a garland.

"I'm happy to help, but I don't know what good I'll be." Tilla's brown shoulders moved in a graceless shrug. "I wouldn't know Fracture magic if it bit me, I'm afraid."

"You'll know," Alhena said darkly.

"I suppose you're right," Tilla said. "But what should I do, if I encounter something?"

"For now? Just . . . tell us." Alhena gave a little sigh. "Tell a priest or another Spirit or Fracture mage, if you know one you trust and who you think will be up to the challenge, but . . . we're trying to figure out who's behind all of it. And maybe knowing where everything's happening will help."

Tilla ran her hands through the grass beneath them. Her face had gone still and keen. *'Like a hunting animal,'* Alhena thought, *'settling into the stalk.'*

"You said your sister had already tried to sound out the Augian Commission?" Tilla asked.

Alhena nodded. "And she met with little luck. They thought her a hysterical female, overreacting to something perfectly normal."

Tilla rolled her eyes. "Never liked them. Half of them were in Ocella's pocket, and the other half were too lazy to care about the corrupt half." She blew out a puff of air, moving a dark lock of hair out of her eyes. "Quinta doesn't like them, either. But don't you dare tell anyone I said that!" she rushed to add, eyes going wide with horror.

"I wouldn't!"

Tilla relaxed. "Couldn't have it getting out that a sacred Vestal didn't trust the sacred Augians. But . . . she doesn't." Tilla's eyes flicked about, as though to see if anyone was listening, but there was still no one anywhere near them. "She doesn't even think the Commission should exist, come to that. Says it's a political cudgel, stripped of the piety and humility that should attend the mages' holy trust."

That did sound like the verdict of a Vestal Virgin. "I think they may have started out with good intentions," Alhena said, thinking of all the history books she had read while trying to help Latona find useful thaumaturgical treatises. "A check on mages' power, as a tribune of the plebs can check the Senate."

"Yes, well," Tilla said, sounding unimpressed, "a great many things begin with good intentions that end elsewise." Alhena could find nothing to disagree with in that assessment. "I'll do what I can. I trust Latona. She's good and brave, even when it costs her to be, and I like that."

Alhena's chest swelled with affection for Tilla and with the relief of knowing she had sounded out the right person. "She is," Alhena said. "I don't think she even always knows it, but she is."

A guileless grin came over Tilla's face. "Your family, like mine, breeds remarkable women." She reached over, tweaking Alhena's hair playfully. "You included." Alhena knew she was growing pink-cheeked and knew there was nothing she could do to stop it. "You should wear your hair down more. It's so lovely like this." Tilla lifted a portion of the bright red curtain, fluffing the curls out. "I don't know how you keep it knotted up so tightly most of the time. Doesn't it give you headaches?"

Alhena wasn't usually the teasing sort, but she felt easy enough with Tilla to be emboldened. "You only say that because your hair's never met a pin it liked."

"Too true!" Tilla laughed, and Alhena was terribly glad she hadn't given offense. "I can't abide constrictions of any kind, really. Lucky it was Quinta and not me who was favored by Vesta!"

Alhena joined in her laughter, but then said, "If you had been, you might be more like her, and she more like you. Our elements may not define us, but they help to shape us." More strongly in some than others.

Tilla was as near a mortal incarnation of wild Diana as she could imagine, and Ama Rubellia a perfect vessel for Venus's power, but Vibia Sempronia had gone the other direction from her natural gifts, taming the unpredictability of Fracture with tight control. *'Still a shaping, though.'*

Tilla angled away from Alhena and put out a hand. After a moment, a rabbit nosed its way from underneath a nearby shrub. Tentatively at first, then with lightning speed, the little creature darted across the grass and onto their blanket. "Go on," Tilla said. "You can pet her. She won't bite. Or run away. I've got her."

Tilla worked magic with such ease that a pang of envy struck Alhena. Her own gifts required such *work*, and some days seemed harder to lure than any rabbit.

"This is what I'm good at," Tilla said, "and I do flatter myself that I am *very* good at it." Tilla's words had a bittersweet edge to them, though, lacking some of her usual bluster and half-mad confidence.

"You are," Alhena agreed, running a finger between the rabbit's ears. The gray-brown fur was coarser than she had expected. *'Perhaps because she's wild, not hutch-raised.'* She enjoyed how the rabbit's nose twitched, its eyes looking trustingly up at Tilla.

"It won't save cities, but it's my gift. All any of us can do is our best by what the gods give us." With one brown finger, she lightly bopped the tip of the rabbit's nose, then moved to scratch its ears. Her fingers brushed against Alhena's, warm and swift. "So!" she said brightly, shrugging off the brief somber shadow. "If your sister thinks an army of hares or pigeons might help her quest, I am at her service!"

"You never know," Alhena said, leaning her shoulder lightly against Terentilla's. "It might be just the thing. I—I mean, Latona will be very grateful."

Tilla's head turned toward her. Her brown eyes were so big, and it made Alhena aware of how close they were sitting. "And you?"

"And—and me." Alhena ducked her head. "These fiends, they've been . . . I keep dreaming about them. Not proper prophecies, at least not often. But I hear them, some nights, and the things they say . . ." But she could not echo their words, not even under broad daylight, not even with ever-hardy Tilla beside her. It shook her soul to think of them.

Tilla dropped her head onto Alhena's shoulder, a comforting nuzzle. "Then whatever I can do, I shall."

They sat in pleasant silence a few moments longer, stroking the complaisant rabbit, until the sky darkened. The sun had dipped below the tree line. "I'd best be off home," Tilla said. "I'm wanted for dinner somewhere-or-other tonight, my father said." She withdrew her hand from the rabbit, and Alhena did the same. Alhena couldn't see or feel Tilla release her magic, but she saw the effect: the rabbit sat up a bit, suddenly aware of its vulnerable position out in the open, then dashed for the nearest cover, a gray-brown streak across the grass, making for an oleander bush.

Tilla leaned over and, quick as a darting rabbit, bussed a kiss onto Alhena's cheek. A friendly kiss, Alhena thought—but Tilla's fingers brushed through her hair, and her heart seemed to grow larger and louder in her chest.

"See you at the Crispiniae's dinner tomorrow?" Tilla asked. Alhena could only nod dumbly, not certain what sensation was swirling around inside her, unruly and tempestuous, wild as untended vines growing up a mountain cliff. "Good!" And then she was off, long-limbed and fleet-footed, leaving her attendant to scamper after her in a panic.

Mus came over to give Alhena a hand up off the ground. "Is all well, Domina?"

"Y-Yes." Alhena blinked down the path, where Tilla had disappeared so fast that she might've been a nymph, turning herself into leaves and bark. "I think so."

XXXV

OUTSIDE TOLETUM

Fourteen thousand men had lined up the first time that Sempronius marched toward Toletum. Now there were scarcely nine. Nearly three thousand had died in the dark, falling beneath a mist of fiends and the heavy blows of Iberian blades, and two thousand more were too injured to fight. Only a third of the Fourteenth was still standing, and many of those were not at their heartiest.

It had taken Hanath a few days to scrape up enough of the herbal concoction for all of her riders. Sempronius had weathered the delay with mounting anxiety, fearing every hour that they would hear the Tartessi were crossing the Tagus and would have the legions pinched between themselves and the Lusetani. As soon as Hanath had confirmed that all of her horsewomen had achieved the necessary particulars, Sempronius gave the order for the legions to form up. At last, he had an advantage he could press.

The tattered remnants of the three legions pointed themselves not at Toletum's walls, but toward the western curve of the Tagus River. If the splitting of the legions had achieved anything, it was better intelligence as to the lay of the land. Sempronius now knew where the Lusetani were encamped, and he knew what the best route there would be. Hanath's female cavalry rode alongside the front lines on both flanks. At the first sighting of the magic-men, they would be off to dispatch the threat before it could fully manifest. The male cavalry remained at the rearguard, ready to reinforce when they would be in no danger of succumbing to the *akdraugi*.

Marching through the woods remained a discomfort. After the attack outside of Segontia, Sempronius would never be at ease marching in such thin lines again. His attention was primed, waiting for another trap.

The Lusetani had scouts of their own, of course, and so the legions were met by the magic-men before they reached the camp. Hanath needed no instructions; as soon as they were visible, she gave a sharp whistle to her girls, and they sprang into action.

As Hanath and the other women thundered across the field, kicking up reddish dust, Sempronius kept his eyes fixed on the magic-men. He could make out no details of their appearances, just a blur of long-haired men wearing robes in shades of blue and green. But there were other figures with them—naked figures, Sempronius realized after a moment.

Crimson suddenly burst onto the color palette at the far end of the field. Beside Sempronius, Felix cursed. He wasn't alone in expressing horror at the sight of human sacrifice just a thousand strides away. Not many of the legionaries would be able to see over their shields, but those mounted on horses could. *'All the better,'* Sempronius thought. *'As if the akdraugi themselves weren't bad enough, now our people know how the damn things are summoned.'* Abhorrence of such a foul practice would encourage even greater retributive ferocity from the Aventans.

He wondered if his sister would have felt it, the rent that the Lusetani magic-men made in the world, at the moment they made it. He had so many questions. Was it the slitting of throats that opened the gate, the physical breach, or some accompanying ritual? Were the *akdraugi* called to the blood itself, or was it the act of death that they needed? Would any blood do, or only human, or only the blood of their enemies? If he was right, and the Lusetani blood magic had much in common with Fracture magic, then Vibia might have been able to tell him. For Sempronius, the magical sensation came along a moment later, the pull of the netherworld calling out to the Shadow in his blood.

Only for a moment, though. Then Hanath's spear found its first mark, deep in a magic-man's chest.

A few of the magic-men fled as soon as they could, dropping the corpses of their victims unceremoniously to the dust. Sempronius could feel the *akdraugi* rising, but no enervating mist appeared, and no harrowing keening split the air. *'So there is some ongoing ritual which must be held. Something Hanath did not afford them the time to complete.'*

But Sempronius had to set aside the thaumaturgically analytical portion of his mind; it was the general, not the mage, who was wanted now, for the Lusetani warriors had assembled and were charging, with or without their *akdraugi* comrades.

Nine thousand Aventan legionaries would have advantage enough against a similar number of undisciplined warriors with inferior armor and weaponry. Few things, though, made an Aventan legion fight so hard as the desire to defeat an enemy who had humiliated them. The legions pushed forward with vigor—a vigor that Sempronius hoped would take the Lusetani by surprise, if they had become accustomed to fighting foes already weakened by the presence of their fiends.

The ground seemed to shake as the first line of the Lusetani crashed into the wall of Aventan shields, so much more solid and unyielding than they had been two days earlier. At the far end of the field, Hanath and the cavalry wheeled about and started back toward the right flank of the infantry force, taking shots at the Lusetani warriors as they passed. Their charge was not without casualty; one horse went down to a Lusetani sword, and Sempronius did not imagine its rider would be permitted to escape. But the women rode hard and fierce, back to join the hundreds of male riders who had been held apart from that initial charge.

A whistle from Sempronius echoed down the lines. The back half of the legionaries began to fan out, coming around on both sides of the main force. These were the freshest men, those of the Tenth who had suffered least in the previous battle. Their forces swung wide, then closed toward the Lusetani as though their entire lines were attached to the central vanguard by a massive hinge.

Seeing themselves soon to be surrounded, the Lusetani broke. The battle swiftly turned into a rout, with the cavalry chasing down and spearing as many of the retreating Lusetani as they could. There were fewer of the enemy, though, than Sempronius had counted on.

Once the battle was done, he found out why. The Lusetani had not sent their full forces out to meet the legions. The rest had taken what they could from their camp and fled across the river. Their war-king must have been among them, or else he had been among the first to break off the attack, for Sempronius could find no man matching his description among the Lusetani dead.

"Cowards," Felix grumbled.

"Clever, though," Sempronius said. "And it keeps us from enjoying too great a victory." He grinned over at his young tribune. "But I say we enjoy what victory we've got for all it's worth."

Dark moods never sat on Felix's face for long, and he answered Sempronius's grin. "Too true, General." He nodded toward Toletum's walls, off in the distance. "Let's see what sort of a welcome Gaius Vitellius has prepared for us!"

Sempronius spurred his horse on, giving orders to the tribunes and centurions to leave off looting the Lusetani camp for now. Time for that later. Once the legionaries were back in lines and the cavalry had returned from chasing down what straggling retreaters they could reach,

Sempronius positioned himself at the head of the force. "Victory on the field is ours!" he bellowed, and the legions answered with a great cheer. "We have robbed these Lusetani devils of the men who summoned fiends and demons to fight alongside them! And you, my brave men—you *survived*! With the very forces of the underworld thrown at you, you have *prevailed*!" Another rousing cheer. "I think these Lusetani will think twice before again assuming that the men of Aven can be chased off by ghosts and spirits!" He pointed toward Hanath, sitting tall in her saddle. "And let us not forget the allies to whom we owe so much, who turned the tide against the Lusetani!"

Sempronius elected not to draw too much attention to the fact that it was the auxiliary *women* to whom they owed their lives; much as he appreciated it, too many of the legionaries would little like the reminder. Most had no idea what the battle strategy had been, much less the biological imperative that made it possible. *'But I will make certain that history remembers you and yours, Lady Hanath. You will have your due.'*

Sempronius whirled his horse around, his crimson cloak snapping with the swift motion. "Now—Let us go to the walls of Toletum and liberate our brothers!"

◇◇◇◇◇◇◇◇◇◇◇◇

TAGUS RIVER

Sakarbik shook Neitin awake. She had fallen asleep shortly after feeding Matigentis. "What's wrong?" Neitin asked. "Mati—"

"He's fine," Sakarbik said. "Playing with your sisters. But something has happened." She put out an arm and hoisted Neitin to her feet. "I felt it, even here—the thread of that Bailar's magic snapping. The men will be returning."

Neitin started out of her tent. "I should make the camp ready—" She halted. "But—"

Sakarbik shook her head. "We do not yet know if they will need succor or if we will all need to flee."

"I can make myself ready to meet them, at least. Alert my sisters and my uncle. Bring Mati to me." As Sakarbik slipped off to do Neitin's bidding, Neitin changed into a clean shift, tied a bright blue belt around her waist, and jerked a comb through her hair. She slipped on her golden bracelets and rings, popped golden hoops through her ears, and at last bound the golden diadem Ekialde had given her around her brow. Whatever was about to happen, she would meet it as a queen, and give Bailar no cause to sneer at her.

She stood at the edge of camp a long while, watching for signs of movement across the dark sky and rocky field, holding Matigentis to her chest. "One of you would know," she said after a long silence, "if—that is to say, if my husband—"

Otiger was standing to her right side, Sakarbik to her left. Both had, like Neitin, thrown on a few items of ceremonial clothing: for Otiger, a deerskin cloak, despite how warm the night air was; for Sakarbik, a beaded shawl, tied around her waist. Neitin felt them exchange a glance over her head. Otiger cleared his throat. "I cannot say for sure, beloved niece," he admitted. "The stars have spelled no doom for him this night, that I have seen."

Neitin blew air out through her nose in dissatisfaction with that answer. "The damn tree . . ." She scuffed at the ground with one toe. "You magic-men gave his blood to a *tree*, when you made him *erregerra*. The tree will reflect it, if he thrives or suffers, but what good does that do us here?" A harder kick at the dirt. "Why not enchant a rock? Or a bird? Something we could bring with us?" Otiger did not reply. He hadn't been at that ceremony and it was none of his doing, and Neitin hadn't expected any sort of answer anyway, even if he had been there. The magic-men rarely saw fit to share their insights with the uninitiated.

In the moonless night, they heard the stampede of footsteps before they saw the men following the river toward the camp. Their haste did not bolster Neitin's confidence.

Ekialde was not among them, she quickly realized. He would have been at the front, leading, and she could not see him as the men drew closer. Instead, his second-in-command, Angeru, strode purposefully toward the camp, bellowing orders to strike and pack as soon as he was within shouting range.

Neitin rushed to meet him, frightened by the implications. "Angeru, where is my husband?"

He bowed his head in acknowledgment of her. "Alive, lady, fear not. But we are in danger. The Aventans somehow broke through the spells that Bailar was casting. We must retreat to a safer location until we can figure out how they did it, and how we may mount a defense."

Sakarbik was at her elbow. "Aventans do not use magic on the battlefield," she said. "How could they have—"

"No idea. Ladies, you should make ready." His brusque tone softened a touch as he met Neitin's eyes. "The *erregerra* will return soon. He led a feint against the Aventans to cover our retreat, but they will not have tarried long."

◇◇◇◇◇◇◇◇◇◇◇◇◇◇◇◇◇

TOLETUM

The tribune who stood beyond the gates of Toletum was familiar, though Sempronius had not seen the young man in many years. But he had Aula Vitellia's copper hair, Vitellia Latona's pert nose, and Vitellia Alhena's blue eyes, and thus he could only be Gaius Vitellius, the surviving son of Censor Aulus Vitellius. This beleaguered man had kept three cohorts alive in the middle of Iberia since the previous autumn. He could not be much above twenty-five, but the past few months had taken their toll. Like everyone in Toletum, he was thinner than he should be, and paler, despite the summer sun.

What troubled Sempronius most, though, was the haze of Shadow hanging over him. Darkness inescapable, clinging to his shoulders like the promise of a shroud. It set a chill on Sempronius's arms, thinking of what could cause a shade like that to haunt over youthful vitality.

He had mustered the garrison into their lines, though, and snapped a salute when Sempronius approached. "Tribune Vitellius of Legio Eight Gemina, turning over duty of my vexillation to the honored Praetor Sempronius Tarren."

"At ease."

Tribune Vitellius's arm fell to his side. "Sir, if you would care to join me in the officers' quarters? I believe we have much information to trade with each other."

"Of course, Tribune." Sempronius turned to Felix. "Have our centurions relieve the garrison. Post our freshest men on the walls and send out scouts to make sure the Lusetani aren't creeping back. I want intelligence on their direction before dawn."

"Sir."

"Once you've got the centurions in order, come join us."

XXXVI

The officers' quarters were in a squat building not far from the city's central square. Despite how hot it had been that day, the room was not overly stuffy, perhaps due to the open windows near the high ceiling. Most of the room was taken up with a long table, currently almost obscured by piles of papers. Four cots were lined up against the walls, though only two showed signs of recent occupation.

When Sempronius entered with Tribune Vitellius and General Onidius, the room's only occupant was a short, lean man with dusty brown hair and a slightly overgrown beard that had a touch of red to it. Like Vitellius, he had a harried and wan look to him, though he seemed to have more energy in his blood than the weary tribune, and Sempronius marked no cast of Shadow looming over him. He rose, brown eyes taking in Sempronius's and Onidius's uniforms, then flicking to Vitellius for an explanation.

"Generals," Vitellius said, "this is Bartasco of the Arevaci."

"Lord Bartasco," Sempronius said, according him a gesture of respect. "I know you by your wife's praise." He smiled. "And lest you fear, Lady Hanath will be with us shortly. She insisted on leading a patrol around the city to make sure no Lusetani lay in wait to ambush us later tonight."

A faint smile touched Bartasco's lips. "Yes, that does sound like her."

"We owe our success to her—but more on that in a moment." Aware that the others would not take their ease until he did, Sempronius jerked open the knot beneath his chin and removed his helmet. "I am Sempronius Tarren, Praetor of Cantabria, General of Legio Ten Equestris, and overall commander of Aventan operations here in Iberia. This is Onidius Praectus, commander of Legio Eight Gemina." He glanced over at Vitellius, who barely seemed to register this introduction to his new commander. "In a moment we'll be joined by my senior tribune, Autronius Felix." He jerked out a chair and took a seat. Only then did Onidius begin removing his own helmet. "Tribune, I must commend you—and I intend to do so formally. I'll be recommending you for the Crown of the

Preserver." That military honor, though not as prestigious as the Grass Crown or Civic Crown, was infrequently bestowed—and technically Sempronius would have to convince the citizens of Toletum to offer it to Vitellius—but it heralded that the bearer had served as the shield and savior to the lives of Aventan citizens or allies, and certainly Gaius Vitellius had earned that honor.

At the moment, however, he little looked like a hero. Now that they were out of public view, exhaustion had taken him over completely, and the Shadow dogging him seemed to fill the whole room. "All we did was stay alive," Vitellius said, hollow-throated. "Those of us who could manage it, anyway."

"And that alone is no small feat."

"You should—" Vitellius swallowed, then tried again. "That is, I would recommend an award for the fishers of Toletum as well. Their efforts made the difference between life and starvation for us this past month and more."

Sempronius nodded. "I shall see it done." He continued as Onidius, then Vitellius and Bartasco, sat down. "Lord Bartasco, I would give you the same crown were you an Aventan citizen. As it is, there is an equivalent honor for auxiliaries." Bartasco waved a hand dismissively, but forbore any demurral when Sempronius added, "There is an accompanying monetary award, as well."

The door cracked open. "Please," Felix said, already yanking his helmet off as he kicked the door shut behind him, "tell me there is wine." He tossed his helmet aside and ruffled his hands through his dark, sweat-damp curls. "Else I'm going back out there with the lads. Nothing like a good bowl of grape to end a day of killing, eh?"

Vitellius's jaw hung agape, and Sempronius guessed that he was unsettled by Felix's irreverence. Onidius remained tolerantly expressionless, but Bartasco's lips twitched in the direction of a smile again. He jerked his head toward a side cabinet. "We've an amphora in there. Help yourself."

Felix did—and, to his credit, poured cups for everyone else as well. "So what's the news?" he asked, after taking a deep swig. "How did you manage to keep the devils from devouring you for so long?"

"I'd sooner hear how you sent them back to Tartarus," Vitellius said, too quickly. Sempronius probed with his magic at the Shadow, just a touch. This young man had a secret, something he did not want to admit.

Well, Sempronius could be tolerant for a time, and so he shared the story—the march from Segontia, the stalemate, the devastating attack launched a few days prior, and finally, their unexpected deliverance via the Arevaci women. The revelation regarding the source of the ladies' immunity to the *akdraugi* finally cracked through Vitellius's dispassion. First confusion, then shock, then revulsion progressed over his face, then the tribune rubbed at his forehead. "I suppose we must . . . we must be grateful for the reprieve, however . . . unsavory its origins."

Sempronius wasn't sure he would have described it as "unsavory," but Vitellius's discomfort with the subject seemed to exceed what Felix and Sempronius had experienced, for all that he had three sisters. "It was unexpected, but most welcome," Sempronius said.

"Do the ranking men know?"

Sempronius shook his head. "We kept the information to senior staff, at least for now."

Vitellius nodded. "Well. It does, at least, tell us that this magic is not unconquerable. If we can find one chink in their armor, we can find another." His voice was stronger, surer, when discussing practicalities.

"The blood of life," Bartasco said, tugging absently at his beard. "Yes, there may be much worth examining in that. I will tell our magic-men to put their heads to it."

"So," Sempronius said, "that is the story, up to when we arrived at your gates. Now, tell me what has occurred here these past months."

The tale that Vitellius spun was enough to harrow any man's soul—or would have been, had Sempronius not faced the *akdraugi* himself by now. Men haunted and hounded outside the city, then trapped within it. That much, he already knew from Hanath. But how matters had worsened since her departure, that, Vitellius could tell him. The tribune gave an account of their losses—though he was strangely sparse in his descriptions, almost chary with what he revealed.

"Three thousand dead, between our legions," Onidius said, sighing. "Not the start we might have wished for. May the gods damn Lucretius Rabirus. He should've brought his legions straight here, not dallied in Gades and then turned marauder along the Baetis."

Vitellius's blue eyes registered shock. "He—What?"

"Praetor Rabirus," Sempronius said, his words slow and cautious, "has acted in . . . let us call it error, rather than flagrant disregard. And in doing so, he has caused more problems than he solved." Sempronius waved a hand. "We can fill you in on that later." With a solid victory under him, Sempronius would write to the Senate and insist they order Rabirus to do his duty until such time as new recruits could be levied.

"We will mourn all our fallen, as is appropriate," Bartasco said. Iberian vowels tumbled about in his Truscan words. "But—and I would not want you to think me flippant, gentleman—but should we not take this moment to celebrate victory over the foes that have plagued us for so long? Should not our men and women feel that liberty?"

"We have nothing to celebrate *with*, Bartasco," Vitellius said, wearily.

"But we do," Sempronius said. "Our own supplies and plenty of loot from the Lusetani war-camp. Bartasco is right. We should give the men this night to glory in their survival." Not to mention that a formal celebration would likely curtail any urges toward less appropriate ways of marking the end of the siege. "A sacrifice to the gods, to start, to give thanks for their ever-watchful eyes, and then a proper celebration, or at least as much of one as we can manage." He looked to Onidius. "Do you agree?"

"I do, Sempronius. Mars knows we could all use a little relief after dealing with those fiends."

"Excellent. Why don't you go introduce yourself to the centurions of the Eighth, start getting them integrated back with their fellow cohorts? Bartasco, you should seek out your lady wife."

"With pleasure, General."

"Felix, go see about taking Bartasco's suggestion and making it reality."

"With even greater pleasure, General." Felix grinned, gave a sloppy salute, and was out the door. Onidius and Bartasco were close behind him, and Sempronius's eyes landed on Vitellius.

◇◇◇◇◇◇◇◇◇◇◇◇

Vitellius knew he had not been dismissed for a reason. Sempronius Tarren had a reputation for insight, but even a fool of a commander would know that he had not yet received all pertinent information about the siege. General Sempronius's cool brown eyes, though, pierced him to the core, flaying away his obfuscations.

"Now, Tribune, if you would be so good as to fill in the edges of the story of this siege."

Vitellius's eyes dropped to the table, still covered in papers, most of which were now irrelevant. "It isn't . . . It's only a problem that should now be resolved, since the Lusetani magic-men have been killed or driven off."

"But if it might rear its head again, I should know about it."

"I know." And he did. Vitellius wasn't trying to hide anything from Sempronius. Only it was so hard to speak of, such a blow to have endured out here in the wilderness, bereft of comfort. "We . . . have had illness." He hastened to add, "It isn't contagious. It was sent by the Lusetani, in their mist. No one caught it except that way, so if they're not here to send it again . . . But it . . . it hurt our numbers. More of our casualties were due to this plague than to combat. And . . ." His eyes drifted toward one of the empty cots. "I'm afraid Bartasco and I both lost our seconds to it."

Vitellius could feel the weight of Sempronius's regard on him, but the general could not possibly judge him worse than he judged himself. *He* had brought Mennenius to this gods-forsaken place. He had been the one to ask that Mennenius come along on the vexillation. He had decided to keep the cohorts together, rather than sending Mennenius and half their number toward the coast before the siege tightened around them.

"I grieve for your loss," the general said at last. He stood, rounded to the table to stand beside Vitellius, then clasped his shoulder. "You have had to endure much more than any vexillation leader ought to have. To lose a friend on top of that is a heavy burden for the gods to have laid upon you."

The reaction surprised him. Vitellius's old commander, Sallust, would not have been so empathetic. "Thank you, sir."

"This is your victory as well. You should celebrate it with us. But if you chose to get some rest instead, no one could blame you."

Vitellius needed no convincing. He chose rest.

◇◇◇◇◇◇◇◇◇◇◇◇◇◇◇

Only once he was satisfied that he had drawn the whole story, miserable details and all, out of Tribune Vitellius did Sempronius leave the command quarters. As the relieving army brought in food, drink, and oil for lamps, he went past them toward the Aventan temple at the far end of the square. No grand sky-reaching pediments here, but a plain mud-colored building with a flat low ceiling. The wooden statues it housed were small and poorly carved things, but Sempronius found a certain nobility in their rough-hewn features. The figure in the center was obviously Jupiter, and to his right was Mars, but the female statue on his left might have been either Juno or Minerva.

The proper sacrifice would've been a white bull, of course, but Sempronius didn't think there were any as near as Tarraco. The gods would have to make due with a pair of spotted goats, his gratitude, and a promise for a more fitting animal given over to them at some point in the future. He gave thanks to his patron deities as well, for guiding him. *'And while I am not known to you, gods of the Arevaci, I am grateful to you as well.'*

By the time Sempronius emerged back into the streets, the local citizens had struck up music. Not now the booming military drums or blaring trumpets that had been a thin shield against the *akdraugi*, but cheerful tunes, bouncing with the rattle of sistrums and the lilt of flutes. He saw Hanath, returned from her patrol, embracing her husband Bartasco, tears in both their eyes. *'An odd pair,'* Sempronius thought, *'and yet, a fitting one.'* The incandescence of their love was obvious, and a sudden wistful pang struck Sempronius.

The Iberians were dancing in the streets, much to the bemusement of many of the Aventans. In the city of Aven, dance was typically relegated to religious rites or theatrical entertainment, not an activity for citizens to engage in. A handful of the legionaries were country folk, though, who sometimes danced at festivals, or else were men who had spent enough time in Nedhena or border towns to have picked up an affinity for the terpsichorean arts, so the Iberians were not alone in their frolicking.

Sempronius sat aside, along with General Onidius, all of the patrician tribunes, and most of the centurions, whatever their origin. Men who needed to maintain a strong sense of authority could hardly cavort in the streets. There was still merriment to be had, in wine and the improvised feast. Sempronius listened as the men around him traded stories of what they had encountered. *'No doubt by the time these stories reach Aven, each man here will have personally driven off a thousand fiends with nothing but his fortitude and a glare.'* If it helped bolster their spirits for the next fight, Sempronius was glad for their hyperbole.

In the midst of the festivities, a woman sauntered toward Sempronius, an impish look in her eyes and a distinctive sway in her narrow hips. Sempronius recognized her as one of the Arevaci maids that traveled with Hanath. The legionaries had been warned to stay well away from them—not that any needed warning after they saw what Hanath could do with a spear, or what the girls themselves could do with arrows. Blood-shed maintained a healthy respect. Yet here was this girl, bold as brass, striding up to him with a come-hither smile on her face.

"General Sempronius," she purred, refilling his cup to the brim with wine. "So much to celebrate, is there not?" Her Truscan had both Iberian and Numidian accents; she must have learned it from Hanath.

"Indeed there is," Sempronius replied. "At last, we have a victory worth writing home for."

"I am wondering," the girl went on, "if you might not be looking for a more private way to celebrate?" She set down the wine jug, and her fingers curled around his shoulder. "The gods, I think, would want us to feel alive on such a night."

Sempronius took her hand, feeling the strong muscles in her fingers and palm. "I thank you, my dear." She *was* lovely. Lithe muscles, well-toned from years of an active lifestyle. A fall of brown hair, a few shades darker than his own. Warm hazel eyes, full lips, healthy teeth, clear skin, and—he could not help but notice as he glanced her over—high, round breasts, just the kind that appealed to most Aventan men. In an objective assessment, she was a winsome girl, and likely pleasant bedsport. But Sempronius brought her hand to his lips, kissed it, then gently let it fall. "I am afraid my attentions could not possibly do you justice," he said. The girl blinked, then pouted. She knew she had been turned down, but Sempronius hoped in such a way that she could take no offense. "If I might—" He gestured toward Autronius Felix, dicing at the far end of the table with a pair of centurions. "My tribune there, Felix, is a fine man, and, reputation would have it, an attentive lover." Bolder than he would speak to an Aventan woman, but a risk he thought worth taking to divert this Arevaci maid.

The girl regarded him a long moment. Then those kissable lips turned up at the corners. She shrugged her shoulder, her tunic slipping low on one side. "Whoever waits for you in Aven, General," she said, "I hope she knows what a fortunate woman she is." Then she sashayed over toward Autronius Felix, who wasted no time in looping an arm around her waist and pressing his lips to her neck. She giggled, evidently no worse off for having been spurned by a general. A tribune, it seemed, would do just as well.

Sempronius smiled, raising his cup again—carefully, considering how close to overflowing it had been filled. A pretty girl, and lively, but those attributes alone had never been quite enough to captivate his attention or move him to the worship of Venus. He required something else, something extraordinary. Even Aebutia, his wife, had stirred only obligatory interest. She had been an exemplary wife: soft-spoken, doe-eyed, with a fine plump figure and supple rosy skin. He had cared for her, honored her intelligence, trusted her ability to manage a household, been attentive to her in public, and done his duty in private, but she had never moved him to true passion. He had never thought much about it, but now he wondered. *'What was lacking, in such an excellent specimen of Aventan womanhood?'*

Nothing, of course. There had been no fault in Aebutia. But then, a man might look at a sumptuous banquet and yet feel no appetite.

Sempronius could not help but compare her in his memory and the Arevaci girl in the present to the woman who *had* so thoroughly captivated him, enough that he yearned for her across a distance of thousands of miles, and no less for the separation of these many months. Vitellia Latona was a beauty, to be sure: her patroness, Venus, had done well by her, bestowing not only magical gifts, but voluptuous curves, shining golden hair, and eyes as bright as emeralds. But Aven was full of beautiful women.

No, something else in her struck him to the core. Her intellect, her generous spirit, her vivid sensuality—all these played a part, but even more so, the strength he sensed in her, the fortitude. That core of steel beneath the loveliness. The strength which had allowed her to endure a Dictator's predations, a world gone mad, an attack from a vicious Fracture mage. All he had seen in her, and all he suspected she could be, if she found the temerity to reach for her ambitions.

Just thinking of her heated his blood. He thought of the words in her most recent letter to him, the evident passion with which she contemplated the thaumaturgical mysteries, the elegant pen strokes with which she wrote her valedictory 'Ever yours in friendship.' He remembered the look on her face the day he had left with the Tenth Legion, the yearning in her eyes, the words unspoken in the press of her hand against his. He remembered her focus, desperate yet so strong, when she purged poison from his blood, saving his life. He remembered her dressed in fuchsia and gold at the Saturnalian revels—and he remembered that gorgeous gown sliding off, revealing nature's glory.

Sempronius glanced again at the Arevaci girl, now sitting happily on Felix's lap, and wondered briefly if he had been a fool, not to take relief where it was freely offered. But no. *'What an empty experience that would be, and unfair to the girl.'*

Felix could enjoy the girl's charms—and would, Sempronius had no doubt. Sometimes Sempronius envied the younger man his ability to enjoy pleasure wherever it could be found. Felix never lacked for willing, sportive partners, when he wanted them.

Sempronius, in the meantime, would content himself with memory— memory, and hope for the future.

XXXVII

On a damp afternoon a few days after the Ides of September, Latona received a summons at her husband's home—not from her sister, as she often expected, nor from Vibia or Rubellia with news about the Discordians, but from her father.

The note was terse, and it informed Latona that she would be attending her father before dinner that evening, rather than asking her to do so. *'Juno preserve me . . .'* A constricting pressure settled around Latona's chest, heavy with dread. She was not sure who to be afraid for. The last time she had received such an abrupt summons, it was with news that her brother had nearly been shipwrecked. *'If there have been letters from Iberia . . .'* Latona's imagination roiled with possible disasters.

When she arrived at the Vitellian domus, there was no sign of Aula, so Latona could get no early warning as to the reason for her summons. She was directed to her father's *tablinum* and found him pacing behind his desk. "Sit." As she tentatively obeyed the order, Aulus dismissed the servants, including Merula, and closed both the doors to the room. A creeping suspicion itched on Latona's skin. Few aspects of patrician life ever took place out of earshot of some slave or servant.

At length, Aulus sat down. Latona could feel turmoil in him: anger, confusion, a hint of despair, the frustration of a loss of words. Aula would, perhaps, have been peppering him with questions. Latona sat quietly, her hands folded neatly in her lap, as silent as the heavy air.

"I went to the Forum today." That, of course, was no surprise; he did so most days when he was in Aven. "I try to make myself available, in case anyone who might not otherwise have access to me needs to speak with me about the electoral rolls. But today I was approached, not with a question about income requirements or property rights, but a strange tale about my *daughter*."

Relief and dismay warred for dominion of her spirit. *'He has not received news from Iberia. He is not going to tell me Gaius is dead. He is not going to tell me Sempronius is dead.'*

But her own secret, it seemed, was out.

Latona kept her eyes downcast, watching her fingers, her thumb rubbing over the nails of the opposite hand. *'I suppose I could not count on his ignorance forever.'* She had been lucky for quite a long time, really. As their circle of trust expanded, as they were more active in the city where there were so many more eyes and ears, discovery had become inevitable.

"I was all astonishment, of course," Aulus said. "Oh, I've heard what Buteo and Gratianus are saying from the pulpit, but I had dismissed it as hyperbole. Now I find they have underplayed the reality. Fiends and foul spirits, the stuff of nightmares and torments. All true! Stalking the streets! Haunting good people and—" Aulus broke off, rubbing at his forehead. "But, fear not, this fellow tells me. The problem has been taken care of. By my *daughter*." Still Latona did not move nor speak nor even raise her eyes. "Is it true?"

All the Vitelliae had tempers, or so familial legend went. Some of their ancestors had been famous for it. It was said to be why they turned out at least one Fire mage in almost every generation, and why there were so many famed warriors and generals in their line. Aulus's had never been bright-burning, though. His older brother, Latona had heard, had been the one who had burned hot—so hot that he came to an early end during the Albine Wars, and perhaps that was why Aulus had learned moderation. In this moment, though, she could feel the fury in him, barely banked, ready to explode with the full force of Vulcan's flames.

And she felt her own, rising to meet it.

"You already know it must be," she replied, biting off each consonant, as though that might choke down the swiftly kindling fire, "or else we would not be having this conversation."

His fist came down hard on his desk, a heavy thump that rattled the lamps and the inkpots. "Jupiter's thunder, Latona! I cannot—After all the care we have shown, after all the—the effort we have gone to, to keep you out of trouble!"

"I was not *in* trouble. I was rescuing others from it."

"Rescuing!" Aulus barked incredulously. "Of all the absurd—"

Latona almost bit her tongue. Hearing her work, all that she had taught herself and all that she had fought for, called "absurd" rankled her. "I will not apologize, not to you nor anyone, for I am not sorry. I was in a position to offer aid and assistance, and so I did."

"You are dabbling in affairs with a depth you cannot—"

"I was tutored at the knee of the High Priestess of Juno," Latona said. "And since I lost that advantage too early in life, I have been patching the holes in my education." A flash of her eyes dared Aulus to deny that her tuition had been foreshortened. "I have read books I'm sure no one else has touched in decades. I have sought counsel from learned mages."

"Matters such as these are the province of the Augian Commiss—"

"I *went* to the Augian Commission," Latona protested. "Salonius Decur as good as called me hysterical, utterly dismissed my concerns."

Aulus pinched the bridge of his nose. "I am sure you have the best of intentions, Latona," he said, exasperated, "but this is beyond your purview. It is for the *best* that your education never extended to such dire matters. Whatever your natural power—and I do credit that you have quite a bit—these *things* you've been facing are still too dangerous." An incredulous laugh burst out of him. "Fiends and hauntings! Latona, I cannot express—These things require the attention of someone with not just power but *experience*, and I cannot believe that you were fool enough to take them on anyway."

Tight pressure mounted in Latona's cheeks and in the back of her throat. Angry tears welled behind her eyes. Rather than letting them flow, she instead gave vent to words that felt like they had been blocked up inside her for years, her voice a low and furious growl. "And I cannot believe you would continue to deny me my birthright. My whole life, you have barred me from answering Juno's call. The best education and experience I have is *here*." She pounded a fist against her chest. "This magic is *mine*. It is in every beat of my heart. It speaks to me in ways that defy words." She drew a shaking breath. "I have no way to make you understand what that feels like. I wish that you would trust me and my estimation of my skills—as once, I think, you must have trusted my mother."

The astonishment on Aulus's face crumpled into something else, a muddle of remembrance and grief and, perhaps, shock that his middle daughter would choose that thread to pull on. But that passed swiftly into indignation. "You do me a discredit, daughter. Your mother never flung herself headlong into such situations. And you shall proceed no further."

"It would be blasphemous to forbid me to exercise the gifts that are mine," Latona countered. If calling upon her mother wouldn't work, perhaps piety would.

"Exercise them however you like within the safety of this house or a temple, but there will be no more tramping about the city, no more confronting unknown powers out in the open!"

Or perhaps not.

Latona propelled herself out of her seat. "I do not consent to this restriction. I am not a child!" Every flame in the room flared slightly, eager and hungry. *'If I could do it now, if I could call them to me, then he would see, there would be no denying then that I was born to do more than sit at dinner tables looking lovely and calm.'* Despite her silent begging, the lamps flared white in sympathy with her rage, but the flames stayed in place.

"Must I inform your husband, then?" Aulus snapped. "Must I tell him of all this and remind him of his duty to protect you, even from yourself?"

"*Would* you?" Latona challenged. She realized she was baring her teeth as she spoke. "Be honest with yourself, Father, and then ask if you really think Numerius Herennius is a man worthy of setting bounds on my behavior. If it is *right* and *just* that he govern me."

It was a gamble. Aulus had made the match, after all, with her safety in mind. But he was not so ruled by pride as other men. He could admit when he had made a mistake, and he had long been aware of how unsuitable the situation was. Untenable, in Latona's opinion, and perhaps, if she could persuade her father of that, there might be a respectable way out of it. And the hint was there, in that he was only *threatening* to tell Herennius, not declaring he would do so. In that he had not done so already.

After a moment, Aulus's shoulders sagged, and he passed a hand over his brow. In that moment, Latona realized what she never had before: that she had a stronger will than her father.

She stepped closer to him, letting some of the fury bleed out of her tone in favor of somber certainty. "I regret that the power I was born with frightens you, Father, and I hope never to bring you shame. Nor do I have any desire to conduct myself in a way that would jeopardize your career, or Gaius's. But I will no longer duck my head and turn aside when the gods are seeking someone to stand as their champion."

"Their champion." This time, Aulus's echo held less disdain, but was still soaked with disbelief.

"You have always told us—*all* of your children, not just Gaius—that we have obligations. That we must serve Aven and the gods to the best of our abilities." She spread her hands wide. "The gods have given me these gifts. I can use them to help Aven. And I *will*." No more hedging, no more hiding, not from her family. "Father, how could I do anything less? It would be shirking my duties. *Then* I could not hold my head up in the temple or among our friends. Inaction, not action, would be the shame."

Aulus was still rubbing at his forehead, staring off blankly. "It is not the shame, beloved daughter, that concerns me," Aulus said at last, his voice thin. "It is the danger."

Through her Spirit magic, Latona felt a surge of emotion from her father: a woe and a hopelessness, a helplessness. She *knew* that feeling, had suffered it so often in the days of Ocella's Dictatorship. In sympathy, she took her father's hand and squeezed it.

With an uncertain smile, he patted her with his other hand. "I worry for Gaius's safety, you know, but I expected that. Every man of our station expects to send his sons to war." His eyes, so like her own, crinkled sadly. "I never expected to fear for a daughter in the same way."

"My fate is the will of the gods, no less than Gaius's," Latona said. "Juno has called me to this. And I promise you, I do not act with disregard for my safety. I always have Merula with me, and usually Vibia, and when circumstances require it, we have fierce and honorable guards."

Aulus's brow creased. "Who—?"

"Men who are clients to your friend Sempronius Tarren. The fiends struck in their neighborhood, and since we dispatched them, they have continued to aid us out of both gratitude and duty."

His eyes briefly closed, and his lips worked in a soundless prayer. Then he took her face between his hands. "Promise me," he said, "that you will be discreet. As discreet as you can. That you will not needlessly endanger yourself."

She heard what he was asking: that she continue to make herself small, as she had always done. That she not draw any more attention than could be helped. That she do no more than was necessary.

But he would not stand in her way. That was a victory, in and of itself, and she would take it. So she nodded, and kissed his cheek, and made a promise she had little intention of keeping. "Of course, Father."

XXXVIII

CENTRAL IBERIA

The Lusetani moved higher into the mountains to the south, away from the Tagus River, returning to the campsite they had occupied during the winter. Ekialde's persuasion had kept the Vettoni loyal for the time being, but it was a grim procession away from the river. Those few who spoke did so in low voices, and the Lusetani and Vettoni eyed each other uncertainly.

Neitin, riding in a wagon with her swaddled son, watched those around her, disliking the signs of suspicion and fear that she read on their faces. *'We should turn this whole procession westward and go home. The Aventans will pursue us if we stay here, a threat to them and their allies. If we retreated further, back downriver, surely they would not follow.'* Ill luck for the Vettoni and Counei, whose lands were closer to the Aventan and Tyrian towns, but then, they had known that when they signed on to Ekialde's mad dream. The Lusetani could fade back into the forests and perhaps escape further notice.

Even as she thought it, though, a pain in her heart reminded her that the time for such a passive end to the conflict was long gone. The Aventans would neither forget nor forgive what Bailar had done to them. They would neither forget nor forgive their curse-hounded brethren, the magical plague, the thousands left dead on the fields outside Toletum. They would remember, and they would come for retribution.

"At least," Ekialde said, walking alongside Neitin's wagon, "we left them weakened. So much that they could not follow us immediately. Their numbers have been depleted. They will have to take time to recover and regroup before they can strike out against us. And now . . ." His brow creased in thought. "Now we shall return to fighting the way we know best. Quick strikes out of the woods." He cut his eyes sideways at Bailar, walking near him. "We were foolish to try and fight in the style of the east, no matter what magic aided us. Now that we have lost so many of our magic-men, we must fall back on our natural strengths."

"I do regret that loss," Bailar said, "but, great *erregerra*, we are not without magical powers, still. Enough of us survived to be of use, and we can call for reinforcements from the western villages, those who were unwilling to join the war effort when we first passed through."

"If they were unwilling before," Neitin said, "do you think hearing that their comrades have been slain will motivate them to action now?"

Bailar ignored her as though her words were no more than the rustling of leaves in the wind, but Ekialde grumbled his concurrence. "It is a valid question, wife—and I do not mean to rely upon the hope that they will provide a new safeguard."

"The greatest shame," Bailar said, "is that we could not recover the bodies of the fallen." Neitin started to nod tightly, for she could at least agree with that need, but then Bailar continued. "Especially if we had gotten to them before their blood cooled. The blood of magic-men has great power in it. We could have done a lot with that."

Nausea roiled in Neitin's gut, and she found herself clutching a fist to her stomach, as though that might help. "Is that all you can think of?"

He waved a hand. "I think of what is necessary for your husband's victory. That is my chiefest concern."

"Some victory you've given me," Ekialde said. Neitin was glad to hear the heat in his voice. "Most of your magic-men lost, near a thousand of my fighters dead, and who knows how long I can keep the Vettoni loyal."

"They acknowledged you as *erregerra*. They will not turn their backs now. As for the magic-men, there are others we can call upon."

"Are you not sorry for their deaths?" Neitin said, brown eyes wide. This dispassion was low, even by the trench-deep standards to which she held Bailar. "They were your friends, your brothers in magic."

"They were my friends," Bailar said, "and they were fools. They should have broken off their work as soon as they realized they were in danger." He shook his head. "I must ask the stars what went wrong. It's to do with that Numidian creature, I'm sure of it. She was the one leading the charges that felled our magic-men. Further proof that the Arevaci are our enemies, as though allying with Aven weren't good enough. They have allowed themselves to be polluted by the ways of the people from around the Middle Sea."

Neitin blew air out through her nostrils. *'You speak as though you know all,'* she thought, glaring at Bailar. *'But you don't. You have no idea who it is you're facing, or what powers they might bring to bear.'*

TOLETUM

"You were right to stay here as long as you did, last winter," Sempronius told Gaius Vitellius, on the morning they were to depart Toletum at last. "Please don't think that my deciding to leave now is a criticism of your choice."

"It's your prerogative, sir," Vitellius replied.

"Perhaps," Sempronius said. His blond freedman was helping him don his armor. "But you've the makings of an able commander in you."

Vitellius's head wagged. "I don't know about that, sir."

A silent moment followed, broken only by the clank of metal and the soft rub of leather against fabric. "If you would like," Sempronius said, tugging at a strap to help settle the weight of his cuirass, "I could send you all the way back to Aven." His dark eyes were steady on Vitellius, his expression free of judgment. "You've more than done your duty to the Eighth Legion. You'd have been home a year ago, if not for our friend Ekialde and his ambitions." He paused, rotating his shoulders. "There would be no dishonor. To the contrary, I should think they would welcome you as a hero, who held Iberia out of chaos."

Briefly, Vitellius's heart lurched with longing. To go *home*, to see his father and sisters again, to meet his niece. To set aside his armor, his duty done. To devote himself instead to law and politics. Not a quiet life, to be sure, and still a purposeful one. But a less bloody life. A life where lives wouldn't depend on his decision alone, and where, if a friend died, it wouldn't be his fault.

"No, sir," he heard himself say. "I began this endeavor, and I mean to see it through."

Sempronius stepped forward to clap him on the shoulder, as General Sallust had often done. It was a different gesture from Sempronius, however. Less empty. He held Vitellius's shoulder until Vitellius looked him in the eye. "Then you should know that you can trust your instincts. They have not misguided you yet."

Vitellius wet his lips with his tongue, searching for the words. He'd never had trouble expressing himself before, but since the damned spirits and the damned plague and Mennenius's damned death, he hardly seemed to be able to string thoughts together. "It is hard, sir," he said, "to trust one's instincts, when one's instincts led to so many deaths."

"It wasn't your instincts that led to their deaths," Sempronius said. "It was Lusetani blood-magic. But I know saying that doesn't change the responsibility you feel. It's *good*, that you feel responsible. A commander who isn't concerned for the lives under his control will be careless with them." He gave Vitellius a little jostle. "But you cannot let that responsibility drag you into waters so deep that you cannot rise from them."

He released Vitellius's shoulder then. He took his helmet from his man and tucked it under his arm.

"Ride with me today, then, if you don't want to go back to Aven. Onidius will spare you for the space of an afternoon—and if you're amenable, perhaps longer as well."

"You're thinking of rearranging the cohorts?" Vitellius asked. It made sense, with the losses each legion had suffered. Better to get two at full strength and fill the third with new recruits than to have all three weakened.

Sempronius nodded. "I wouldn't want to separate you from your cohort, of course, not with all you've been through together. Well, we can speak more on that later. Today, we shall talk strategy. You, Felix, the Lord Bartasco, the Lady Hanath, and I." Sempronius let a slight grin creep onto his features, and there was a spark in his eyes. Far more animated than Vitellius had ever seen in Governor Sallust. Far more keen. "We shall come up with a plan that will bring victory for Aven, and vengeance to lift the souls of the dead off of your shoulders."

◇◇◇◇◇◇◇◇◇◇◇◇◇◇◇

NEAR CORDUBA, BAETIS RIVER

Rabirus received two messages just before the Kalends of October.

The first came by way of a bird that Rabirus was growing to hate the sight of: one of Sempronius Tarren's, or rather one belonging to his pet Air mage. Word would have reached Sempronius by now of Rabirus's escapades with the Tartessi, and Rabirus opened the letter expecting a prolix castigation. Instead, the letter contained an account of the Aventan victory at the Battle of Toletum and the lifting of the siege upon that city. Sempronius had at last discovered a way to counter the Lusetani magic; his cavalry had slain a great many of their magic-men, and though their war-king had not been taken or killed, the Lusetani forces had scattered.

'He'll be trumpeting this news back in Aven as well.' Rabirus had been counting on his own victories overshadowing Sempronius's entrenchment. He had taken two more villages near Corduba, one of which had actually been the camp of some of the bandit slavers who had been harassing the city. There had been few citizens of Corduba left, as most had already been sent to Olissippo for trade, but redeeming those from captivity had won Rabirus a small measure of regard in the town. He had sent a cavalry unit in pursuit, to try to overtake the traders before they reached Lusetani territory. Finally, his own good news to share, his own tale of victory to be read out in the Curia and the Forum. *'Just when I thought I was getting ahead . . .'* But Rabirus's luck had turned again, so swiftly. *'What's victory over a few raiders compared to liberating the largest town in central Iberia?'* Even if it was no more than huts on a hill, the people of Aven would know no different, and the story would sound impressive enough to swell Sempronius's reputation all the further.

Sour as that was, the lack of chastisement concerned Rabirus almost as much. A man like Sempronius wouldn't let such a thing slide. An enemy's error was something to take advantage of. If Sempronius was not chastising him privately, then some public condemnation would be forthcoming, Rabirus was sure. *'But the serpent will bide his time, wait until he can do the most damage.'*

The second message came that night, as he sat down to write a letter of his own, to Arrius Buteo. When a knock sounded at his door, he called "Enter!" but did not bother to rise. He outranked everyone else in the camp, of course, and if they were going to pester him of an evening, they should know they were trespassing on his time.

Two men entered: one, the junior tribune set to attend Rabirus that night, and the other, a sturdy-looking man with dark hair and a foxy face. Keen, Rabirus assessed him. He had the look of a military tribune and could easily have been the son of some senatorial family of middling regard—but Rabirus did not recognize him. He seemed scarcely older than Rabirus's own son, and was not in military kit, but a simple deep-blue tunic with a maroon cloak.

"Sir," said the tribune, "this young man said you would be wanting to speak with him? Said he has news from Aven."

The young man had no letters with him, so whatever news he had must have been locked inside his head. Rabirus was somewhat inclined to turn him away for his presumption, but again, something in the keenness of his face caught his interest. "Very well, then. Let him in. I'll call for you if you're needed."

Once the door shut, the young man strode toward Rabirus's desk, inclining his head politely, but not subserviently. "Praetor Rabirus. Thank you for your time."

"Who are you?" Rabirus saw no need to be anything but blunt. "And what news have you?"

"I'm called Publius."

Rabirus arched an eyebrow. "And your *nomen*? Who are your people?"

But the young man shook his head. "That isn't important right now. All you need to know is that I represent someone in Aven. Someone whose interests align with yours."

Rabirus settled back in his chair, crossing his arms over his chest. "Well, Publius No-One, from Nowhere, you'd best speak quickly to make your worth known to me." He shrugged, his expression a dismissive sneer. "I already know a great many men in Aven whose interests align with mine. I know who they are, and I know I can trust them."

"Senators," Publius said. "Politicians. You know *those* men. I represent someone from . . . a different arena, shall we call it?" Visibly unconcerned by Rabirus's derision, Publius ambled across the tent, trailing his fingers along the edge of Rabirus's desk. "He regrets he could not meet with you in person, but he is not in a position that allows for travel." A short, mirthless laugh passed from Publius's lips. "Nor is it the sort of thing he could safely commit to a letter."

Rabirus gave no vocal response, but stared at the young man, endeavoring to communicate in every line of his body that he had yet to be impressed and that this whole matter was swiftly growing tedious.

Publius did not seem to notice. He glanced around the tent idly as he spoke, his eyes roving over the sparse furnishings and decorations. "My patron became aware, some months ago, of your recent efforts to direct political matters in your favor." Publius turned to face Rabirus, his expression suddenly sharp. "Fires on the Aventine and curses in the Forum? Whatever next, Praetor? Knives in the Curia?"

At that, Rabirus tensed and sat forward. "Speak carefully," he growled. "What does your patron think he knows?"

Publius chuckled. "It took a little time to fit the pieces together, I'll grant you. After all, poor Pinarius Scaeva was hardly in a state to give a solid accounting of the events. Such a pity, when a mage falls to pieces like that, but I suppose when one plays with dangerous toys—"

"Publius," Rabirus said, his voice hard. "Enough. I am intrigued, I will confess it. But I do not work with men whose names I do not know. Tell me whom you represent, or you can head straight back to Aven, for all I care." Publius's fair eyes gazed at him a long moment. Rabirus was being weighed, appraised, and he did not care for the feeling. *'Another in the long series of indignities I've suffered in this gods-forsaken hinterland.'*

At length, Publius's expression relaxed, as he seemed to come to some sort of decision. "Yes. I think it should be safe enough." Rabirus made an impatient gesture. "I was sent here by my patron, Sextus Durmius."

It took a moment for the information to fit into the correct mental slot, but then Rabirus fit the name to a man: a man wearing the black-bordered toga of a mage, standing in a place of honor in the Curia. "Durmius Argus, you mean. *Commissioner* Durmius Argus."

"The same."

An incredulous huff of air left Rabirus's nostrils. "If you had led with that, we might have arrived more swiftly at a profitable conversation!" Rabirus had never known which members of the Augian Commission had been on Ocella's payroll, peaceably looking the other way when one of Ocella's pet mages crossed a line in doing his bidding, and which of them had been suborned even further, procuring mages with particular talents for Ocella when the need arose. Ocella's paranoia led him to keep his various informers and supporters hidden from each other at times, and the mages in his employ, he kept most secret of all. Even Rabirus, as good as Ocella's right hand in the last years of his power, had not known all of their identities.

Now, it seemed, he could make a fair guess at one of them, at least.

Rabirus gestured to the other chair in the room, sitting across from his desk. "Make yourself comfortable, if you wish," he said, "and then tell me how it is that Commissioner Durmius, who I thought to be concerned with overseeing only Aven's magical citizens, knows of my work in defense of the city."

Publius did not rush to sit, but still moved with a casualness bordering on insolence. Who *was* this young man, and where had he come by such self-regard?

"When Pinarius Scaeva was found wandering the smoldering Aventine Hill last year," Publius explained, easing himself into the chair, "it naturally raised some concern. A priest with a divine blessing on him, a man who had served the Temple of Janus well and faithfully for years, suddenly out of his wits? What had happened?" He spread his hands in an open gesture. "Well, the Commission was called upon to investigate."

'The Vitellian woman had something to do with it. I don't know how, but she managed to overcome him, and something about that broke his mind.' But Rabirus would not say that to Publius. If neither he nor the Commissioner had figured that out already, it was information Rabirus would keep close. For all that it might be information he could call down against her, it might cut against him as well. Ordering an attack on a patrician matron was certainly something that could be used against him, if the Commissioner proved an unreliable ally. *'And if it became generally known, my career would be over.'* No one would vote for a man who had ordered such a breach of the *leges tabulae magicae*. Even Arrius Buteo might shrink away from him for that.

'I did what I had to. I do what I have to, for the good of Aven, to protect us all. What transgressions I take upon my soul in the meantime are no one's concern but mine.'

"Exactly how the Commissioner got through to Scaeva, I cannot say." Publius shrugged loosely. "I'm not a mage, myself."

Rabirus wasn't willing to take that statement at face value, not without more information about Publius Of Unknown Origins.

"But he managed to make some sense of Scaeva's ramblings and the shattered remnants of his memory. And you, Praetor, figured prominently in the story, such as we could piece it together."

Rabirus remained still, unwilling to show what a chill was now coursing through his veins. For all that Publius seemed amiable, it was concerning that such matters could be pulled from Scaeva's mind, even in his broken state. Not that Rabirus was ashamed of what he had done, but he knew how many of the common people would not read his actions in the right tenor.

A slow smile crawled over Publius's face. "No need to fear, Praetor. I assure you, the Commissioner and our other allies understand entirely what you have done and why you have done it." He laughed, oddly high-pitched, too mirthful for the conversation. "Why! If we were going to seek legal action against you, it wouldn't have been me turning up on your doorstep! You'd have been recalled by the Senate and hauled into court—if, of course, you hadn't chosen to flee into genteel exile rather than face prosecution." Another sly smile. "No doubt you know plenty of safe bolt-holes. Bithynia, perhaps, or Palmyrea. I'm sure you have friends there, who would take you in."

Was that a threat, of some kind? Rabirus had to assume so. *'Just because a dog fawns does not mean it will not bite.'* If he failed to please, failed to fall in line with whatever Commissioner Durmius wanted . . .

Rabirus cleared his throat, trying to look unconcerned. "So he has the measure of me, it would seem. What is it, then, that sends you here?"

"The Commissioner knows that you served at Ocella's right hand, but he knows, too, that it was at best a stop-gap, a way to keep hold of the reins of power against the day when proper order could be restored."

Rabirus nodded. "That has always been my aim," he said. "The *mos maiorum* should dictate our ends as well as our means."

"Ah." Publius held up a corrective finger. "There's where Dictator Ocella had it wrong, and where you do as well, if you'll forgive me, Praetor. If restoration of proper order is your desired end, you must work at it through a different means."

Rabirus's eyes narrowed. "Explain."

"Imposing order on an unwilling populace, on the defiant and the willfully ignorant—that's never going to work. The people of Aven have grown fractious and stubborn. They do not *want* order, not inflicted upon them by severe laws and restrictions."

"And what remedy is it that Commissioner Argus proposes?"

A sly smile. "Just the opposite, of course. Feed the chaos until the world bloats itself on madness. Lean into the disorder already present in their lives, and give them surfeit of it until they sicken." He came forward swiftly. "Then, only then, will the people cry out for order and justice."

"An overcorrection, you mean." Rabirus was still, considering. "Let the disease run its full course."

"As with a fever. Sometimes it must burn hotter before the body can return to health and vigor." Again, the sly grin. "You know this, deep down, Praetor. If you didn't, you would never have engaged Pinarius Scaeva."

With a small shrug, Rabirus shook his head. "He was a useful tool. It might have been another."

"Oh, no, Praetor. That you chose Scaeva was far more than chance. He has been an agent for our cause since long before you engaged his services." Publius reached inside his tunic, drawing out a pendant of some kind, on a long chain. Bronze, Rabirus could see. Unhurriedly,

Publius unhooked the clasp, then leaned forward, passing the pendant over to Rabirus.

A disk, about the size of Rabirus's palm, with words engraved on one side, around the image of an apple. Brow creasing, he turned the disk over and saw the embossed image there: a woman with long, streaming hair, dressed in battle raiment, with spiked wings protruding from her back. Her shoes were sharply pointed; her gown had a checkered pattern on it. One hand clasped a trident, cruelly barbed; the other, another apple.

Only with considerable discipline did Rabirus manage to keep his jaw from gaping in astonishment. "Discordia," he breathed. "You cannot be serious."

"Oh, quite serious," Publius said, "as is the Commissioner, and others who believe that the tablet needs to be scraped clean before the new order can be written upon it. What better way than embracing the Lady Discordia's capacity for destruction?"

The room felt over-warm. Rabirus's nostrils flared as he struggled to maintain composure. The implications staggered him. A Discordian in the Temple of Janus. A Discordian on the Augian Commission. A Discordian wandering freely into the midst of his army. How many more might there be?

"We suspected you did not know Scaeva's true allegiance," Publius said. "Had you known, would you have chosen another tool?"

The knee-jerk reaction was to say of course, he would never have contracted a member of a blasphemous and forbidden cult—but the words stuck in Rabirus's throat. "No," he admitted at last. "No, I daresay I would not."

"There you are, then."

A contemplative silence fell over the room. Rabirus turned the pendant over and over in his hand, as though some message might reveal itself. "You still haven't said what it is that brought you here."

For the first time, the placid amusement faded from Publius's eyes. "We have a problem, in the city. We've put some efforts into motion, but we've met with pushback far earlier than anticipated. I won't bore you with the thaumaturgical details—but we would like you to return to Aven to help amplify the message we are trying to send."

"Why not treat with Arrius Buteo, then? That man can amplify a message like no one I've ever known. And he's conveniently already in the city."

"We don't trust Arrius Buteo," Publius said, some of the smugness returning to his expression. "We don't know him as well as we know you." He spoke lightly, but Rabirus heard the threat nonetheless. *'Do as we require, or everyone else will know what we do.'*

Not that Rabirus was unwilling to return to civilization, but the prospect presented any number of problems. "How am I supposed to justify leaving Baelonia months before my term is up? With legions still in the field?"

Publius shrugged. "That is not my knot to unravel. But we would be much obliged if you worked it out quickly. The autumn storms will be starting soon—and it would be most convenient if you were to return to the city before the elections."

◆ AUTUMNUS ◆

Splinter the Fifth

The cracking season.

That was how Corinna thought of autumn. A season when everything started to fall apart. Proserpina descended to the Underworld, Demeter mourned, and the world slipped away from health and into trembling decay. Others might think of harvests and hunts and elections, but Corinna saw the edges of the world crisping and crackling and crumbling. Every fallen leaf a wound.

It would knit itself back together in a few months' time, of course, ragged flesh cooled with the winter rains and well-stitched by spring's greenery. *'But someday, some year, maybe not . . .'* Perhaps there would come a time when infection would set in and the world could not repair itself. The cracks between the worlds could widen, gulfs and breaches too great ever to be repaired. *'What fine chaos that would be.'* Perhaps it had been so, in the earliest days of the world, when the gods-before-gods reigned. Discordia was born then, the daughter of dark night. And all the other children of Nox, too, noble and ignoble both: spirits of sleep and death, dreams and nightmares, fate and vengeance and slaughter. *'Such things thrive in a broken world.'*

Corinna knew this, and her heart yearned for it. Order crowded out splendor, and ever had. Men put laws around the world to try to tame it, but surely the grandchildren of Chaos could not forever be mewed up within such boundaries.

'The dead can pass through to us, through those cracks. If they were wider, maybe we could pass the other way. Maybe we could reach not just the world of the dead, but the world of the gods. Or other worlds yet unknown . . .'

Corinna walked barefoot in the street, the autumn wind catching at her unbound hair, and she smiled to think of such a possibility.

XXXIX

Latona nearly collided with her husband in her haste to depart the house. *'Damn, damn, and damn.'* She had hoped to get out before Herennius returned from the Forum. A message had come, about a Discordian curse breaking out in a warehouse connected to the Domitiae—the sort of fiend that manifested in daylight, and Latona was determined to do something about it.

Herennius caught her by the arm, harder than was truly necessary, since she'd already come to a halt in the vestibule. "Where are you off to in such a rush?"

"To see Vibia Mellanis." It was not a lie. She'd sent a message for Vibia to meet her at the southeastern end of the Circus Maximus, so they could walk together—in the protective company of Merula and whichever bodyguards Vibia chose to bring along. The afflicted warehouse stood in the Velabrium, the crowded market district wedged between the Capitoline and Palatine Hills, a short distance from the Temple of Portunus— the god of keys, and thus one with dominion over Fracture. Latona hadn't yet decided if that was a good or ill omen.

Herennius's expression darkened into a glower. "Vibia Sempronia, you mean?"

Latona lifted her eyebrows. "Yes."

"Sempronius Tarren's sister."

"Yes," Latona said, her shoulders drawing together and a tension stretching down her arms. "All his life, so far as I understand it."

Herennius's lower lip bulged out slightly, then he huffed. "I had not realized you and she were so friendly."

"Our families are closely allied, which has been a boon, considering his recent victories." The story of the Battle of Toletum had been the talk of Aven since word arrived at the end of September, and all the Popularist families had been celebrating. "And we are both mages, besides, and with the Cantrinalia coming up—"

"I've had a complaint about you."

"A *complaint*?" Latona echoed, with a scoffing laugh. "As though I'm some negligent foreman on one of your farms?"

"From Aemilia Fullia," Herennius went on, ignoring her protest.

Latona swayed back slightly. "If Aemilia has a problem with me, she can—"

"Apparently she has *tried* to reason with you, but found you recalcitrant." Herennius's upper lip curled. "Which is not much of a struggle to imagine." Latona tried to pull her arm away from him, but he jerked her back—and this time, it was *Merula's* tension she sensed, spiking like a legionary's *pilum*, ready for the throw. "Is it true?" he demanded. "What she says, is it true?"

Latona cocked her head slightly, a false smile on her lips. "You would have to enlighten me as to the nature of her complaint."

"That you have been—" Finally he released her, so he could gesticulate wildly with both hands. "—gallivanting around the city, inserting yourself where you're not—"

"Where I have been asked to intervene," Latona said. Herennius blinked in astonishment to have been cut off. Latona's teeth were on edge. *'I took this chiding from my father, but by Juno, I will not take it from you.'* She drew herself into a solid and balanced stance, lifting her chin. "I am a mage. People in this city have been afflicted with magical troubles. It is my duty and my honor to help address them."

Herennius wagged a finger at her. "It is the prerogative of the Augian Commission to investigate and deal with such matters."

"The Augian Commission refuses to acknowledge the problem exists." Latona's voice was crisp and tart as a fresh apple. "Think of it as charity work, if it soothes you to do so."

"Aemilia Fullia asked me to take you in hand." He made as if to grab her again, but Latona twisted out of his reach. His face flushed, embarrassed at the fumble, and he did not try again. "To put a stop to your unwomanly ambition."

There was heat building in her blood, warmth pooling in her palms. "Yes." The word hissed slightly. "That does sound like dear Aemilia."

Herennius's dull eyes blinked rapidly in befuddlement. "She's the High Priestess of Juno. You owe her your deference."

"I owe what I am to Juno herself, and to Venus, and I shall do as *they* bid me." Latona pivoted away from him and stalked toward the door. The slave stationed there was gaping at the scene, so Merula pushed him out of the way and opened it herself.

"Do you truly have no care for how your actions reflect on your family?" Herennius bellowed. "On me? On your father and brother? People are talking."

She stopped at the door, hand against the frame. Yes. People were talking. Aemilia Fullia was talking, and probably Arrius Buteo and his cronies. Once, such rumors would have been enough to intimidate her. But people were talking on the Esquiline, too, and in the overlooked corners of the city, and the word *they* spoke was "defender."

She could never explain that to Herennius. Hard enough, to break through to her father. Herennius would never, if he were given a hundred lifetimes, ever understand.

Latona turned, fire-eyed, back to her husband. "Let them," she said. "Some things are more important."

◇◇◇◇◇◇◇◇◇◇◇◇◇◇◇◇

When Latona turned up outside the Circus Maximus, color was high in her cheeks, and her jaw was set so hard her teeth were grinding. *'That can't be a good sign,'* Vibia thought. Not this the elegant dinner-party conversant, nor the doggedly determined mage who had tramped across muddy field with her skirts around her knees. Latona's eyes were half-wild, almost rolling, and Merula, at her side, had an expression of concern on her boxy face.

'No sense being tender-footed about it,' Vibia thought, and bluntly asked, "What on Tellus's good green earth is the matter with you?"

"Nothing," Latona bit off. Then she gave herself a shake, though little of the tension left her. "My husband. He's just—" She blew air out through her nostrils. "He's not an easy man."

Vibia gave silent thanks to Juno and any other responsible gods, once again, for Taius Mella. Trusting, supportive Taius, who when she said she needed to be about on mages' business, supplied her with whatever she said she required—even when that meant giving her a pair of well-muscled bully-boys to accompany her into a less-refined part of the city. "Are you going to be all right?" When Latona made a dismissive noise, looking off into the distance and waggling her fingers, Vibia shifted to stand directly before her and snapped her fingers once, right in front of that pert little nose. "I mean it. If you're distracted, this will be a disaster. I shan't blame

you if you need to take the time to pull yourself together, but I most definitely shall if you charge in with scattered wits and get us both in trouble."

Affronted defiance flared briefly behind Latona's eyes, but swiftly settled. "You're right," she said. "I'm sorry." Her posture deflated, and she
passed a hand over her eyes. "I can use this emotion, not let it control me.
I promise." The vow, Vibia suspected, was not entirely directed at her.
"And the walk will do me a world of good."

And, strangely, it did seem to. For Vibia, there was little pleasure in
navigating crowded streets, but Latona seemed to come alive as they
walked with the stadium, quiet today, on one side and a tight-packed row
of workshops and merchants' stalls on the other. Her eyes lost their far-
away furor and instead looked to the colorful trays outside the shops with
evident interest, no matter if they displayed glass-beaded jewelry, painted
dishes, or flowers and figurines intended for temple devotions. To Vibia's
ears, the cacophony was an irritation and the scents almost overwhelming: smoke from bread ovens and workshop forges, chisels hitting stone,
hammers striking metal, fish and spices all mingled in confusion, vendors
crying out enticements or cursing at their neighbors. Yet Latona seemed
to relish it. Her step became lighter, her limbs looser, her eyes brighter.
When she nearly tripped over a pair of girls who ran into the street, chasing a yellow cat away from their pastry stall, she laughed, catching one of
the ragged creatures before she tumbled into the dirt and setting her back
on her feet.

'Perhaps it's a Spirit thing.' All magical power came from somewhere,
after all. Vibia drew upon breaks and boundaries for hers, but Spirit's
power was bred in life itself.

'The Spirit can't be all, though, for Sempronius is like that, too.' Her
brother could scarcely walk from one corner to the next without encountering something that delighted him or someone to talk to. His enemies
called it a ploy, but Vibia knew the truth: he simply *liked* people.

They were met near the Temple of Portunus by a gray-haired man
with a scar upon his cheek. A former legionary, Vibia guessed, who had
served his time under the banner before making a life in the city. Like
Sempronius, the Domitiae had patrons among the city's collegia, and the
man identified himself as second-in-command of the upper Velabrium.
"Ladies, I am bid to bring you to the afflicted place," he said. His voice
had the gruff and untutored tones of southern Truscum. "It's safe
enough," he said, glancing at Vibia's club-toting attendants, "but 's a bit
of a warren, if y'take me. Easy to get lost, so stay close."

The day seemed to grow darker as they cut through the narrow streets of the Velabrium, where the buildings were in some places so close together that their little group could only pass single file. *'Gods, what a fire trap.'* The blaze on the Aventine the previous year had been bad enough, but a fire here would be utterly ruinous. *'So why not attack here, if the Optimates wanted to cause a real disruption?'* The answer, she realized, was likely that the Optimates themselves had major investments here, but few in the Aventine docks and emporia.

Vibia felt the warehouse, full of throbbing malignancy, even before their guide paused in front of a door, wide enough to admit carts, and nervously gestured. "This is it, ladies. We think . . ." He glanced over his shoulder, as though afraid the building was listening to him. "There have been accidents here, more than seems regular. We thought it odd, but . . . there were so many possible reasons." His hand circled in the air in front of him. "New slaves, poorly trained. A drunk foreman. Someone stealing things in the night and not putting the crates back where they belong. Simple explanations, yes?"

'Yes,' Vibia thought. *'The same simple explanations the Optimates are pushing in the Forum. Negligence. Slack morals. People from elsewhere who don't know how to do things properly. And the gods punishing us all for allowing these degradations.'* She folded her arms tightly, clutching at the fabric of her tunic, at once eager to get on with it and wishing she could run away. Within the warehouse walls, a horrid ache cried out for attention.

"Then, we started seeing . . . things." He shifted his weight from foot to foot. "First we thought it was smoke—and you can imagine what an alarm that set up—but then . . . then it was different. Some of the workers, they started . . ." His brow creased. "Dunno how to explain it, really, ladies. They weren't themselves. Started picking fights out of nowhere. No words, even, would just haul off and punch someone."

Vibia met Latona's eyes with a sidelong glance. *'True to the pattern.'*

"Then some started falling down, shaking and sweating like they'd been cursed by Apollo," the man went on. "None ever had troubles like that before. We've done all the proper sacrifices, had a priest come in and cleanse, but it keeps . . . it keeps . . ."

Latona stepped forward, laying gentle fingers on the man's shoulders. "We shall do what we can. Open the door, please."

Vibia checked the pins holding her crimson mantle in place. Already it was growing warm. Merula had a crimson scarf now, too, knotted around her head to hold her dark hair back from her face, then woven into her plait. Vibia's men would remain outside, but Merula refused, as ever, to be left behind. *'Just as well. Latona's the only one not wearing her own weaving, so it might be her that needs the tackling this time.'*

It was quieter inside the warehouse, with the noises of the market muffled, particularly once the door slid shut behind them. For a panicked moment, Vibia feared this was a trap: that the door would be bolted behind them, that the Discordians or the Optimates or whatever hellish alliance bound them together had discovered a way to eliminate the women who were undoing their work.

'Breathe. Your own men are outside, and armed. They would not allow that.'

XL

Latona could feel the tear in the world, horribly strong and more tangible than any they'd encountered before. She remembered losing teeth as a girl, her tongue probing the strange gap in her mouth afterward. *'Not just a tear, this time . . . a sinking hole, a widening breach . . .'*

Pain tightened beneath her heart. *'The last time I was in a warehouse like this, I almost died.'*

She could not let panic take control of her. She thought of the first Discordian grotesquerie she had discovered, on the hill in Stabiae, and how her sisters had helped her then. *'With me,'* she heard Alhena's voice in her mind. *'With us.'* For them, as much as for the rest of Aven, she had to keep her head, no matter how great a challenge the Fracture magic presented for her composure.

This place was nowhere near so empty as the Aventine warehouse. Crates upon crates were stacked in neat rows. Dust swirled in the pale shafts of light created by thin windows at the top of the walls. A few oil lamps hung near the door; Merula carefully took one down, wrapping the chain around her hand. "Flames for you, Domina."

Latona nodded her thanks. The more Fire energy she could draw upon, the better defense she would be able to mount. Swallowing around the lump in her throat, she looked to Vibia, waiting for the Fracture mage to point them in the right direction.

All the color had drained from Vibia's face, and her fingers were plucking at her mantle, fanning it up off her shoulders. "It burns, Latona." Her voice was still her own, but strangely hollow. "Much worse than before. It *hurts.*"

Latona caught her fingers and pulled them away from the fabric. "Let it lie. It's working."

"I know, I know . . ." She took a step forward, gesturing Latona and Merula along.

The air grew thicker as they trod deeper into the warehouse, or perhaps it only seemed so. Quieter, too, insulated by all those crates, until

Latona felt certain that she could hear her fellows' heartbeats. Or could she only feel them, thrumming through her Spirit magic?

Vibia sucked in a breath. A smoky wisp had appeared, a few paces ahead of them, hardly visible at first in the gloom. It spread itself out over the edge of a crate, and as the wooden slats began to crackle and splinter, the fiend grew larger and brighter. In another moment, there were others, directly in front of them and spreading down the next row.

"They're calling me," Vibia gasped. "Can't you hear them?" She staggered forward, one hand outstretched, then shrank back. Nearby, one of the crates cracked open, its slats shattered by the fiends' devouring force. Lentils spilled forth, clacking and rattling as they poured onto the dirt floor.

'If they're attacking the food stores—and now, just after the harvests have come in—'

But there was no time to think of that now. More and more of the fiends appeared, hovering around the women. *'Evidently we make a choicer meal than lentils or scraps of wood.'* They were clustering closest to Vibia. She remembered Pinarius Scaeva telling her how sweet it was, to devour another mage's energy; perhaps that was why few showed any interest in Merula. *'Why Vibia and not me? Even with the mantle on, they're aiming for her.'* Like calling to like, perhaps; Fracture magic seeking its own level.

Latona reached out with Spirit, trying to grasp the flow of energy between Vibia and the spirits. They were trying to open chasms around her, aiming to suck her and her power in; Vibia, in turn, had dug herself magical gulches as a defense mechanism, but she could not keep up with so many at once. The smoky forms danced and darted toward her, seeking out vulnerable points both physical and spiritual.

Latona closed her eyes briefly, then opened them again with her magical senses better primed. She almost wished she hadn't, so bright was the red glow that met her. The scarf in Merula's hair glowed softly, but Vibia's looked like iron in a forge, heated nearly to the melting point. No wonder Vibia wanted to tear it off. *'It's working harder, but it's working. They can't possess her while it does. I hope.'*

But she could not use her own magic to bolster Vibia, not now. Latona had to engage the *lemures*, or at least try.

Merula's lamp flickered as Latona drew on Fire's strength to feed Spirit. This time, before she sent Spirit out toward the fiends, she tried to think of a shield. *'Fire protects. That's what the rhyme says. So protect me now.'* Like a glassblower at his art, she spun her magic, thinking of shaping its force as she had learned to shape flames.

Trepidation twinged at her. No one had taught her how to do this. Rubellia had provided some guidance, and there had been hints in the texts she had studied, but no one had shown her, no one had walked her through the steps. *'Juno's mercy, I don't even know if it can be done.'*

She shoved aside the twinge. Not long ago she had told her father that her magic was her own, that her magic itself taught her and guided her, the gift of the gods and their hand upon her brow. *'If that is so, then what must be done can be done and will be done. Use Fire to shape Spirit, as heat shapes metal.'*

Trusting in the magic she had spun out to shield her, Latona sent a blast of Spirit energy at one of the *lemures* nearest to her. It was not one of those trying to menace Vibia, but one poking in curiously from the column of high-stacked crates to their right. Its sepulchral keening rose to an angry shriek—but instead of swooping down upon her, it darted away. Nor did it strike back at her with that harpoon-like power. Her own magic remained under her control. Heartened, Latona pushed her magic further, giving thaumaturgical chase. The fiend moved swiftly, but before it disappeared from view, Latona thought she saw it grow thin, like overstretched cloth.

But her effort had caught the attention of the others. Several now surged at her from both sides, much closer than they had dared to come before. Merula hissed in sudden pain, and magic flared from her scarf, bright red, protecting her.

Instinct told her to run, to put distance between herself and the devouring spirits—but instead, she shoved herself between them and Vibia. "Leave us!" she found herself shouting. "Leave this place and go back to the void you came from!" She touched Vibia, who straightened as though suddenly wakened by the touch. "Vibia, the charm, find the charm!" She started to turn away, but Vibia seized her hand, gripping her fingers so tightly that it hurt.

"Stay with me." Something between an order and a plea. "It's easier to keep my head clear."

Latona reached for Merula with her other hand. "Stay close." Latona imagined her shield of Fire-forged Spirit again, calling to mind what the legionaries carried: solid oak covered by leather, painted a defiant red.

Then she imagined a row of them, locking together into an impregnable wall.

Vibia began to creep down the line of crates, tugging Latona along with her. Her eyes were closed, as though not seeing the fiends made them easier to dispel; she was following magical instinct alone.

'*Loose pila,*' Latona thought, as she held her shield firm in her mind while at the same time lashing out with a pulse of Spirit magic.

The fiends around her howled, high and fierce like the wind before a storm. She should have been afraid. A sensible woman would have been afraid. But with the warmth of her magic flowing in her blood, with the strength of it standing as a shield between her and the darkness, fear gave way to anger. She scowled at the presumption of these little fiends. '*Don't like Spirit magic flung at you, hm? Well, I don't like Fracture magic poisoning my city.*' She set her jaw. '*My will is stronger than yours, so it's you who will have to learn to bear disappointment.*'

A blast of cold air hit them all, strong enough to knock Latona into Vibia and to make Merula stagger. Latona's hairs stood on end everywhere. Whatever rent had been made in the world to summon these fiends, surely this air had come through it, like Pluto's own breath, far too icy for early October.

"We're close," Vibia said, opening her eyes again and examining the nearby crates. "I can feel—"

Another gust of wind whipped at them. The chill seeped into Latona's blood, sapping her strength. The Fracture magic battered at her protective barriers. It wanted to take her power, split it off from its source, spin it away from its intended focus. The brighter she burned, the more it yearned to devour her. '*A colder corpse than most.*' Pinarius Scaeva's harrowing words echoed in her mind again, followed by those that the fiends had spoken through Vibia: '*Flesh is sweet and souls are sweeter and mages sweetest of all.*'

Latona's fingers clenched into claw-like shapes, as though she could rip the fiends apart with her nails. She pushed back again, her Spirit magic against the smoky *lemures* dipping nearer.

"We will have you . . ." The words came from nowhere, and everywhere. Not loud, not by themselves, but like a whistle underneath the wind, the lyrical accompaniment to their wretched shrieks. Vibia's thin shoulders shuddered, and even fearless Merula's hand was shaking.

"We will have you . . . We hunger, and we will have you . . ."

'No. No! I will not have it!' A surge of anger rolled through Latona. The air around her seemed to shimmer gold, gold with hints of volcanic red, her magic suffusing the dusky light around them. "How *dare* you?" she shouted, not sure if she was talking to the fiends or the mage who had sent them or both. "How dare you prey on this place and these people? I will not have it!"

The golden aura around her burned brighter, hotter, even as her fury mounted. In loosing her anger, Latona seemed to have found an untapped well of power, and now she drank from it greedily.

"I am Vitellia Latona, blessed by Juno and Venus, and I tell you *I will not have it*! This city and these people are under *my* protection!"

The Fracture magic pushed against hers, like an overstuffed pillow refusing to yield to the pressure of a hand. Still she gave a mental shove. "Merula, here—" Vibia's voice was thready, hardly audible above the unnatural wind and the howling fiends. Vibia drew Merula over to a particular crate; Merula set down her lamp, and Latona heard the scrabbling of metal against wood. She stood with her back nearly pressed against Vibia's, one arm still pulled behind her, hand clasped tightly with the other mage's, all her effort bent on keeping the three of them within her shield. Through the red-gold haze of her magic, Latona could see the fiends swarming around them. Dozens of them by now, formless shadows moving fast as the winds.

They were *furious*, and Latona was glad for it. Their rage was her victory. "That's right!" she yelled. "You can't have them! You can't have me, and you can't have them. You can't have *anyone*!"

A *crack!* sounded behind Latona: wood giving way. "There!" Merula said. Only then did Vibia release Latona's hand: Latona heard the slide of metal against cloth, then a slow rip, and Vibia's muttered prayers.

Latona's skin was hot and cold all at the same time, all the fine hairs standing on end as the blaze of her magic defended against the invading darkness still trying to break her control. *'It's this hard for me, and I know what I'm up against. What they could do to those unable to defend themselves—'*

The thought spawned new rage, and Latona gave herself over to it until there was nothing in her but this molten wrath, golden and glowing and pure.

"I don't know who you sent you, but I know this: You. Will. Go. *Back!*" Latona stamped her foot, and with that, fueled by the frustration and indignation that had been building up through months of hunting and fighting and never feeling like she was winning, she sent out an enormous blast of Spirit energy.

The noise from the *lemures* reached a deafening volume, a high and harrowing screech like a thousand owls crying out at once—and then, they all cut off, leaving an even more deafening silence behind to haunt the warehouse. The smoky shapes still hung in the air, frozen, and Latona's breath caught in her chest.

"Got it!" Vibia cried, but before the sound had fully left her lips, a blast of wind stronger than all the others erupted from behind Latona, hurling all three of them to the floor. Merula neatly turned her momentum into a controlled tumble off to Latona's left, but Latona barely caught herself on her hands, and Vibia landed on top of Latona, her elbows jabbing sharply into Latona's back. She rolled inelegantly off, getting a face full of dirt as she tried to right herself.

Latona arched up, looking to the ceiling.

Not a fiend in sight.

◇◇◇◇◇◇◇◇◇◇◇◇◇◇

Vibia rolled again, onto her back this time. She could barely summon the strength for that much. She didn't want to look again at the charm she had found in the box that Merula had split open. There were too many bones for one animal, tangled and intertwined, wrapped together with scraps of fur and horsehair and the gods only knew what else.

Her hand flopped about on the floor next to her until she found the hilt of her bronze dagger: a specially consecrated blade she had recently acquired, and had taken to tucking within her belts. Without that, the charm might have taken much longer to unwind. *'Could Latona have held them off longer?'* She had heard Latona shouting, and her enchanted mantle had felt like a curtain of fire hanging over her hair. Whatever the woman had done, it had kept Vibia's head clear long enough. *'Just barely.'* If the fiends hadn't gotten to her, she would soon have been overwhelmed by the sheer force of so much magic acting upon her.

Vibia turned her head sideways. Merula was already up and on her feet, kicking at the dirt where a few of the bones had spilled onto the packed earth floor. Latona was on her hands and knees, eyes cast upward. Vibia coughed, attracting Latona's attention.

"Are you—?" Latona asked.

Weakly, Vibia nodded. "I need a moment. That . . ." She could hardly put into words how much it had taken out of her. Just holding herself together, even with Latona's assistance, had been a mental feat. Battling the Discordian charm on top of it had her limp as a wrung-out towel. "We have to end it soon." Vibia tugged her tunic away from her chest; she was sweat-damp all over. "I can't keep doing this, Latona. I can't."

"You were brilliant, Vibia." Ever so earnest, Vitellia Latona, ever so hale.

"Not everyone has your strength," Vibia said. The words tasted more sour than she had intended. Latona didn't deserve her pique, and so Vibia managed to trap the following thought before it left her tongue. *'Or your stubbornness.'*

XLI

Central Iberia

West of Toletum, the Tagus River sluiced its way through fewer jagged hills and high plateaus, and into bumpy red hills spattered with clumps of thick green forests. They had not gone far—Sempronius was loath to remove himself from the security of either Arevaci territory or Aventan towns entirely—but it was enough to show subtle changes in the landscape.

They were digging in near a point where another river met the Tagus from the north. Corvinus didn't think highly of the location. The tributary, silty and yellow and scarcely two wagon's-widths across, had no name. Its sluggishness troubled the Water in Corvinus's nature, and he knew it would be troubling Sempronius as well. All the same, the place had defensive advantages. Sempronius had set up camp for his three legions a short distance downriver and on the south bank, heeding Bartasco's advice that both the tributary and the Tagus would soon swell with the autumn rains. Two camps, in fact, each on a hilltop, within sight of each other, providing solid command of the surrounding area. The commanders had, by mutual agreement, split the Eighth Legion: Vitellius's cohorts were encamped with the Tenth, along with a few others, while Onidius took the rest of the legion to the second hill to combine forces with the much-battered Fourteenth.

The Lusetani, they had heard, had pulled back even farther west, though no one believed they were in full retreat. They seemed to have scattered, though. Eustix's birds and Hanath's riders alike brought back reports of small skirmishes between their allies and their foes, of towns harassed but not overrun and put to the sword as they had been before the Aventan victory at Toletum.

Corvinus found Sempronius not in the command tent of the Tenth Legion's camp, but in the open air of the camp's central road, receiving a delegation of Iberians. When first they had come to the region, Corvinus had been unable to tell one set from another, though he knew the Arevaci and the Edetani considered themselves distinct and separate peoples, not only from their enemy Lusetani, but from each other—and from the

Cossetans, the Counei, and certainly from the hated Vettoni. It had taken Corvinus some time to learn the distinctions. Now, though, he could see the subtle differences in how they knotted their garments, in the decorative style of their brooches and bracelets. These visitors were strangers, and Corvinus could not place them in his mental roll.

Sempronius was deep in conversation, his brow seriously furrowed, but Bartasco of the Arevaci stood nearby, burly arms folded over his chest. He didn't look disgruntled, precisely—but nor did he look pleased. Corvinus came alongside of him.

Bartasco lifted an eyebrow at his approach and gestured toward the strangers with one hand. "Your general, I think, seeks an accord with these Tartessi, though recently we would have cut them down like wheat, had we encountered them in the open."

That explained their unfamiliar signifiers, then. "They were not enemies until other Aventans made them so," Corvinus replied. "If they can be made friends, we will have a greater advantage against the Vettoni and Lusetani."

"I do not doubt the wisdom there," Bartasco allowed. "But it seems a cold thing to me." He watched Sempronius with the Tartessi contemplatively a moment longer, then turned away. "Come." He gestured Corvinus along with him. "I see you working every moment you are awake. Do your weary bones the favor of sharing a cup of wine with me."

Corvinus had other errands to be about, but Bartasco was the highest-ranking man among their allies, and Corvinus dared not risk offending him with refusal. "I shall be glad to, Lord Bartasco."

They walked down the central path past the quaestorium, where the Tenth Legion's supply officer was huddled with engineers, discussing where best to find the timber necessary to finish turning the camp into a proper winter fortress. Everywhere, legionaries were at work: placing stones for latrine drainage or joining wooden beams to raise barracks, all under the careful direction of the engineers. Other men were on the field beneath the hilltop camp, drilling. Sempronius was no ruthless commander, but nor was idleness tolerated. *'Every man to his duty,'* Corvinus thought, *'for the General does hate waste, of effort and energy as much as of resources.'*

They settled into Bartasco's tent, standing near the westward gate. It was round where the Aventan command tent was square and cast in colors of green and brown rather than scarlet, but otherwise differed little.

Corvinus had not noticed how chilly the afternoon had become until the warmth of the brazier reached him.

"You are, if I have it right, not Aventan-born," Bartasco said, when they had settled into low canvas chairs, and he had filled two cups with the golden wine that seemed to be the preference in this part of Iberia.

"That is correct. I was born in Albina, in the high mountains north of Truscum."

Bartasco sat forward, elbows on his knees, his cup between his hands. "And you did not, I think, come to Aven by choice."

A wry smile touched Corvinus's lips. "That is a gentle way of phrasing it," he said. "I was taken as a slave, yes, when I was quite young, during Aven's conquest of my homeland."

Bartasco's head wagged in sympathy. "Poor luck."

Enslavement had no legal structure among the Iberians, as it did in the nations of the eastern Middle Sea, and so it was, Corvinus had observed, often considered a pitiable condition, but not a necessarily irreversible one. A person taken by a rival tribe might eventually transition into their new community, through work or marriage—or they might escape and return home, free again. In Aven, the condition's mutability was of a different sort, tied to the whim of the enslaver. A house slave might reasonably expect manumission upon a master's death, if not earlier. Public slaves, too, could be freed after a term of service; it was a popular custom invoked by politicians, to honor one god or another. Those slaves consigned to the fields or mines faced steeper odds against freedom and, often, grimmer fates. *'Fortuna has far more work to do when she wishes to redeem the victims of such a massive system, so codified and regulated, and reinforced by the might of the Aventan military.'*

Bartasco went on, as though following Corvinus's unspoken thought. "Yet now you stand, a free man, at the right hand of a general."

"Aven's laws manumit any slave who demonstrates a magical blessing. It is considered an ill thing, to keep in bondage one whom the gods favor." It had not been the only turn of Fortuna's wheel to have helped Corvinus out of catastrophe and into his present circumstances; the first had been due to sheer cleverness, when someone at the latifundium he'd been sold to noticed that the little pale-haired boy had a talent for numbers. He'd been bought then by the Sempronian household, to train as a clerk, escaping what otherwise would have been a hard and likely quite short life in the fields. "I was not yet ten when my talents came to the fore. I was freed, but remained with the Sempronian family for my education. Then, when the dominus inherited, he promoted me."

"Why not return home, once you were free to do so?"

To a natural-born Aventan, Corvinus might have answered less honestly. "One life was stolen from me. There was no getting it back. A man must live the life in front of him, not the one behind."

"You have observed Aven with double eyes, then," Bartasco said, "as an outsider and an insider, together."

Slowly, Corvinus nodded. "Yes, I suppose that is the truth of it."

Bartasco took a ruminating sip of his wine. "I would wish you to tell me, then, as someone who has seen its workings with perhaps a keener awareness than those born to its world, of the bones of Aven. I have seen much of its muscle. I know a little now, I think, of its soul. But what makes it stand?"

Corvinus's brow creased in thought before he replied, weighing his words; Bartasco had asked in sincerity, and Corvinus would do him the credit of answering with gravity. "Patrons and clients."

One of Bartasco's thick eyebrows quirked toward his hairline. "Eh?"

"It is the system upon which Aven's society is built. Men—whole families, really, sometimes whole cities—bound together by vows of fidelity and mutual advantage."

Bartasco snorted. "That word. You Aventans do like to think in terms of advantage." Then he frowned. "Or *do* you think of yourself as Aventan?"

"Certainly." That response came easily, without forethought. Losing his first family, his first nation and identity, that was an act of violence nothing would ever change. The tragedy played out in every nation of the world, so far as Corvinus knew, and was no less a calamity for being common. At first, becoming Aventan had been a matter of survival. Now, Corvinus could no longer imagine the person he might have been without that conversion. "I have been Aventan far longer than I have been anything else. Its gods have been good to me."

Corvinus did not say that his own had not been; probably they had tried their best. He had not been old enough to know them. Another phantom pain, a half-remembered loss.

Clearing his throat, he continued: "And, yes, we do tend to seek benefit. Aven is the child of Tyre, Athaeca, and long-burnt Ilion—trading peoples, all. Everything is a transaction, even how we deal with the gods. The patron is a man of some wealth or stature. To the client, he offers his protection and the advantages of his station—that might be loans of money, or it might be financial advice. He might arrange good marriage opportunities for the client's children, or set them up in business ventures."

"And in return, this patron? He gets . . . ?"

"Loyalty."

"Ah. A jewel beyond price in any society."

Corvinus sipped the wine, a touch too sweet for his liking. "Quite often that loyalty takes the form of political support. When a man goes to the Forum to make a speech, his clients attend him. Their voice in the crowd encourages others to listen, and their presence communicates that a man is well-regarded and supported by others of varying social station." He smiled, a touch ruefully. "It can seem very dry and mercantile, I know, but it's . . ." Corvinus weighed the thought, weighed all he had learned of Aven since coming within its walls. "It's sacred. It's like the guest-right. A bond may be formally dissolved by mutual agreement—I became client to the Semproniae when I was freed, but I could have chosen another patron, if I wished. To betray that bond while it stood, however?" He shook his head at the unthinkable proposition. "That would be like turning against your own kin."

Bartasco was quiet a moment, and Corvinus was content to let him be. Outside, he heard the discordant song of the legion at work: hammering and thumping and cursing.

"I have heard tell," Bartasco said at last, "that you Aventans refer to Numidia and Cyrenaica as 'client kingdoms.'"

"And Bithynia and Phrygia," Corvinus affirmed.

"And that arrangement—Does the word 'client' mean the same for a kingdom as for a man?"

Corvinus began to understand the nature of Bartasco's inquiry. "You wonder what Aven intends for Iberia, if we are to become further entrenched here."

"We would not be bondsmen, as your people—" Bartasco rumbled a bit, belatedly awkward. "Forgive me, friend, but it is—"

"It is the truth. The tribes of Albina lost a war, and our bodies were the spoils." Corvinus rarely smiled, but his lips quirked up at one end, just a touch. "Had it been otherwise, perhaps Praetor Sempronius might have been in thrall to me, and not the other way around."

Bartasco snorted his recognition of the vagaries of fate, then said, "The Arevaci fight alongside Aven, not against her, and many of us have lived alongside Aventans in peace." He scrubbed at his beard with the back of one hand. "I do not say the Lusetani have done right, in attacking Aven. But their aggression did not come out of nowhere. We see more Aventans in Iberia every year. Even forts like this may grow into towns and cities. If we are to continue living together and in peace, we must determine what that will mean."

Many Aventans might take Bartasco for a simple man—a pleasant and companionable barbarian, but a barbarian nonetheless. But Corvinus could tell, even on short acquaintance, that that would be a shallow assessment. *This is a man trying to determine the course of a nation, though he controls only a small portion of it.* Numidia, Bithynia, and the rest all had single monarchs making their decisions. It made signing a treaty a simple matter. Albina had had no such cohesion, to its sorrow— and nor did Iberia.

Bartasco knocked back the rest of his wine and stood up. Corvinus did the same, though he had to take a larger swig to empty his cup. "I thank you, friend Corvinus, for your perspective. I have much and more to consider."

"Lord Bartasco," Corvinus ventured, attempting to inject more warmth into his tone than he knew it typically carried, "I am Sempronius's client, and his friend besides, but he would want me to give you honest counsel, not sway you unjustly. I hope you will come to me with future considerations."

For the first time in the conversation, Bartasco's face broke into its easy, broad smile, and he clapped Corvinus on the shoulder. "I will do so."

When they returned to the Aventan command tent, the Tartessi were just departing. Sempronius looked satisfied. "An accord," he announced, when Corvinus and Bartasco reached him. "Not quite an alliance, but I will take whatever steps I can toward the restoration of amity. We'll be paying a sum in recompense for what they suffered at the hands of Rabirus's legions—"

'Rabirus and the Optimates won't like that at all,' Corvinus thought.

"—and in return for that and some favorable trade concessions in Toletum and the port towns, they're going to hold the pass between the two rivers. The Vettoni keep rabbiting off that direction, it seems, so perhaps we can choke them on one side or the other."

Before Sempronius could explain any further terms, swift footsteps approached them up the central road. "Sir!"

They turned to find Felix with a bigger grin on his face than anything besides a pretty girl usually got out of him. Beside him was most certainly *not* a pretty girl, but a solidly built man of middle years, with black-and-gray hair and a few days' worth of scruff on his chin, wearing the armor and crested helm of a tribune. Yet Corvinus did not recognize him, and by now he knew all the tribunes of the Tenth, Eighth, and Fourteenth well.

A wicked gleam was in Felix's dark eyes as he saluted to Sempronius, then gestured to the man. "Sir, you most definitely want to hear what our friend here has to say."

◇◇◇◇◇◇◇◇◇◇◇◇◇◇◇

CITY OF AVEN

"You should have picked a swifter boat."

Rabirus had sent a message ahead from Ostia, telling Arrius Buteo to anticipate his arrival back in the city, but he had not expected to find his ally waiting for him on the Aventine dock, with a face full of scowls. Buteo was alone but for a pair of protective-looking slaves; no clients or other senators attended him. He held a rolled-up scroll which he slapped against Rabirus's chest the moment Rabirus approached him, leaving the slaves behind to unload his trunks and find a cart for them. "What is this?"

"News," Buteo said. "From Iberia. And why in the name of all the gods did you leave?"

"I wanted to be here for the elections," Rabirus murmured, unfurling the scroll. "And Baelonia isn't in revolt the way Cantabria is. My legions will winter just fine in Gades."

"Will they?" Buteo said, a little too pointedly. Rabirus's eyes fell to the paper.

It was a letter to the Senate, penned by Sempronius Tarren, out of his winter camps west of Toletum. Amid the usual tedious updates was a note that the stray cohort from Legio IV Sanguineus, besieged in Toletum all those long months, was pleased to have been reunited with their fellows, for the rest of the legion had come north to join them.

"I sent them to Gades with the Second," Rabirus said, in a dull tone of disbelief. "I turned east to the nearer port, but they were meant to go on to Gades with Cominius Pavo . . ."

"The Second went," Buteo snapped. "The Fourth, it would seem, did not."

Rabirus's fingers clenched around the paper, crushing it, until Buteo smacked his hand and snatched it away from him. "The mutinous bastards." He thought of the recalcitrant prefect, who had scorned Rabirus's tactics. The surly engineer, who had nearly let them get drowned by the rising river. The centurions, who looked more to their prefect than their general. "Those sons of bitches, I'll see them decimated!"

"A hard time you'll have of that, if they join Sempronius Tarren's heroic efforts. People won't stand for it. They can understand decimating a legion that's shirked its duty, played the coward, betrayed its commander, but—"

"They *have* betrayed their—"

"How will people understand that, when you're the one here in Aven?" Buteo gestured wildly at the docks. "You're the one that left your post!"

"The Second obeyed me!"

"So why didn't the Fourth?" Buteo's pale eyes were icy with disdain, the sort of look he usually reserved for the Popularists. Rabirus didn't care for being on the receiving end of it. "This many men, deciding as one to disobey orders? And the Second did nothing to stop them?"

"We don't know the Second didn't—"

"It speaks of a failure in the commander, not in the men!" Buteo barked, loudly enough that the heads of nearby dockworkers and merchants turned toward them. "What in Jupiter's name happened out there?"

Rabirus's own slaves paused in their work, goggling at the pair of quarreling senators, until Rabirus made an impatient gesture at them to continue. Rabirus began pacing, dragging both hands through his hair. It had been a gamble, returning to Aven before his year as praetor was up. But nothing in Iberia had gone the way he intended. For months and months, all his efforts had gone awry. Even if his strange visitor's suggestion to come back home hadn't come with an underlying threat, Rabirus would have been tempted. Returning to Aven, he had hoped, would change his luck. "I can fix this."

"No." Buteo sniffed through that enormous nose of his. "You can't. You can keep your head down and stay out of our way until after the elections."

Rabirus rounded on Buteo. "After all I have done—all I have sacrificed for our cause—you would turn on me thus?"

"I would not have a liability standing beside me in the Forum when I am trying to secure election for a full slate of our people!" Buteo hissed. "We have a tremendous opportunity this year to restore some sanity to Aven's government. Half the Popularists are in Iberia, and the other half are chasing their own tails. And when I tell you what's been happening here—I tell you, the gods have shown their minds, Rabirus, they are speaking their displeasure in every neighborhood of Aven, and the people will flock to us as they seek safety and—"

"The gods are what?"

"—reassurance and—what?" Buteo scowled at being thrown off his speech. "There have been omens. Strange things occurring in the lesser neighborhoods."

"What sort of strange things?"

Buteo's face creased in mingled confusion and annoyance. "Things we can make use of, so what does it matter?" He shrugged the folds of his toga back into proper position on his shoulder. "Accidents, fights, some reports of haunting spirits—all signs of negligence and lethargy, if you ask me, *precisely* what happens when the low plebs ignore the *mos maiorum* in favor of hedonism, and so I've been saying in the Forum, Rabirus, and I tell you it is *working*."

Buteo kept speaking, but Rabirus was hardly listening. His mind went back to the strange visitor in his tent in Iberia. *'We've put some efforts into motion, but we've met with pushback far earlier than anticipated.'* Accidents and fights, he knew these could be the weapons of Discordia. He had benefited from them the previous year. *'Haunting spirits, though . . .'* Similar to the complaints from Toletum. *'If I can find a way to link these things . . .'*

His belongings were all off the boat by now, guarded by a pair of slaves while another went to fetch a cart. Rabirus sat down heavily on one of his trunks, and Buteo came to loom over him. "Rabirus? Rabirus, I must have you understand—"

"I'll stay out of the way the next two months, if you think it best," Rabirus said. "We can come up with a viable excuse for the Fourth. As for why I'm here—why, because Sempronius Tarren's reports continue to be hyperbolic nonsense. I am more needed here, at home, among the good people of Aven, than I am in Baelonia. And I have brought tax revenues home, let the people mark *that*."

"Sempronius Tarren will want his command extended," Buteo pointed out. "If you can convince people he truly has been exaggerating, you might be of *some* use."

"How gracious of you." Rabirus rubbed irritably at his chin. His boy had nicked it shaving, and the cut itched. *'I must find Durmius Argus. And I must send back to Iberia . . .'* How Sempronius Tarren had won the Fourth away from him, he was not certain—but the man would pay for the transgression. *'That man. That damned demagogue, he'll bring everything to ruin.'* Maybe these Discordians were right, and a period of chaos was necessary to clear the way for proper order, but Sempronius Tarren would keep the nation churning in pandemonium forever. *'He'll take Aven so far from itself that we forget what we are, who we are. Our proud nation will never have the chance to correct to our noble origins. He'd see us polluted with foreign hedonism and vice, he encourages the plebs to upend tradition and harmonious structure for the sake of their own selfish desires, and he would sit at the center of it all, scooping up as much power and wealth to himself as he can manage.'*

Sudden fury propelled Rabirus to his feet, and Buteo hastily stepped away.

'Damn the man. Damn him! Ocella tried to cast him down, yet he survived. I tried to rid the city of him, and yet he persists. What would the gods have me do to protect Aven from that wretched instigator?' Rabirus kicked the nearest trunk, hard—and heard something unexpected. Inside the trunk, something had shifted and clattered. Nothing should *clatter* in a wooden box filled with tunics and cloaks. Rabirus snapped his fingers to the nearest slave. "Open that."

Unquestioningly, the slave obeyed. He pulled the pin that held the trunk closed, and when he lifted the lid, the interior gave way.

Rabirus knelt to examine it more closely, and Buteo came to stand over his shoulder. A false panel had been placed inside the lid, so cunningly and tightly that Rabirus had never noticed it, all these long months traveling. That panel now lay atop the neatly folded tunics, and with it, what it had concealed: a sheet of hammered bronze, carved with deep lines. Rabirus could not understand the words; such things were always written in a kind of code, known only to practitioners of the art. But he knew what it was.

"A curse tablet," Buteo hissed behind him. "Rabirus—"

"Throw that in the river," Rabirus said, standing. No sooner had the slave moved to do so than he countermanded, "No! Wait." The slave paused, hand still outstretched. "Wrap it in something. Don't touch it, and in Jupiter's name keep it away from me. But I would know whose work that is."

Whoever's hand had cast the curse, however, Rabirus had no doubt who was behind it. *'It may have been in my trunk all the time I was in Iberia. Since I left Aven, perhaps!'* All his ill luck was now explained: every delay, every misstep, every gods-damned insect bite pocking his skin. It was almost as heartening as enraging, to know his misfortune had not been his fault. *'Curse-hounded through Iberia, no wonder I could never get ahead there.'*

Now he would be free of it—and Sempronius Tarren would suffer in recompense.

XLII

Latona sat at the desk she had, much to her husband's irritation, moved from the back corner of the garden and into the domus's main sitting-room. Since he would not cede her space for an office, she took it and dared him to contravene her. Herennius grumbled to himself and flung caustic words at her, deriding yet another sign of her imprudence and her inappropriately masculine aspirations—but he did not have the desk moved.

Elbows on the table, fingers clenched in her hair, Latona stared at a list of every suspected or confirmed Discordian curse in the city thus far. *'There must be a pattern. There must, there must.'* There were obvious clusters: the Popularist strongholds of the Esquiline and Aventine had been hit most frequently, and Latona half-wished she could take that as confirmation of her suspicions, that the Discordians were in league with the Optimates. But the very worst curse so far had been in the Velabrium, where the denizens were of mixed factions, or no faction in particular, and even the Optimate-friendly plebeian neighborhoods, where lived families who had been poor in Aven as long as the patricians had been rich there, had suffered. Merula's instincts, too, had been correct: the dormitories of the public slaves reported hauntings and accidents.

'They do avoid patricians, though, the thrice-damned cowards.' Whoever the Discordians were, they were not so devoted to total chaos as to risk attacking those with greater power to defend themselves. *'Yet, at least. If they continue to grow stronger . . .'*

Footsteps padded into the room. "Post for you, Domina." Merula handed over three papers. Two were thin folded notes; the third, much thicker and less crisp, as though it had been in transit far longer.

Latona's heart quickened as she stood. "Thank you, Merula." She removed herself from the desk to a nearby couch, tucking her feet up underneath her and reaching for the wrap that had fallen from her shoulders sometime during her study. "Is it chilly in here today?" she asked, draping the soft forest green wool around her shoulders.

"A bit, Domina." Without further instruction, Merula barked at one of Herennius's hovering slaves to light more lamps and stoke the brazier.

With great discipline, Latona tended to the shorter notes first: one was an invitation to join the rest of her family in dining with the Terentiae the next evening; the other, a swiftly jotted note from Davina, reporting a fight outside of her bathhouse, where the combatants, once separated, seemed to have no idea why they had quarreled. Latona tossed that onto her desk, to add to her list.

The third, as she had anticipated, bore the dark wax and falcon-in-flight seal of Sempronius Tarren. Biting her lower lip softly, Latona curled herself more comfortably over a rolled pillow and began to read.

'My dear friend—

'I greet you from the top of a nameless hill above a nameless river. Already it has begun to snow here. Your brother tells me it held off until December last year, but weather in Iberia runs more to the extremes than it does in Truscum. The summer was hot and dry as a bread oven, the autumn has been damp and foggy, with a swiftly descending chill. The Iberians say this heralds a sharp and long winter. We have prepared as best we may, but the Lusetani predations left much of the countryside either stripped bare or ill-planted in the first place. The eastern coast, however, has not fared so ill, and I believe we can bring in provisions enough before the snow falls thick enough to block what paths pass for roads here.'

Latona smiled to read that. *I expect you're already planning improvements to those roads, aren't you?* She pitied the legionaries who would, no doubt, find themselves put to leveling ground and laying brick, if the weather held and no Lusetani appeared to trouble them until spring.

'I have spent winters in strange places afore now. In Abydosia, you can hardly think of it as winter. Their seasons go by flood and drought, not by heat and chill. In Numidia, the northern reaches were mild, if rainy, but the southern mountains had snowstorms as fierce as any in the Albine ranges. We shall see what the season brings in Iberia. Yet as I must endure it, whatever it is, I shall find a way to think it beautiful. Pale flakes look well on ocher dust, I find, like the dappling on a fawn.'

Not many people, she knew, would think Sempronius Tarren to be much of a poet. Certainly he would not be likely to append the moniker to himself. Yet the romantic urge was there, and most often when he spoke of places. She had heard it in his love for the City of Aven and could feel it whenever he wrote to her, describing a far-off mountain range or the serpentine twists of the Tagus River. *'He ought to have been another Odysseus, another Jason, traveling always to discover new lands and wonders . . .'*

But no. He was not shaped for that life any more than Latona could rest easily too long away from Aven. They were, both of them, bound to the city's soul. Whatever other splendors were out there, nothing would ever compare. His next words gave the proof to that:

'I had not expected to wrap up this endeavor in a single year, but I must also confess, it would be a fine thing to be home. Missing the elections is trouble enough to my conscience—though I hope I have provided sufficient reason for the Senate to extend my command, I must still worry over how all the other offices will shake out. There are other things to miss, as well. I cannot think to find so invigorating a Saturnalia, for example, as I last enjoyed in Aven.'

Heat rushed upon Latona's cheeks. *'Wicked man.'* It was as close as he had come, in any letter, to alluding to their delicious transgression the year before.

'Your letters have been a great comfort to me, Vitellia Latona. I have often felt as though I could hear your voice across the miles. It is not only the news from the city that I have been grateful for—though I certainly welcome your diligence in that regard. But there are few enough people to whom I feel I can speak so freely and honestly, and I cherish that you trust me enough to do the same.'

His next words touched her to the core: a comfort, almost like a promise, edging near that strange, intense tenderness which he had expressed at his departure, but had held off from putting into print.

'You are remarkable, Lady Latona, and I think—I dare to hope—that you have begun to realize it. Yet I am all the more certain that, whatever you have expressed in your letters, it must pale next to the golden glow of your reality. When this endeavor ends and I return to Aven, I shall be more eager than I can say with dignity to see for myself.'

It was Latona's ill fortune that her husband happened upon her while the pleasured flush was still on her cheeks and while the smile still ghosted over her lips.

"Wife," Herennius said, planting his hands on his hips in what he evidently thought was a posture of authority. "I demand to see that correspondence."

Latona blinked at him. "Certainly not."

His cheeks grew florid. "I demand it."

Latona rose from her couch and handed the letter to Merula, who secreted it somewhere on her person. As she did so, she let the hem of her tunic lift just enough for the blade strapped to her thigh to catch the light from the many gleaming lamps. An unsubtle maneuver, perhaps, but Latona would not chide her for it. "I refuse," Latona said, squaring her shoulders.

"It comes from Iberia, does it not?"

"I receive much correspondence from—"

"Do not try to pretend it is all from your brother!" Herennius's nostrils flared. "I will not allow you to make a fool of me!"

Latona summoned one of her most charming smiles and said, as sweetly as she could manage, "If you have a reputation for absurdity in this city, it must be entirely to your own credit, and none of my doing." She lifted her chin, unafraid to let him see the naked acrimony in her eyes.

"*I* am not the shame-bringer in this family," Herennius countered. "Though I am heartily tired of hearing gossip about my wife's imprudent behavior. Bad enough when it was Ocella, but—"

"When *what* was Ocella?" Latona advanced on him, but Herennius shifted, unwilling to look her in the eye.

"I should have known then, I suppose, what a taste you had for powerful men."

An itch began in Latona's fingers and crept up her arms, her magic prickling with her growing fury. "A *taste*?" she managed to say, through gritted teeth. "You think what happened with Ocella was to my *taste*?" Before he could respond, she went on. "You don't even know what happened. You never asked, never wanted to know, all too content to turn your head aside and—"

A sudden thought struck her. She remembered what Maia Domitia had said a month ago, when she'd met her at the temple: *'I wish my husband had just taken the bribe he was offered.'*

Latona's hands clenched with sudden rage. *"All* too content," she repeated. "As though there were something in it for you, if you feigned ignorance, if you made no fuss."

She saw it, a flinch in his cheek muscle, a little twitch. Felt it, too, in the slough of his emotions, as his self-righteousness faltered. "I don't know what you're talking about."

His tone was utterly unconvincing. "What benefits did you get, *husband*? For such a wealthy man, for a man owning such tempting property, you came through Ocella's reign remarkably unscathed. Improved, even, in your finances." Her breath became ragged and she trembled as rage suffused her blood. "Tell me. Tell me now. When I bargained for my family—"

A half-sob caught in her throat; she could remember it too well, in so many details. The dawn, bright and clear, but with high, wispy clouds threatening rain later in the day. Aula's shriek, bringing her from the garden. The smell of blood covering the tiles of Lucius Quinctilius's atrium. The tears on Aula's face, and Lucia's, as they stared down his murderers. Dictator Ocella's eyes, cold as stones beneath river-water.

"When I sacrificed myself to keep them safe, what did *you* get?" Still no answer. Latona strode toward him, a sizzle like lightning crawling through her blood. "What did you get?" she again demanded. "You must have had a price, to look aside. What was the bounty you took, for your wife's virtue?"

Herennius looked aside, his gaze cast into some dim corner of the room. "There was no payment," he said. "It wasn't like that. It wasn't . . ." A muscle in his cheek twitched. "The farm, near the Rubicon. The Dictator had taken it off some . . . some proscribed man. It was a gift. Gratitude for my . . . my understanding." Any abashment at the admission swiftly gave way to indignation, however. "And as for your virtue, you had little care enough for it yourself. You drew the Dictator's eye; you must have known what would follow. Perhaps you intended it."

Tears rose to the corners of Latona's eyes, not of sorrow but of incandescent rage. But of *course* Herennius was so small a man as to think she had invited her own violation. Latona had not thought she could hate him so much as she did in this moment. This man, whom her father had intended to protect her, had stood aside and let Ocella do as he pleased, happily accepting a few acres of wheat and pasture. Through the bile rising in her throat, she managed to choke out, "A farm. A dead man's farm." The words tasted acid on her tongue, and she hoped Herennius could hear every ounce of her contempt in them. "I knew you for a coward, Herennius, but I never thought you a simpleton, nor did I know that your dignity could be bought so *cheaply.*"

The crack of his hand against her cheek was loud—loud as a clap of thunder. Had it only sounded so because it rang inside of her own head?

A heavy moment passed. Herennius stepped back, his feet shuffling against the tiles of the floor. Latona let her head hang to the side for a moment, fury brimming inside of her. For a moment, she thought she could kill him for the indignity done to her. Slowly, she dropped her hand from her cheek. Slowly, she met Herennius's eyes.

Whatever he saw in her face staggered him. Face pale, he retreated a step. He had gone too far, and he knew it. Still, peremptory arrogance ruled in him. "Wife—" he began.

A sudden crashing noise. Every oil lamp in the room shattered. Now Herennius skittered back almost into the atrium. She had frightened him, and she was glad of it. Her Fire magic filled the space with heat, the lamp oil blazing where it stood. Slaves rushed to douse sofa cushions and fabric hangings—at least they did around the corners of the room. No one dared come within several feet of Latona and Herennius.

"Domina." Merula's voice, somewhere behind her, held a note of warning. Latona was familiar with that tone; Rubellia used it on her from time to time. It was how one approached something dangerous, an animal you thought might bite. *'And by the gods, I could. Right now, I could.'* She had seen so much violence in others in her life, but she had rarely felt it within herself. Now, her heart burned with fury.

She probed Herennius with Spirit magic. Terror, utter terror, vibrating and uncertain. She had scared him. *'Good.'* She wanted him scared. She wanted him to *hurt.*

"Domina." Merula, again, and now Latona looked down at herself. Only then did she realize that her fists were clenched, as though she might strike Herennius in return. That, though, was not what had concerned Merula enough to speak. Clenched, her fists were—and glowing. Flames from the brazier had leapt to her hands, eager for her to use them in her own defense.

'Ah.'

Herennius was not merely scared; he was terrified. *'What scares him the most, I wonder?'* Pure physical fear of the harm she might do him, if she chose? Fear that she might have such anger and vigor in her? Or a larger fear, fear that she was demonstrating powers that no mage was supposed to have? *'No. His mind is not big enough for that.'*

Dimly, Latona could hear the usual noise of the street beyond the house, but it seemed to be coming from much farther away. Between two breaths, the world seemed to freeze: *'Guide me, Juno . . .'*

A deep breath filled her lungs, then released in a sigh. She flexed her fingers in a slow, deliberate motion. Herennius stood stock-still as she strode past him to the atrium, his saucer-wide eyes following her. She knelt, slowly and deliberately, then thrust both of her hands into the impluvium pool. The water hissed and even steamed a little; the cool water stung, but Latona let it douse the energy she had been building. It felt a bit like betrayal, to rid herself of her flickering little allies.

A moment later, she cupped some water and splashed it on her face. Then she stood and walked back toward Herennius, stopping still a few strides away from him. "I suppose it's no surprise that it comes to this."

"Vitellia, I—"

"Herennius," she said, speaking in a very careful pace as she chose each word and spoke it with precision. "This marriage is at an end." He sucked in his breath as though to say something, and she held up a hand to halt him. "Let us not demean ourselves with further arguments. It was an arrangement made in a different time, when I, at least, was a different person. It has been unsuitable for years. It has now crossed the line into entirely inappropriate." She turned to Merula—and noticed, only then, that the girl had her dagger in her hand. *'Bless her instincts . . . and her restraint.'* Latona wanted out of this house, but murder was hardly likely to be conducive to her future. "Merula, please bring my personal things. A few gowns, my cosmetics and perfumes, my jewelry, my private altar." She strode back to the couch, ignoring Herennius, and picked up her soft green wrap. "That will be sufficient for now. We shall send my father's men for the rest in the morning."

"Latona—" Herennius had, at last, found his voice. "Latona, please don't be hasty."

"I divorce you," Latona said, swinging her wrap over her shoulders and watching as Merula skittered—a little too eagerly, perhaps—toward her sleeping cubicle. Latona turned to her desk and began gathering up her papers, slipping them into a box of polished ebony.

"Latona," Herennius started again. "Please." He seemed to have recovered from his fright and was angling back toward his usual concerns. "This will be embarrassing for both of us."

"Perhaps," Latona admitted, tucking the letter-box under her arm. "But I am tired of enduring private humiliation for the sake of avoiding public embarrassment. I divorce you." She had to say it three times, for formality's sake, and there were witnesses enough to make it official. "Look on the bright side, Herennius. You care little for politics, and I care little for trade. Your friends will support you; mine shall support me. I imagine we can keep public unpleasantness to a minimum."

"Latona—"

"I divorce you." She finally turned to look at him again. "There. It is done."

"But what—how—how are we going to explain this?" Herennius's tone was strangely hollow. Confusion, not sorrow.

Latona's shoulders moved in a careless shrug. "I'm sure we can come up with a suitable explanation. My father decided to look for other opportunities. You are pursuing some merchant's daughter to secure yourself a plum trade."

Herennius snorted. "I can't give a financial reason. No one would believe it, not with the dowry you came with."

And which now, Latona reflected with some pleasure, Herennius would have to give back to her father. "Then perhaps we make the most shocking choice of all and tell the truth," she said, a sigh in her voice. "That we do not like each other." He stared, unable to contradict her. "At the moment I am too angry and too tired to much care what story we spin out of it." Merula re-entered the room, carrying a small chest. "Are we ready?"

"Yes, Domina." Merula could not keep a grin off her face, and by the baleful look Herennius gave her, he had noticed.

Latona had never been better pleased by Merula's insolence. "Then let us be off." And without another look in Herennius's direction, Latona turned and stalked toward the front door.

XLIII

Latona's cheeks were still burning a furious red when she came to the door of her father's home. She had hardly noticed the surroundings as they moved through the streets winding up the Palatine Hill. Her arms were folded across her chest and she rubbed them for warmth. She ought to have changed gowns before leaving, put on a warmer tunic and sturdier shoes, but she had not wanted to stay in that house a moment longer than strictly necessary—not so much out of pique as fearing that Herennius might find his courage and attempt to bar her from leaving.

As Merula pounded briskly on the door, Latona turned, gazing out at the city. Abruptly she remembered the previous year's Cantrinalia, after which she and Sempronius Tarren had stood in this same spot, watching the sun set over the red rooftops of Aven, warm with promise. A new feeling pierced through the fury and the indignation: hope.

A sudden gust of wind, crisp and cool and smelling of damp leaves, snatched at her hair, and she shivered. Merula was still knocking, and now cursing under her breath. "Diana's tits, where is that fool boy?"

When the door at last did open, the fool boy in question got a tongue-lashing in rapid Phrygian. From his furrowed brow and jutted-out lower lip, Latona guessed that he did not speak the language. Merula's tone was impossible to mistake, however, and once Latona was safely and warmly bustled inside, sighing with relief as the warmth from the hypocaust came over her, she switched to Truscan. "—to leave your lady standing out on the street! I'll be having words with Paenas, mark me right now! Now go! No, do not be going to the Lady Aula yourself, clearly you cannot be trusted! Find me someone better equipped!"

The hapless lad ran from the room, tripping over his own feet as he went. Latona thought about chastising Merula for her harshness, but could not quite summon the energy. It hardly mattered, anyway, for Merula's rancor had alerted Aula to her presence. "Merula, dear," came the sweet voice, preceding Aula into the atrium. "I'm not sure what Urco did to incur your wrath, but it's a bit uncouth to reduce the lad to tears, whatever the—" As she rounded a column, her voice trailed off. She had caught sight of her sister. "Latona? My darling, what's . . . what's the matter?" Her eyes went from Latona's face to the chest Merula was toting.

"As it happens," Latona said, "I suspect you'll be pleased." She looked to Merula. "To my old bedroom, if you please." And back to Aula. "I'll be resuming occupancy, full-time. I hope no one minds."

"Minds?" Aula's face split in a wide grin. "You've actually done it! You have, haven't you? Please say you have." At Latona's nod, Aula broke into a squeal. "Then I'm *ecstatic*! Oh, my honey, you don't know how long I've been wanting—well, better late than never, I suppose, but all the same—" Her face volleyed suddenly from delight to a mildly disconcerted frown. "Oh. Dear. Father."

"Yes," Latona said, rueful. "Father. Is he in?"

Aula shook her head. "Dining with Rufilius Albinicus tonight."

Latona's lips quirked up. "And he left you at home?"

Aula's mouth returned the smirk. "With Young Rufilius in Iberia with the Fourteenth, there's not much of a reason for me to go, now is there? Much though I admire and respect Old Albinicus, of course." Aula reached out and seized Latona's hands. "Come on, dearest. I'll fetch Alhena, and you can tell us all about what finally persuaded you to shuck off that useless crustacean of a husband."

◇◇◇◇◇◇◇◇◇◇◇◇

Latona had both her sisters at her side when she told the story to their father. Not that much explanation was needed, once Aulus inspected the red mark on Latona's cheek. It would be bruised and purple upon the morrow; Latona wondered if Rubellia could teach her a charm to cover it. That was one discipline of Venus she had not yet tried.

"Oh, daughter. I am sorry." He shook his head. "I *had* come to realize that Numerius Herennius was not quite the exemplary match that I had hoped he might grow into, but that he would resort to . . ." The words seemed to catch in his throat; Aulus appeared unwilling to put name to the abuse. To his credit, he did not ask what Latona might have done to provoke Herennius to hit her. The Vitelliae had never considered that the legal right to beat one's wife justified the moral failing of actually doing so.

When she expounded further, about the farm taken in trade for her chastity, Aulus actually hung his head in shame. "I am sorry," he said again, huskier this time. "I . . . judged him ill." Latona only nodded, not wishing to make him feel worse, but unwilling to exonerate him from responsibility. "Will there be trouble?"

Latona shrugged. "I doubt he'll raise any objections, lest I should publicly proclaim him a wife-beater and a panderer. Getting divorced is bad enough without creating an immense scandal out of it."

At the word "scandal," Aulus winced slightly. After another moment, he stood, placing his hands behind his back and pacing around the room. Alhena's slender fingers intertwined with Latona's, and Aula's hand was at the base of her back.

'He is disappointed,' Latona thought, watching the creases around her father's eyes and jowls. *'But is he disappointed in me?'* A divorce was not world-ending for patricians of their status—but nor was it something to throw a celebration over, however Aula might feel to the contrary. Latona wondered if Aulus was figuring out how to explain the situation to his friends.

And then, despite her chagrin at dismaying her father in this way, Latona felt a little, rebellious surge of insolent anger rising in her breast. *'He's known for ages that this was an unsuitable match, but he never saved me from it before now. He could have had me divorce Herennius as soon as Dictator Ocella was dead. It would have made perfectly clear that the marriage was only for the convenience of protection in the first place, and no one could have blamed us for ending the farce once that threat had passed. Now it will look . . . well, I don't know like what, but I'm sure we're about to find out.'*

But at long last, Aulus came to rest in front of her. He placed a hand gently on each shoulder and kissed Latona upon her brow. A blessing Latona wished she did not need.

◇◇◇◇◇◇◇◇◇◇◇◇

Rabirus had seen Durmius Argus before, many times. Members of the Augian Commission were frequently on hand in their black-bordered togas when the Senate met or during legal proceedings, to ensure that no magical tampering took place. Yet the man's face had never impressed itself into Rabirus's memory, and looking at him now, Rabirus struggled to find anything notable about him. Dark hair, middling brown eyes, neither tall nor short, neither slim nor sturdy, with a vaguely amiable smile and an utterly forgettable air about him. Rabirus wondered, first, if he cultivated such a nondescript presence, the better to achieve his goals without attracting undue attention, and second, if it was magical in nature, a subtle charm nudging observers' eyes and thoughts away.

That thought put a crease in his brow. Rabirus little liked being manipulated.

"Praetor Rabirus," Durmius said. His voice had an oily quality. "How good of you to cut your travels short on my behalf."

'He speaks as though I had been taking a pleasure cruise around Crater Bay, not leading legions on the other side of the Middle Sea.' But Rabirus swallowed his annoyance. "Your messenger was most persuasive."

"Please, do sit." Durmius sank into a curule-style chair, and Rabirus did the same. They were ensconced in his study, with a slave standing outside the door but none within. Durmius folded his hands across his slightly rounded belly, fingers interlaced. "I imagine my friend Publius's message came as quite a shock to you."

"I confess, I had not anticipated finding a devotee of Discord among the mages of the Augian Commission," Rabirus said. "I had not thought any of your talents ran to Fracture."

"Nor do they," Durmius explained. "Not all of Lady Discordia's followers are blessed with her talents, any more than all those who honor Jupiter or Juno are Spirit mages. *That* is my gift, incidentally, and I love the god who gave it to me no less for also appreciating Discordia's place in our world." He spoke of it so reasonably, as if it were ordinary thaumaturgical discourse and not consideration of dark magics and banished cults. "No, my role is not in working Discordia's will directly, but in providing some cover for those who do."

"There are many who would say," Rabirus began, carefully, "that such use of magic is anathema to the gods' blessing. A perversion of sacred purpose."

Durmius spread his hands wide. "Is not Discordia a goddess as well? Does she not deserve her due?"

Rabirus had no easy answer. There was a logic in that, to be sure. "And how have you served the goddess among the Commission?"

"A few of my fellows have been convinced to see the truth of our world," Durmius said. "Our job is so much more than petty quarrels about misplaced curses, you know. More even than keeping magic out of the Curia and the Forum. No, our sacred trust is to do whatever necessary to ensure the gods continue to bless Aven. Recent generations have forgotten this, doing only as they are told by the mandate of the Senate."

"Have they?" Rabirus drawled. "And have you noticed ill effects on the city?"

"Oh, certainly, Praetor." Durmius looked quite sad. "But it has come on so slowly, you see, most of the populace has not. Think back to the days of kings, and before that, the days of legend. Was not magic so much stronger then? Mortal men could work wonders. Our gifts now are so thin and weak by comparison."

"And you believe Discordia can . . . what, restore the greater magics to the world?"

"Chaos itself has been said by some to generate magical potential, as perhaps it did in the dawn of the world," Durmius said, "but I believe the greater power is in drawing the gods' eyes back to us. We must be *worthy* of their regard."

Rabirus nodded. This, he could understand. "Aven has deviated far from the intentions of our noble ancestors."

For the first time, Durmius's smile became more than bland, taking on a self-satisfied edge. "We are correcting the course, Praetor, as we must. As I believe Publius told you—we can call upon Discordia to help us unmake what needs destruction, and then we may profitably build upon a stronger foundation." Then the satisfaction vanished, and his thumbs waggled circles around each other. "But not all the Commissioners are stalwart enough men, I fear. Some have had to be . . . encouraged to look the other way."

"Bribery?" Rabirus asked, almost glad to find such petty corruption in a man so aglow in ideals.

"Among other things," Durmius answered lightly. "But as we have become more . . . active . . . we're attracting more attention, and I must confess myself unequal to the task of tending to all of it. This is where you can help us: in diverting public attention away from Discordia's servants, and in casting our actions in a light that will help to clear the path for a grander future."

A simple enough charge. "I shall encourage the people to think of it as when a fire destroys a building. Though we may mourn the loss, it is an opportunity to create something stronger upon the ashes."

"Just so!" Durmius's cheeks lit with pleasure. "Just so."

"But, Commissioner," Rabirus said, "if I am to protect your—Discordia's—servants and their actions, I must know more of these people and what they are doing." He sat forward a bit, his elbow on the lacquered edge of his chair. *'And I would have some leverage over you, friend Durmius, if you're going to hold Pinarius Scaeva over me.'*

"Certainly, certainly." Durmius reached for a small bell and gave it a sharp ring. "I cannot give you the names of all Discordia's servants. Even *I* do not know them all. Safer that way." His eyes glinted; it had been the mandate of Ocella's court, as they both knew. "But I can introduce you to one for whom I have great affection, and she can tell you more about her efforts."

"She?" Rabirus asked, surprised, as the door opened, admitting a young woman. Durmius rose to greet her, and Rabirus decided to err on the side of showing her the same respect.

The girl looked perfect. *Too* perfect, a woman carved of alabaster stone. Her garments were pure white and sat on her with such precision that she might have been an unpainted statue. Even when she moved, her steps were so small that her gown hardly seemed to ripple.

When she raised her eyes to Rabirus's face, though, he knew in an instant that no one who saw this woman could ever forget her. Her gaze had an intensity that startled, a world apart from her brother's pleasantly bland aspect. *'Ocella had eyes like that,'* he remembered, as the hairs on his forearms stood on end. A vibrant blue, shocking as lightning, cold as ice.

"Praetor Rabirus," Durmius said, placing a hand against the young woman's back, "it is my great honor to introduce my sister, Anca Corinna."

Rabirus's first thought was that Durmius had handed him too great a prize, revealing his own kin as a Discordian. The second was that if he was willing to do so, he must feel very secure indeed. "Lady Corinna," Rabirus said, inclining his head. "A pleasure." He glanced to Durmius. "Her name—?"

"She's my half sister, from my mother's second marriage," Durmius said, explaining why she was an Anca Corinna and not a Sexta Durmia.

"Ever since birth, I have been a fragment." Her voice had a slight musical note to it, though the effect was more unsettling than pleasant.

"She is a Fracture mage of rare ability," Durmius said proudly. "And quite a fine poet."

Corinna cocked her head, drawing nearer to Rabirus. "We've met before, you know."

"Impossible," Rabirus replied. "I would have remembered."

"No," Corinna said, "but I do not blame you, for I was cloaked and hooded then, being smuggled on and off Capraia."

Understanding dawned. *'One of Ocella's girls, then. Or one of his pet mages. Or both.'* Ocella had hated the Discordians, banished them from Aven. Had he known the girl's divine loyalty, he would have thrown her off Capraia's highest sea-cliff. *'But I had no notion of Pinarius Scaeva's affiliation. Ocella could have made use of this girl for his own purposes and never been the wiser.'*

"I am pleased to make your acquaintance now," Rabirus said. "Your brother tells me you can illuminate my understanding of your . . . efforts."

Corinna moved to a chair and folded herself neatly into it. "We had much to practice, with blood and bone." Durmius smiled indulgently, as though his sister had not opened with a thoroughly disturbing statement. "But it's become easier, to invite the lady in. Listen as you walk the streets, and you will hear her at work."

Rabirus's gaze slid from the young woman to Durmius. *'Does he think this an adequate explanation?'*

"No doubt your friend Buteo has informed you," Durmius said, "of the troubles the city has had since midsummer."

"Fights and accidents, he said. And hauntings."

"All for Discordia," Corinna's lilting voice confirmed. "Curse dirt—"

"A trick we borrowed from your friend Scaeva," Durmius interjected.

"—and little charms, to weaken wood and stone. But the doors, the bronze doors, those are my favorites, I must confess, sir." Her face lit with pleasure; Rabirus was put in mind of a death mask in a lararium, shining with a flame behind it. "They open the way for the fiends, and they delight, oh, they delight in this world of ours."

"*Lemures,*" Durmius explained. "Among other such spirits. They disrupt common lives and foment terror. It's been useful in certain neighborhoods. I think by the time of the elections, we may have driven some to utter chaos."

"They are so hungry," Corinna said, and it took Rabirus a moment to realize she meant her fiends and not the people of Aven. "Ever so hungry, and so grateful for the chance to feed—" Her expression darkened so swiftly that Rabirus took a step back. "But someone keeps *closing* the bronze doors and sending them back." Her hands curled into claws, pressing into her thighs and marring the marble perfection of her appearance. Swift as a summer storm, tears sprang from her eyes, and her breath came hard and shallow. "I hate her, I *hate* her, she closes every breach she finds, she sews the world back together." Corinna shook her head, forcefully enough that dark locks of curly hair slipped free of their pins. "She wants broken things put back together, she doesn't *understand*!"

"Ssshh, shh, shh." Durmius dropped to his knees in front of his sister, catching her hands before they could rend her garments. "Easy, my dear. You'll have your chance." He sent an apologetic look over his shoulder at Rabirus. "Forgive her. Fracture magic takes its toll on the mage more than many elements, and she's been working ever so hard lately."

The contrast between the polished lady who had entered the room and the increasingly wild-eyed waif in the chair was alarming, true, but Rabirus had fixed upon her words. "Who?" he asked her. "Who has been stymieing your efforts?"

Corinna sniffled, her body starting to rock in the chair. "The golden one," she said. "She brings others, one of them a traitor to our gift, others bright and dark, but it's glitter-gold behind it all, glowing with such horrible shine. I *hate* her!"

"But who is it?" Rabirus demanded, even as suspicion began to well in his mind. "Do you know her? Who is she?"

"Oh, I know her," Corinna snarled, her voice dropping low and losing its musicality. "I know her of old, and so do you. She was there, there, there on the island, though she did not shimmer so then. Now she's all ablaze, the Spirit mage." Corinna's eyes flared wide as she pronounced the name as though it were a death sentence: "Vitellia Latona."

XLIV

Sempronius did not often dream.

He had never been sure why. Some Shadow mages had a particular talent for it, walking through the curtains of the sleeping world with deftness, but it was not a gift that had manifested in Sempronius. Sometimes he thought it was because all the imagination in his soul was bent to a purpose: to the dream of Aven, the glorious city and nation-center that he knew it could be. Perhaps, with so much of his cerebral capacity dedicated there, none was left over for Morpheus to play with. Sometimes he wondered what he was missing out on, if there was some glorious world that others entered that he could not. But the waking world was enough to be getting on with, and so most of the time, he was glad enough to rest without mental distraction.

And, if he did not dream, nor was he often visited by nightmares. For that, he was more grateful than ever, knowing the lingering effect the *akdraugi* had visited on so many men, particularly those who had been barricaded inside Toletum for months. The legions' healers had been taxed to their utmost, trying to find succor for men who still woke with horrors, long after their last encounter with the *akdraugi*. The legions had encountered no such eldritch terrors since Toletum. Sempronius feared the Lusetani were regathering their magical strength, but in the meantime, they had encountered only warriors of a mundane nature and chased them all around Iberia's central plateaus. The men fought without breaking, but in the night, some of them woke howling. The healer-mages tried to purge internal demons; the healer-priests beseeched Asclepius; the healer-surgeons threw up their hands in despair, for these horrors were nothing they could cut out of a man.

If not dreaming spared Sempronius that torment, he would gladly accept the trade.

On the night before the Kalends of November, though, Morpheus did see fit to visit him with a message.

He found himself back in Abydosia, standing under a dark sky on the banks of that land's massive, dark-rolling river. Except it wasn't rolling; the Iteru lay still and quiet, unnaturally so. Not frozen. Sempronius had seen frozen rivers, high in the mountains in winter, but the Iteru would never freeze, not unless Pluto himself ascended from the netherworld and dragged its waters back below with him. And the river did not have the glossy sheen of ice atop it. Rather it was as if the Iteru had simply decided not to flow.

He looked up, trying to gauge the season by the stars, but thick cloud cover had blotted them out. Behind him, he heard the rustling of grass and the laughter of jackals. Then, as his gaze dropped back to the river, he did see movement. Not the usual flow of water, but the ripples that came with something moving beneath.

Crocodiles, he realized. Slowly moving toward him, their tails betraying them only to the sharp-sighted. Black shapes under black water under a black night. Three, headed straight for him. He took a step backward, but as soon as he did, the jackals hiding somewhere in the grasses grew louder. He could only watch, then, as the crocodiles came toward him, dark shapes full of hungry malice—

In the waking world, Sempronius's eyes flew wide, but before he moved a muscle, he examined his tent. Corvinus lay asleep on a cot near the doors, bundled under blankets. He heard nothing unusual, only Corvinus's slow, steady breath and the breeze buffeting the canvas walls. It was too late at night for any activity in the camp. Even the sentries would be still at their posts.

But then, a faint scrape, off to the left side of the tent. As Sempronius's eyes adjusted to the dark, he fixed them in the direction of the sound.

One—two—three shapes, crawling through the darkness.

Moving as slowly as he could, Sempronius slipped a hand under his pillow, gripping the hilt of the dagger he kept there. He forced himself to wait, tensing his muscles, until one of the three figures had moved within striking distance.

Then, Sempronius was on his feet as swiftly as he could manage, whipping the bedsheet away from himself and toward the other two attackers, while lunging at the closest with his dagger. *"Corvinus!"* he roared, even as his blade missed its mark, his opponent twisting just out of its way.

The attackers had leather armor and curved blades slightly longer than his own, though not the size of a *gladius*. Sempronius had only his sleeping tunic and the dagger. But he couldn't allow poor odds to make him timid. He stabbed again at the first attacker, then turned to ram the second with his shoulder, knocking him off balance.

Corvinus had woken at Sempronius's shout and immediately ripped the ties from the tent flaps. "Lictors! To the praetor!"

A hot pain flared in Sempronius's hip; one of the enemy blades had made contact. Sempronius seized the edge of a table and swung it hard, overturning it in the direction of his attackers, then did the same with a chair. Anything to keep them at a distance, for just another moment. He flung a dish at one of them, then an inkpot—anything he could lay his hands on. Inelegant fighting, to be sure, but Sempronius had always thought it better to stay alive, no matter how ridiculous he looked. He backed up toward the tent wall, snatching up a pillow as he went: a poor shield, but at least something he could use to help deflect the blades coming at him.

Two of Sempronius's lictors came rushing in, followed by Autronius Felix, fire in his eyes. Though the lictors were in full kit, Felix was no better armored than Sempronius, but that wasn't about to stop him joining the fight. With a mighty bellow, he hurled himself at the attacker closest to the door, bearing him to the ground and punching with abandon. Felix wrested the blade from the man's hand and immediately buried it in his throat.

Only one of the other attackers turned to fend off the lictors; the man closest to Sempronius kept his attention doggedly fixed on his initial target. Instinctively, Sempronius reached out for his Shadow magic. It came easily in the midnight-black tent. He could have used it to disappear, or as near to it as made no difference, but he couldn't do that in front of the lictors. So instead he flung his power at his assailant's eyes.

It wouldn't make much difference in such a dark room, but it was enough. Sempronius saw the blink of confusion as the temporary blindness hit, saw the man lose focus on him. In that breath of hesitation, Sempronius stepped forward and drove his blade into his attacker's gut, then shoved him backward, right into a lictor's sword.

The third man was already on the ground. Sempronius couldn't see his wounds, but they had not been immediately fatal. The would-be assassin was wheezing wetly, gulping for air.

Sempronius knelt beside him. "Who sent you? Tell me, and we may be able to find you a medic." The man gave a damp chuckle, shaking his head, then grimaced in pain. Sempronius tried again, in Tyrian. This time, he saw a flicker of understanding in the man's eyes, but still, there was no response. "Tell me!" Sempronius demanded. "We have mage-healers, we can—"

The attacker snarled something then, in an Iberian dialect that Sempronius had not yet mastered. He committed the words to memory, though, even as the man coughed up a glob of blood—then spat it at him, and died.

"Sir!" Both lictors snapped to attention, and the more senior of them spoke. "Sir, I cannot—There's no excuse, sir, I—"

Sempronius held up a hand. "A moment, please." Swiftly, he wiped his face with the sleeve of his tunic, then, pushing past the lictors, Felix, and Corvinus, he stepped outside of the tent.

The night breeze snapped over his sweat- and blood-damp skin. A half moon hung low in the sky, grazing the top of the camp's wall. Sempronius closed his eyes and thanked the gods for his deliverance. *'Pluto and Nox, Jupiter and Mars and Juno and anyone else who had a hand in this, I throw myself before your feet in gratitude. Whichever of you sent me that dream of warning, I owe you a white bull.'*

He stepped back into his tent to find Corvinus lighting lamps while Felix and the lictors examined the corpses.

Corvinus cleared his throat. "Sir, you're—" He gestured at the wound on his hip. "I'll fetch a medic."

"Wake Gaius Vitellius, too, while you're at it."

"Already here, sir," came the young man's voice, from the tent flap. "I heard the commotion and—"

"Good lad," Sempronius said. "Then, Corvinus, find a handful of centurions and set them to searching the camp for anyone else who doesn't belong."

"Yes, sir."

Vitellius rubbed at his face, still clearing sleep from his eyes. "What in Mars's name happened?"

"The General was attacked," Felix said, a bit sharply, holding his blood-covered hands up in the light.

"Yes, I can see that," Vitellius shot back. "But how?"

It was a fair question. A fortified camp was not the same thing as a marching camp, or even a less permanent standing camp. They had walls of timber, proper gates, watchtowers—all things that should have made it impossible for even a few of the enemy to sneak inside. *'It would have been harder still if we'd traded my command tent for a building.'* But Sempronius had insisted that barracks and stables take precedence.

"Was it an attempt by Ekialde, do you think?" asked Felix.

Sempronius considered. "Perhaps. Perhaps not. There does seem to be magic about it."

Felix snorted. "I should hope so. If three armed assassins got into a fortified Aventan camp with*out* magic, we should all hang up our shields and go home right now."

But Vitellius, who had, of course, been among the Iberians much longer, was shaking his head. "I don't know. For all their perfidious magic, the Iberians are like the Tennic tribes when it comes to warfare and honor. All that time I was out in the open, before Toletum, and Ekialde never sent assassins after me. He waited until he could face me in battle. He tried to ensorcel me, then, but he made the attempt face to face, sword in hand. This subterfuge, knives in the night . . ." Vitellius shook his head. "I would not swear beyond all doubt that it isn't the Lusetani. They may be learning perfidies anew. But it doesn't strike me as Ekialde's style."

"We are meant to think he's behind it, at least." Felix brought a light next to one of the dead men; he had unmistakably Iberian features, broad-faced and russet-toned.

"Go find Bartasco and Hanath," Sempronius said, nodding to Vitellius. "I want to ask them about this."

◇◇◇◇◇◇◇◇◇◇◇◇◇◇

Perfunctorily, Bartasco and Hanath examined the dead bodies: checking their weapons, their jewelry, flipping them over to get a better look at their clothing and their tattoos. Then they stood, looking at each other. "Counei, I think," Hanath said. "And far from home."

"I agree." Bartasco turned to Sempronius. "Southern tribes, for certain. You can tell that from the weave of their garments and those tassels on their sleeves. None of the central tribes favor that style."

"And the weapons," Hanath said. "The grip is much different than what we use."

"But this—" Bartasco nudged with his foot at one man's head. Two earrings were studded into his upper ear. "This is how the Counei, in particular, communicate rank."

Felix swore in a grumble. "Another tribe has turned against us?"

"Perhaps not," Bartasco said. "These may be mercenaries, only."

"Their lands do not stand so very far from the Lusetani," Hanath countered. "They may have been suborned through fear or bribes or gods know what persuasion."

"Bad news for us if they have." Sempronius pinched at the bridge of his nose, then went to his desk, unearthing the map of Iberia that the scout Dorsus had been helping him to compile. He was glad Corvinus wasn't in the room to see him do so. Sempronius had wiped the blood from his hands and pressed a wad of fabric onto his injured hip, but he was nowhere near pristine enough for his steward to consider him allowed near papers. "Bartasco, show me. Where are the Counei villages?"

"Far south," Bartasco said, gesturing. "The Tartessi are not far from here, you know, near Corduba, between the rivers. But the Counei are not mountain people, not river people, even. They live in the flatlands near the sea. Some south of Olissippo, but mostly eastward, toward the mouth of the Baetis."

He had pointed to the city of Gades.

"Son of a *bitch*," Felix muttered.

Bartasco and Hanath glanced among the three Aventan leaders: Sempronius and Vitellius stony-faced, Felix ruddy and cursing. "We're missing something," Hanath said.

Sempronius looked at the lictors. "Gentlemen, if you could remove these bodies. Strip them of anything valuable or identifying. We may need to send a message to someone later on. Summon the healer-mages to look the bodies over for marks of magic. The Arevaci magic-men may be able to discern whatever charm allowed them to get into our camp unnoticed." Bartasco nodded approvingly. "Once they're done, have someone drag the bodies to the forest line. The wolves and crows can have them."

At that moment, Corvinus returned, with one of the legion's physicians in tow. Sempronius held up a hand to detain them. "I promise I'll subject myself to your ministrations in due course," he said, "but I am in no danger of bleeding to death, and there are more important matters."

The medic ducked his head deferentially, but Corvinus gave him a hard glare. "Dominus, I must object—"

"Yes, Corvinus, I know you must. Come in, and you may chastise me to your heart's content once we're done." He looked again to the medic. "I'll visit you in the infirmary shortly."

The medic nodded. "I shall make sure the building is warmed ahead of your arrival." The medic couldn't resist one admonition before parting, however. "Do drink something while you're still here. Water for your health and wine for the pain."

Corvinus set about pouring a cup for him. No one else spoke while the lictors dragged the bodies of the assassins out of the tent. Once they were gone, Felix stuck his head out of the tent, looking around, then nodded in assurance that no one was lingering outside.

"So what's set all of your feathers a-ruffle?" Hanath asked, while Felix knotted the tent flaps back together—those that Corvinus hadn't torn in his haste to summon help.

Sempronius was in the middle of swallowing the well-watered wine that Corvinus had pressed on him, so Vitellius supplied the answer. "Lucretius Rabirus, who was recently abandoned by the Fourth Legion. His seat is in Gades."

"Not that he's in it," Felix grumbled. "The Fourth left him because they couldn't believe he was withdrawing entirely from conflict. But he may have sent these men our way before he tucked tail and fled back to Aven."

Bartasco looked from Sempronius, to the map, to the bloodstained rugs where the dead bodies had lain. "You think he sent these men to kill you?"

"I cannot say for sure, of course, but it would not be the first time he has tried."

Bartasco nodded solemnly. "Son of a bitch, indeed. To kill a man in honorable combat is one thing, but this . . ."

Hanath's lips had curled in disgust. "This is how it was done in Numidia, in years past. The lords feuded, and they were as likely to send a single assassin into a rival's tent as to face them on the field. Dishonorable, but often effective."

Sempronius gave her a rueful smile. "I believe those words could sum up Rabirus's overall method of engaging with the world."

◇◇◇◇◇◇◇◇◇◇◇◇

After Sempronius let the medic stitch up the gash on his hip, the others eventually went back to their own tents and presumably to sleep. Against Corvinus's objections, Sempronius chose to stay awake, walking the camp until the sun rose.

The mages wanted to wait for daylight to examine the would-be assassins' bodies. Sempronius questioned the already-chastened sentries himself—as much to make sure the centurions weren't misapplying blame as anything else. If they had missed anything mundane, they'd be executed for dereliction of duty. *'But men should not be blamed for supernatural hoodwinking.'*

As he suspected, no sentry had seen or heard anything abnormal. They had all been at their posts, alert, and each man could vouch for the others.

As a white dawn rose over the plateau, setting a crisp frost on the ground, Sempronius returned to his tent. Little though he liked to admit to physical failings of any kind, he collapsed on his cot, exhausted, as Corvinus began tying up the tent flaps behind them. He stared up, lacing his fingers together on top of his chest. "I may need to rethink my strategy here, Corvinus."

"Sir?"

"Mars prohibits magic on the battlefield," Sempronius murmured. "But with what our enemies are willing to use against us, it may be time to test the bounds of that proscription. I cannot think that he wants his armies at such a wretched disadvantage."

Corvinus sat in a chair near Sempronius's cot, looking concerned. "Dominus, you don't mean to . . . to flout Mars?"

"I hope to honor Mars in all my deeds," Sempronius said. "And I've no desire to risk exposure. I just think we might want to explore options." And it couldn't be blasphemy, not really, if done to serve the gods in the end.

XLV

Central Iberia

It was even colder than it had been the night that Matigentis had been born, though winter had not yet come in truth. More than a month, yet, till the winter solstice. *'My child has not even had a name for half a year.'* A strange thought, somehow.

Mati no longer needed to be carried everywhere, though Neitin hated to have him out of sight. He could pull himself up to stand, and he had recently become absolutely unstoppable when crawling. His speed was astonishing, not only to see so small a body moving so fast, but because he moved across the earth with the trusting innocence of one who had never yet encountered pain. Utterly fearless, Mati had wanted to investigate everything, hauling himself up onto the cots and benches in his mother's tent. Every time he called out "Ma!" Neitin's heart twisted.

Tonight, he had been left in the custody of his doting aunts, while Sakarbik led Neitin out of the camp and into a copse of trees at the riverside.

"But why tonight?" Neitin hissed, burrowing her cheeks into her cloak. It was spotted and soft, made from the fur of wildcats. Ekialde had bestowed it upon her as a bride-gift.

"The moon," Sakarbik said, shrugging off her own woolen cloak. She wore only a short-sleeved tunic underneath.

'Does the magic within her keep her warm?' Neitin wondered. *'Or is it just stubbornness?'*

Sakarbik looked skyward. The moon itself was not visible, but a silver effulgence glowed from behind the spiky evergreens. "Full moons and new moons are for amateurs," she said. "The real power comes here, at the cusp of things. That's where you can seize real power, at the time when the world *wants* to turn and change, not when it's teeming or fallow."

"And we stand halfway between autumn and winter, so it could be doubly powerful."

Sakarbik twitched an eyebrow, as though suppressing the instinct to look impressed that Neitin had sorted it out. "Just so." She took a few steps away from Neitin, turning her face again to the sky and spreading her arms wide. Her palms were up, her fingers spread, not so much as though she would receive the gods' grace, but as if she intended to claw it from heaven. She began chanting, her voice low and musical. Neitin had heard her sing before, lullabies to Matigentis, but out here in the wilderness, the sound *fit* better. Singing to the stars, Sakarbik's voice had in it the wolf's howl, the rush of river water, the rumble of far-off thunder.

Neitin crouched down to rest her legs, rocking back and forth on her heels with her cloak wrapped tightly around her. Magic had always made her nervous, for all that her uncle practiced it, and had done all her life. Watching rituals set her heart to fluttering. It was all too uncertain, too far beyond the realm of daily life.

Sakarbik's song put her in mind of her youth, in the days before she had gone up into the *mendi* to wed Ekialde, the promising second son of a chieftain who was friendly with her father. Baking bread and combing her sisters' hair, those had been Neitin's joys. Splashing in the river, welcoming the hunters back from the forest, and laughing with abandon, as she had not felt light-hearted enough to do in months.

'Where did it go wrong?'

Not when she wed. That, too, had been utter joy and delight. She knew she had wed a warrior, of course, but at first, his raids had been the usual sort. No, things had only gone off course on another night like this one, when she sat in the dirt, watching as magic-men assembled and declared that her husband had been chosen by the gods to lead their people against the mighty force of Aven.

'Would that the gods had left well enough alone. We might have been happy.'

Sakarbik's invocation crooned softer, until it dwindled into silence. She stood still for a moment, then turned, startlingly swiftly, and crossed back to Neitin, who scrambled back to her feet. "Can you be brave?" Sakarbik demanded. "As brave as you need to be?"

"I—Yes." What other answer, after all, was there?

"Good." Fast as a striking snake, Sakarbik's hand shot out and snatched the talisman from around Neitin's throat—the one made of clay and Ekialde's blood. She had never been comfortable wearing it, since it had come from Bailar's hands, even if the blood had been freely given by her husband, not stolen from some unsuspecting soul. All the same, she gasped, clutching a hand to her chest. Her neck felt suspiciously light.

Sakarbik held her hand to the sky. "Endovelicos of many faces, Endovelicos who blesses my sight, here!" Her fist tightened with impossible strength, crushing the talisman. She cast it before her, the crumbling clay disappearing into the earth.

Sakarbik stepped back, side by side with Neitin, looking expectantly at the space between the trees. Neitin didn't dare ask what she was waiting for.

An owl screeched, alarmingly close to them. Neitin found herself thinking with sympathy of whatever mouse or rabbit was destined to be a meal this night. A stiff breeze caught her from behind, pushing her cloak flat against her arms and calves. It carried the scent of fresh pine with it, and at that moment, the half-moon crested into visibility.

A mist began to appear in mid-air, condensing into swaying forms. The sight was, by now, all too familiar to Neitin. She sucked in her breath. Her mind wanted to run, to flee, but her feet refused to move.

Sakarbik's hands clamped on her shoulders. "Don't be afraid."

"You've betrayed me!" Neitin hissed. "The fiends—"

A hard shake rattled her teeth. "Don't be a fool, either! *Look*, little wife, little mother! What do your damn eyes tell you?"

Despite that her knees seemed to have turned to water, Neitin did as she was told. Her throat worked anxiously, but as she peered at the spirits hovering nearby, she did not feel the same anguished dread as when Bailar summoned his *akdraugi*. Nor, when she managed to look past her fear, did they have the same appearance.

These spirits had no more of a fixed form than the *akdraugi*, but instead of moving in sharp gusts and aping demonic faces, they were soft, rounded, bouncing gently in mid-air. One bobbed a little nearer her, then seemed to shy away again. They had a warmth to them, in their golden glow, but they did not feel comfortable. In gazing on them, Neitin experienced the breath-stopping awe that she had the first time her father had taken her to Olissippo, to see the Endless Ocean: a sense of her own smallness, her own insignificance, staring into the face of eternity. "What—What are they?"

"*Besteki*, little wife. Good spirits." Another shake of her shoulders, though less violent this time. "It has taken me quite a bit of time and effort to work out how to invite them into the waking world, I don't mind telling you."

A helpless half-laugh bubbled out of Neitin, then she clapped a hand over her mouth, lest the spirits take offense.

"They cannot stay long," Sakarbik went on. "There is too much tainted soil in these parts. They do not like places where the *akdraugi* have been." This was the camp where Bailar and Ekialde had first tried summoning the demons, before they had moved closer to Toletum. Sakarbik had not been with them then, could not have known, but for her magic. "I think I may be able to persuade them to look after you and your child, and keep you from harm." Sakarbik paused, drawing a long breath, then huffing it out through her nose. Neitin had a flash of insight: whatever Sakarbik was about to say, she knew it would not go over well. "But I do not think they will do so here."

Neitin blinked over her shoulder at the Cossetan magic-woman. "What do you mean?"

"What I said. Here, where the *akdraugi* have run rampant, where they might be summoned up again at any time. Where so many men have taken blood in their names." Her lip curled in disgust. "Where so many souls are rotting."

The *besteki* flared slightly, as if in agreement with her words. Neitin's thigh muscles trembled, but she swallowed and tried to stand up straighter, shrugging off Sakarbik's hands. "What good will they do us, then, if they will not stay?"

"A great deal," Sakarbik answered, "if you do not stay here, either."

Neitin whipped about, strange though it felt to turn her back on the *besteki*, like disrespecting an honored chieftain. "What do you—" She bit her tongue before she could ask the same question again. "Where else is there to be?"

The yellow in Sakarbik's hazel eyes was indiscernible in the darkness, but her exasperation was easy enough to perceive. "You have a father, I think? Far to the east?"

"I do."

"You would be safe there? He would receive you and your son gladly?"

Neitin's head nodded—without her permission, and as soon as she realized she was doing it, she shook herself fiercely. "I cannot believe this. You would have me abandon my husband, my people, in the middle of a war?"

"Your husband has polluted himself," Sakarbik hissed. "He deserves abandonment."

"He is coming to see sense!" Neitin protested.

"For how long? See it yourself, little wife! Without Bailar's magic, the Aventan legions are cutting through our raiders like so much cheese.

Already he is losing control of the Vettoni, while the Arevaci and Edetani stand fast with their scale-armored, scarlet-cloaked friends. When others begin to peel away—when even the men of other Lusetani villages question the wisdom of continuing to fight—how long will your husband resist Bailar's sweet song, which might lure them back?"

Neitin's lower lip quivered. She wanted, so much, to insist on Ekialde's stalwartness. He was the *erregerra*, chosen of the gods, surely he had in him the strength to resist such temptation. Surely he would continue his fight on more honorable terms—or, better yet, give it up entirely and return home, as she had begged him to do for so long.

But she could not lie to herself so shamelessly, and so she said nothing.

Sakarbik seized Neitin's chin and bent until they were nearly nose to nose. "If you stay here, little wife, you die. The stars are quite clear on this."

She might have been lying. She was Cossetan; she had few reasons for honesty with Neitin, whatever oaths she had sworn.

"And Mati?" Neitin asked.

Sakarbik's face reflected the glow from the *besteki*, warmer and brighter now, as if they had grown closer behind Neitin's back. She did not dare turn to look but held Sakarbik's unblinking gaze. "He may live, if you stay here," Sakarbik said, "but he will not grow into anything a mother would wish. Whatever monster Bailar has made of your husband, he shall do worse to your son. The stars have shown me a grotesque future for him, gore-soaked and foul."

She might have been lying. But Neitin did not think so. The easiest lie would have been to promise Mati's death. Only the truth could be more horrible. "And you? What do the stars tell you of yourself?"

Sakarbik's head wagged side to side. "No, little wife. I do not ask for myself. I need not. I pledged myself to you, did I not? And so there is my course. If you go, I go, and perhaps we both live. If you stay here and die, then surely, I die, too, if not at Bailar's knife, then under the lash in some foreign land."

Neitin's chest ached as though she had run a league, and the chill in the air had invaded her very bones. Her eyes stung with tears, quickly blinked away.

"Very well." A harsh whisper was the best she could manage. "I will follow the *besteki*."

Sakarbik released a hissing breath. Relief, Neitin realized. Had all of her anger and exasperation been cloaking fear? That thought, more than anything else, persuaded her that she had made the right choice.

"The *besteki* will give me a signal, when the time is right for us to leave," she said. "But be ready. I think it will not be long."

∞∞∞∞∞∞∞∞∞∞

CITY OF AVEN

The Terentiae's garden was wilder than that which one would find behind a usual Aventan domus. Its paths were simple packed earth, not pebbled or tiled, and wound irregular patterns around unpruned trees and shrubs. There were few flowers at this time of year, but the cypress trees remained verdant, and here and there, white and pink ginger plants lent color to the surroundings. A brazier had been placed in the midst of the miniature wilderness, and Terentilla and Alhena lay on a blanket beside it, sipping warm spiced wine and trading stories.

Alhena told herself she had come only to see if Tilla had learned anything new about the Discordian threat, or if she had had the chance to speak to her Vestal sister about it. Easier to tell herself that than to examine why the thought of spending time with Tilla set her pulse eagerly racing. They dispensed with the critical information swiftly, then spent the rest of the afternoon at leisure: talking about the latest comedy in the amphitheater, playing speedy rounds of *calculi* on a wooden board, and playing music. Alhena could handle a cithara passably well, and Tilla had skill on the panpipe. "Mama thinks it's half a disgrace, me preferring such a common instrument," she said, grinning, "but Papa thought it fitting for an Earth mage, so no one has tried to take it away from me."

She trilled a few swift, lilting melodies, then, as Alhena flopped back onto a pillow, gazing up at the gray November sky, a low and lulling Ionian tune.

Alhena wasn't sure how long she sat, listening to the music, before the world around her faded away and she found herself again surrounded by green hills. As had happened before, the land cracked at the surface and peeled away, exposing the tangle of bones beneath. The sight no longer startled her so much, but the rattling noise they made still jarred her senses, and the putrid reek of the fat glistening on them assaulted her nose. But she gritted her teeth, and this time, when the strange bronze doors appeared, she walked toward them without hesitation.

"Show me," she demanded. The doors emanated the same strange heat as before, and the words appeared, burning on the door as though written in the light of hot coals. "Show me where you began."

Dimly, she felt a press on her hand—her real hand, not the hand of her dream-body. And that gave her an idea.

Alhena reached out for the door. *'It can't hurt you, not really. It's only a vision.'* Telling herself that did little good when she pressed her hand to the burning bronze. Pain seared through her, and her instinct was to jerk back, as one would from a hot cauldron, but she forced herself to keep contact with the doors. The words on them were swirling faster and faster now, and the pain scorched up her arm, making it feel as though her hand were on fire and the rest of her were about to catch. She screamed through the agony.

As from far away, she heard Tilla's voice. "Alhena? Alhena, what's the matter—"

Alhena had no idea if Tilla could hear her or not, but she refused to give up, for she could see cracks beginning to form in the door, beginning under her hand and spiderwebbing outward. "Show me! Show me what made you, show me who made you!"

All at once, the door shattered. Alhena had to close her eyes against the blaze of bronze light, and when she opened them again, the scene had changed.

Not now the endless country hills she had seen in her spring vision, but the seven hills of Aven itself. For a moment, she seemed to be hovering above them: then, she was in their midst, moving at the speed of dreams, gliding faster than true footsteps could ever carry her. She found herself in the middle of the Forum, but such as she had never seen it: empty, utterly empty. Even in the days of the Dictator, there had always been *someone* about—a public slave sweeping temple steps, an administrator running to his duties. To Alhena now, however, the Forum was cast in stark colors, as though it were about to storm, and not a soul but she transgressed there.

'Proserpina, if you have given me this vision a-purpose, if you want me to follow this path so that I can help my sister . . . tell me which way to go.'

A long moment passed. Perhaps the goddess was not attending her devotee's dreams at this moment. But then, a stiff breeze whipped up behind Alhena, catching at her garments and turning her slightly toward the right. *'Right it is, then.'*

Alhena let the wind guide her, impossibly fleet-footed, down the Via

Sacra, between the Palatine and the Carinae. Then up, cutting north along the city wall. On the eastern side of the wall here, she knew, were the necropolis and lime pits. The wind nudged her back west again, however, before she reached the Volscian Gate. *'Remember this, remember each crossroads,'* she told herself. *'You must be able to find it again.'*

When the wind abruptly stopped nudging her, Alhena found herself in front of a building made of bones.

A domus, she thought, with a high bronze door, but the walls were all gleaming white bone, interlocked and stacked twelve feet high. She heard whispers behind the door, the voices of the fiends. *'We hunger, little prophetess, we hunger . . . so many souls in this city, so many meals . . .'*

But Alhena paid them no heed. *'I know where to find you now. I know how to catch you!'*

Alhena shook herself out of the vision. It took a moment to return fully to her natural senses. Her limbs felt sluggish, and her vision blurred when first she tried to focus on Tilla's brown face. Only then did she notice her friend's panic. "Alhena!" Tilla gasped, hauling her to a sitting position. Her hands clasped Alhena's face. "Are you—"

"I'm fine, Tilla, truly, I'm—"

"That was terrifying! You went all pale and still and cold and—Does that happen to you all the time? I was so—so—!"

Still dazed, it took Alhena a moment to realize that Tilla was kissing her cheeks in feverish relief. Then her brow, then her hair, then her cheeks again, and then—*'Proserpina help me'*—her lips. No quick peck this time, but lingering softness. Even more astonishing, Alhena found herself returning the kiss. One of them sighed; Alhena wasn't sure who. Tilla's hands were callused, slightly rough as they stroked Alhena's neck, but her mouth was soft and sweet and an utter revelation.

Alhena's heart was pounding fit to burst from her chest. She had been kissed before, chaste and bloodless, before poor, dead Tarpeius had left on his campaign. That had been pleasant, she supposed, but *this*—this stoked a need somewhere inside Alhena that only magic had ever touched before, a secret heart-inside-her-heart that she had never known to look for. *'Mercy, is this what my sisters have felt?'*

That thought jolted her out of the sudden cloud of bliss. *'My sisters—I have to tell them—'*

Alhena broke away from Terentilla, though not without regret. "Oh, Tilla, this is lovely, but we haven't time."

Tilla sat back on her heels, her head whipping about the garden.

"You're right. Gods. I'm sorry. I wasn't thinking. I just—You scared me so—But someone might—"

Alhena had never heard strong, surefooted Tilla sound so flustered. *'Was she as surprised as I was?'* She would have to unravel that later. "That's not what I mean." Alhena clambered to her feet and put a hand down for Tilla. "We need to get to my sisters, *right now*."

XLVI

The place *reeked* of Discordian magic. Vibia wondered if the others sensed it as she did. Latona, perhaps. To Vibia, they may as well have been walking into a charnel house. Splintered bones and rotting flesh, grave dirt and pyre ash, that was what this half-crumbled house smelled like.

Rubellia had been with Latona and Vibia when the two younger girls had come crashing into the Vitellian domus, hands clasped and babbling. Once the story came out, they had sent Tilla back home. The girl hadn't wanted to go, but Rubellia had sensibly pointed out that they would need someone who knew where they had gone, in case something went wrong. Even then, Tilla had lingered until Alhena pressed her hand and whispered something in her ear.

Rubellia and Alhena, at least, seemed to have the sense to be afraid. Alhena, for all her determination to face the foe, looked like Iphigenia being led to the sacrificial altar, and Rubellia's normally serene expression was drawn and pale, the apples of her cheeks hollow. Merula's face was as mulishly impassive as ever. *'And then there's Latona.'* Fear hardly seemed to touch her when she had the bit between her teeth. It had been their salvation in the warehouse, but Vibia was wary of it nonetheless. Fear, in sensible amounts, led to caution. A lack of it often led to foolhardy behavior. *'Foolhardy and ferocious. Like Sempronius.'* Vibia couldn't decide whether to admire or disdain it, in either of them.

The house near the Servian Wall was in a poor district of the city—not a slum like the Subura, but forgotten, squeezed between more vibrant areas. This house looked to have been abandoned for some time. The paint on the door was flaking off, and ivy had overgrown the walls.

"This is it," Alhena confirmed, then swallowed heavily. "This is what I saw, when I asked Proserpina to show me the genesis of all this malice."

"It certainly *looks* like the sort of place a Fracture mage would favor," Vibia commented.

"Do you think anyone's in there?" Rubellia asked.

All of the women stared for a long moment, as though merely asking the question might reveal the answer. "Latona, can you tell?" Vibia suggested.

Latona frowned, closing her eyes briefly—then stumbled, at the same moment that Vibia felt a lash of malevolence emanating from within the building. Shaking her head, Latona brought herself back upright. "Whatever's in there does not like me," she said. "I mean, maybe not *me*, it might have just reacted to the Spirit magic, but—"

"No," Vibia said. "It doesn't like you, in particular." She cut her eyes sideways at Latona. "Sorry. But the chain of that magic was too focused to be accidental. Whatever's going on in there—it recognized your magical signature."

Latona gave a rueful almost-smile. "Well, if they're expecting company, I'd hate to disappoint them."

"Indeed," Rubellia said, affecting false cheerfulness. "It wouldn't do to be churlish."

Alhena's face had lost all color. Vibia reached out and touched her shoulder. "If you wanted to go back," she said, in as gentle a tone as she could manage with her nerves thrumming, "no one would think the less of you."

But Alhena shook her head. "These things have been infecting my dreams. I deserve the chance to confront them." Her fingers wrapped into the crimson scarf tied about her hair, identical to the ones Rubellia and Merula wore, though shorter than Vibia's mantle. Latona had been hard at work since absconding from her husband's house, it seemed—a development Vibia had scarcely had time to process since learning of it a few days earlier. She could hardly blame any woman for wishing to be free of such a creature as Numerius Herennius, and she no longer thought Latona so wantonly ambitious as once she had, but disquiet still lurked in the back of her mind, particularly as concerned her brother.

Merula approached the door first, testing it gingerly, then giving it a hard shove. Another blast of magic emanated from the building. Vibia gritted her teeth against the shock of it. This magic was wild, aggressive, bucking like a horse that had slipped its bridle. Everything she detested in Fracture magic. *'Even the Bacchan cults constrain their excesses and indulgences to certain festival days, recognizing that such things are best in counterpoint to the rules of civilization. The Discordians would see chaos take over every aspect of life.'*

From within the house, a faint keening noise swelled. *"Lemures?"* Alhena asked, voice trembling.

"Of some sort," Vibia replied. "Not *umbrae*, I should think, during the day, but . . ." She sighed, shaking her head.

They all knew what had to be done. They all knew they had to go in. It was what they had come for. But all four mages stood, as though rooted in place, until Vibia puffed out a breath. "Janus protect me." She lunged for the door, practically hurling herself through it before she could think better of it.

She had only a moment to see what lay beyond—painted columns and walls leading off to inner chambers, dry ivy and dead trees standing in clay pots, a few torches stuck into sconces—before a searing pain seized her head. The air was thick with *lemures*. More than there had been in the fields and vineyards of Stabiae, more than in the Velabrium warehouse, more than Vibia would have imagined could cram themselves into one place, a choking cloud of black and gray. None had distinct form. Individually, they were weak, but there were many of them, so many, and their keening cries echoed off the neglected walls.

Vibia lurched back, every instinct in body and soul alike telling her to run for her life, but even as she shrank away, Latona plunged forward. Someone slipped a hand into Vibia's. Alhena, she realized a moment later. The poor thing was all a-tremble, but the look of stubborn determination had not left her face.

"The fiends hunger," Alhena warbled. "That's what the voice said, in my vision. The fiends hunger, and our city is a feast."

Alone among them, Rubellia was looking at the other mages rather than at the wispy figures darting and weaving around them. "Latona . . . Latona, something strange is happening, I can feel it, but not quite . . . I can't quite tell . . ."

All four mages reacted in a shared instant. Latona gave a violent jerk, as though something had speared her through the middle. Alhena shrieked, her knees going out from under her. Rubellia gasped, clutching at her chest. And Vibia reeled, the pain in her head turning to a radiant flash of agony. Merula alone seemed unaffected, flattening herself against a wall and looking about to find a mortal assailant.

Rubellia's highly primed empathy must have sensed it first. Latona's energies had been focused elsewhere, but Rubellia had picked up on it—and Vibia could tell what had happened. She wasn't sure if the fiends themselves were doing it, or if the women had tripped some curse by entering the space, but Fracture magic had ripped into each of them. A sucking, draining force, tearing their own magic out of them. *'Gods, this had better not create another void,'* Vibia thought through the drumming pain in her head, *'because without Sempronius here, I really don't know how to deal with that.'*

Vibia's mantle was blazing hot against her skin; the others' must have been, too. *'How much worse would this curse be without its protection?'* Then, a more alarming thought: *'How much can the Fire magic in these consume before they lose their strength? What if they give out entirely?'* Alhena's might have done so already; she had pressed the heels of her hands into her eyes and was kicking her feet against the ground, caught in the throes of some horrific vision. Merula dove for her, strong arms locking about the young woman to keep her from hurting herself.

"Get her out!" Latona yelled over the fiends' howling. Wretched conflict wrote itself on Merula's face as she looked from her mistress to horror-stricken Alhena, but at last she nodded and started dragging Alhena toward the door. Or trying to, anyway. Alhena was half a dead weight and half a struggling wildcat, tasking even Merula's abilities in wrestling.

Vibia could feel Fracture magic rising in her, like calling to like, bubbling up from within, eager to join its fellows. She clenched her fists, struggling to keep control. If she let loose, her magic might multiply the fiends around them into a veritable army, or it might amplify what was already happening to the other three.

'And what is happening to—' But that answer came swiftly enough. Rubellia's magic was strongest in empathy, and now she was laughing and sobbing at the same time, gasping and wailing and sighing. Vibia could sense the shape of what the Discordian magic had done: wrested control from Rubellia, then tumbled her emotions like dice. Rubellia clutched at the wall, frantic with her efforts to master herself.

"No!"

It was Latona who shouted, a defiant bark over the howls of the *lemures*. As Vibia watched, one of the fiends flickered and guttered out. Latona had her hand toward it and was making a pulling motion back toward her own chest. Her face had contorted with rage, eyes blazing. She wasn't scared—or if she was, no trace of it showed in her body. She was furious.

'Is that her? Or is it something of the fiends getting into her?'

Vibia's own control was slipping. The wild magic that had whipped loose was an aggravation. Her own magic resonated with it, and for the first time since she had been very young, she felt the unwelcome sensation of something inside her chest yearning to burst free. Like an unbroken yearling stamping and tossing its head, her magic wanted to be given head.

'*Stop it,*' she thought, ordering her powers to calm themselves. '*Discordian magic is seductive, but it is everything we have set ourselves against.*'

But it howled in her ears, and its pull drew her like a lodestone. '*Is this how Sempronius felt, facing that void?*' A temptation of magic, dangled before her eyes like a jewel on a chain, and all she would have to do was grab for it. These fiends didn't care who made them; they knew no loyalty. They knew only power; they respected only power.

Vibia shook her head violently. '*Stop!*' Since childhood, she had learned control. '*And I will be damned if I relinquish it to some half-baked terrors now.*'

But on they came, the smoky wisps darting around her. A metallic scent hung in the air, bronze and blood, and Vibia wasn't sure how much longer she could keep her own thoughts barricaded against the intruding onslaught from the fiends.

Then, fingers grasped her, an arm went around her shoulders, and the air seemed to clear. Latona had worked her way over, and Vibia felt the same lessening of pressure as she had in the warehouse, along with that sunburn-warm sensation on her skin: Latona, flooding her with Spirit magic, gifting her energy and focus. It hurt now as it never had before, the invasion of her inimical element, driving out the Discordian influence, but Vibia welcomed the pain, like plunging into a cold bath, a clarifying shock.

There was a curtain at the far end of the vestibule, ragged and half-torn from its rod. When Latona pulled it aside, both women fell over as the blast of magic beyond hit them—or perhaps it was only the overwhelming odor of death and decay.

There, in the middle of the atrium, in the dry impluvium pool, was a pile of bones as tall as a man, knotted together with dirt-smeared and rotting fibers.

"They're all coming from that," Vibia said, trying to stand back up, but only able to get as far as her hands and knees. The Fracture magic rolling off the mass of bones was staggering. "I can't—It would take me ages to unravel all of that, even with the consecrated knives."

Frowning, Latona looked around them. She crawled over to the wall, using it to help herself stand back up. Then she snatched at one of the torches jammed in a sconce. '*Someone had to light that,*' Vibia thought.

All the other charms had been laid some time before Vibia and Latona had found them—maybe days, maybe weeks, maybe only hours, but long enough that the mage left no trace of themselves. *'Someone is here, or was within the hour.'*

Latona tossed the torch at the pile of bones, but though a few of the scraps of fabric holding the mess together caught flame, it wasn't enough, not nearly enough to consume the curse. They'd all be driven mad long before the fire had time to do its work, and already Vibia could see the Fracture magic picking the flames apart, threatening to douse them.

Latona walked toward the heap, staggered to her knees, gritted her teeth, kept crawling. Vibia, still on the floor, shook her head in disbelief. "Latona, what are you—Oh!" Vibia cried out as Latona shoved her hands right into the flames where they were brightest. Gaping in awe and terror, Vibia watched as the fire grew, all around Latona's fingers, yet Latona showed no sign of fear or pain. She withdrew her hand, cupping a tiny blaze in her palm as though it were some small pet. This she deposited higher on the pile, where it caught and burned white. Again and again, Latona plucked flames with her hand and redistributed them. Only once did she glance over her shoulder at Vibia. "I-It's working!" Vibia croaked. As the conflagration grew, it ate at the curse.

The *lemures* could feel it too. They shrieked louder and left off tormenting Alhena and Rubellia, swarming to defend their gateway from the netherworld.

Latona's hands might have been immune to the fire, but her clothing was not. When a flame snapped out at the edge of her gown, she had to leap back, frantically beating the fabric to extinguish it. Rubellia lurched toward them, her face streaked with tear-tracks. She kept her distance from the pile of bones, but reached out with both hands, and the fire grew brighter, hotter. Vibia felt the Fracture magic snapping, and where it did, the flames turned an unnatural blue.

With hungry eyes, Vibia watched the heap of sacrificial remains, though she was hardly aware of the gruesome spectacle of bones and rotting sinew anymore. All her senses were primed for the magic gorging forth from the mound. As Rubellia and Latona worked together to heighten the blaze, a tendril of the curse whipped loose from the whole. Vibia seized on it with her own magic, giving it a mental yank.

The howling cacophony around them grew sharply louder, protesting her work. Vibia ground her teeth together, despite the pain that shot through her temples, and redoubled her efforts. *'Unwind, unbind. I can break you, I know I can. My magic is that of beginnings and endings, and you? You end here, now.'*

Now the entire pile of bones was ablaze, all the flammable material catching. The *lemures* left in the room vibrated with anger, their cries surging to a roar of indignant fury. Behind them, Alhena had stopped sobbing; Vibia hoped it was because Merula had finally hauled her out of the building. With sweat drenching her forehead and back, she continued tearing at the bindings of the Discordian curse, ripping each tangled strain of magic from its moorings. As the fire devoured the charm, Vibia shredded its power with her own.

A blast of frigid air blew through the house. No, not blew, Vibia realized—it was sucking in, into the void that lay invisible, somewhere beyond the mound of tangled carcasses. The *lemures* were being dragged back to their home, whatever part of the netherworld they had come from. Their smoky forms distended and stretched, and Vibia could feel the splintering Fracture magic as each one lost its grip on the world and sank back into oblivion.

Latona was caught off guard by the sudden rush of air and might have stumbled fully into the flames, had Rubellia not seized her by the elbows and jerked her back. They both fell then, landing in a heap near Vibia. Latona flung out an arm. Vibia grabbed it, then reached for Rubellia with the other, the three women clinging to each other as the fiends shrieked their displeasure, whirling and twisting around them in a malignant haze.

XLVII

When the last of the *lemures* disappeared, its howl echoed behind it. The tear in the world still throbbed like an open sore, a blight on the fabric of the world.

The flames blazing on the heap of bones were *wrong* now, not the healthy orange glow Latona had seized from the torch. Now the fire burned cerulean and azure. *'The effect of the curse? Or because they're now burning on the boundary between two worlds?'* Breaking the curse-charm alone had not been enough, not when such a gash had been rent in the natural world. Something had to be done to seal it. *'Fire magic can cauterize a wound, and Spirit magic can counter Fracture. Maybe if I . . .'*

Latona's forehead creased as she contemplated what she could sense and see of the metaphysical laceration. Jagged bronze edges, where the curse had torn through, visible to her magical sensibilities beneath the fire and bones that her eyes perceived. She reached out for the flames with her magic, drawing power from them, then focused all her attention on that gash. *'Like a blade over flesh,'* she thought. Then she swallowed uncomfortably. *'Not that I've ever done such a thing.'* But she had heard about it, read about it. *'And you did heal Sempronius. And you've healed these tears in the earth before. This one is just . . . much, much larger.'*

She used the Fire to fuel her Spirit, blending the two together as she sought to draw the ragged edges of the world together. She heard, as if from far away, a hissing noise. *'I hope that means this is working . . .'*

Perhaps because they had already incinerated the charm that had forced open the crack between the worlds, this gash did not fight her as others had done. No sensation of splinters beneath her skin, no pricking at the edges of her mind. Just a massive hole, gaping open, which her Spirit magic struggled to close. She felt a hand on her back—Rubellia's, she thought, though she did not turn to look—giving her support when her body began to sag with the effort. Slowly, finally, the balance of power shifted, and Spirit began to close the wound that Fracture had left.

Vibia let out a reedy sigh, and then the flames went out all at once.

Latona felt their sudden absence like a dousing of cold water over her head, and from Rubellia's shiver, suspected she felt the same.

The air inside the house brightened, the smoke wafting away like an early morning fog burned off by the sun. Latona exchanged nervous looks with Rubellia and Vibia, their limbs still all in a tangled heap, none willing to believe the fight was over yet. Just as Pinarius Scaeva had used her own magic against her, tearing into her well of power and churning it into the void he had created, the *lemures* had reached into each of the mages present and taken their strength. *'Or tried to, at least.'* They had not reckoned with the fortitude of Latona's fury.

A high, girlish scream started in the vestibule and rushed toward them. Vibia spun around, hands outthrust, as though to intercept whatever new demon the Discordian magic had hurled at them—but there was no demon. Only Alhena, wild-eyed, with Merula at her heels and a branch clutched in her pale hands, evidently torn from one of the long-dead trees which must once have decorated the atrium in verdant splendor.

Alhena ran straight for the charred and sagging mound of bones and whacked it with the branch, sending bones and other crisped remnants of the curse scattering with an almost comical clatter. Screaming in rage, Alhena knocked at the pile again and again, until her breath grew ragged and her violent cries gave way to hysterical sobs.

Eventually, she let the branch drop from fingers that were now red and swollen, then collapsed backward, joining the heap of mages on the floor. Latona scooted closer to her, releasing her grip on Rubellia and Vibia so that she could wrap her arms around her sister. "Damn them," Alhena rasped. She swiped inelegantly at her nose with the back of her hand. "May Dis devour their rotten souls, every one of them." Latona wasn't sure if she meant the *lemures* or the Discordians who had summoned them into this world, but in either case, she agreed.

"Domina?" Such quavering uncertainty did not belong in Merula's voice, and Latona was almost as alarmed to see the trepidation on Merula's broad face as she had been to see the *lemures*. "Domina, you are all—You are safe?"

"As can be, Merula," Latona answered. Her own voice was hoarse. *'Was I shouting more than I realized?'*

Merula narrowed her eyes at the pile of bones. "What is needful now?"

"Helping us up off of this damned floor would be a start," Vibia said, holding out a hand. Merula hauled her up with less grace than Latona suspected Vibia was used to, then went to assist Rubellia.

Latona stayed on the floor a moment, squeezing Alhena tightly. She had no comforting words to offer. She tried instead to merely offer her sister a soothing burst of empathic energy—but the effort of dispelling the *lemures* and closing off the Fracture magic had left her utterly drained. Latona wasn't sure she had the strength to extinguish a candle.

Then Rubellia reached down, gently drawing Alhena out of Latona's arms. Latona felt the soft glow of Rubellia's magic settling over them both, but mostly wrapping around Alhena like a warm blanket.

Merula cocked her head at Latona. "You can stand, Domina?"

"I think so."

"Good." Unceremoniously, Merula reached beneath Latona's armpits and hauled her up. Then, quietly, she added, "That was terrifying, Domina. And I do not like being terrified."

"I know, my dear." Latona cupped her cheek, smiling slightly. "You could have stayed outside, you know."

Merula snorted. "You are knowing me better than that, Domina." She turned away, looking at the pile of charred remains, then bent to pick up Alhena's stick. "She fought like a tiger, you know, when I am trying to get her out."

"Yes, well," Latona said, smiling over at her sister, "we're all stubborn women, under the Vitellian roof."

"Latona," Rubellia said softly, "I'm taking her outside." She stroked Alhena's hair lightly. "Fresh air, yes? Nothing so restorative."

Latona nodded. "We'll be out in a moment. I just want to make sure that . . . that everything's settled, here."

As Rubellia guided a still-sniffling Alhena out of the house, Merula started prodding at the partially collapsed tower of blackened bones. Vibia sidled up beside Latona. Her sable hair was, like Alhena's, torn totally loose of its bonds, and her skin was pink and puffy with exertion. She looked strong, though, much stronger than Latona felt, and was already setting to work adjusting the pins and belts of her gown, neatening her appearance back to something approximating its customary precision. "Someone was here," she said. "Very recently." She jerked her head at the torches in their wall sconces.

"Someone might *still* be here," Latona said. "Though I don't know how they could've missed all of that."

"Oh," a voice said, "they didn't."

On the far side of the atrium, a woman stood beneath an arch that led back toward the other rooms. Vibia stopped dead in her tracks, clutching at Latona's arm so hard her fingernails would leave marks. Merula whipped the stick in her hand up like a club, ready to strike.

The woman was perhaps twenty, with nearly translucent alabaster skin and raven-dark hair that hung loose about her shoulders. Her face belonged on a statue of some goddess, so even and flawless were her features. But her eyes blazed with implacable hatred, and the air around her shimmered bronze in Latona's magical sight.

"The pair of you," the woman said, her tone strangely song-like. "Glitter-gold and the knife's edge. Such a lot of trouble you've been."

"*We've* been trouble?" Vibia snapped. "You're the one—"

"You keep spoiling things," the woman went on, ignoring Vibia. "You're shutting all the doors. You *can't* do that, you just *can't*. And you broke my friend Scaeva's mind, the two of you."

It had been Alhena, not Latona, who had helped Vibia in that, but if this girl was misinformed, Latona would not correct her.

"You've shielded yourselves well. I'll have to work around that." She cocked her head to the side, contemplative. "But only your minds and your magic. Your bodies . . ." A sudden grin flashed, ghoulish on the perfect face. "That, I can work with."

Her hand snapped out, splaying against the nearest column, and before either Latona or Vibia could react, the arch above began to shake. Bits of plaster fell to the ground as the ceiling cracked and shuddered.

"Latona, she's bringing down the—*Run!*" Vibia shouted, bolting back toward the atrium. Latona was right on her heels—or had intended to be, but found herself falling instead.

'*No, no, no . . .*'

A weight landed on her back: the Fracture mage, one leg on either side of Latona's body, pushing her into the tiled floor. Then, just as swiftly, the weight lifted—was *flung* from her. Merula had whacked the stranger with her stick so hard that it broke, then hauled her off Latona. She struck the Fracture mage several times, swift and effective, but when her hand went for the dagger at her thigh, the woman reached up and snatched the kerchief from Merula's hair. She wasn't fast enough, not entirely. Merula's blade flashed, and red blossomed in a long line along the stranger's arm.

Then a terrible noise pierced Latona's ears, worse than the snaps and pops of rupturing plaster all around her, worse than the shrieks of the *lemures*: Merula, screaming in utter agony. Unthinkable sound, unimaginable. "Merula!" Latona shouted, trying to push up and go to her, but her limbs refused to respond, sapped of all strength.

Before she could figure out what had happened, Latona was knocked prone again. The Fracture mage clasped her hands around Latona's head. "I'm afraid I lied," she said, in that same lilting tone. "Your magic wasn't very well-shielded at all, not anymore. Weak, weak, but don't blame yourself, glitter-gold. Anyone would be, after dealing with my trap."

'Her trap. She—' Latona struggled, trying to get to her feet, but it was as though her muscles would not obey her. *'She intended all that to happen. She set that spectacle so that we would spend all our energy on it, and leave ourselves vulnerable.'*

Chips and dust continued to fall from the ceiling, plinking like hard rain all around them. "I'm afraid I just can't have you interfering, glitter-gold, no, no, that won't do at all." A shattering pain came into Latona's head, as though the woman's hands were crushing her skull like an egg. She screamed, or tried to, but she no longer had even that much strength. "Say hello to the fiends for me, beauty."

Latona's world erupted, blinding white followed by the black weight of oblivion.

XLVIII

Merula had known pain, thought herself well-girded against it. She had been beaten by the people who had enslaved her. She had endured blows and cuts from the gladiatrix who trained her to fight. Never had she felt such a wracking torment. Everywhere her skin had touched that of the Fracture mage, her body erupted into horrible pangs, as though her bones were breaking and stabbing their way through her skin. When the woman threw her off, Merula could do nothing, her every sense too swamped by astonishing agony.

Then, all at once, it stopped. The pain, the crumbling plaster, the tremors in the walls, all ceased, leaving a terrible stillness. Merula glanced at her limbs briefly, to assure herself they were not broken in truth, then sprang up, snatching her fallen knife, ready to carve that bitch-dog of a Fracture mage to ribbons.

But the woman had vanished. *'She could not be getting far. I could still—'*

The thought tangled as Merula's eyes took in Lady Latona, left in an ignoble heap on the cracked tile floor, as still as death.

"Domina?" Merula scrambled to Latona's side, rolled her onto her back. "No, no, no, no." The domina was limp as a rag, her eyes closed, her cheeks ashen. "Domina! You must wake!" Panic rose in her chest. She placed a hand to Latona's cheek. Warm, despite its pallor. A good sign. Her fingers went to the domina's throat, pressing at the side of her windpipe. Merula held her own breath, waiting—then released it in a ragged sigh when a pulse beat faintly against her fingertips.

At that moment, Vibia rushed back in, accompanied now by Rubellia and Alhena. "I thought you followed—" Vibia began, breathless. "Where did she—?"

Merula looked up at them, eyes blazing with fury. "I am going to *kill* her."

⬦⬦⬦⬦⬦⬦⬦⬦⬦⬦⬦

'My fault, my fault, my fault.'

The words thumped in Alhena's mind with each footstep as she and

Vibia ran through crowded streets, too panicked to care if anyone recognized them. Not likely, in this part of town, anyway. They had to get help, and the nearest friend they could trust was halfway up the Esquiline. Merula, fuming and cursing and swearing vengeance, had stayed behind to guard her mistress, while Rubellia desperately tried to rouse her. *'Please, please let Rubellia wake her. If I hadn't had that vision—if I hadn't told her we had to go, right now—it was a trap, and I led her right into it, how didn't I see it was a trap? My fault, my fault, my fault.'*

Alhena had been outside with Rubellia, still trying to gather herself together, when the Discordian house had shaken as though Vulcan had stamped his feet beneath it. Vibia had hit the front door, then turned, with a horrified expression on her face. "They didn't follow—I thought she was bringing the whole building down!" Vibia had shouted in explanation, but only a column and a bunch of ceiling tiles had fallen. By the time they reached the garden again, the Discordian mage had disappeared, and Latona lay on the floor, unconscious and surrounded by dust and shattered plaster.

Thinking of her sister had Alhena weeping, which did not make running any easier. Her lungs burned with effort, and her eyes were so wet she could hardly see where she was going. But Vibia had her firmly by the hand, and she allowed herself to be tugged along until they reached a tavern with a rearing horse and the word VATINIAE painted on the side.

"Vatinius Obir!" Vibia shouted, as soon as they were in the door. "Your captain, *now!*"

The tall man emerged from a back room, brow creased in worry. "Ladies? Is there—"

"My sister!" Alhena gasped, half-doubled with exertion. "Please—"

But Obir was already on his feet. "She is hurt? In trouble?"

"Both," Alhena half-sobbed.

Obir turned his head to his nearest associate, a tall pale man, sharp with sudden alertness. "Get a litter. The small light one, fast as you can." Then he snapped his fingers at a scrawny boy. "Go fetch a healer. Bring him to the domus of Aulus Vitellius, southern face of the Palatine, green door."

<hr />

Latona had not woken by the time they returned to her, and Alhena broke out sobbing anew as Obir lifted her, with a gentleness that seemed odd in so muscular a man, into the litter and drew the curtains around her. As they rushed for the Vitellian domus, Alhena half-heard Rubellia and Vibia coming up with a plausible story. "Her father will never let her out of the house again if he finds she was hurt on this business," Rubellia said, voice thick with tears, "and she would never forgive us for that."

"An accident, then," Vibia said. No tears in her, but her voice crackled like dry paper. "In the marketplace. A collapsing stall, a fallen beam."

When they reached the door, Vibia rushed in without preamble, issuing instructions to every slave and servant who caught her eye, and Alhena followed, drawn in her wake, too overwhelmed with tears to speak. Obir carried Latona in and lay her on a couch.

Aula ran into the atrium, wide-eyed with terror. When she saw Latona, she shrieked, her knees going out from under her. Vatinius Obir swooped to catch her by the arms, hauling her upright. "She lives, Lady, she lives!"

"No, no, not again, I can't, not her, not her!" Aula wailed.

"She lives, she *lives*!" Obir insisted, over and over, until Aula tore her eyes from Latona and looked at him, scarce comprehending.

"Sh-She—?"

"She's alive." Vibia came forward, and with Obir's help, navigated Aula onto the couch opposite Latona. "We—" But then Aulus rushed in, and Vibia lowered her voice. "I'll explain properly later." She raised her chin, striding over to Aulus. "There's been an accident." And as Vibia and Rubellia, between them, spun the story they had agreed on, lying with all their combined art, Alhena sank to her knees beside Aula, clutching at her sister's leg as though she were still a small child seeking comfort. Aula's hand sank into Alhena's hair; the other covered her eyes, as though she could not bear to look at Latona. Alhena could not bring herself to look away.

'*My fault, my fault, Latona, I'm so sorry, I'm so sorry.*'

◇◇◇◇◇◇◇◇◇◇◇◇◇◇◇

'*She should not be so still.*'

Latona's restless energy often irritated Vibia, but now, seeing her laid out as though waiting for a shroud, her stillness was a horror. Only a faint rising of her chest gave sign that she yet lived. No flutter of her fingers, no twirling of her hair, no gaze taking in every wonder of the world around her.

They had moved Latona from the couch in the atrium to her own bed. Only Vibia sat with her now. Everyone else, it seemed, was weeping. Aulus was at the household shrine, imploring the gods to save his girl. Aula and Alhena were on a couch, crying into each other's shoulders. Rubellia had recovered herself enough to consult with the healer, but tears continued to flow down her cheeks unchecked, though her voice was smooth and controlled. Vatinius Obir had absented himself as discreetly as possible. Vibia pitied the horror and sorrow she had seen in Obir's eyes. *'My brother will have both our heads for not taking better care of her.'* Even Merula's eyes were wet, though her expression as she paced the atrium was of fury, not despair.

Vibia sat at Latona's side, dry-eyed. Tears had never come easily to her. She didn't think she had cried since she had put aside the toys and charms of childhood. But that did not mean she was not in agony. *'Damn you, Latona. When did you become important to me?'*

The healer had come and inspected her head. A bad blow, he agreed, but there was no blood, and he could feel no fracturing of her skull. "There is no reason she should not wake," he had proclaimed, and promptly suggested a number of sacrifices Aulus could make, to speed the process along.

"Please wake," Vibia whispered to the too-tranquil face, still sungolden even this late in autumn. "You're not really going to leave me to deal with this Discordian nonsense, are you?" Her voice felt strangely thick. "I'm only involved because of you. It would be absolutely wretched of you to shirk your portion of the responsibilities now. And can you imagine, if I had to avenge you? Utterly ridiculous. No. I absolutely refuse." Her nostrils twitched, and she swallowed around a lump in her throat. "Do you understand me? I won't do it. And that means you can't—It means you *have* to wake. You have to wake up."

But Latona did not stir.

A rustle of skirts heralded Rubellia's return to the room. "Did you get anything more useful out of that charlatan?" Vibia asked.

"He recommends valerian, white willow bark, and ginger when she wakes," Rubellia said, coming to stand beside Vibia's chair. "And plenty of rest."

Vibia snorted in derision. "Any fool could come up with that treatment plan. I hope Aulus didn't pay him for coming here and doing nothing." Absurdly, her voice broke slightly on "nothing."

Rubellia leaned in close to Vibia and dropped her voice. "Vibia, it's beyond his ability. We need to get a healer-mage in here, and even then . . ." She shook her head. "I've been trying to sense her, but . . . it's like she's not in there. I've been with injured people before, but it's not like . . . it's not like this. It's not only the knock to her head." Rubellia glanced about again, affirming that no one would overhear them. "From what Merula said, that Fracture mage attacked them both. What she did to Merula was temporary, it faded as soon as the mage left, but this—"

"Clearly is not." Vibia pinched the bridge of her nose, squeezing her eyes shut. *'Focus. You should be able to see this. You should be able to figure this out.'*

Shards of Fracture magic sliced into her awareness. An incredible concentration of them, barbed and angry, but Vibia could not find their origin. They were tied to no token, no charm, nothing that Vibia could locate.

"I don't know," she whispered in defeat. "I don't know what this is, and I don't know how to fix it."

Rubellia gave her arm a squeeze, perhaps in sympathy, then drifted out of the bedroom again, going to commiserate with Aula and Alhena. Vibia leaned over Latona, touching her shoulder. If there was any consolation to be found, it was that she had not gone cold. To the contrary, she was quite warm to the touch. Not feverish, for her skin had no flush nor sweat, but that same sun-bright heat that Vibia had felt from Latona's magic. *'Perhaps she's fighting within, even now.'*

Vibia bent close to Latona's ear. "Wake up, damn you," she said, almost in a growl. "You *have* to wake up. If you die, my brother might well plunge on into Pluto's realm to drag you back out, and really, none of us have the time for that nonsense, so *wake up.*"

But Latona remained insensible as a statue.

GLOSSARY

AB URBE CONDITA: literally, "from the founding of the city." How the Romans/Aventans measure years, in time since what we consider 753 BCE, the legendary founding of the city.

AEDILE: a mid-level magistrate responsible for public buildings, the public games, and the supply of grain to the city. Elected by the Tribal Assembly. Men generally served this office between their quaestorship and praetorship, though it was not strictly necessary to be elected as praetor.

AUGIAN COMMISSION: the group of mages dedicated to preserving the provisions of the *Lex cantatia Augiae* and keeping order among Aven's magically-gifted citizens.

CAMPUS MARTIUS: the Field of Mars, a large open space used for military training and for elections.

CENATORIA: a simpler and less-burdensome garment than the toga, worn by men on informal occasions.

CENSOR: a magistrate responsible for maintaining the census and electoral rolls, supervising public morality, and some aspects of government finances. A man had to have served as consul to be elected as censor. Elected by the Centuriate Assembly.

CENTURIATE ASSEMBLY: one of three voting assemblies which gathered for legislative, electoral, and judicial purposes. Originally a military organization, but later expanded and ranked by wealth rather than military status. Only the Centuriate Assembly could declare war or elect the highest-ranking magistrates: praetors, consuls, and censors.

COLLEGIA: assemblies with legal purpose and some authority which could function as guilds, religious organizations, or social clubs. Most common were the crossroads colleges, which were neighborhood associations formed around shrines placed at intersections.

CONSUL: the highest and most prestigious political office in the Republic. The Centuriate Assembly elected two consuls to serve together for a one-year term. Consuls held executive power. They convened and presided over the Senate, negotiated with foreign states, and served as commanders-in-chief of the legions.

CURIA: the Senate House.

CURSUS HONORUM: literally, the course of offices; the sequential order of public offices held by politicians in the Republic.

DICTATOR: a magistrate entrusted by the Senate with full power and authority to act unilaterally. A temporary office intended to be held for no more than six months.

DOMINUS/DOMINA: literally, "master/mistress," but also translates as the equivalent of "Lord/Lady" when used in conjunction with a name.

DOMUS: house. In the city, generally referred to a free-standing building occupied by a single family.

EQUESTRIAN: one of the property classes, ranking below the Senators but above the rest.

FIVE CLASSES: property classes including all those who held land but did not have enough wealth to qualify as Equestrians or Senators.

FORUM: a large open-air market, often surrounded by a mixture of temples and shops. The largest forum in Aven, generally referred to as *the* Forum, was the center of political, mercantile, and spiritual life.

GARUM: a popular condiment made from fermenting fish.

HEAD COUNT: the property-less class, with no land and little wealth.

INSULA: apartment. Blocks of insulae could be five to seven stories, with the largest and most luxurious apartments on the bottom floor and the smallest and most miserable at the top.

IDES: in March, May, July, and October, the fifteenth day of the month; in all other months, the thirteenth day.

KALENDS: the first day of a month.

LATIFUNDIUM: a large agricultural estate under private ownership.

LEGES TABULAE MAGICAE: a section of Aventan law governing the behavior of mages, particularly with regard to interactions with non-magical citizens.

LEX CANTATIA AUGIAE: an Aventan law preventing the ascension of magically-gifted citizens to the ranks of aedile, praetor, consul, or censor.

LICTOR: a civil servant who acted as a bodyguard to high-ranking public officials.

MOS MAIORUM: the "proper way of things." An informal code based on precedent and custom, elevated to dogmatic status by the Optimates.

NONES: in March, May, July, and October, the seventh day of the month; in all other months, the fifth day.

OPTIMATES: one of the two most prominent political factions in Aven, dedicated to conservatism, relative isolationism, and the preservation of power among the elite.

PATRONS AND CLIENTS: a system in which the patron, a man of higher social status and clout, served as protector, sponsor, and benefactor of the client, who in turn provided support and assistance to his patron.

PENATES: household gods.

PONTIFICAL COLLEGE: an institution consisting of the highest-ranking priests of the state religion.

POPULARISTS: one of the two most prominent political factions in Aven, favoring expansion of civic rights and economic opportunity.

PRAETOR: a magistrate ranking just below a consul. Praetors had municipal and judicial duties, but might also serve as commanders of legions or as local governors. Their specific duties fluctuated greatly at different points in history.

QUAESTOR: the first rank of the *cursus honorum*, requisite for entry to the Senate, responsible for the state treasury and audits.

QUINTILIS: the month we know as July.

SENATE: the Assembly consisting of the most experienced politicians. The Senate dictated foreign and military policy and directed domestic policy but could not actually pass laws.

SENATORS: both the highest-ranking and wealthiest social class and those men who served in the Senate.

SEXTILIS: the month we know as August.

THERMOPOLIUM: a quick-service restaurant for food on the go.

TRIBUNE: a title with several meanings. A tribune of the plebs acted as a check on the Senate and the Assemblies, able to exercise veto power over the actions of consuls and other magistrates. A military tribune commanded portions of the army, subordinate to praetors and consuls; these were usually men in their early twenties, getting military experience before beginning the cursus honorum. Other mid-ranking officers were also styled tribune, generally those who were members of a commander's staff.

VILLA: a large home outside of a city. This might be a villa rustica, a country estate, or a villa maritima, a seaside home.

Acknowledgments

This book came together across a few years of personal trials, geopolitical struggle, and societal upheaval. I say "came together," but that's an awfully passive phrase for the labor of wrangling, molding, hammering, and sometimes just plain kicking-in-the-shins that this narrative required. I owe a great debt to the people who got me through these years, and so I give my fervent and enduring thanks to:

-My parents, who have never failed to encourage their very strange child in her flights of fancy. I love you, and I am so grateful for your support and guidance.

-My publishing team: agent, Connor Goldsmith; editor, Betsy Wollheim; managing editor, Josh Starr; publicist, Alexis Nixon; and every other professional whose hands and eyes have helped to shape this project and coax it out into the world.

-The many scholars whose work I have leaned on while creating the world of Aven. A full list of the books, podcasts, documentaries, and other assorted sources I have used are available on my website (cassmorriswrites.com).

-The Sirens community, the Authors 18 group, and so many other writer-friends. It is so crucial in this business to have a supportive network, and I am continually delighted by the generosity and grace demonstrated by these wonderful people.

-My wonderful Patreon members, whose support has kept me going both materially and emotionally, and particularly to the Consuls: Bruce and Mary Morris, Marcell Williams, Solomon Romney, and Robert Mee.

-Lin-Manuel Miranda, who has done more than he knows to lift my spirits during challenging times.

-Noah, whose support has been unflagging, whose enthusiasm is boundless, and whose championing of a ridiculous rarepair ship in this series never fails to bring me glee.

Onward to Book Three. Audaces Fortuna iuvat!